Bradley Greenburg grew up along the Wabash River in Tippecanoe County, Indiana, just a half mile from an early 18th-century French trading post called Fort Ouiatenon and a few miles from Prophetstown and the Battle of Tippecanoe site. He teaches Renaissance drama and English literature at Northeastern Illinois University in Chicago, Illinois. This is his first novel.

When Lilacs Last in the Dooryard Bloomed

Bradley Greenburg

SANDSTONEPRESS
HIGHLAND | SCOTLAND

First published in Great Britain
and the United States of America in 2014
Sandstone Press Ltd
PO Box 5725
One High Street
Dingwall
Ross-shire
IV15 9WJ
Scotland.

www.sandstonepress.com

Editor: Moira Forsyth

The publisher acknowledges support from
Creative Scotland towards publication of this volume.

ISBN: 978-1-908737-87-8
ISBNe: 978-1-908737-88-5

Cover design by David Wardle at Bold and Noble, Hitchin
Typesetting by Iolaire Typesetting, Newtonmore
Printed and bound by Totem, Poland

for KLO

sine te nihil sum

Acknowledgements

Many of the places in this novel are real. All characters are invented.

I want to thank local historian Robert Kriebel, whose work was a constant inspiration. Thanks also to the Tippecanoe County Historical Museum (whose grass I mowed as a teenager) and the Tippecanoe Battlefield Museum in Battle Ground. Leonard J. Moore's *Citizen Klansmen: The Ku Klux Klan in Indiana, 1921–1928* was invaluable for insights into Klan activites in Indiana. Eric Foner's *Reconstruction: America's Unfinished Revolution, 1863–1877* gave me an epigraph and a clear understanding of the postbellum political landscape.

A number of readers nurtured the manuscript throughout its eventful life: Paul Cirone, Chi Eze, Giosuè Ghisalberti, Kyle Copas, Gina Buccola, Peter Kanelos, Carrie Brecke, Mike Galligan, Nancy Wrinkle, Brigid Pasulka. The team at Sandstone have been a pleasure to work with at every turn. Editorial Director Moira Forsyth has made this a much better novel.

Thanks also to my mother, Malissa, for her abiding patience and courage. Finally, I want to express my deepest thanks and love to my wife, Kris, and my son, Xavi, for the best support anyone could ever ask for.

Slavery is dead, the negro is not, there is the misfortune.

Cincinnati *Enquirer*, 22 May 1865

The past is not behind us but beneath our feet.

Philippe Sollers

Book One

Coosa County, Alabama

Nashville, Tennessee

Tippecanoe County, Indiana

1863–1868

One

Clayton McGhee turned six the year he was emancipated by proclamation. He asked his granny what emancipation meant and she said it was like being let into a fancy store but with no money to buy anything.

Clayton's grandfather and father were accomplished carpenters. Before the war they had been allowed to practice their craft independently, even though they were the property of the Meecker family. They kept their own house and were required to tender a yearly sum in exchange for being available to do work for others. Three hundred dollars in installments, the rest saved to buy their children. Clayton watched his grandfather painstakingly count the stack of greenbacks on the oak table where they took meals, awed at what a little paper and ink could do.

Clayton was born on a cornshuck mattress in their cabin along Hatchet Creek outside the little town of Goodwater in the northeast corner of Coosa County, Alabama. Amos and his son James – Clayton's grandfather and father – traveled the muddy broken roads up to Sylacauga and down to Alexander City to do one job after another, always carrying their papers from Meecker folded in an oilskin in case anyone asked what they were doing traveling so freely.

Many did.

Work became increasingly plentiful as the war emptied Alabama of its able-bodied men. It was peace that brought them scarcity. In the early days of what the distant federal government called Reconstruction it became dangerous to compete with white builders in the small towns and so the family moved first to Montgomery, then Nashville. A black carpenter who could hand-make windows and cabinets, lay flooring, and turn stock on a lathe seemed now an affront. Employers shook their heads and told them all the work they had was pulling nails out of old boards or, at best, working pitman in a sawmill. Gone were the days when a customer would grace them with an appreciative smile after pulling out a drawer, turning it over, examining its dovetails and testing its carriage for straightness, or pressing a finger on the muntins in a window to see if they would bow from the rails. So they pounded and shoveled, sawed and sweated while they watched white men knock together inferior houses and barns and town buildings that would be lucky to survive a stiff March wind.

In the late spring of 1868 the two older generations of McGhees came to the conclusion that emancipation in the South, practically speaking, might never arrive. Clayton had not been privy to these discussions but he could tell something was about to change by his mother's eyes. When he asked what was going on, she diverted her gaze, feigning interest in a rip in his britches that had been there through two washings. His father's subsequent preparation and departure for the country above the Ohio River was supposed to be accomplished without fuss. But young boys, like dogs, can always sense change.

James rode out of town on an early April morning just after the sun came up.

Clayton stood with his brothers in the pale light and waved. After they had eaten a silent breakfast, Amos sat them on the front steps and told them where their father had gone.

Granny kept vigil with her Bible each night her son was away. His grandfather sat in his rocking chair inside a cloud of pipesmoke watching her run a thin finger under the fine black type. Though she could not read them, the words brought her comfort. It was Clayton's job to read aloud. His

4

mother, Lily, brocaded tiny flowers into muslin near the edge of the hoop that held a bonnet she hoped to sell. On the floor by the hearth, his brothers played at something with small blocks of wood they'd found and imagined into toys. The old woman turned the pages until a satisfaction descended upon her. She took between her crooked fingers the faded red bookmark sewn into the binding and marked the page. Handed it to her grandson.

"Boys," his mother would say, looking up at him with a smile set upon her concentration. They left their game and clambered into chairs.

Clayton read from where his granny left off, now and then glancing at the door to see if it would open.

Clayton McGhee learned to read from Lenore Peacham, in whose store he had worked since their arrival in Nashville in the autumn of 1866. It was called Peacham's Dry Goods but even after the war ended the stock scarcely matched the description. Stores sold what they could get. When there was flour they sold flour. When berries and tomatoes and beans were in season they offered them. When bolts of cambric and gingham, or even huckaback, came available they reprised their role as the purveyors of millinery and sundries. The Peacham store had a generous awning and long benches on either side of the door which were never without takers. In their first week in town Clayton was sent by his granny to buy flour, sugar, and molasses. She put the coins firmly in his hand, gave him detailed instructions as to amounts, then made him repeat them back to her. Don't bring me no magic beans, she'd said, slapping his behind and sending him running. Though it was only two streets away, Clayton had been nervous. Montgomery was a small town that just kept going. Nashville felt huge.

In the street he repeated the weight of each item as he walked, cautiously minding the horses and wagons that trundled by in every direction. He stopped to admire the artistry of a burly fellow who rolled a full beer barrel down a wooden ramp, tipped it on its end, then spun it at an angle onto the groaning boards of the sidewalk and in the front doors of a saloon. A teamster yelled at him to get the hell out of the way and he ran into the mouth of an alley as a man in a blood-colored suit roared past, whipping a matched pair of jet black horses.

His heart was beating like mad and he remembered clearly his granny's other admonition: he was *not* to get killed on his way to or from the store.

On a bench out front of Peacham's sat three old men engaged in an animated discussion about something he could not catch. They paid him no mind. Inside it smelt of wet leather and lye soap. On a high shelf on the far wall he spotted the telltale colorful glow that meant candy. The man behind the counter had wavy hair that reached past his collar and wore a full length apron so white and without wrinkles Clayton thought it might crack when he moved. He had light skin and in combination with the hair gave off an air of sophistication. Clayton placed his order. Without a word the clerk measured and packaged each item into a parcel, which he neatly wrapped in brown butcher paper, then made some calculations on a pad of paper.

"That'll be forty eight cents."

Clayton held out his hand with the coins and the man took all but two of the silver ones and one of the coppers.

"I thought at first you was here because of the sign," the clerk said.

"What sign?"

"Yonder by the door in the window."

Clayton craned his neck but could not see it. "No sir, I didn't notice no sign."

The man shook the coins in his hand and blew on them like dice before depositing them in a cash box he retrieved then placed back behind the counter. With the knuckle of his index finger he smoothed his downy mustache with such deliberateness that Clayton supposed he either once had, or dearly wished for, a thicker one.

"How old are you?" he asked.

"Nine, I reckon."

"You reckon." The man leaned over the counter and sized him up. "Can you read or do figures?"

"No sir." Clayton was not sure he should be talking to a stranger, but the man did not speak to him as a child and this loosened his tongue. "My daddy can read some but he says they'll be time enough to teach me when we get settled."

"The sign ain't for you then. You all headed west?"

The clerk leaned with his elbows on the zinc, looking conspiratorially left, right, then over Clayton's head. He continued, not waiting for an answer.

"I'm lighting out for San Fran Cisco the first chance I get. A man with a decent stake can get rich as Midas out there. Even a colored fella. Hell, they got chinks and messicans and I don't know what all. Man like me can pass for white no problemo."

Before Clayton could think how to answer the apron man abruptly disappeared and began fussing with something behind the display case. Distorted by the curved glass Clayton could see him duckwalk to the end and then stand up with a feather duster and a polishing cloth.

In a loud voice he said, "Young man, if there isn't anything else I suggest you get along now."

Clayton felt a hand on his shoulder. An older woman's voice asked, "Did my son the famous gambler get you what you came for?"

He glanced at the man who smiled pleadingly.

"Yes ma'am."

She hefted the parcel and handed it to Clayton. "You baking a pie?"

"No ma'am. I mean, my granny. Maybe." He stood holding the parcel.

"You aren't allergic to pie, are you?" she asked.

"No ma'am." He thought for a few seconds. "I'm whatever the opposite is of allergic to pie."

She laughed at his earnestness and asked, "Was there anything else we could help you with?"

"I was interested in that sign you put up."

She looked him up and down.

"How old are you?"

"He's ten or eleven, he reckons," apron man said.

"Can you read and do some figuring?"

"I read the sign, didn't I?"

The apron man's name turned out to be Ben and the woman his mother Miss Lenore, as everyone called her. She and her husband had been freed in 1849 when their owner got what she called Gold Fever and disappeared to California. Her husband had been sent for with excited promises of easy riches and had left her with their little son and gone off to make a fortune. She had long since given up hope he would ever return.

The sign in the window advertised their need for a delivery boy and this suited Clayton fine. She explained to him what she called the terms and he nodded his head not knowing what else to do. He supposed he could do all the things she described, except the obvious ones. Maybe reading and counting would not matter. When he returned home, out of breath and clearly excited, his granny told him to slow down and come out with it. When he told her he had got a job she looked pleased and called for his mother who was out tending their little garden. The two women regarded him with pride and then with skepticism and then as their faces clouded over he understood that they could not be fooled. Granny marched him back to Peacham's with her hand behind his neck, impervious to the traffic of wagons or men.

There she politely thanked Miss Lenore and informed her that her grandson could no more read nor figure than a mule. She surprised both of them by saying, "Well, then I shall have to teach him."

It would never cease being a wonder to Clayton McGhee that a stack of paper, made from humble wood pulp and potash, sewn and glued along one edge, printed about with tiny figures in simple iron gall, could transport you anywhere in this world or another. Miss Lenore had been a patient teacher and he was reading simple sentences inside of a month. By Christmas he could read the Lord's Prayer out of the Bible and did so to his brothers' astonishment at the holiday dinner. Granny couldn't stop remarking how tickled she was. Her grandson knew she had him marked out for a preacherman.

Every Friday he handed over his wages to his mother who counted them into two piles. The larger one she swept into a leather pouch that was hidden from everyone but her. The smaller he was allowed to spend or save as he wished. By the spring he had accumulated the enormous sum of two dollars. To accomplish this he stayed well clear of the bright jars of candy at the store. Once a week, on Saturdays when they changed the displays, he permitted himself a long look at the toys in the windows at Loveman's, a larger and more prosperous version of Peacham's. The two dollars was intended for a special trip to Abraham Setliff's bookshop in the Commercial Hotel building on Cedar Street.

His first mistake was to ask Ben whether it was possible for coloreds to shop there. Ben replied that there was no place he wouldn't go in this town. Which of course meant that he had no desire to go into any establishment dull enough to sell books. Since, for Clayton, Setliff's held potentially infinite pleasures, such bravado did not come so easy. The area around the Commercial frightened him. As its name suggested, it was the center of activity for those with deals to make and money to spend, populated with rich folks and swells, out of town buyers and sellers, shifty characters in search of a mark. It wasn't just that Nashville was whiter here at its center. He was used to that. In Montgomery it had been the same: the closer you got to the Capitol and its towering white columns, its fenced lawn and groups of men doing business in the shade, the more exposed he felt. If a negro was in that part of town he was working for somebody.

The second he walked in the door and the unseen bell tinkled his arrival he knew he ought to have asked Miss Lenore. There were two men huddled at an ornately carved table at the far end of the room looking at a folio volume. They stopped what they were doing and the man Clayton figured to be the bookseller removed his spectacles and straightened up laboriously. The other man continued scanning the open book, then carefully turned a large cream-colored page. In the uncomfortable silence he could hear the snap of the brittle paper. Clayton took in the contents of the room, aware that he might not be free to browse at his leisure. Books in dark shades of leather and cloth covered the walls from floor to ceiling. Two lower bookcases, one longer than the other, were also filled, the shorter one topped with a glass case in which open volumes were displayed. A step ladder had been set up in one corner. Above it high on the shelf near a narrow window was a black void where several books had been removed. He dug his hand into his pocket and clutched the two shiny silver dollars with such force that he could feel the stars that ringed the seated lady Liberty.

"Something I can do for you? There isn't any work here if that is what you've come looking for." Setliff's manner of speaking was slow and deliberate, as though he were used to pointing out obscure passages in old books.

The man at the table turned another page, this time nearly licking his fingers before thinking better of it. His tongue stayed out as he read silently to himself.

10

"I already got me a job. I come to buy a book."

"You are picking up a book then for your employer. Very good. Was it ordered or something we have in stock?"

"No sir, I mean, it ain't neither one." Clayton stood up straighter. "It's for my own self."

"You wish to buy a book."

"Yes sir."

"To read."

"To read, yes sir."

Clayton had worked too many hours around Ben, whose voice answered in his head, *Is they other kinds of books?*

Setliff pinched the bridge of his nose and then replaced his spectacles. His pursed lips slowly formed themselves into a sardonic grin. He laughed without opening his mouth. The other man did not look up.

"I've had little urchins in here before. I may be but a bookseller but I can put my foot up your backside quicker than you'd think. Now get out of my store before I tan your black hide."

Clayton weighed his coins and his options. Setliff had not stepped around the table nor closed any of the thirty or so feet between them. Based on the older man's languid disposition and overall bookishness he reckoned this was not a distance he could cover quickly. Clayton wanted to defend himself, to make it clear he worked as hard as any grown man for his savings, to give an account of how toothsome his expectations had grown with each penny, nickel, and dime until they gnawed at him. It was clear that he was not going to obtain any satisfaction from the bookshop or its owner. But that did not mean he had to go away empty-handed.

The man at the table turned another page, his lips moving without interruption.

He opened the door a crack and let it rest against the jamb. It had to be wrenched open when he entered and he did not want to have it stick against his exit. Setliff stared at him

11

warily but with a bird-like patience. As suddenly and swiftly as he could he leapt to the glass-topped shelf nearest him and ran his finger across the spines. He could feel the titles embossed at various depths but could not read them in his haste. When he saw movement out of the corner of his eye he made his selection. With the book tucked under his arm he reached into his pocket, drew out the dollar coins and pitched them at the advancing figure. He heard their silvery sound as he grabbed the door handle. As he ran from the shop he hoped they had not hit the bookseller in the teeth or shattered the glass of his spectacles.

He did not stop until he reached the alley behind the store and only then chanced a look to see if anyone was chasing him.

In the quiet that followed the terrible young ruffian's startling act, Setliff closed the door until it was secure in its frame. He considered locking it. Still too early, no matter the reason. He could feel himself shaking from all the excitement as he bent down to retrieve the glittering coins. Newly minted, solid currency, the eagle sharp and unworn. With the toe of his shoe he felt the space where the book had been.

"Irv!"

The man did not look up.

"Irv! I sold the Defoe."

"I heard you. Two new dollars. You overcharged him."

"You can chase the black bastard if you want."

"He got what he deserved. He was damned obstreperous."

Clayton thought he would never make it back to Peacham's. He had never run so fast nor been so scared in his life. He expected every grown man or woman to get hold of him and bind him for his long-legged pursuer. At the back door he caught his breath and drank a dipper of water from the bucket. When he was sure no one was coming he sat on the top step to examine his purchase. The book was leather-bound and thick. The first page was dark green, then a blank sheet, then the title page, which he read out as best he could: The LIFE and Strange Surprizing ADVENTURES of ROBINSON CRUSOE, of York. Mariner: Who lived Eight and Twenty Years, all alone in an un-inhabited island on the Coast of America, on the Mouth of the Great River Oroonoque; Having been cast on Shore by Shipwreck, wherein all the Men perished but himself. WITH An Account how he was at last as strangely deliver'd by PYRATES.

Clayton smiled. He couldn't get all the words, but he got "shipwreck" and "pirates." Best of all he had heard of this story.

"What you got there?"

It was Miss Lenore. She opened the screen door and leaned out. He held the title page up for her to see.

"Robinson Crusoe. Well now. That is quite a tale. And a nice book too. Where'd you come by it?"

"Setliff's. Over in the Commercial."

"You don't say. How is Mr. Setliff doing?"

"All right. Busy with somebody so I showed myself around."

"What made you fix on this here book?"

"It's got a island and pirates. Not a lot of pictures but what it has are pretty good. Mr. Setliff said boys what had been in there before me liked it."

"Recommended it to you, did he?"

"Yes ma'am. Recommended it."

"How much you give fer it?"

"Two dollars."

She closed the door behind her and sat on the step above him.

"Flip to the end. No, the inside of the back cover. Look up in the corner for a pencil mark."

He held the page closer so he could make out the figure.

"One point zero zero."

"What does that tell you?"

His heart sank. How many weeks of walking in the heat and the rain with a heavy box or sack did that dollar stand for? How many back-breaking bags had he unloaded right here from wagons to get to a whole dollar?

Clayton felt her hand on the top of his head.

"I bet you by the time we're done reading that book and you find out what happened to old Crusoe and his boy Friday you won't remember how much you paid."

Two

In Louisville James McGhee asked at a surveyor's office if they had a map of Indiana. The fellow unrolled it on a table, battening its corners with flat stones. James tried to fix as many details in his head as he could.

"What is your business up there?" the surveyor asked.

"Looking to buy a farm," he replied.

"You would be best off getting upstate. Southern part is full of hills and hollows." He traced a line across the map just below the capital at its center. "Cultivating land below here, on a rocky pitch with mules . . . " He shook his head, poked the page further north with his finger. "You want to keep going until you find fertile, flatter ground. River valley if you can get it."

James thanked him and pointed his horse towards the bridge. He wondered if that were the only reason.

He expected it to feel different once he crossed out of Kentucky, since over the Ohio was the North and what had been thought of for so long as the road to the Promised Land. Not heaven exactly, but possibilities. So many whispered stories about Canada and the settlements of freemen around Lake Champlain and the mountains. He knew such sentiment existed in the East. But it was common knowledge that especially after the passage of the Fugitive Slave Act, escaping northwest above the Ohio River Valley was not safe.

As his horse clopped off the end planking of the bridgeway he looked at the white faces of the people milling around the low market stalls eyeing bolts of cloth, pewter and copper household goods, tallow candles and catches and an assortment of made things floated down the Ohio. He dismounted and stopped at a toy stall, nodded hello to the toymaker, a red-faced balding German wearing an apron made of bed ticking. The man looked up without expression through spectacles worn low on his stippled nose and went back to carving the propeller of a gee-haw whimmy diddle with a jackknife. The light wood curled into a pile at his feet. James examined the toys: stringed buzz saws, cornhusk and apple dolls, a variety of flutes and whistles, drums, and an army of intricately carved and painted soldiers. He picked up a cavalryman and the knife stopped. The eyes came up again through the glass, stayed fixed on him. James realized that he had no idea of his place here, whether he ought to be shopping amongst others openly like this, and if looking at toys, which he knew his boys would so love to have, was appropriate. The German was silent and watchful as the cavalryman was mustered back into his ranks. James nodded and moved carefully through the crowd.

People in this new state, if not exactly friendly, did not appear to be hostile either. At least not in public. He made his way through Jeffersonville without incident, stopping at a farrier to have a loose shoe seen to, the grizzle-bearded man taking his custom without comment beyond the exchange of coins.

This, even, is a kind of progress, James thought.

In Morgan County he stopped at the town hall in the county seat to ask did they have any land for sale. The woman went into the back office without saying a word. A man in a vest with bright glass buttons down the front came out and told him in a low voice that indeed there was no land for sale anywhere in the county and that he doubted very much if anyone would sell him any if there was.

"I already had my hat off," James would say later, "and now I bowed my head and backed out the door slow and deliberate and got the horse, calm as I could manage, fingers shaking near too much to gather the reins, and rode on out of there." His fright had come not from being put in his place, for he knew that as well as his last name, but in not being given place at all.

He pushed the horse as hard as he dared for the rest of the day but made fewer miles than he wished. It was knobby country with oxbow roads and ramshackle farms. In clearings that ran ragged up murky hollows he glimpsed cabins built of rough-hewn logs, without visible livestock, and whether coincidental or not, unmended fences. Not a lick of whitewash or other sign of prosperity. That night he slept miserably in a stand of maples in a cold rain, too scared to creep into a barn or any building that might bring him trouble.

From there he kept north, through more attractive land that sprouted tidy farms and barking dogs, following the roads when he could and steering with the sun along creeks to the northeast when the trace either petered out or went the wrong way. He stopped after two days riding in Lebanon, in Boone County, noticing right away the dirty, foulmo-uthed kids playing in the streets. They were behind him in a gaggle by the time he reached the courthouse. He quickly dismounted, tied up, and went inside to make his inquiries. In the land office a man sat at a desk paring his fingernails and whistling a brisk tune. After James had stood at the counter for several minutes the man said, "We are closed for lunch."

"I'm sorry sir, but it can't be past ten in the morning," James offered.

The clerk stared out at the walnut trees swaying in the May breeze. "We take long lunches here, boy," he replied. "Sometimes all day," he added, getting out of his chair with a groan and going into a back room.

James wondered whether there would be an end to this. He had not seen any black folks since Louisville and wondered now if there were any outside the big towns. Maybe he ought to ride back south and find something closer to where there were

17

people of his color, then there would be . . . What? The worst land and the butt-end of a society being built out of defeat? James had no doubts that things were better than they were, but better than slavery was about like saying better than dead. It didn't mean you could work, go to school, eat regular, go to sleep at night and not have to worry about who might be out there. His father, getting old now and having a hard time working, was already grumbling about how at least before he paid his yearly due and folks – white folks, even, he'd say, finger pointed at the sky – would hire him for his skill.

Now look at us, he'd say, showing his hands and their shovel and pick calluses. *Digging like goddamn plantation laborers.* His mother would slap her knees and rise to escape such talk, saying over her shoulder, *Don't you take the Lord's name that way Amos McGhee!* Up north seemed the only option James could see in getting out of such thinking, the resignation sewn into the fabric of the South.

He knew a town was getting close when small, ill-constructed dwellings began to appear in the fringe of woods on either side of a canal. These were built, it looked to him, from scraps of other, better places. Smoke rose from the insides of some, but he saw none of their occupants. A quarter mile later he came to a man astraddle an overturned stump looking intently at the water or something across it as though rapt in thought. He was shabbily dressed, the skin of his elbows poking through ragged homespun sleeves resting on filthy worsted trousers. The hat pulled tight onto his head was spangled with stains. Three cane poles arced delicately over the bank, their lines disappearing into the water below pieces of painted cork. The man did not turn until James was nearly upon him. When he did, a little startled, he said only a low, polite "how do," not looking up or blinded somewhat by the afternoon sun, since he took no notice of a stranger riding beside what must have been a familiar stretch of water for him. And not a hint of notice of seeing a black man astride a horse come along in the middle of a May day. James touched the brim of his hat, returned the same greeting. He thought better of asking *any luck?* since he could see a stringer stuck low in the bank pulled taut by a roil of fins and tails.

A rail bed curved out of the woods to join the stretch of canal. It appeared newly built, the steel bright and cold-looking. James regarded the rocks tumbled below the tie-ends, tar balled and glistening, littered with coal dust and shakes. He hoped there weren't children hereabouts with too much time on their devilworkshop hands.

The canal angled to follow the river's course. It moved brown-green, the surface furred by cottonwood down, a flat-bottomed boat rowing upstream against the far bank. This river wasn't so different from those in Alabama. Silty and sluggish, though here a milk and coffee brown instead of reddish clay. None of these rivers seemed able to cheerfully reflect the sky like the ocean was supposed to do.

"That must be a damn fine sight," he said to the horse.

James followed the towpath until it brought him to a street. He took it, moving up a graded bank, over the rail tracks, their shine a mark of civilization after so much green and brown. With trepidation born of recent experience he entered the outskirts of the river town still not knowing what it was called but with a greater curiosity upon him.

The houses at its edge were built with purpose and well cared for, the yards fenced with smart outbuildings freshly whitewashed, a few chickens pecking the fences clean of bugs. A yellow mutt followed him in the road at a distance, barked once out of habit rather than enthusiasm, and retreated back to the shade of a dogwood tree. And then there it was, a sign announcing the name of the town:

LaFayette
Welcomes You
Founded: 1825

19

After so many miles on the back of a horse, sleeping on a thin bedroll and eating the same food out of a sack, plagued by the feeling that he would never find a place for them to settle and how he would deliver this news to the family waiting in anticipation back in Tennessee, such words, no matter how shallow their inscription, touched him. Even though it was only a piece of wood, it was the first welcome he'd had since he set out.

James remembered the name of the river now. The Wabash. Ain't there a song about it? He couldn't remember, thought maybe it was another river, tried to think where Stephen Foster was from and was sure it was Kentucky or Ohio. He would have to get better at knowing the states and their ways if he was going to live here. It surprised him to think this way all of a sudden, faint hope a new feeling. He sat straight in his saddle and gathered himself to find something, anything here.

The street turned out to be Front Street. It ran alongside the canal, separated by houses and then a tannery, whose smoke and steam were visible just before the acrid smell. The tannery was a low wood affair, long and narrow beside the river with open doorways on both ends big enough for wagons to pass all the way through. A canal boat was pulling into the docking area, loaded high with bundles of raw hides, ropes stretched across the mottled skins, the bulkers waiting to unload the cargo. Even from this distance he could see the knotted muscles of their forearms. One man poled to keep the boat in the center of the channel while another led a team of draft horses on the towpath. James heard him call the horses to pull and could make out the faint creak of ropes and tackle against the wood stanchions in the bow of the boat.

The railroad tracks became visible again as Front Street came to an end. The houses on First Street were orderly and well-built: four-square with two floors, elaborate two-story with a perpendicular addition, and saltboxes. The chimneys were set inside the walls instead of outside as they were in the South. Holds the heat that way, he realized, thinking for the first time how different the seasons must be up here. At one of the houses a woman was tending a garden, hoeing between early radishes and onions, her children playing in a sandbox. A street came in from the right and he saw the sign, Alabama Street, and stopped the horse. Well now, that was a surprise. The buildings were commercial here and rose at least three stories. There was a hardware store, a livery, and what appeared to be a laundry, though it had no sign. On the sidewalk planking people tended to their business. Vegetables were arranged in bushel baskets beneath an awning, a barber poll turned bright red and white against pale limestone. A man with a cart and bell called out his enthusiasm and skill for the sharpening of cutlery. A seller of fish received a late-day delivery of ice from a stout bald man sweating a block with tongs on his shoulder, sawdust stuck to his shining head. No one seemed to notice him. Or if they did there was no sign of it. He kept his head down and followed a dray heaped with straw, fragrant and familiar.

James stayed behind the dray as it turned at Columbia, then onto Third at the corner of the courthouse square. The courthouse itself was a luminous mass of white limestone, columned up the front, with a greensward on one side where smartly dressed folks sat on benches beneath a fringe of new oak leaves. They passed Main Street and left the square, turning at Ferry and then into the open bay of a livery. James sat his horse in the street and watched the driver dismount so that he could get the wagon backed into place. To do this he took hold of the bridle and brought the horse forward until its head was nearly touching the boards of the stall on the far wall. He then pulled the bridle down so that the horse's nose sank to its chest and with his other hand patted it as far back on its hindquarters as he could reach, all the time saying "back now" in the same cadence. As hard as it is for

21

a horse to back up in harness to a heavy wagon, they made it look smooth. The bed of the wagon four feet from the bin the driver said "whoa" and the horse stopped.

As the man pitchforked straw James rode up and said, "That's a mighty good backin up horse you got there."

The man's back was to him and he stayed bent at his work. "Yep."

"Sorry to bother you while you're workin, but I needs some oats for the horse. You know whose place this is?"

"Name of McRae. Probly no here though, got boy works in late afternoons." With a hand on his lower back he straightened up, put a knuckle to one side of his nose and blew the other side over the wagon.

James looked around but there was no boy or other attendant in sight.

"I don't see nobody."

The man turned. He was short and wore once blue overalls stained in the front, shirtless, a fire of curly red hair on his head and licking out the top of the bib, his oval face and sharp nose skirted with an untended beard flecked with escaped straw. He had a friendly grin that dissipated to an open stare as he saw James sitting there. An unexpected curiosity.

"Well. We get not too many negro folks round here, cept on canal boat or upriver packet sometimes. Must be you rode in."

James had never heard such an accent, with its choppy sing-song, the voice slightly high-pitched for such a stocky fellow.

"Yessir. My people is carpenters, build just about anything. We aim to buy some land up here and commence to farmin." More detail than James had intended spilling out in his sentence, as though he had unwrapped it from an oilskin to declare his right to be sitting here, having goals and plans.

"Why you don't do that down there where you got more peoples? Seem strange to come all da way up here away from your kind."

22

James waited to see what this meant by the man's body language. The question had the familiar challenge to it but without the inflection he was used to hearing, the implicit warning that lay inside such seeming plainspokenness. The man stood leaning on the pitchfork, with neither belligerence nor attitude.

Maybe he just wanted to know.

"If it was simple we'd stay down there. Trouble is they's too much that can't be fixed by a war, won or not."

"From what I read in papers it is maybe worse now."

"Yessir. For some folks it is. They'd rather be back with the devil they knows. They ain't prepared to be free."

"Well, to be honest I do not know whether you get welcome here. For me a good Christian should have been against that slave business. Jesus say all of this pretty clearly in the book of Matthew. Judge a man by his deeds. If he prove different, well . . . I tell you one thing, when I arrive in this country and join up with Union army, this was in sixty-four, we fought beside a negro regiment – "

A scream shattered the quiet of the barn, spooking the dray horse and knocking the man over hard in the bed of the wagon. As he fell he struck the edge of his forehead on the side rail. James tried to steady his own horse and saw that the man did not get up. The screaming continued. A woman. And another voice, a boy's maybe, yelling for someone to let go. At the far end of the barn another bay door let out into an alley. James could see through the gloom the back of a brick building across a stretch of cobblestones.

He spurred his horse around the dray and across the center aisle, urging with his knees against her hesitancy. The sound of gruffer voices. A man's phlegmed laugh, his lungs laboring, a whooped cough, a slap, the crack of heels. The horse stopped at the threshold, the edge of late afternoon sunlight drawing a line downalley. James jerked the reins, forcing the reluctant animal over the lip of bricks and into the bright light. The mare's steel hooves rung on the cobbles, the alley a mass of sound and confused movement toward which he reined and was on them.

The sudden appearance of the horse startled two men, a boy of fourteen or so, and a woman in a yellow dress. The boy's brown wool hat lay on the stones and his nose was bloody. The smaller, slighter man had a handful of the boy's collar in his scraped fist. On the ground a bigger man was astraddle the woman, his elbow across her throat while the other hand fumbled beneath the layers of her petticoats for flesh. The man holding the boy took a step towards the intruder, free hand over his eyes to block the light. His thick mustache covered a gap-toothed sneer, the gold in his mouth glistering in the hard light.

"Mind your business and move on."

The woman thrashed and gurgled over the elbow, desperate and guttural, the man still foraging, moving his hips. James knew he should turn and ride off, go to the next town, or head back south and admit defeat.

"Nosir. I cain't do that. You turn that boy loose and get your friend up offen her."

The man leaned forward, took an unsteady step, wrenched the boy's neck to get a better grip.

"Well *Jee*zus. Will you look here Walt? This nigger wants us to stop. Thinks he's in charge." He turned but Walt was not listening. He laughed his phlegmatic laugh and spat a thick gob. "You get back on your boat you know what's good for you, sambo. I ain't gonna fucking say it again."

Out of the back of his belt he drew a knife, held it up glinting, its brass shank the color of the tooth but cleaner. James reached behind him and removed his Hawken rifle from its strap atop the bedroll, doubled the reins in his left fist and brought the gun around.

"You shoot me you'll hang quicker'n shit."

"I ain't interested in shootin you," James said slowly. Then he pivoted the heavy rifle around his palm and slammed the stock down on top of the man's head. He crumpled without a word and the knife bounced metallic between the front legs of the horse. At this sound Walt turned, his mouth a downturned slash in a red-brown beard, hand drawn out of yellow cotton. He sat back on his heels and tried to pull a heavy Colt Navy out of his belt but the barrel was too long and he was wrestling it as James took three quick running steps off the horse and swung the Hawken into his chest. The impact made the sound of a blunt axe on a soft tree. The woman screamed as the boy ran down the alley, nails in the soles of his boots clicking. Walt fell backwards with the force of the blow, writhing and curling up on his side. James put his boot on the whiskered neck, reached down and pulled the Colt the rest of the way out of his belt to put it in his own. The woman's honey-colored hair was badly disheveled, her eye makeup had run down her cheeks, and a small leak of blood ran the cusp of one nostril. She stared at him as she sat shaking in her dandelion dress. When she backed away he stood still, empty palm out to reassure her he meant no harm.

That bright yellow was the last thing he remembered until he woke up on his back on the cold hard floor of a jail cell. Or so he found out once he struggled to his feet, feeling the back of his head which, he said, was sure to be stove clean in if the pain was any indication. His fingers found a large knot and a crust of dried blood. His eyes adjusted in the halflight making out a cot hung by chains to the wall, a bucket, the lattice of iron bars. It smelt fetid and dank, of old sweat and decay. A man groaned somewhere.

Oh Lord, he thought, *I must have killed one of them men.*

He sat against the wall and put his head in his hands and waited.

Three

Miss Lenore had been right about the tale. It was slow going at first, but with her help Clayton soon became deeply absorbed in Crusoe's adventures. He managed only a few pages a day due to his habit of rereading passages he liked. And he liked a great many of them.

He confided in Miss Lenore his worry that he'd come to the end too soon. She reassured him there were many, many more books in the world. That may be, he replied, but I only got this one.

Clayton was finding the evening Bible reading more and more difficult. Before his father left the book of Exodus had been exciting. Now an adventure story made him afraid for the main character's life. He could not keep from imagining what was happening to James in light of Crusoe's story. There were big differences, of course. His father was not free to journey as he liked to make a fortune; there was a necessity to his travel. But he thought Crusoe must have felt the same way: he had to leave home and take risks in order to have a better life. Amos had explained to the boys that James had gone to do just this. Since it was Crusoe's story, Clayton at first identified with this adventurous young man. And when he nearly died in the first sea voyage, and then was captured by Barbary pirates in the second, Clayton felt a deep kinship with his narrator as each day's reading brought new challenges and solutions. But when Crusoe escaped the Moors with the slave boy he was faced with a decision that divided his loyalties. As much as Clayton wanted to be like

Robinson Crusoe – brave, resourceful, clever – he could not stop thinking about how that slave boy felt. Hadn't his father been a slave boy? And his grandfather before him? He knew he was the first boy in family memory who was *not* a slave, but this didn't erase the fact that he'd been born that way.

It was a relief when Crusoe and the boy were rescued by the Portuguese Captain. But then Crusoe sells him. Just like that: from companion to commerce. Crusoe starts a plantation in Brazil and decides that the only way it can work is with slave labor, which he attempts to get by sailing to West Africa. It is during this journey that he is shipwrecked on his famous island. Clayton was starting to think that this man was getting what he deserved. How many times had Amos told him that those who sow the wind reap the whirlwind? He reckoned that adventures were fine, but they ought not be pursued at the expense of others. Didn't it ever occur to Crusoe that the slave boy had feelings? Did he give any thought to whether the Africans he might get to work in far-off Brazil would not find it much of an adventure?

Clayton judged Crusoe to be a man who understood these questions better once he was alone on the island and discovered that not only were there fierce, dark-skinned natives with a claim on his new home, but that they would also happily eat him. The money he had made and the land he owned wouldn't mean a fig to the cannibals. With this turn of events Clayton settled into a happier relationship with his narrator. He appreciated his fear and vulnerability, the lack of mastery his skin color had previously afforded him. As an outsider Crusoe was a good companion. He didn't want him to get eaten, but he was glad the cannibals had shown up to give him a fuller understanding of what it felt like to be reduced to being food or a possession.

On a rainy May morning Clayton sat on the left-hand bench in front of Peacham's reading. Or trying to. The three old men who were inveterate inhabitants of the right-hand bench – who Ben called the Three Wise Men to their faces and the Three Blind Mice behind their backs – were carrying on about horses. Each one had been a groom before the war and swore up and down that they had been witness to the finest piece of horse flesh anyone had ever laid a curry comb to. Lies and exaggerations ensued, wagers made without regard to scale or monetary sufficiency. He tried to ignore them but they cackled and thumped the sidewalk with their canes. Miss Lenore came out to hush them a little, which she accomplished by standing in the frame of the door. As fearless as they were in the presence of a headstrong, willful animal, they had no illusions about who held the bridle hereabouts.

She came and sat by Clayton and glanced over to check the page number he was on. It was hard to concentrate with her sitting there.

"These old fools bothering you?"

"No ma'am," he lied. She knew better.

"I'll get the law over here quick as a cat if they're disturbing anybody. I can't have any loitering round this place."

The three old men laughed at this latest installment of the No Loitering game.

Filly Joe, weathered and toothless, his hat so battered it looked like it had started its life as another piece of haberdashery entirely, said: "Miss Lenore, you know we keep this here pew free of lingerers and layabouts. They ain't no more tolerated than the devil his self."

"For what I'm payin you all to rope in custom I'd expect to be a little busier."

"There ain't many bodies a stirring in this weather. Charley wants to know what that boy is reading." He pointed with his stick at Clayton. Charley, whose last name nobody knew, was built in the same manner as Filly Joe, but with a jagged scar that cut at an angle from his hairline to just below his ear. The puckered flesh was pale pink and the eyeless socket wept a liquid attended to with an ever-present red handkerchief.

"Why you asking me?"

"That durn boy won't no more tell us what he's a doin than that son of yourn will show us a little card trick. You cain't get young folks to do nothing nowadays."

His cronies nodded their heads like crows on a branch.

"How bout you fellas make a pick up for me over at the depot and I'll fix you beans and cornbread for dinner."

Clayton suppressed a smile as the three men hoisted themselves off their perch with groans and sharp words for one another. This was the only time they moved about, other than getting to the store from their boardinghouse. Lenore could have sent Clayton or Ben to fetch whatever little thing the station master held on to for her, but she knew it did them good to have a purpose. As they shuffled off Ben's voice rang out from inside.

"See how they run, see how they run. Did you ever see such a sight in your life?"

They crossed the street still locked in animated conversation taking no heed of the wagon that reined up and stopped for them. At the grocer's they paused to hail one of the shoppers bent over a bin of potatoes or onions, no doubt dispensing advice regarding the choosing of root vegetables. At the corner drugstore they spoke with the postman who was on his way out. They were still talking to him when he broke away to resume his rounds. When they were out of sight the street fell into a hush, the skies opening up in a serious downpour.

The rain made its din on the tin overhang undisturbed by the chatter of old men.

Clayton resumed his reading and Miss Lenore sat quietly next to him.

Unable to hitch his attention to the motion of the plot he closed the book.

"What's on your mind?" she asked.

"Not knowing what's happening to him. Been having bad dreams too. Daddy in a big stew pot with painted cannibals dancing all around."

"Have you ever heard the saying 'What's without remedy should be without regard'?"

He shook his head.

"Try not to fret, Clay. It can't be as bad as it is in any book."

A heavy door wauled open on its hinges, light spilling into the edge of the cell from down the passage. James stood up, legs and back stiff, his head throbbing. He hadn't realized how thirsty he was. A man with a bucket stood at the bars. James couldn't see much of his features except his slight build. He wore a vest over a white shirt with a star pinned to it that caught the furtive light.

"Put your ass on that cot yonder."

James did so. A round of keys rattled at the lock. He opened the door a foot and slid the bucket inside.

"There's water in there."

"Obliged."

The door clicked shut.

"What's your name?"

"James McGhee, with a h."

Telling him something with that. Letters.

"Noted. What's a man like you doing in this part of the country on a horse? You come up or down?"

"Up. From Tennessee."

"Mighty long ride. What's your business?"

"Well, there ain't been much work for folks in the trades, for carpenterin and such, since the war – "

"I'd a thought they'd be need for that with what Sherman and the others did down there."

"Yessir. My folks, black folks, ain't a lot of call for us who has skills by them who'd as soon not be reminded of Sherman

30

and such, as you say. We come up from Alabama. I rode up this way lookin to buy some land to start farmin on. Ain't nothin in the South for us now."

"I spect not."

"Beg pardon, but where's my horse and my things what was on her? I mean, beggin your pardon but them men was . . . I was – "

He lurched off the cot and turned, putting his forehead on the cool of the iron frame, trying to hold in his guts.

"Slow down. We'll sort this out when Walt can talk or his brother wakes up."

He clutched his stomach, wrapping his arms as hard as he could around himself.

"But shorely them two ain't gone tell the truth, expecially with me – "

"With you beating the tar out of them?" The man laughed a little behind his mustache, raised his hat up and scratched his head. "I reckon they ain't likely to confess to nothin."

"I meant with someone else to blame, fella like me, I spect they'll cotton right to that."

"I spect they will, and like I said, we'll get it sorted out in due time." He put the keys on his belt and started back the way he came.

"Why'nt you ask the lady?" James said after him. He rose and leaned against the bars, pressing his forehead against more cold iron.

"Says she don't remember anything." The heavy door chirred open.

"What about the boy?" Silence. The light stayed constant, faint along the passage between the cells and the flagstone wall. Footfalls back. James retreated.

"What boy?"

"They was a boy there too, getting treated rough, what got the man the cracked head." James started to reach up to the back of his own head and stopped.

31

"What'd he look like?"

James described him. Told how he ran out of the alley. The man drew his hand down his chin and neck against his whiskers.

"Sit tight," he said and strode down the passage shutting the door behind him, darkening the cell.

"Ain't much else *to* do," James whispered to himself quietly. He eased down on his side on the cot, pulled his knees up, and tried not to worry, tried not to think about his horse, his money, the future.

"McGhee. Wake up."

James rolled over to a white hot pain. He swung his legs around and felt the back of his head instinctively, trying to see who was there. The sheriff again, if it was the sheriff. Had they talked about that? He couldn't remember. His body ached and the pain kept time in his head like far-off thunder.

It sounded like a thousand keys in the lock.

"Come on with me."

"Where we goin?"

"Bound to be better than this, ain't it?"

He sat still, listening for any other sounds.

"They's fryin pans and then they's fires."

The man laughed and held the door, gesturing toward the light.

James walked along the darkened cells, a hush but for his shuffle on the stone floor. The door of his cell clicked behind him. He took the two steps up, past an open heavy door into a sparsely furnished room. The walls were brick. Wedged in one corner a desk (oak, James noticed without having to think about it), two slat-backed wooden chairs facing it, a potbellied stove in another corner with a redbone hound stretched out next to it. Against one wall a cabinet with rifles, a sawed-off shotgun, brace of pistols hanging from pegs, all locked behind a wire grille. Through a window James could see that it was late evening or early morning, the street empty of people. On one of the chairs was his hat. He picked it up, felt inside, fingers coming away clean. The door was shut heavily and the man hung the keys on a fob at his belt, walked around the desk and sat down, gesturing for James to do the same. James looked him over. Sandy mustache, turned down at the ends, thin nose, freckles, light eyebrows and lashes, boyish but not young, the crow's feet around his eyes deep. The eyes were sparkling and sharp. Lawman eyes.

"The boy told me what happened. The woman got her memory back once I told her what he said. She confirmed it and filled in the gaps. Walt's story was a might different. Had some real imaginative moments, him defending her honor against that black devil and so forth."

"That boy belong to her?"

"Not hardly. She ain't got much honor neither."

"That still don't give them no right to do her that way or a boy like that."

"Agreed. Man from the paper was here earlier asking after what happened, said he'd spoken to Cmicky about seeing a negro on a horse then heard there'd been some commotion behind McRae's Livery."

"Who'd you say?"

"Cmicky. Polack drives a dray and delivers things."

"I done forgot about him. He all right? I reckon he cracked his head pretty good."

"A passel of cracked heads yesterday." He picked up a short briarwood pipe off his desk, struck a match off the bricks behind him and lit it, hands cupped around the bowl. James thought of his Uncle Willis, long dead now, and his mouth harp. Smoke lifted gently between them.

"He'll live. Got a bandage on it like he's playing the fife in the 4th of July parade."

"It morning or evening out there?"

"Morning. I bet you're hungry. Girl from the Lahr House

is bringing breakfast over. Ought to be here any minute."

"Thank you kindly. You the sheriff?"

"I am. Name's Colegrove."

A knock on the door and a girl came in with a heavy basket covered by a checked cloth, trailing an aroma that made James sit all the way forward in his chair. He was starved.

The girl set the basket on the desk and sneaked a look at James.

"I'll be back with coffee," she said.

"OK, thanks Emily."

The sheriff stood up, sat his pipe in the ashtray, took the cover off the basket and put his nose in. His eyes said he liked the smell. He cleared one side of the desk and began unloading, taking out ham, eggs, crocks of butter and preserves – grape, it looked like, and something pale yellow, and raspberry full of seeds – a pitcher of milk, and a stack of biscuits. James felt lightheaded, his stomach an impossibly small burning thing making him swallow to keep from retching. He had to clasp his hands in his lap to keep from grabbing something and wolfing it down.

"Go on then, you must be starved." He handed James a plate.

James stood, leaned over, made a modest pile of eggs, took a piece of ham, picked up a biscuit and smelled it, opened it with his thumbs, was too hungry to care that they weren't any too clean, slathered butter and jam on it. He sat with the plate in his lap and ate it all without pausing. Colegrove was still buttering his biscuit when James looked up, plate empty. The girl came in with the coffee, looked at James' plate as though she expected to find something fascinating there. She sat the pot down leaving a cloth wrapped around the handle and went out again.

"Well, don't be shy, tuck in there again."

James did as before. He held up a biscuit while the sheriff poured coffee into red enamel cups.

34

"You know I never tasted a biscuit till after the war was over. We never ate nothin but cornbread."

"Why's that?"

"Daddy always said *Biscuits is for white folks*. That never made a damn bit of sense to me. I know what he means now, but I still like biscuits."

They ate in silence. The dog stretched and rolled over onto its other side, yawning widemouthed and licking its paw before easing back into rhythmic breathing. James was amazed it could sleep with so much food in the room. Maybe dogs were different up here. From outside came the sound of wagons rolling by in the street, footsteps drumming on the wooden walkway, the falsetto of a boy hawking newspapers off along the street somewhere. The town was waking up.

"Am I free to go?" James had suddenly thought of his horse, the money sewed into the saddle, all that was left to do. He set his plate gingerly in the basket, nearly as clean as when he'd received it.

"If you can write you need to sign out a sworn statement, then you can be on your way." James nodded and wiped his hands on his trousers. "I want to say thanks for what you done, since there ain't much chance Polly Sevier, the woman in the yella dress, is going to, nor the boy, nor, come to think of it, Walt and his brother who are lucky they didn't do something a hell of a lot worse. Drunk bastards. Anyway, best I could do was feed you breakfast and get your horse for you. She's tied up in front. I had her rubbed down and fed."

"Can I pay you? They ain't – "

"No call for that. What you going to do now?"

James finished his coffee. He took his hat from the other chair, settled it firmly on his head, snugging it down over his eyes gently as far as the bump in back.

"Go over to the land office I reckon. Lord willin they'll be somethin for sale, or at least somethin they'll sell me, if you know what I mean."

"It's across the street in the courthouse, second floor. When you get up there ask for Marjorie Lane. Tall slim woman. The man who runs it, you don't want much truck with him if you can help it. I don't think he likes, uh, southerners."

"Yessir. Obliged."

The sheriff held out his hand and James shook it. A small courtesy between men, but James felt it differently, the first white hand he'd been offered in the North.

It was by far the nicest courthouse he had set foot in yet. White plastered walls, blond oak floors, a wide walnut stairway, its newels and rails shined a deep brown. Ornamental brass gas lights hung at intervals. James wondered when they used them, since the building was lit brightly by its floor-to-ceiling windows. On the second floor he found the land office, the sign marking it at a right angle from the wall over the door.

This office looked like the others: as long as a rail car, counter up front with a few chairs for people to wait in, three desks in a line under high windows. A rank of file cabinets covered the other wall. At the back of the room hung a large plat map of the county, the river clearly visible slicing through it with the density of the town a shadow in the center on its eastern bank. James shut the door. A clerk sitting at the nearest desk rose to meet him. The man was short, his head not reaching much higher out of the chair than in it, and fat. He wore a maroon waistcoat and gray trousers which made a chafing sound when he walked. His wispy, thinning hair was drawn forward framing a clean-shaven face that would have been boyish if the look it held were not so stern.

There was no sign of Marjorie Lane.

"What office you looking for boy?"

James removed his hat.

"This here office, the land office."

The man stared James in the eye but said nothing, his face

impassive. As if the stranger's reply required some thinking. James felt a rising tension but did not want to show it.

"Your boat leave you?"

"No sir," he said, genuinely surprised. "I didn't come on no boat."

"Is that so. Most folk like you come through on a boat. Come in and go right back out. Maybe take a drink at Martin's tavern off the towpath but that's about all."

"Is Marjorie Lane here today?"

The man interlaced his fingers on the counter and stared at them. His elbows barely reached a comfortable place on the edge.

"There is nothing Miss Lane can do for you that I cannot. Now what is it that you want?"

James did not think it wise to leave now and come back later, since perhaps she had taken sick or was on holiday. Maybe the sheriff had been fooling with him.

"Well sir," James said slowly, looking down at the hat he held in front of him with both hands, biding his time. He chose his words carefully. "I'm interested in buyin a farm or some land to farm on."

The man's short fingers played his knuckles, rhythmically. One thumb orbited the other.

"So either a farm, with a house and outbuildings, perhaps accoutrements, or land, arable of course. That's what you are *interested* in?" he offered, the mockery clear despite his level tone.

James squeezed his hat, thought how nice it would feel to have his hands on that neck. He tried to remind himself what his mama would say a good Christian would do.

Before he could come up with anything in response, the clerk went on.

"If you could get a piece of land, some acreage, say, then what would you do? Sleep on the ground? In the *trees*, perhaps?"

"No sir, there'd be no need for that. My daddy and I would – "

"So there are more of you? Good god."

"Yessir, they's seven of us, including my boys. As I was commencin to say, we'd build our own house and such. We skilled – "

"*Skilled*. Yes, well, that may be what they call what your kind did before the war, but it's *different* up here, you see."

"I don't think – "

But he was cut off by the man, his face flushed with some inner exertion. He slapped the palms of his hands on the counter to emphasize his words.

"There is nothing for sale. Now please leave this office and reboard your boat."

Four

James McGhee had ridden a long way and was tired. He had slept in the open on hard ground, eaten stale food, been cursed at, lied to, chased by dogs and children, and even saved a woman from harm who did not bother to thank or even acknowledge him.

Now he was angry.

He was brought up to be submissive to white people. There hadn't been any choice in that. He knew how to repress his wants and shunt his thoughts to survival. Live for a better day, his mama had told him. Turn the other cheek. He felt just about out of cheeks to turn. His fury rose up in him and he watched it rush past its usual mark without cease.

He let it.

When his fists slammed down on the counter his expression of rage shocked the fat clerk who jumped back is if he had been struck. In a panic he turned toward his desk, intending perhaps to arm himself with something there or put some furniture between his person and this crazed black intruder. In doing so got his feet tangled. He stumbled and reached out to grasp the edge of the desk but he misjudged the distance and his forehead struck it with a dull crack.

James held still, waiting to see if the man would stir. When there was no movement he dropped his hat on the counter and let himself through the low swinging door that separated it from the wall.

"Mister?" he said in a quiet voice.

There was no response. He advanced cautiously, afraid the man would come to and just as scared that he would not.

James bent down and shook him gently, then leaned over and put his ear to the man's back. He was breathing. As carefully as he could he rolled him over to see how grievously he'd hit his head. He folded his handkerchief into a square to dab at the blood. There was a darkening bruise and swelling but he wasn't bleeding badly.

He had to think. If the man died and he was found alone with him they would never believe it was an accident. His horse was close by. With a little luck he could be miles from town before the man was discovered. But if he died when he could have been saved by the timely fetching of a doctor . . . .well, that was a kind of murder too. The sheriff seemed a good man. If he had to trust someone to believe him there was no better option. Having a plan made him feel calmer.

When he heard the door open his heart hammered in his chest.

Marjorie Lane wedged the door open with her foot, a steaming cup of tea held perilously in one hand, a parcel cradled under her other arm. She thrust her head in to appeal to Tumwater to get up and help her. When there was no answer she suppressed her irritation, managing to wriggle through without dropping anything or spilling too much tea.

"Wendell?"

There was a hat on the counter.

"Where on earth have you gone?"

When the stranger stood up she did not scream but her cup crashed to the floor and the parcel fell into the spreading puddle of chamomile. He was tall, black, bareheaded, and held a bloody cloth.

Truth was, she was surprised she had not opened the door on a scene like this before. Wendell Tumwater was not renowned for his politeness. Marjorie had no trouble guessing what he had done to a black man to upset him so.

"What on earth is going on in here?" she asked. She went

40

through the swinging half-door and saw her colleague flat on his back, his forehead cut and bruised. She knew she should be scared, but the man had backed up and around the desk.

"Miz Lane?"

This surprised her.

"How do you know my name?"

James took a deep breath, let it out slowly.

"It was an accident, ma'am. Sheriff Colegrove told me to speak to you. Said the man who works here might not be too helpful. I rode up here from Tennessee and I need to find a place for me and my family to settle, have a farm, keep to ourselves. The man here wouldn't listen to me and I got mad and it scared him and he tripped and whopped his head on the desk."

"We need to get a doctor. It looks pretty bad."

"Yes, ma'am. I was gonna get the sheriff, but probly better the way you say."

"Please stay here. I'll be back as soon as I can."

"Name's McGhee, ma'am, James McGhee."

He wasn't sure why he told her this, but reckoned it made sense to be as cooperative as he could.

James waited for ten excruciating minutes, periodically checking to see if the clerk was still breathing. He kept the handkerchief on the cut. Marjorie Lane returned with a doctor in a black suit followed by Sheriff Colegrove.

The doctor went straight to Tumwater and opened his bag. James stood up and backed away, the examination proceeding with no indication he was there. The sheriff caught James's eye and gestured towards the far end of the room, where they moved to talk in front of the filing cabinets.

"I told Marjorie your business here and she'll see what she can find once we get him seen to," Colegrove said quietly. James had been looking at his feet, expecting to be told to move along and not come back. He met the sheriff's gaze.

"You a good man, Mr. Colegrove."

"It's the least I could do. I don't support Tumwater and his friends."

"We ain't had too much help from white folks. We won't forget this."

"Who's to say I might not need me a carpenter one day here soon? My house is awful drafty. Be seein you." He pulled his pipe out of his shirt pocket, knocked it against the sole of his boot then blew through the stem to clear it. Marjorie looked at him disapprovingly, as if to remind him that he was indoors. He turned back, a thoughtful look on his face.

"I almost forgot to ask you. You didn't hit him did you? I mean, I can understand if you did, but that'll make things complicated. He may not look like much, but there's more like him than you'd think."

"No sir, it's the way I told it to Miz Lane. I swear."

Colegrove spoke a few words to Marjorie then let himself out, holding the door for a man who wrestled a stretcher into the office. James watched as they lifted the fat clerk onto the canvas, hoisted him up, and navigated out and into the hallway.

"Mr. McGhee." Her friendly smile was a relief. "I will take a look in the plat book and the survey lists to see what is available."

"Yes ma'am. I'm thankful for your help. If they's a broom I'd be glad to sweep up that crockery yonder."

She rummaged beneath the counter and came up with a straw whisk broom and a file folder.

"This will have to do for a dustpan. It's all we have. And don't thank me yet. We have yet to see if there is anything to be had."

James gathered up the larger fragments, placing them carefully in the small steel bin next to the door. The chamomile smelled like spring and James suddenly felt as though it had been months since he sat on the porch of their house in Nashville watching Lily planting slips, prettying their most recent temporary home. It had only been two weeks, maybe less.

Marjorie went to the back wall and put her finger on the large map, drawing it along the river from the town south by west, on the opposite bank and out into the county. On a table beneath the map she untied the string and opened a large folio, ran her finger down a column of names and numbers, stopped, then held it in place carefully as she drew out another smaller binder of loose sheets of heavier paper, many embossed with a seal, some yellowed, others worn with folding. She found the one she was looking for and took it out.

"Come here please."

James approached and she put her finger back on the map, pointing to a small rectangle on the other side of the river, a finger's breadth away from it, southwest of the town. It had a number written on it and this she directed him to in the folio.

"You see here, this parcel, eighty acres, was owned by the Metzgers – "

"What happened to them?"

"It was only the old man at the end and they, well, they found him dead there, in the . . . I'm not sure exactly. I do think those circumstances have hindered its sale. A bit spooky or unlucky for some folks."

She seemed not to want to talk any more about that subject and James was in no position to push her.

"We way beyond worryin about luck, Miz Lane. What kind of land is it and how much do they want?"

"It says here seventy-six acres of tillage, pasture, and orchard, a creek, and four acres of homestead. Outbuildings, barn, cabin. And there's a note."

She turned the page and ran her finger down a list of names, stopping half way.

"House uninhabitable. Barn and outbuildings in sag, no, sad, shape." She looked at him, her eyebrows arched quizzically. "A rather impressionistic entry by someone, but I think

43

it's clear that things had not been kept up out there. They will certainly have gotten worse in the year that Mr. Metzger has been dead."

"How much?"

"Well, the winter was a pretty rough one and – "

"No ma'am, how much does it cost?"

She opened a drawer and pulled out a ledger, opened its glossy red cover, checked the number again from the folio, and found the entry.

"It has been assessed at four hundred ten dollars. It would be more, but with the decrepit state of the buildings it's only a shade above what it would be just for the land."

James thought of the money he had sewed into his saddle. Four hundred thirty-one dollars. It wouldn't leave him much left over, but he figured he'd need little for the ride home. He felt suddenly tired, as though age had overtaken him here of a sudden, the ride up country, the uncertainty, the imagining of those older faces, the smaller ones, their hopes and fears. The back of his head ached.

And then he saw it.

As he had when he'd ridden in and come upon the river flowing in the distance, the patchwork of farms and houses and the bluff on the other side, the feeling of calm and possibility that had come over him.

"I'll take it."

"Don't you want to ride out and take a look first? See how bad the buildings are?"

"Are there other places you can sell me for the same price with good buildings?"

"Well, no, there's really nothing else, except some tracts of woods at the east end of the county."

"Then I'll take it. How do we do this?"

"According to the records, Mr. Metzger was the last surviving member of his family and the estate was put into foreclosure to pay his debts. The county seized it for nonpayment

44

of back taxes and paid off his creditors against its value. All of which means you will have to go to the Assessor's Office down the hall, since they handle sales and act as the cashier for the county. Can I ask how you are going to pay for this?"

"Cash money."

"Let me walk you down there. You'll have to wait a couple of minutes while I get the paperwork together."

James untied his horse from the hitching rail in front of the courthouse, led her over to the trough, and patted her neck while she drank her fill. Tucked into his saddle, where the greenbacks had been meticulously sewn, having been so carefully saved and counted, stacked, recounted, was the old oilskin in which they used to keep their papers, now protecting the bill of sale for the new farm. He had to smile. The horse took its nose out of the trough, swung around, blew water out of its nostrils. Its near eye regarded him as though he were suddenly a stranger.

"What, you never seen a man smile before?" He had to admit that she probably hadn't. Not in a good while.

It had been a couple of hours since Marjorie left him in the Assessor's with the nice gray-haired lady to finish his paperwork. She said she had some things to attend to and passed the briefest of looks with him as she said goodbye.

James walked his horse back to the sheriff's office, tied up, and knocked on the door. Colegrove sat behind his desk, running an oiled piece of white cotton through the barrel of a partially disassembled Colt Dragoon. He looked up, removed the wire-rimmed spectacles from behind his ears and sat them beside the pistol's cylinder.

"Marjorie find you anything?"

"Bought us a place downriver a few miles. Round eighty acres."

"Marjorie say whose it was?"

"Metzger."

"She tell you the buildings are for shit out there? I don't think the house even has a passable roof anymore. Doubt the barn's anything but a buzzard roost."

"That don't matter, we aim – "

"She tell you about the old man?"

"Only that they found him dead out there someway. A might skittish about the details and I didn't press, beggars not being choosers and all."

"Just as well." He reached for his pipe. "It is pretty land over there, I'll tell you that. You get the buildings and such straightened out you'll have you a nice farm."

James tried to think what to say next. The deed of sale in the oilskin seemed less powerful now as a talisman, unable to guarantee him safe passage where there was bad blood.

"I don't want no trouble when we all come back up this way."

"I understand." Colegrove put both boots flat on the floor and sat up in his chair, gripped the edge of the desk with his free hand and pointed at James with the stem of his pipe. "Look McGhee, it won't be easy for you folks here. Different maybe, but not easy with the likes of that fat man and his friends. They don't care much for anything different around this county and they pretty much run things off the river and the canal and now the railroad. Big plans for this place. I wouldn't get between them and theirs, if you know what I mean."

"We want to be left to ourselves, get on with our lives."

"You'll still have to come to town, trade with folks, participate in life here whether you want to or not."

"We pretty good at stayin out of view and harm's way. Spect we'll just have to be careful."

"Let's hope harm leaves well enough alone."

"Yessir. You know what they say – "

The heavy, ironbound door to the cells swung slowly open on its poorly oiled hinges, a sound that made James cringe.

46

Through it backed a small figure sweeping the end of the hall with a broom. He turned, saw James standing there and stopped, dustpan held out in front of him. The boy from the alley.

The sheriff broke the uncomfortable silence.

"You two haven't really met one another. McGhee, this here is my boy Charles Junior, but everyone calls him June. June, this here is James McGhee."

James extended his right hand. After several awkward seconds June shook it but did not meet the older man's eyes.

"You got something you want to say to Mr. McGhee?"

"Thanks mister," the boy said.

He looked over to his father who gave him a nod. He put the broom and dustpan next to the door, opened it enough to get through and was out on the sidewalk and gone.

Colegrove shifted his weight in the chair, picked up the barrel of the Colt, sighted down its length with one eye.

"Boy's had a hard time. Started when his mama got sick. She was the only one he would really talk to. After she died it ain't been easy for him."

"I reckon not," James replied, trying not to think how far away his own family was.

"He got into some trouble a few weeks back. I thought working at the livery for a few hours after school would do him some good. Figured maybe I'd get Cmicky to teach him to work horses. Hell, I never can find the time myself. You got any boys, McGhee?"

"Three of em."

He opened the other eye.

"That's a handful. Your wife must be worth her weight in gold."

James stood still.

"Shit, I'm sorry," Colegrove said. "I didn't mean nothin by that. An expression is all."

"I know it," James replied.

47

"He's a good boy, but a dark mood gets a hold of him and he don't have no reason about him."

"How long ago, you don't mind my askin."

James thought he had overstepped a boundary when Colegrove stared at him. The strength seemed to go out of the man and he said in a quiet voice, "Right before Christmas."

"I'm truly sorry for you and your boy, sheriff." He wanted to ask whether there had been any news about Tumwater's injury, but it didn't seem proper.

James put his hat on though it still hurt to do so. He extended his hand. The sheriff stood, took it.

"Godspeed. We'll be seein you before long I expect."

"Yessir, you will. Thanks again for the meal this mornin," James replied, remembering the biscuits, wondering how long till he'd eat another one.

"No trouble. Least I could do for the boy and for bashing your head in that way."

James laughed. It had not occurred to him before that it was Charles Colegrove who knocked him out.

Five

James recounted his journey at the table after a long sleep and a huge meal. Nearly a whole chicken and most of a row of collards. The boys sat rapt, elbows on the table supporting their chins as he told of riding up through Kentucky, across the wide Ohio, of Louisville and the hams he'd seen hanging, the toymaker across the bridge. In Clayton's mind his tall, strong father rode upright, proud on his horse through the city and across the river. He had to remind himself that there was a bridge and that his picture of the horse chesting the water was inaccurate.

Marjorie Lane figured as something of a hero in James's story, as did the sheriff for not taking the white man's side in the aftermath of the accident in the Land Office. James described the farm as best he could and now gestured for Lily to hand him the oilskin on its lanyard, from which he drew the deed and bill of sale. Here Amos had questions and moved his chair closer to the table. The two men discussed the buildings, what they would need to do, supplies and strategies. Amos made some sketches with a stub of pencil on the inside back cover of a Witherby Tool Company catalog they kept in a drawer of the sideboard. As the men made plans, the boys began to yawn and lose interest. Lily put her hand on each head and gesturing for them to follow her, to get ready for bed. Their protests were quieted by the look James gave them.

On the way north they most often found people civil, if not hospitable, especially when they understood that the wagon

49

and the laden horse were not stopping to settle down. The few provisions they'd needed and provender for the horses had been bought from the backs of stores and liveries with little talk beyond exchange, a word of thanks, a nod.

Each day was measured in miles of washed-out and rutted track. Occasionally there was a smoother pike with a toll, the old man coming out of his little house at their approach to collect his pennies. The visible world was monotonously bordered by a wall of trees, other times a slough with mossy stumps sticking up for perched birds, or tallgrass prairie, waving with the breeze like an inland sea, hissing, fragrant, impenetrable.

West of Indianapolis they spent the night beneath their stretched canvas cover outside the village of Brownsburg and got directions to the Crawfordsville Road that led into Montgomery County. They crossed Big Walnut Creek and Raccoon Creek via covered bridge, a novelty the boys had come to look forward to since entering this new state, taking turns hollering for the echo it made. They had been told to stop this after two bridges but could not help it, poking each other in the ribs to see who would have the courage to break the silence, earning the pretend ire of their grandfather, who swung around scowling in mock menace, the boys pretending to button their lips, eyes in the rafters.

Pushing on through Crawfordsville – a town that appeared to have been established longer than any others they'd seen in many days, which even had a college, its brick buildings impressive in a country of wood frame and butted logs – they came to Sugar Creek, which all agreed was a fine looking stretch of water. James called a halt. "I can smell you boys all the way over here. What do y'all say to a swim?" he asked. They jumped from the wagon and tore their clothes off. In seconds they were splashing and dunking each other. The water was clear and shallow enough not to be dangerous, and the women watched them frolic while the men hunted a spring to replenish their water stock.

Clayton had never seen his father so talkative and animated as they rattled the last miles to where he had promised a view of the river valley below where the farm lay.

And true to his word, it had been fine. The day was clear and nearly windless. Redwing blackbirds made bullying chatter along the edge of the meadow. In tilled fields crows and grackles congregated in black flocks. They stopped the wagon and turned it, each member of the family finding a place to stand. His father helped his grandmother up so that she could see too. Before them was a green valley cut by a light brown river, here and there a patch of rowed crops, a shed or a house, the sun picking out sand bars, a gap in the trees that James pointed to as the canal, a flash of white where a packet boat slid southwest, poled slowly by bare-chested men. His father had already described all of this and each of them had a version of it in his or her head, now coming to bear upon the reality of their new beginning.

James turned the wagon and they descended into the valley, Clayton riding the horse with his brothers behind him, like three spoons in a drawer. They crossed at the village of Granville, composed of a few wood frame houses and a store, gray weathered clapboards in need of a whitewashing, awning and porch lined with straight-backed chairs and joint stools, one topped with a curled-up, enormous orange cat. The residents about on this day were treated to a sight the likes of which they had never seen. A wagon filled with possessions, furniture, provisions and tools, tied in a high heap and clanking off the sides, rolling by with a young negro couple flanked by an older negro couple. Behind, a bay mare with three boys, two on the saddle and one on the blanket, skin the color of polished boots, hair like dark new wool. They returned the onlookers' gaze with open curiosity.

James and Amos tipped their hats to the older men who sat chairs on the porch of the store, to a woman planting flowers along a picket fence, and to a horseman riding the other way

51

who stopped in the road as they passed him. James thought it just as well that no one asked any questions, preferring anonymity to neighborliness.

They had decided back in Tennessee to take the longer way round and come to the property from downriver rather than passing through LaFayette. Most of what they needed to get started was in the wagon. They would introduce themselves to the town as gradually as possible.

After Granville the road angled down gently to the river, low and placid this time of year. Alongside it grew milkweed and hazel, enormous bushes of honeysuckle alive with bees and butterflies, plum brush, sumac and grape vines presenting a wall of vegetation. The road at times seemed carved through it. Which it had been. The descent let out onto a broad flood plain, the rougher bush giving way to tall prairie grasses cut through by streams draining the higher ground, marked by willows and the brown tops of cattails. Some of the prairie had been cleared and rectangles of corn, short of knee high, contrasted dark green with the lighter grasses. What dirt they could see down here, visible between the ordered rows, was dark and rich-looking. Like something you could eat. There were also fields of wheat and rye, still green and delicate, mixed plots of beans, tomatoes, runners of squash and melon, a few flop-eared pale orange blossoms still on the vines. From the higher point in the road they could see two cabins at the bluff-edge of the prairie upriver, high enough to avoid the normal flooding but precipitously close to a big flood if it were to come. It had been easier to build below the slope and the tree line, the river bottom close by to put a boat in. It was much the same across the way on the opposite bank, except for the bluff, which rose more sharply to a string of humpbacked hills covered in thick forest. On her map, Marjorie Lane had shown James a road up through these hills to the top of the bluff and the flatter ground of the farm. From the river road there was an Indian trace that followed a fall of stones and water called Indian Creek. She told him this was the only way they could reach the farm, short of coming all the way into town and winding their way back over high ground.

On paper this had not looked too difficult.

They crossed the uncovered wooden bridge, a rudimentary platform of planks laid over a trestle of logs driven into the mud and the bank, low to the water. The planks were not all securely nailed down and their ends came up as the heavy wheels rolled over them, making a slapping sound as they subsided. James stopped the wagon, handed the reins to his father, climbed down and took the reins of the horse from Clayton. A spooked animal might go right over the edge. He let the wagon lead them across slowly, patting the mare's neck as they went to calm her on the hollow surface that her hesitant hoofs clearly did not like. When they reached the other side James reached into a burlap bag and gave each of the horses a carrot. He climbed back up onto the seat.

"That bridge is a week's hard rain from endin up downriver in pieces," remarked Amos.

"I wouldn't want to be on it with the water comin down through here," James replied. "Good news is we won't need to cross it again unless we want to." This last phrase, they all realized, was a significant departure from *have to*.

The ascent up the trace was not easy. The boys had to dismount and walk the horse ahead, staying clear of the wagon in case it broke loose and careened downhill. At the steepest places the women walked ahead with the boys while Amos led the team from the front, both hands on the bridle of the big gelding, James in a crouch on the seat with his hands on the brake. In case of a broken harness or hitch failure, he would try to set it and stop the wagon. If this didn't work he would try to leap off. After a hundred nervous yards they came level, then another short pitch and they reached the top. Amos sat down on a stump and emptied the pea gravel and sand out of his boots, wiped his gray head with a handkerchief. He smiled at his grandsons.

"Boys, my old body's about give out. I think you all are gone have to carry me the rest of the way. Come on."

Clayton and Sam were pulled under their grandfather's big arms, taking one each over their shoulders like a yoke, heaving as hard and as loud as they could while the old man pretended to be lifted up. He slouched over them, nearly collapsing their bony legs, Elijah now pushing at his rear end. Slushing through the gravel, pirouetting, nearly going over, Sam lifted off his feet, across the road to the high grass and all falling in, Elijah piling in on top. James and Lily laughed, relieved to have made it without mishap, their boys safe, while Granny fussed over to them hauling Elijah out.

"You durned old fool they's probly snakes and god knows what in there."

Then she was pulled over herself and onto her husband's broad belly, laughing .

The first thing Clayton noticed was how green it was.

Middle Tennessee had been green in its way. A stifling verdancy that saw summer engulf spring like a snake, swallowing it with only the bare outline of its having been. Here the palette was sharper, the shades of greens and browns, the blue of the sky, clouds like blown ships, were all distinct. Later he would remember the South as a watercolor landscape, shapes and colors bleeding into one another, while he saw his new home as an engraving, hatched with a finer point.

From a distance the house, barn, and outbuildings looked picturesque. The homestead had been well chosen: a flat tongue of land cleared between two ravines, one with a stream cutting down its length, falling over the face of the slope and zigzagging down on a bed of hardwood leaves to the prairie. There was two hundred yards between ravines, whose beginnings were tree-lined with oaks, hackberries, maples and hickories, the understory thick with sassafras and mulberry, poison ivy beneath and nettles at the edge. Stands of horseweeds poked out where nothing had been cut for a few years, prospecting, as were clumps of low sumac along the track that led to the farm. Amos and James could see the shape of this, the outline of possibility, already mentally sharpening the scythe blade and swinging it, whispering back the weeds, putting order back to the creep of nature. The women stared hard at the house, seeing in its subtle lean and dullness a decrepitude that would certainly be worse inside, on the lived surface. They understood the work that lay ahead. Granny put her arm around the younger woman. Lily gave her a faint smile, her face full of determination. The boys saw so much to explore they nearly fell off the horse craning their necks around their older brother, receiving elbows from him as he steadied the unbalanced animal. Only Clayton understood that there would be so much to do that there would be scarce time to build forts or hunt crawdads in the creek. But when it was finished, or at least caught up some, what a space was here to stretch out in. He took a deep breath of air crammed with summer promise. He let it out slowly then reached back and held onto his brothers, kicking the horse into a canter.

Upon closer inspection, the only buildings that would not have to be completely rebuilt were the smokehouse and the corn crib, preserved by constant use rather than care. Care had, indeed, been withheld from the house, barn, stock corral and fences, all of which looked to have been abandoned to the elements for more than a few years. Clayton wondered how the old man had lived out here for so long without looking after what sustained him. If he had been seen to by neighbors they had come a good distance to do it. The well was ringed by field stone, the carriage for the bucket fashioned out of squared logs. Its rusted wheel turned sluggishly. The rope had either rotted away and fallen in or been taken off. There was no bucket. Amos went to the wagon and fetched one along with a length of rope, which he uncoiled and tied to the handle, lowering it down until it splashed. It came up heavy and full but choked with leaves. Amos put his nose to it and nodded his satisfaction at the smell: vegetal but sweet.

He called Clayton over. "Drop the bucket, pull it up full, dump the leaves, then do it again until it comes up clear." At first he refused to let his little brothers help, pushing them away when they tried to pull with him, until the blisters started and he had no choice.

Beneath the canvas shelter they rested tired limbs, trying to stave off awareness of the great labor that lay ahead. The pain was leavened by the awareness that they were doing it for themselves. Every cut's trueness, every joint's squareness was a contribution to their future. The first days in the early July heat were spent pulling things out of the house and outbuildings to see what, if anything, was salvageable, and to get a better idea of how deteriorated the structures were. Granny remarked that they might ought to leave the old wardrobe, the china cabinet with the glass removed, broken chairs, a two-legged table nailed to the wall, boxes of chipped china and tarnished, mismatched tableware, *all that junk*, since it was likely the only thing holding the place up.

The barn was worse.

There were rats and buzzards, several families of possum and raccoon, and groundhogs dug in below the foundation. Amos said it reminded him of a circus train with all the animals riding in one car. When they opened the bay doors the decayed hinges molted a cascade of rust, the top one on the right side door disintegrating completely. They struggled to brace it by bending it around to rest against the building until they could fix or replace it. With the doors open there emerged the stink of rotted hay and animal flesh. Clayton held his nose. James told him to take his brothers and get back a little ways, since they weren't sure what might come out of there. They did so readily. Sam and Elijah looked suddenly scared. They peered into the maw of the barn, wondering what it might hold. Something ran through the weeds to one side, its passage bending them in its wake. Then a commotion broke out somewhere inside. Up high in the rafters. It was Sam who pointed at the sky and said "Look!" Five or six giant, dark birds had taken wing and flapped slowly until swallowed up by the trees.

"Clayton, you take your brothers to the house to help your Mama and Granny and then get on back here. Bring a shovel and both rakes from the wagon." Protests from the younger boys were quieted by a look from their father. They went on dragging their bare feet as slowly as they could get away with. Amos stood in the doorway, hands on his hips.

"What you want to do first, son?"

"Wait till that boy gets back with a shovel. I ain't goin in there without something to swing."

The floor was dirt, the central bay empty but for a few scattered boards, bent nails pricking out of them. On the left, where the barn had its longer slope, were stalls, cracks of light showing in a few places where there were doors to the outside or shut windows. Across the bay was another set of doors letting out into the fenced barnlot and beyond this a corral.

"I spose it'd be too good a luck to find this here full of shiny oiled equipment," Amos said.

"Mm hm." James was not in the mood to hear any criticism. He turned away and watched Clayton struggle across with the tools. He took the shovel from him and went in. The light was bad and the smell stronger, like an unlimed outhouse. The ladder to the loft felt solid.

"Get on up there boy. Open that hay mow door, let some light in, tell us what we got."

Clayton looked at his father to see if he was serious. He was. Clayton's sense of importance, swelling after leaving his brothers with the women, now felt like a hard lump in his gut. Like he'd swallowed a rock that couldn't go one way or the other. His grandfather took the rakes from him.

He went so slowly up the first few rungs that James swatted him on the rear with the shovel and said, "Come on now, quit foolin and get up there." Clayton was not fooling. He was instead trying to get his arms and legs to work. He was afraid of the birds, whose red, hairless necks and heads he had seen bobbing ominously only minutes before. What their beaks could do he did not want to know. Nor whether they had teeth or how they would react in the dark of the loft to an intruder. At the top he stood unsteadily, peering into the dimness for any sign of movement. A faint light came in through the chinks where the swinging doors met. The hole in the roof behind him cast his shadow dark against the deeper gray. He went forward by reaching one foot out and holding his body back, as though feeling for the edge of a cliff, ready at any second to retreat to the ladder. Half a dozen of these steps and then a rustle, like little feet ticking across a wood floor. Hundreds of them.

He stopped.

Fifteen feet to go. Clayton decided that it was like cold water: better to jump in and get it over with. He let out a yell and ran for the door and an explosion of flapping and screeching was all around his head, the air clotted with down and dust, stiff feathers brushing his arms up now in defense. Something sharp cut his forearm and he cried out and went down curling up, waiting for them to descend on him to rip his flesh. He could feel the disturbed air of their movement, turbulent and foul-smelling, dead flesh wafting over him.

Then quiet but for a roaring in his ears, which he realized

was from his pressing them with the palms of his hands. His father's voice said something. He opened his eyes but could see no birds for the thick swirling dust. Pushing himself up he went for the doors, threw the latch and kicked them open, sending them groaning around to slap against the building. He sat down, breathing heavily, his father's head rising up from the ladder.

"You hurt? Still got both your eyes?" James had a crooked smile on his face.

"It ain't funny." Clayton held his arm, began to cry. His desire to keep up with the men was gone. James reached the rake and shovel into the loft, pulled himself up over the edge, scanning the rafters full of nests and covered in shit.

"Let's see under there." James pried the boy's hand away. "Best get that seen to. Go on to your granny, tell her what happened."

Clayton's fear overtook him now as he cried more in earnest.

"Go on now."

At the bottom of the ladder Amos stopped raking old hay and pieces of wood into a pile so that he could rub the boy's head, dust and pieces of straw flying out like a beaten rug. Clayton took the offered handkerchief and wiped his eyes as he walked to the house.

Six

It took a week to get the barn cleared out, first of its living residents and then of what they had left behind. Some were not content to escape with their lives and came back to reestablish themselves, the possums and groundhogs mainly, and had to be exterminated. Granny stewed two of the possums. The young groundhogs they roasted, the meat dark and greasy but fine compared to the frowzy salt pork and dried beef they had been eating for weeks. The raccoons still prowled the place but had the good sense not to go where people had settled back in. With the hole in the roof patched, the buzzards had no ready entrance and exit. After a few days in the trees, circling above the barn roof during the repair, hoping the humans would lose interest and leave them to their roost, they departed for some other aerie. To Clayton and his brothers fell the task of cleaning the loft. They used brooms to dig out the nest materials from the rafters – grasses, twigs, feathers, congealed masses of indeterminate composition, pieces of cloth and string – then swept it all outside through the double doors.

One night after supper Elijah asked how the buzzards got that cloth to put in their nests. Amos replied around the stem of his pipe, "It come off of little children, I reckon. Them birds swoop down and with their sharp beaks strip off just what they need."

The boys looked at their granny who gave them the little shake of the head that let them know he was funning.

Still, they imagined what that would be like, the giant bird descending with its beady eyes and red, loose skin whooshing out of the sky, no place to run, the fabric ripping, the flesh with it. Elijah and Sam looked at their older brother, at his arm with its healing gash, glad they had been sent to the house that day.

While the boys cleaned out the barn there was much to do to make the house livable. The first decision was whether to tear it down and use the materials to build another. Leaving what was already standing had the obvious advantage of convenience, since they could repair with more speed and move in out from under their makeshift tent camp faster. Problem was they would have a dwelling that would be less functional – dark, drafty in winter, stifling in summer, crowded. Not to mention, James pointed out, they would only be putting off the inevitable, since a rot had set in lord knows how deep in the wood.

They would start over. Roughing it as they had been wasn't so bad. It was made more tolerable each day by their progress and the sort of progress it was. Free, or at least unencumbered by what someone else thought they ought to be doing because of who they were, or appeared to be.

Once the barn was sorted they moved the wagon and the canvas into its shelter along with the rest of their belongings. The horses had been bedding in the newly mucked stalls for a few days and the place smelled of freshly cut grass and animal. At the edge of the big doors they dug out a shallow hole and moved the fire ring, iron tripod, cauldron and kettle. In the evening they sat in the chairs they had brought, built by Amos the year after he had married Clara – chestnut with rush seats, woven by Clara's mama before she died, who had learned the skill as a girl growing up in Charleston, South Carolina. To pass the time between the end of supper and bedtime they sang songs, Granny insisting on hymns since there was no telling when they might set foot inside a church again. Or they told stories, Amos dipping into his stock of tall tales, life experience, hearsay, trickster stories, and a few things granny termed "unchristian" but which always tickled the boys.

"Thing about a house is, you got to see it before you pick up the first tool or piece of wood."

"What you mean, see it?"

Clayton and his grandfather sat with their legs dangling at the edge of the hayloft, the boy's bare heels thumping rhythmically against the barn wood. The sun had been up an hour and the dew was beginning to lift out of the prairie grass in flat waves of mist. Clayton thought it so peaceful before the sun made it hot and focused the humidity, before the work got started and he fitted his hand to some tool or other. So much to do. But he was learning to carpenter, and enjoyed it to his surprise.

"Craft ain't only in the hands, boy. It's in the imagination."

"Hmm," Clayton replied. He really did not see what his grandfather saw, even if he stared as hard as he could at the spot where the old house had stood. He could imagine a house and could change it from one variety to another, but it was either a house or it wasn't. The process that made it a finished building eluded him. He might as well try to imagine a body without its skin.

They had disassembled the Metzger house carefully, pre-serving its materiel as best they could. Some of it was not salvageable, rotted out from the freeze and thaw of seeped water or mold or termites. Some of the weatherboards they could reuse. A few of the studs and joists, and many of the wide floorboards, would need only a sanding and refinish. The roof had the most damage, having been made hastily, or perhaps without the skill or determination to make it last. Instead of shingles the Metzgers had used tulip poplar bark, which is easier to get and form into roofing, but

62

wears much faster than nailed shingles. Enough water had found the gaps that the rafters had rotted and begun to sag the beams down, the roof beginning to look like the house had exhaled and couldn't breathe in again. All of this wood they stacked in a separate pile, in the event there was some use for it.

Clayton and his brothers had spent most of their time pulling nails. The boards had to be clean to be of any use. Any nails that were straight enough to drive they set aside. The others went into a box to be melted down later and turned into something else. New nails perhaps. During this tedious process the younger boys had to be watched closely, as their attention wandered and they used the claws of their hammers to chop at the wood or to dig in the ground. More than once their father jerked one of them to his feet by the arm and reminded him what business they were about. The play they imagined all around them had dwindled considerably. Clayton was bored with this at first but then found that if he was careful he could pull the nails straight, and even straighten the crooked ones, if he levered the metal out just so. This also left a board less scarred and split. He realized that this would make a tighter, more weather-resistant house. Their house. He looked at his brothers, pulling at the misshaped heads, gouging the wood, attention wandering to a butterfly or a spider in the pile, and it occurred to him that even this small task contributed to what they were building.

"When we was pullin them nails outta all them boards, I tried real hard to do it careful so's the nails might come out straight and the wood left whole."

Amos put his big hand on his grandson's knee. "You seen that they was more than pieces of metal stuck in wood, some dumb chore you was told to do that made no sense, had nothin to do with you. That's a man's way of lookin. When you see how all the little things is connected, you on your way."

Clayton smiled. His grandfather stood up with a theatrical groan, knee joints cracking, then held out his hand and lifted the boy off his feet to follow him down the ladder. To work.

Clayton hung on to the gunwale of the wagon bed as it rattled across the prairie leaving a wake in the tall grass. If a fish had jumped up out of the waving green he wouldn't have been surprised. When they reached the woods Clayton handed over the axes, two heavy iron wedges, and a sledgehammer. James and Amos took these and waded through the grass and into the shade of trees. Clayton dropped two small hand axes, watched carefully where they fell shushed into invisibility, then clambered over the side. Feeling with his toes he picked them up and followed. Bearing an axe in each hand he thought of how they'd played Indian back in Tennessee, sneaking them out of the tool shed and chasing one another through the fields and scrub woods. As he entered the trees, where it was quiet and considerably darker, he was mindful that it had not been too long since that was a deadly game around these parts. Spooked, he hurried after.

He found them fifty yards into the woods. His grandfather appeared to be hugging a large white oak, his ear to its massive trunk. His father was nowhere to be seen. He heard a thunk, then another. Clayton moved closer. James was on the other side striking the tree with the sledge, gripping it right up near the head. Amos nodded to his son and they moved off again, picking up the tools, James pausing to chop a blaze into the bole. They came to another large tree which grew straight and very tall. They stopped and set the tools down. James turned to his son.

"Well boy, what kind of tree is this?"

"Oak?"

"What kind?"

"Um . . . white?"

"Nope. That other'n was." He waited. "Look at the leaves."

They were spiny, spiked at the ends, narrower and finer than the other tree.

"Red oak."

"Good. Now what's the difference?"

"White's good for about everything, but hard and heavy. Red rots in the ground."

"All right. Now what are we gonna do with these two trees?"

Clayton thought about it. He closed his eyes and tried to do as his grandfather had taught him. First he imagined the lumber they had salvaged from the old house, and what had been thrown onto the junk pile. What were they missing?

"Well, I think maybe them big beams at the bottom of the house, the ones holdin it up, looked rotted and buggy, and it might not be a good idea to build everything resting on them. Like Granny's Bible story about building a house on sand."

Amos laughed. "That's right, boy."

"So white oak for that." He remembered the state of the roof, its sad deflation and its sitting now wholly in the pile of cast-off. "Red oak for the roof."

"Why?" his father asked.

He smiled, looked at his grandfather.

"Like water off a duck's back."

"That's right. Red oak keeps the water out or the whiskey in," Amos said. Then, in mock seriousness, "Boy, don't say that around your granny."

Clayton didn't have to be told that.

They picked up the tools and started off deeper into the woods. Clayton hefted the hand axe, hoping they had left the job to him.

"Ain't we gonna mark this one?" he called, arm reared back and at the ready.

His father stopped, put down the sledge and axe and walked back, his right overalls pocket burdened low with the weight of the wedge.

"Take a good look at that tree, son."

Clayton did, sighting up its height into the regularly spaced branches which waved at the top in the slight breeze. It appeared straight and was thick enough. He looked at his father, considered tapping the tree as they had done with the other. Now that he thought about it, they had not even done it to this one.

"Look at the bark."

He did so. It was no different from all the other bark he'd ever seen. He shrugged.

"Does it go straight up the tree?"

"No, it kinda spirals up. Like a barber pole."

"What's that tell a man who wants to cut house lumber out of it?"

"The grain won't be straight neither?"

"Yessir. Maybe pretty for furniture, but not what we need now."

"Daddy?"

"Yeah."

"How you know a tree sound when you thunkin it?"

"You listen to a lot of trees."

In the next week Clayton worked harder than he ever had in his life. Each night he could barely hold himself up after he'd eaten. Not even his favorite story from his grandfather – Brer Fox, the snake-bit hoe handle, Stagolee, John Henry, or even his creepy favorite, Aunty Tucky – could keep him from turning in early to his straw-filled bed of striped ticking where he was asleep before he could even think about the day.

They felled the white oak and a red, Clayton getting to put his ear to the latter, which he thought rang prettily. Contrary to what he thought happened in tree chopping, where you chopped and it fell over, getting these big trees to fall safely and in the right direction was technically difficult. It took a whole morning to get them down. Both men were soaked through with sweat by the time the last crash echoed through the forest, upsetting the birds and leaving a thorough silence in its wake. Clayton watched as best he could, but had to stand back behind a deadfall, instructed to get as low as possible if the tree fell towards him. The toppling of the first tree was far more dramatic than he'd expected. Trees that size didn't simply keel over. The chopped end often leapt wounded into the air before being pulled this way and that by its branches first in the canopy and then by the trunk striking others on its way down. The base of the felled tree never landed next to the stump and often jumped back toward where the axeman had been standing, as if striking out at its assailant. This left Clayton in no doubt about the damage this could inflict to a body.

Once the felling was over they went to work cleaning the downed trunks of limbs. Clayton was now able to get in and work with his hand axe. With a barking spud they removed the bark, which stuck in places, it being too late in the summer for it to ease off like shed skin. The logs were then lined out, which Clayton saw was the emergence of a squared log from a round one, accomplished by standing atop it and chopping carefully along each side and then turning it to repeat the process. After two days of this, bent and handsore, bitten by deer flies and mosquitoes, they had two rough-hewn logs, one sawn into eight foot lengths and the other hewn on three sides and sawn in half. As they walked out to the wagon after the second day, Clayton asked about what they had done so far.

"Daddy, why did you all only chop three sides of that white oak?"

"Well, that round, rough side sticks further in to support the joists and floorboards."

"Oh."

"Why'd you saw the red oak so much shorter? Wouldn't it be easier to get it out of there in one piece?"

"It would," Amos said, behind him, an axe over each shoulder, "if we had Babe the blue ox to do the draggin. But seein as we only got two draft horses, we got to do what we can. That white is gonna be hard enough to get half out at a time."

"Why didn't you all saw that one?"

"Them sills," his father said, "gotta be whole and long enough unless you want to live in a chicken coop."

Clayton had never seen his old granny in better spirits. He wondered if their new place reminded her of a time she deeply missed. He'd often asked about her childhood on the plantation but all she would say was, "I don't recall, child." But she did recall, and Clayton sheltered the fragmented particulars of her recollections in his memory. He gathered them whenever she demonstrated some skill or instructed him in some craft, which she would illustrate with a story of where she learned it. Each time, he noticed, she was a girl being patiently schooled in ways of housekeeping. This never wavered. The family members she named – mother, aunts, cousins – were kind and patient, endlessly knowledgeable, and otherwise never spoken of. His efforts to liberate them from these scenes to determine what happened to them, to progress beyond Granny's girlhood, were met with a dismissive silence. Whatever occurred to tear the narrative of her life so that she could not, or would not, tell it straight through, did not bereave her of the essential skills she practiced every day of her life. Nor of their provenance.

Under her hand the barn began to resemble less a ruined outbuilding than a dwelling temporary but welcoming. Once sleeping accommodations were arranged she set out with

Clayton's mother to make the place look, she said, "like people lived there." One useful remnant from the Metzger family's many years of homesteading was a decayed garden grown over by prairie grass and weeds. Only granny saw it hidden amongst the encroached greenery, pushing back handfuls of lambsquarters and spindly johnsongrass to reveal a perfect stand of rhubarb. She also found potato plants in flower and runner beans snaking along, pods newly sprouted on the vines. There was a gooseberry bush further on but something had picked it clean of fruit. The two women began by scything back the garden weeds and overgrowth, then chopping out everything that wasn't edible with a mattock and spade in order to turn the soil for new crops. This last task accomplished by two hard days of hoeing, the women aided by the boys who picked out and piled rocks from the dark earth. Clayton had never witnessed his brothers so intent upon something that did not involve playing, and knew that his granny must have devised some kind of reward for their attention. At the end of the second day, when he returned from the woods arm-weary and hungry, he noticed that his brothers had built the walls for a rudimentary castle out of the stones they liberated from the churned loam. Clayton shook his head and smiled at the brilliance of it. Instead of working they were playing; each rock they could find was the piece of a larger puzzle. How she would get them to do anything once the castle was a space for their imaginations he had no idea. Invent some new stratagem, he reckoned. She was not a woman who planned to fail.

The garden would be simple for the time being. With the season so advanced they would have to plant and tend carefully. The days were already hot and the nurturing rains of April and May were past; the boys would tote many a bucket of water in the weeks ahead. Packing the wagon in Nashville, Clara and Lily had insisted on bringing as much food as they could carry. This had resulted in a disagreement that made

Clayton aware of how tense his parents and grandparents were, whether they showed it or not.

"Woman, what in tarnation is all this?" Amos asked, beginning to rummage in the sacks and parcels they had stowed in the front of the wagon.

"Mr. McGhee you get on out of there. It ain't none of your business what we bringing to feed this whole bunch." When Granny used the mister before her husband's name it was a good idea to find something else to do, but Clayton was busy wiring a slatted crate together that held Granny's cherished set of china plates packed in straw.

"James, will you tell your mama that if she takes up any more of this wagon with food we gonna have to leave either tools or a little boy behind?"

"You can tell your papa that if he wants to work he's gonna have to eat, and the lord knows – "

"I ain't got time for this here carryin on," James replied, disappearing back around the side of the house. Clayton watched his mother look in that direction and back at her in-laws. She placed her hand on Amos's shoulder and steered him towards where her husband had gone. He could just make out what she said in her soft peacemaker voice.

"Rabbit and dumplings, fried okra, squash and onions with bacon, a mess of greens with a hock, grits with butter. . . ."

Clayton laughed at how easily the big man had been distracted from his concerns, but also realized how good the food sounded. He felt scared at the prospect of a place that would cause his stalwart granny to prepare so zealously. He was accustomed to his father's insistence that they would make do, that they would apply their skills to the problem and it would be solved. But this was different. All those seeds and cuttings, the cured and salted meat, the portable fruits and vegetables wrapped and secreted around jars of preserves, pickles, eggs in vinegar, pili peppers, smoked fish and jerked venison bought from the few Indians who still

70

lived out in the county. Such abundance made present the absence that even such a hardy woman deeply feared. And if granny feared it Clayton knew he ought to be careful not to believe that tools and guns could solve everything where they were going.

Granny had sacks of seed bundled in the wagon and these she laid out in colorful piles on a horse blanket. Clayton's brothers immediately wandered over to look and touch, already transported with possibilities for their use. Lily sent them on their way with a stern reminder of what would happen to them if they interfered with their granny's work. She chose to plant corn, though it would be some time before they saw any ears ripe enough to eat. It would come good in August and be a fine thing on the cob at the end of a hard day. She knew they would have to buy cornmeal when her stock ran out as there was not enough tilled land nor growing season to sustain them. Onions and radishes would grow quickly and these were the first things she sowed along with squash, peas, turnips, beets, and greens. The collards, mustard, and kale would soonest provide them with the fixings for easy meals with the simple addition of water and salt pork. She'd make pone or hoe cakes for the pot liquor. With turnip greens and beet greens and the dandelions they were already eating, everyone would be grumbling for something different. But she knew how to get everyone's mind off it.

Taters.

The sweet potato slips she snapped carefully off the withered tubers kept blind in their burlap. She rooted these in the freshly turned earth, pressing it down with her dark wrinkled fingers to hold them in place. God's little miracles. You stuck them in the ground and kept them upright, added water in abundance and waited. For all the destructive things she'd been privy to in her life this was one example of life's tenacity. And once they got some taters in the ground they were a handful of sugar away from heaven. She'd also get James to shoot a possum and some squirrels and they'd eat just fine. Clara McGhee understood this wouldn't feel like home to them for a while, but she reckoned food would allow a body to feel like it was in the right place.

Seven

Dragging the logs out was tedious work. Clayton had a lot of responsibility with the horses, keeping them calm and lined up while the men connected the chains and watched that they did not slip. He whispered to them reassuringly, fed them strategic nubs of carrot.

They worked the timber in the clear space between the emerging vegetable garden and the foundation where the old house had stood. The fieldstone pillars had been strengthened where there had been cracks. They set rocks from the stream beneath the logs on the short side to support the bottom. Before they set the sills in place and leveled them, squaring off the foundation, they set to work riving the red oak stock for shingles, nailers, and clapboards.

For shingles they sawed a few of the logs into two foot lengths and sat these on an end. James told Clayton to stay with his grandfather and to pay attention. This was a job he had to learn now so they could get the stock ready to season, fit for roofing when they got to it. Clayton noticed right away that his father went faster while his grandfather was more deliberate, more exacting in rendering the wood precisely so that almost none of it had to be discarded into the kindling pile. Amos first explained how you use the froe, the maul, and the riving break to split the bolts thinner and thinner until you have the thickness you need. The froe, Clayton thought, looked like an axe made by someone who had never chopped anything. It consisted of a heavy blade, straight-sided, about eight inches long, sharpened on its top and with an eye for a hickory handle, like a hatchet. You used the maul, which was like a sledgehammer but made out of wood, to drive the blade of the froe, handle up and used for leverage in splitting. The riving break was a thick tree limb they had dragged out of the woods that had a narrow fork used for holding longer pieces such as clapboards. The shingles could be riven on top of one of the still whole logs turned on an end as a rest.

They stood at the first red oak log and Amos drove a wedge carefully into it with measured hits until the wood began to split. When it did so he stopped and put in another wedge toward the center point of the log in order to get the crack to run in that direction. Once split in half this way he started over halfway between the splits to halve the log again, leaving it still standing upright, like he was cutting a cake before handing out any of the pieces. When the log was rendered into radial wedges two inches thick Amos used the froe and the maul to rive the bolts into thinner pieces.

"How thin they need to be?" Clayton asked.

"About half an inch, maybe a little less. Point is they need to be near the same, else you won't have you a flat roof and the water won't run right. Now you try it. Go slow and be careful you set the blade even and flat or it'll run crooked down the grain."

Clayton took up the spare froe and used the back of his hatchet for a maul. He balanced the piece of oak on the log but it came up too high for him to see properly or get any leverage.

"Hold on," Amos said. He dropped a split piece on the ground and put Clayton's stock on it.

"You got to be able to look down into the grain, make your first strike count."

Clayton held the froe blade against the top of the bolt, adjusting its inclination gingerly since this pressure was the only thing holding it up. Press too hard before the blade bit into the wood and it would fall over. He knocked it over twice before he got the right angle with the requisite force.

"Tap it on in some," Amos said, "and if that ain't right pull it out and start again. It won't hurt the end none."

He tapped the blade but it went in at a slight angle. He wrenched it out, knocking the bolt over. He picked it up and tried again, thought he had it straight and whacked it smartly with the blunt end of the hatchet. The froe went down almost halfway with a crack, the green wood splitting cleanly along its crisp grain. It started level but at an angle back toward him, which would give him a thick piece and one that would be too thin. He stopped and looked at his grandfather, who said, "Get on through it and start again. Only way to learn is by doin it."

In an hour he had it figured out. Though he went much slower and fouled the blanks more than the older men he produced a decent pile of shingles by the end of the day. When his father came over at noon Clayton was all smiles as he worked the froe and added to the growing stack of his successful efforts. James nodded and went on with Amos to the barn for his dinner. Granny appeared with a cloth wrapped around something warm. She handed it to him, kissed his cheek, and went back to the barn. A biscuit with ham stuck inside it, a crust of fat along one edge the way he liked it. He wolfed it down and went back to work.

Next day the men laid the sills, setting them true with spirit levels, cutting mortises into their rounded sides for the floor joists. Meanwhile, Clayton worked to finish the shingles, planing them flat where the grain had split at too great an angle, then rounding off each bottom corner so that it would end in a taper. Round ends, Amos explained, shed water better than square ends. Clayton awaited an explanation and the old man chuckled.

"It's called featherin. Remember that old duck's back, boy," and shuffled away.

In the days that followed they cut the tenons of the joists for the sill mortises, framed the studs for the walls, and strengthened these with braces. They built the walls of the house flat on the ground in separate pieces. Finally it dawned on Clayton that they would have to raise these heavy structures, fitting the tenons into the mortise cavities on the sills. They must weigh a couple of hundred pounds, he figured, and were awkwardly shaped for lifting. When he asked about this it was clear his father did not want to talk about it. He leaned into the strokes of his hammer, nails between his lips. He said something about tackle and horses but Clayton neither understood nor pressed him on it.

They set in the floor joists, some of which had to be remade due to rotting of the original stock. A smaller white oak was used for this and after it had been lined and sawed Clayton was instructed in how to cut the tenons with an adze, careful to check that they would fit as snugly as possible.

It was a Friday morning, Clayton reckoned, that found them laying the plank floor, adzing down the high spots and furring up the low ones, fitting the planks where they crossed the joists. After several planks were set down and leveled they bored one-inch diameter holes into every other joist about an inch beyond the last plank, then set iron pins into them. Using wooden wedges driven between the pins and the last plank they tightened up the set of boards until they screamed and then nailed them down. They were hammering the second set of pins when they heard the faint ringing of trace chains, hoof falls, and the banging of a wagon bed. They stopped what they were doing and walked toward the open space where the driveway approached between the house and the barn. His mother and grandmother had been doing some sewing in the shade and came out shielding their eyes, his granny doing so with an embroidery hoop. His brothers were supposed to have been working in the garden but he saw now that they had been digging some sort of fortification around a crude fort-like mound at the far end, out of sight of their father working on the house.

As the buckboard drew closer they could see that the crouching white man who held the reins above the bouncing spring seat was letting his horses run, the wagon sliding back and forth wildly across the ruts of the road. His thick, short legs absorbed the shock until they hit something bigger and his bottom would crash down into the upcoming seat, sending him off his feet entirely.

They could hear his laughter all the way from the road.

He turned sharply into the drive, a wall of dust continuing on north, the wagon barely staying on all four wheels. Finally he checked the horses into a trot. James now recognized the fellow in the wagon from the livery stable who had fallen and cracked his head. This was a different conveyance, bigger, and with two horses instead of one. It was him all right. James recalled his ruddy complexion and teamster's hat pulled down over greasy red hair, a shirt that might once have been white, the arms cut off jaggedly under suspenders and trousers that appeared chewed below the knees. He had him some white legs, James noticed.

He slowed the horses, saying something to them that none of the onlookers could understand. He jumped down nimbly from the wagon. With his pale legs and dirty brown feet Clayton thought this stranger looked like one of the gypsy tumblers he'd seen through the fence of the county fair in Nashville.

"Road is not so good up bluff and we nearly fall down it in loose rocks, but road at top make us want to run," he said. He smiled broadly, showing gaps where two lower teeth should be. "I get carried away with fast horses. Is good to see you again Mr. McGhee." He held out his hand and James shook it.

Small but strong.

"Welcome. Call me James. I don't recollect your name."

"Ah, it is Cmicky. Casimir Cmicky. But everyone call me Cas. I hear from sheriff you buy Metzger place and supposed to arrive over one month ago. When no sign of you in town to buy or trade I make decision to come out, see how you getting along."

He looked around James towards where the house had stood, then at the others standing in a rough semi-circle, trying to hear what they were saying to each other in low family voices.

"You have been doing much work here, I see. I remember you say that you are carpenters and I have no doubts about it. Now I must meet the serious boss-man there with the axe."

He was looking at Clayton, who stood next to his grandfather balancing the head of the adze on his right foot.

"That there is Clayton, my oldest. He comin along with the carpenterin. Ain't cut off no fingers or toes yet."

Cmicky, who was only a couple of inches taller, though twice as heavy, shook the boy's hand. Clayton, unused to having his hand shook, did not grip hard enough and had to grit his teeth as his fingers were mashed together.

"This must be your father," he said, taking the old man's hand and elbow. "Your son is a brave man, sir. There are not too many who would have beaten the fearsome Lecroix brothers."

"I thank you," Amos said. "Them's fine horses you got there."

"You are shrewd judge of horseflesh, Mr. McGhee – "

"Amos."

"Amos. I wish they were mine," said Cmicky, his round, open face still sweat-soaked, "but they belong to McRae who owns the livery. I have to make a pickup for him downriver in Independence and I think, why not drive up bluff and see how black people doing at new farm."

James, unused to making introductions, heard a woman clear her throat behind him.

"Oh, and this here is my wife, Lily, and my mother, Clara."

Cmicky put his hat against his chest and bowed deeply to both women.

James introduced the little boys, who had to be coaxed out from behind their mother with a stern tone, Elijah instructed to get his filthy fingers out of his mouth. The man shook their small hands, the brown disappearing entirely inside the white, Cmicky theatrically addressing them as little men.

"A beautiful family. Now may I see how you are doing with house building?"

Lily stepped across and put her hand on her husband's arm. "Would you like something to eat, or a drink of water?" she asked. "It's no trouble to make a little something." Cmicky patted his pendulous stomach. "No thank you, I ate with the horses before leaving town."

James explained the state of things upon arrival. Cmicky nodded his approval as he looked over the newly laid sills and foundation, the joists mortised in, floorboards coming across with the pins waiting to cinch them tight. He nodded continuously and removed his hat to scratch at his hair and fan at the gnats. Clayton couldn't help but stare at him. The little man was in constant motion, unable to hold still or give the sense that his thoughts could become disconnected from the movements of his body. His father and grandfather were men who would stand and contemplate something for long minutes, their brains temporarily adrift in thought separate from their physical selves. Clayton had found himself repeating many questions to one or the other of them in such a state.

Cmicky regarded the walls they had begun to construct, examining them and rubbing the whiskers along his jawline.

"How you raise these when finished?"

"Well, some rope and a horse, lever them up over a crossbeam – "

"That dangerous work my friend. Horse or rope slip you destroy work or hurt somebody. I see it before out this way. So far from town you perhaps not get doctor in time."

"We'll manage."

"No, my friend, there is no need for this. You give me day and I come back with the wagon and a couple of strong men and we raise walls, also help to get roof beams into place."

"We couldn't ask you – "

"It is not matter of asking. I'm telling you that we will come, so you give me day and we be here. Maybe your wife and your mother can make us supper when all is finished. There is two friend I have who will come out with me. A big Italian, excellent for lifting, and another from down your way. He nice guy, but not right in his mind."

James looked at his father and then at the ground. He had stayed out of town but now town had come to him.

"Make it a week from today. We'll have it all ready to raise. Lily and my mama will put out a spread of vittles you all ain't never et."

Cmicky slapped James's back and broke into a wide grin, took two short steps and pumped Amos's hand like he was running for office. Clayton watched him approach, prepared his hand for a surer grip, but got only a squeeze of the shoulder as he went by.

Back up on the wagon he bent to uncoil the reins then turned around and paused, as if weighing them.

"Clayton, you want to ride to Independence with me? We make pickup, I show you town and canal port there. No need to worry, James. I take care of him. Boy need to get off farm sometimes or he goes crazy. That what happened to me," he said, laughing his gap-toothed laugh.

Clayton looked imploringly at his father, wanting to go, to see what the town was like, to feel the power of those fast horses. Without returning his gaze, James said, "Thanks kindly Mr. Cmicky, but Clayton's got too much to do here and we can't spare him."

"OK James, no problem." He wound the reins around each open hand in a deft circular motion, bringing them down to slap the hindquarters of both horses simultaneously. Their hooves dug into the dirt and the wagon lurched off, its driver turning over his shoulder to shout, "Call me Cas!"

As they went back to work Clayton listened carefully while he imagined the wagon negotiating the face of the bluff. He breathed quietly, straining to hear any sign of a crash, the scream of horses. Nothing. All that remained was the gauzy cloud of dust, broken and scudded along by the south wind.

Eight

Three days later, while they were setting braces in one of the end walls, four men rode out of the tree line from the north. Clayton saw them first. Riders were not an unknown sight, but these stopped, the hoofsmoke of dust kicked up moving low behind them. Clayton was laboring with a mortise axe on a gatepost for the fence they would build around the front of the house. He laid the axe down gently, flat in the grass. Whistling low to the older men he gestured with his head into the distance. The riders moved their horses up in a line, facing them some two hundred yards away. James held his framing hammer, took the nails out of his mouth. Amos used his heavy Bailey plane to shield his eyes against the westering late-afternoon sun. The man on the far left turned in his saddle to reach for something strapped behind him. It glinted in his hand as he brought it around. Clayton saw that his grandfather's grip on the plane handle was no longer a carpenter's.

Without turning James said, "Get to the barn, boy. Stay low to the grass."

Clayton did not move, could not take his eyes off the man who held the long piece of metal to his eye. His father hissed "Go," but he did not. He waited for a puff of smoke or for the other men to make some kind of move, but they sat their horses still. There was another brassy flash as the man collapsed what he was holding in on itself. He had been looking at them through it. The two figures in the middle dismounted, disappearing behind their horses. James craned his neck to see if they were moving somehow into the grass.

Then they were mounted again, four upright figures in a dark line against the pale green prairie. Suddenly the man on the far right wheeled his mount and cantered back into the trees, the other three following. They stood for some minutes, unmoving, the birds flitting around the work site. A group of blue jays made a racket behind them near the barn. Nothing stirred at the tree line. They strained but could hear no sound of horse or rider.

James turned and fixed his son with a fierce glare. "Boy, next time I tell you to do something, you do it. You hear me?" He took Clayton by the upper arm and marched him to the well where he backed him up against the ring of stones. Clayton hung his head.

"Yessir."

He could hear his father breathing heavily, smell the work on him. James put his fist under his son's chin and raised his head, compelling him to look him in the eye. Clayton wanted to explain that he had not been able to move. He could see anger in his father's face mixed with something else, something around the eyes that gave the impression that he was uncertain, his anger tempered with doubt. Clayton felt the wet of the tears run down his cheeks, making them itch, pooling at the corners of his mouth. Abruptly James turned and walked towards the barn. Clayton wiped his face and looked at his grandfather who stood staring into the distance, shading his eyes.

Moments later his father came galloping by. He turned into the road and kicked the horse into a flat run. At the spot where the riders had sat observing he reined up and dismounted. They could see James bend down, working at something. He stood and remounted, carrying some long object. When he rode up to them Clayton could not see what it was until James handed it to Amos.

Clayton was put in mind of the time when he was little and they went to visit his Uncle Willis's grave. This was when they still lived in Alabama. He had not been quite able to grasp that it was his father's uncle, and thus his great uncle, due perhaps to his fascination at the graveyard itself and the grown-ups' reaction to being in it. He had never seen his father so somber and closed up. It had scared him. Death seemed more tangible to him in its effects on the big, strong man who was his father rather than as some force supposed to inhabit the pretty grounds of the cemetery.

His grandfather held the cross. Two pieces of whitewashed wood nailed together, the sharpened bottom darkened with dirt. He inspected it then handed it to James.

"Stuck in the road or in the grass?"

"In the middle of the road."

"Hm." Amos shook his head. He slumped a little, leaned against the well, pulled out his handkerchief and mopped the back of his neck. The creases around his eyes and forehead appeared to Clayton deeper, the skin like a mask over his real face.

"And so far from Alabama," he said in a dry whisper.

Desperate to help in some way Clayton said, "At least they's Christians." But his voice rose up in pitch at the end, unable to keep the questioning from it.

James snapped the crosspiece off.

"Not a word about this to the others, you hear me?"

Clayton nodded.

When the wagon returned a week later it approached slowly, laden with boxes and three reclining figures. Clayton was in the barn helping his mother clean their first crop of onions and red potatoes. At the first telltale sounds of visitors he ran for the door, his mother's voice not enough to stop him.

By the time he reached them the men were already engaged in animated conversation. Cmicky had a great smile on his unshaven face, hands and hat gesturing wildly keeping time with whatever it was he was saying. To his left was the biggest man Clayton had ever seen. His father was a goodly sized fellow but here was someone a full head taller. He had curly black hair surrounding a face that appeared to belong to a younger man, hairless and smooth but for a creased chin and long, straight nose. The effect of a boy's head on such a big body was reassuring somehow. He wore a red and black checked flannel shirt with the sleeves cut off – Clayton considered for a second that with the size of his arms maybe they had *worn* off – and linsey britches held up with gold baling twine. On his feet were some kind of leather sandals.

On the other side of Cmicky stood a man of indeterminate age, due less to any boyish features than to an expression of carelessness, or perhaps blankness. While the face can be deceiving, as it was likely to be, Clayton thought, in the case of the big man, who just happened to look that way, this other man radiated a kind of innocence or vacancy that was connected directly to whatever inner workings there were inside him. There had been a man in Nashville who he passed on his way to work at the store who was known in the neighborhood as "the idiot." He sat in a chair on the porch of his parents' house each day, all day, hands on knees, staring blankly into the distance. The parents had to be vigilant, not of their son, who never moved except to eat or relieve himself, but of the local youth who were in the habit of daring one another to go up on the porch and touch him to see if he would move. Clearly the man standing there in a pair of worn overalls, frayed at the knees, large round head shaved to a shadow of a widow's peak, doughy face with deepset, dark eyes, was not in the same straits as the man on the porch. But he was also not inhabiting the same plane of existence as the rest of them. Clayton noticed this most when he was introduced and shook hands. The man nodded his head and offered a bare pressure without registering his presence with his eyes, which went around the sky, severed from communicative intent.

Clayton was prepared for Cmicky this time and got his hand deep into the grip. He returned the pressure and looked him in the eye as his father had taught him. James told him that before the war a negro man was almost never allowed to shake hands with a white man and if he did was better off lowering his eyes. But now, hard as it was to get used to, they had to shake hands like the white men did with one another or there would always be difference folded into the start of everything. The Italian, whose name was Fabrizio, , had a large, hairy hand, but a gentle one. He was wondering if hard grips were not in inverse proportion to stature.

Cmicky said, "You can call him Fab. He biggest but nicest dago in whole state." He laughed until he coughed then slapped a smiling Fabrizio on the back. "I only joking of course. Being Polack I get away with such things." He turned to the other man. "And this Moberly, from your neck of woods, though now proud Yankee like all of us."

The corners of Moberly's mouth registered the comment but his eyes flitted around as if following the flight of recent birds.

Speaking loud and slow, as if calling across a body of water, Amos asked, "Where you from, Moberly?"

He turned his head on a swivel at the sound, blinking rapidly, answering with a smile that revealed small, even teeth.

"Carolina. And I ain't deaf, just slow. I reckon I can hear well as any man in Christendom."

He had an unmistakable Southern accent, pronouncing his home state with three syllables.

"It is true Amos," Cmicky put in. "That boy has hearing like you will not believe."

"I smell taters," Moberly said softly, his right hand hovering below his chin.

"And smell also," Cmicky added.

Clayton put his fingers to his nose. But if they smelled like potatoes, if the outside of a potato even had a smell, he could not detect it.

Then, to his surprise, around the wagon walked a boy, his attention devoted to something shiny he held up to his mouth. A harmonica.

"And this is June," Cmicky said, "who is finally finished pissing after such a long ride. Clayton, June is about same age as you. Maybe you show him around the place."

The boy leaned against the spokes of one of the tall wagon wheels and shined the little instrument with his shirt tail. Clayton ignored Cmicky's invitation since he would rather stay with the men and be part of the work that would soon commence.

"I can't tell you how obliged I am that you all have come to help us," James broke in. "It's real neighborly of you. Maybe we can get started and work up an appetite, cause my Lily will have more food laid out than you ever seen when it's time to eat."

Cmicky rubbed his hands together.

Clayton asked, "What's in them boxes Mr. Cmicky?"

"Cas, boy, *Cas*."

"Yessir."

Cmicky rolled his eyes. "Polite but stubborn. Like my mother." He crossed himself then walked over to the wagon where they could hear a muffled sound coming from the slatted crates.

"There are pullets and some hens. I noticed you had no chickens here last time and thought you could use eggs and meat. Perhaps save you trip to town."

"You thought right," James said, removing his hat. "That's real nice, but we ain't got much cash money, and – "

"You don't pay no cash. Birds are from Moberly, who is whiz at birds. He take some payment in kind later when you are settled. Maybe fish or venison in winter. It no hurry, right Mobe?"

Moberly nodded his big round head.

"Clay, why don't you and June see these crates up to the

barn," James said. "Spread them out in the far stall, the one you cleaned out yesterday. Ask your granny for some cornmeal to throw in and make sure they got water."

Clayton assessed the job and reckoned he would miss a fair bit of the work he had so looked forward to. They would be raising the walls of the house while he was lugging boxes.

"But Daddy – "

"Don't but me no buts, boy. Get it done and then come and help us."

On the third trip from the barn back to the wagon June said, "you don't stop throwing them crates in there like that you're gonna kill all your chickens."

"They ain't my goddamn chickens," Clayton responded, not caring who heard him curse. He could see Moberly tending the horse, keeping it in a straight line and slow walking it to raise the skeletal wall so that it could be nailed into its foundation. His job. He could keep a horse calm and focused. And here he was moving birdcages.

"It's nothing to me. Only telling you is all." June climbed into the bed of the wagon and pushed the remaining crates to the edge.

"Let's get this done. I got better things to do."

June turned to watch the men laboring to get the awkward wood structure stabilized as it yawed at one end and nearly broke. The big Italian shouted and ran to brace it. Then he looked up at the women and little boys peeling potatoes and cooking over a hot fire.

"Seems to me like we got about the best job there is." In lieu of a smile he pulled out the harmonica and surprised Clayton by playing a snatch of a dancing tune.

"That was pretty good. What was it?"

"It's a reel called 'Drowsy Maggie.'"

"What's a reel?"

"It's dancing music, mostly. Most of my mama's family are musicians. My mama loved to dance."

"Let's dance these birds up to the barn so we can help with the house. You play and I'll carry." Clayton lifted a crate with two skinny brown chickens inside and found the tune with his feet like he'd seen Ben Peacham do at a Sunday dance to impress the ladies of Nashville. Granny looked up from the beans she was snapping and shook her head at such foolishness.

It was a lot more fun than sulking, Clayton had to admit. It had been so long since he'd had a companion his age he'd nearly forgotten how to play. There would still be plenty of work to do when they finished their chore.

Thirty minutes later they reclined on bales of straw amongst a more tranquil collection of clucking fowl, content now with something to peck at besides one another. Dust motes caught the afternoon light.

Carrying chicken crates had turned out to be a good time. With each trip June set a different tune which Clayton tried to match with some fancy made-up dance steps. He'd fallen down twice and they'd laughed, his granny standing up and yelling something that made them laugh all the harder. He was worn out now which pushed away his worry about missing the work on the house. That's what happens, he reckoned, when you hold all that responsibility. You work and work and there doesn't seem to be any outside to it.

He heard a match struck and sat up to June lighting a thin cigar, which he drew on, puffing out a smoke ring.

"You play the harmonica *and* smoke ceegars? You awful big for your britches."

"Here," June said, handing it over, "try it."

Clayton took a big pull and nearly choked to death. June fell off the bale laughing.

"Hold it in and blow it back out. You ain't supposed to inhale it unless you're used to it, which you ain't. If you're gonna puke don't do it thisaway."

Clayton handed it back with his eyes shut tight, coughing, trying to get some air into his ragged throat.

"Where'd you get it? Your daddy smoke them things?"

"Pinched a handful from that cigar store on Fifth Street. The one with the Indian."

"They almost all got a Indian, one's I seen."

"Well, in this here town there's but the one Indian, and the man who owns it would never suspect the sheriff's boy of helping himself to the merchandise. I'll get you some hard candy next time I come out this way. What kind you like?"

"I'll take anything I can get at that price." June offered the cigar again and Clayton raised a hand. "I believe I've had enough of that."

They sat in the quiet for a minute, the dulcet sounds of foraging chickens oddly soothing.

Clayton asked, "What did you mean your mama *loved* to dance? Don't she dance no more?"

June blew out a mouthful of smoke. It swirled and eddied, drawn up and out through the propped-open window. Leaning back, his arm on his raised knee and hand cocked under his head, Clayton thought his new friend looked like an old soul. There was something about him in equal parts joyful and weary.

"She died."

Clayton didn't know if you got used to saying a thing like that, but somehow he knew June hadn't said it very often.

"I'm sorry," Clayton said, feeling bad for having asked. He'd been to funerals and his mama had taught him how to behave. "I didn't know. I reckon maybe she's in a better place now."

June ground the little cigar into the sole of his boot, made sure there was nothing left to catch the barn on fire.

"Could be. But that don't make it no easier. I don't really understand how a place could be better if you got to die to get there."

"From what I've seen that's what folks say to make you feel better. But I don't think you're obliged to believe it. She was your mama and it ain't really none of their business to say where she is or why." Clayton sat up. "You want to know what I think?"

June looked over, his lips drawn together.

"Sure."

"I think wherever she is, every time you play that harmonica she dances."

They lay in companionable silence until June said, "Thanks Clayton." He pushed the harmonica into the pocket of his shirt and stood up. "Why don't we head down and see if we can help your daddy and the others with the house?"

Clayton might have fallen asleep where he sat against the side of the barn, belly tight as a drum, if not for the sound of the Italian licking his fingers and Cmicky belching. It had been a long day and the sun hovered orange and trembling at the edge of the world. They had lifted and nailed, measured and cut and levered, fixed tenons in mortises, cut braces into studs and raised all four walls now ready to have clapboards shiplapped from bottom to top to seal the structure. There was so much still to do – setting rafters on the false plates, putting down collars and shingle lath on the rafters, hanging shingles, gable-end studs to set, cornices to box, rake boards to place, and chimneys to build – but the work of more than two men and a boy had been accomplished and they could now see their way to the finish. Even Granny said it was finally starting to look like something they might could live in.

"James," Cmicky said, sitting on one of the elm stumps they had arrayed in the trampled-down grass on the north side of the barn, "let me ask you something."

Clayton had returned from helping his mother and grandmother haul plates to the barn where they would wash them in the dented and chipped enamel wash pails the boys were now filling with trips from the well. He took up his place against the barn wall, pulled a piece of stiff grass and picked his teeth with it.

"You see any men out here? Not only passing down road. Watching maybe or doing mischief at night?"

The faint look that passed between James and Amos had to do with the smallest muscles beneath the eyes, a constriction of minute effort from one man to the other, asking whether one had seen or heard something he had not let on. Or, maybe more importantly, whether any of this ought to be shared with outsiders. Amos took a drink of his coffee then looked into it. The silence stretched out, its tautness accentuated by each man's posture. Clayton looked from one to the other, hoping that any second they would say something, anything, so that some kind of explanation might follow. Since those riders had come to sit in the road, leaving their whitewashed warning, there had been little talk or humor even from his grandfather.

"Gentlemen," Cmicky continued, leaning forward with hands clasped in front of him, eyes coming up from the ground to regard Amos then James. "There is a war coming. Maybe war is too strong of word, but there is battle for right to live in this county. Black men from South should know what I speak about."

He looked from son to father. No visible response.

"I understand you come up here to escape such matters. But it seems this country will not settle down until it has fought this war over and over. You think it end with North and South?" He smiled grimly, took off his hat to run fingers through his hair the color of deadfall leaves. "There are men who will always want to tell other men what to do, for reasons of money or fears which they call many things. Point is these reasons always fault of ones who suffer. Blacks stupid and lazy, good only for working like animals, happier being slave, take white women given chance, worship devil. Polacks and Italians and Irish dirty and without manners. Want only to drink and make babies and worse, Catholics, caring only for Pope and priests and not for country or nothing else. Same they did to Indians, though at least they had excuse that red men were killing people. You see result though. They not cooperate so they killed or marched off west, someone else's problem."

Clayton sat up slowly, not wanting to call attention to himself. June caught his eye but he looked away. He waited for his father to say something.

"James, you meet Tumwater when you here before?"

James took his jackknife out and the small rectangular whetstone he kept in his pocket, spat on the white surface and slowly began to run one side of the blade in circles. He looked up with one eye.

"I did."

"You think he and men like him let you live out here in peace?"

"We mind our own business they got no reason to quarrel with us."

"That where you wrong, my friend, and you know it."

The blade stopped its metallic circuit. James looked up. Fabrizio, who had been biting his fingernails, spat a last fragment into the grass and put palms on knees, as if ready to rise.

Clayton was surprised when his grandfather spoke.

"Cas, we done been through this with white folks for a long time. We know how this goes. Now we appreciate – "

"No Amos, forgive my rudeness but you do not seem to know what is going on, or perhaps are unwilling to admit it. Old rules from before not apply here. This is frontier, with government, justice, ownership all up for grabs. Strength and organization is all. In town there is group of men who want to control everything and they will do anything to keep this county obedient. Foreigners and blacks make them afraid."

"We don't want nothing from them," James replied. Amos nodded his agreement.

93

"You are black, work for yourselves. This makes a bad example."

Cmicky contemplated his fingers, steepling them together, waited.

"You have a beautiful family James," he continued. "I would hate – "

"Four men on horseback, sat at the tree line yonder, watching us work, left a . . . a . . . " Clayton said these words breathlessly, as if he had run a great distance to do so. He found himself standing. All eyes on him. His father's look sat him down, told him to be quiet now.

"Left us a cross stuck in the road," James added, his voice low but distinct over the whetting of the knife. "Likely they read in the papers about them white sheets down to home. Reckoned since they rid out this far they'd leave us something to remember them by. They been out here a couple other times, at night. Just to look. They ain't killed or took nothing yet."

Clayton looked sharply up at his father, whose eyes were back on the blade, honing its bright edge in deliberate circles. He hugged his knees, imagining men on tall horses stalking the barn, along the fence, standing at the door as they slept, silent wraiths glowing in the moonlight.

"Yet," Cmicky repeated.

Nine

Wendell Tumwater could not sleep.

He walked the town like a sentry, between the hours of eleven and two tracing empty wooden sidewalks beneath the downtown awnings, safe at this time of night from thrown mud, hurtling children, fresh horseshit. While the brats in their beds blissfully dreamed he enjoyed the stillness. Tumwater feared horses, hated children, and despised the Irish who shoveled trash into bins. They were each in their way dirty and unfit and ought to be out on the streets at night, sight unseen, while proper folks conducted their business in the light of day.

He had grown up in Cincinnati, the son of a Presbyterian minister. Like LaFayette it was a river town, though with the difference that it sat strategically at the border between North and South. His father openly opposed those who aided fugitive slaves running north up through Kentucky to Covington, where they would be taken by boat at Fort Thomas across the wide Ohio, then up through the underground railroad to Canada. It incensed him to think they might settle in the state.

Wendell had not been good at much as a child. Overweight and coddled by his mother, he had been uninterested in and untalented at physical activities.

So he became first the listener, then the doer.

This summer, since he encountered the black man in his office, he could not sleep.

In his head he played over and over the meeting with the tall negro who had entered the office hat in hand, asking in his husky voice if *Miz Lane* was there, his plantation accent making him nearly impossible to understand. The attempted assault took on a dramatic clarity: the dark shape looming over him, huge rough hands reaching for his neck like a packet boat rope around a snubbing post, coming tight, pulling him off his feet. After that he recalled only waking up on the office floor, Marjorie Lane standing over him chewing her lip.

The young, newer doctor had arrived, whom he ordinarily would not have let touch him, and administered a sedative. He woke up hours later at home, his wife arched over him brow-furrowed, pressing a cool cloth to his forehead.

After three days his head stopped hurting and he had regained his voice, though he still had a slight ringing in his ears. He went immediately to Sheriff Colegrove's office and berated him for letting his assailant leave town without arrest. Colegrove, in his usual manner, sat in his chair smoking a pipe, pretending to listen intently. Tumwater knew better. The sheriff was not a man who understood the way things ought to be, hiding behind a sense of fairness that showed no respect for the people he served.

"A man like you is no good as a rudder to steer this town," Tumwater said. He tried and failed to keep his voice down. "You will have us in a hell of a mess if order and justice are not restored."

Colegrove took his feet off the desk. His smile made Tumwater boil with anger. He said, "There will be no reprisals against the negro and his family. You understand me?" It maddened the little man that he got orders without argument.

He pointed a fat finger and said, "That's on your head," and stormed out, slamming the door as hard as he could.

The advantage of insomnia was that it gave him time to plan, unencumbered by his duties in the land office or the interruptions of his wife.

With the Independence Day holiday come and gone, Wendell Tumwater's impatience grew to such a pitch that he could scarcely contain himself. On the fourth, attending the parade along Main Street, he was struck by an overwhelming feeling of patriotic zeal. This paroxysm of rightness left him shaken and unable to enjoy the day's artificial pageantry. While he knew full well he did not resemble him in either shape or comportment, he felt the presence of his father's will, his moral rectitude and determination, his love for this new country and how it could be if it would only follow the proper course. As the day dawned on the fifth he was out walking with only the milk wagons and the early shopkeepers for company.

Why was Jeffries waiting so long?

The week after Tumwater's encounter with James McGhee, his neck stiff and the flesh around the stitches at his hairline running from purple-red to green, he was summoned to Jeffries' office on Salem Street. For thirty minutes he held his hat and waited, admiring the soft carpets, velvet coverings on the furniture, the baby grand piano kept in the anteroom. Jeffries and his wife Sylvia had parties there and reportedly hired a piano player who came in by coach. He had never been invited. He imagined the waiters in their waistcoats touring the party. A world he aspired to, though his father would not have liked it. Truth was, he desired fruits for his labors. Why should righteousness beget poverty?

He had never, ever liked that part of the Bible.

A secretary brought him out of his reverie and instructed him to follow her. Henderson Jeffries sat behind an enormous mahogany desk, the light from the window behind him setting his silver hair aglow. Tumwater had to blink repeatedly until his eyes adjusted to the glare.

Jeffries began speaking without any formalities. "I am frustrated with the way things are going. My fellow businessmen have grown complacent, refusing to act aggressively in accordance with the changing times."

"Sir, I – "

"We are," he continued, pointing at the ceiling with his cigar, "in a different world than before the war."

Tumwater nodded vigorously. He moistened his lips in anticipation of delivering a speech he had learned from his father, honed over the years and modified to suit the context, regarding the dangers of the mixing of races, of religious and moral bankruptcy. At the first word he was stopped by the cigar, shaken so as to quiet him. Jeffries went on, surprising Tumwater by mentioning none of these things.

"It is the economic imperative that must drive our strategy. The control of commerce means the control of life and livelihood, of what people have the time, energy, and inclination to think, to want to do, to believe in. Let me give you an example." He sat back in his chair. "The negro families in town. What do you think of them?"

This was an easy one.

"That they'd be better off with their own kind, back down south or in Africa or someplace." Wendell felt the lump on his head involuntarily.

"Why?"

"Well, it's my belief that different peoples ought not to consort with one another. The white race cannot afford to allow its form of government, its institutions and social structure, to be mixed with that of other races. It will bring us down . . . compromise us." Tumwater knew this line of argument chapter and verse, had gleaned it from his father, sharpened it with reading from southern newspapers and pamphlets.

Jeffries held up his hand. "I hear where you are going with this, and it will not do. You can't run a town or a county or a state that way; it simply won't hold up."

"Well sir, I don't – "

"Look at the South. They lost a war of economic imperatives while coercing their citizenry into believing they were fighting for a cause, nebulous as it was. For a way of life, for

98

white supremacy, against an evil invader. Hell, you crawl behind a stone wall and ask five Johnny Rebs what they were fighting for, you get five different answers. That is if they even had one. The South needed its negroes before the war as much as it does now, it's just that the circumstances have changed. Previously their economic and social structure was unified. It has been torn in two and they have chosen to concentrate on the latter, the former having been taken from them. Where they cannot enslave by force they wish to control by custom."

"And you think they are doing the right thing with their negroes? This Klan you read about – "

"Yes and no. They have the Klan because they have lost control of their system of government. Their commercial activities are compromised. No more free labor. Those sheets and hoods tell the story: open intimidation and fear by means of secrecy and symbolism. This is a game without a purpose, a scurrying after scraps. What those people ought to be doing is business with the North, with Europe, opening markets, changing the way they produce goods, manage their trade, influence Washington to bring them into the umbrella of economic prosperity. They are only keeping the negroes down because they have nothing else to dominate. It's a narrow-minded response. I ask you again. Why do we need the negroes who live here?"

"Well – "

"And the Irish and Italians and Poles. What would we have if they were of a sudden all gone from here?"

Tumwater wanted to say "a better place," but knew that this was not the answer Jeffries wanted to hear. He worried the brim of his hat, looked up into the long oval face with its closely trimmed beard the color of a new-minted silver dollar.

"I don't know."

"Your passion is admirable, Wendell, but misplaced. How would you like to take a more active role in things?"

"Things?"

"Yes. In the goings-on of the affairs of this county. In the inner workings of the progress of our little community here."

"I'd like that. What can I do?"

"The answer to my earlier question is that we need these people, Wendell. We need them so that there can be an order to things. Order is based on difference, and difference is based less on the more obvious examples of skin color or religion than it is on *making* the difference mean something. Are you following me? The blacks are different-looking, to be sure, but who's to say this is inferior? You won't find that in so many words in the Bible, and it damn sure is not in the Constitution of this nation. Ask your friends in the South if they found that document congenial to their purposes. If we shipped out all the blacks and Catholics, what would we be left with? Would the resulting homogeneity find its own order?"

Tumwater was getting confused. There were words here he would need to look up in his dictionary and then piece this conversation back together. It was getting away from him.

"I can see by your expression that you don't quite agree."

He tried to make his face go blank, afraid Jeffries would rise and dismiss him and any hope he had of participating in whatever plans were afoot.

"Even if we had your ideal group of white people left here, how would we organize things? Who would do the dirty jobs, the low-paying ones? Classes of people would not change unless we abolished or radically altered the economic system, divided everything up equally, got rid of money and private property and so on. To keep things on the proper footing we would have to make a difference with our own kind. You would be in something of a pickle then, my friend. What argument would you make for this? Or are you a communist?"

"Mr. Jeffries, I can assure you – " Tumwater rose to his feet, flushed.

"Calm down, Wendell."

The fat little man's attempt at acquiescence had emerged sounding like protest. He was glad to have been interrupted, since he had no idea what to say without risk of ruining his opportunities.

"What we must do is maintain control of the economic imperative by using our management of different peoples. There are many ways to do this. What we cannot have are these people doing what they please in an independent manner. For example, the man who gave you that lump on your head is homesteading in the county, free of the town, of the necessity of participating in its commerce. There are others who have aided him and his family, who themselves have been plotting and planning together to raise themselves into a position to influence our commercial activities. We must put a stop to it."

"What can I do?"

"You can put your passion in the right place."

Later that morning, Tumwater sat at his desk fanning himself, trying to concentrate on the plat map he was recopying. The more laborious task of filling in the town lots was finished – an entire day's work – and he had moved on to the village of Chauncey west across the river. With one finger on the grid and his pen poised at his place on the list of names, he checked these against the old map at his elbow. Every few minutes he had to stop, wipe his face and forehead with a handkerchief, and then fan himself with a stiff piece of blank deed parchment. It would not do to drip onto the fresh map. Outside the window, open as high as it could go, the trees sat impassively, their leaves barely rustling in the turgid air. Even the flies sat still. Back to the map and list, he came to the name Metzger, crossed off, the name McGhee penciled in above it in the willowy script of Marjorie Lane. Tumwater looked back at the map, moved his finger one grid to the north, where he had just seen the name "Lecroix" crossed out. He checked the plat number against the entry in the ledger.

Of course. Earlier in the year the Lecroix brothers had shown up and demanded their farm back. The county had seized it over unpaid back taxes while they were away. Tumwater had tried to explain this to them at first patiently, but when they began shouting at him, threatening to commit violence then and there he had hastily closed the office and gone straight to the sheriff.

He again checked the plat map against the ledger to confirm that their parcel backed up against the McGhee land. It did. The ledger contained a further detail. A slice of what had been Lecroix land was now owned by the McGhees.

There was the answer.

Fan the embers of grudge into the fires of acquisitiveness. The Lecroix brothers could have been harnessed for such rough business anyway, but what could they be incited to do with a motive? He remembered now the account from McRae himself of the split head of Walt Lecroix, fingered his own diminished bump, wiped his face with the damp handkerchief, and smiled his little smile.

Jeffries' secretary, Miss Van Ryke, with her horsy nose and slight Dutch accent, would not let him past her desk, no matter how he drew himself up. Invoking his earlier meeting with her boss did no good, nor did the tone he used to cow his wife make the slightest dent in her composure. He agreed to wait, assuring her that she would regret it if he were not back by the time his lunch hour was up. Her polite smile in return to this admitted no possibility of rue. Tumwater sat in the same comfortable spot as before, racking his brain for reasons to dislike Hollanders.

When Jeffries admitted him with a wave of his hand he looked at his watch and said, "Five minutes." His plan, still

ill-formed but growing, tumbled out. Jeffries folded his arms. He reached into the small pocket in his vest, snapped open the gold watch, gave it a quick glance, and repocketed it.

"I've had men out there," Jeffries said, "doing a few things, laying the seeds for something bigger. Hired them off the river, paid with cash and whiskey, sent them back from wherever they came. If we are to embark on this more ambitious plan of yours we will need to proceed deliberately and decisively. I do not want anyone left to tell the tale. Just the example made, swift and without mercy. Do you understand me? From now on it is in your hands. I will see to financing, and you will come to me only when it is absolutely necessary. Anything you need, any information to relay or exchange, you will come and see Miss Van Ryke. She will take it from there."

On his way out he looked into the secretary's eyes, nodding slightly to acknowledge his new place in the affairs of the Jeffries circle. Her blue eyes locked onto him and betrayed not even the slightest recognition.

Ten

Clayton picked his way carefully down the ravine carved into the flank of the bluff. He took his time, not wanting to fall on his burned hand. The iron pot had scorched him where he'd touched it with the heel and base of his thumb. Granny rigged a sling out of an old flour sack and sent him off to gather more berries with his brothers. This he removed and pushed behind a rack of hay in the barn loft.

James had been quick to anger since Cas had pressed him about confronting the men who had ridden out and planted the cross in the road. His father was not generally a moody man. Clayton knew him to get this way only when something was weighing heavy on his mind. Earlier in the morning they had built a roof truss. In gauging whether the three of them were going to be able to hoist and nail it to the top plate Clayton's grip gave out and the awkward triangular support twisted and fell to the ground. It hadn't been his fault but hours of work had been wasted and James yelled at him to get up to the barn with his mama. Clayton had stood there, hoping this might pass. When he said he was sorry his father ignored him and set to work pulling apart the fractured pieces of wood. His grandfather put a gentle hand behind his neck and steered him away from where they were working.

At the bottom of the ravine the creek resumed its habitual shape and purpose, running on flatter ground that sloped gently and then leveled into the flood plain of the river. He climbed out of the creek bed and stood in the shade of the last trees, shielding his eyes to look across the expanse of prairie for most of a mile until another line of trees marked the passage of the river. From this slight elevation he saw the wrinkle in the grass where the river road ran away to town and in the other direction to Black Rock and Independence. Beyond it the creek took its time across the treeless expanse to where it fed the Wabash. In the barn he'd pocketed a round of string and on the workbench made three crude hooks out of spent nails that sat in a bucket waiting to be smelted. It was hours till supper. Clayton figured he could sulk while he tried to get his brothers to mind or he could make himself useful and catch some fish. He had yet to explore the river or the sweep of prairie beyond the ravine's end and could see no reason to squander the opportunity.

Walking in the tall grass was harder than he expected. It was up to his chest near the tree line but as the ground became flatter and the soil richer it rose higher and higher. It grew to his chin by the time he reached the road. Once there he paused to peer out, making sure the way was clear. Not that he expected a busy thoroughfare, but he would rather get to the river without having to talk to anyone about who he was or what he was doing. The road's surface was pocked with holes and in the center baked hard and flat. Like inverted train tracks deep ruts left by wagon wheels ran parallel into the golden distance. There was a plank bridge where the creek crossed and Clayton could not help stomping his foot to see if it made a hollow sound. It did but nothing like the covered bridges they had seen on their way north. The racket flushed a covey of quail out of the grass and the avian explosion of wingbeats scared him. He immediately checked the road for other people. He had not been alone in months, he realized. It gave him an odd comfort to be afraid and not have to worry about whether anyone noticed.

Beyond the road the ground was soft and marshy. After he walked out of his shoe in the muck he slowed down. He found that if he stepped at an angle onto the grass, bending it beneath his foot like a mat, he wouldn't sink nearly as much and could go faster. With the grass reaching above his head he was forced to gather himself and jump up to get his bearings. With such unsure footing this led to several falls, each of which saw him covered in a little more mud. At least it kept the horse flies off.

It took him a good while to cross the prairie. When he lost his way he checked the position of the sun and then struck out in the direction of the creek. At first he tried walking in it but this became impossible. After the road it did not flow along a bed of sand and rocks but sticky, soft mud from which he feared he would never remove himself. He stayed in the grass and aimed for a line of unmistakable sycamores until they loomed overhead, their white trunks cheerful and sturdy after so much grass. The prairie ended at a stand of sumac and he had to bend down and force his way through thin branches. The woods here arose from a sea of low weeds he did not recognize and stands of nettles he avoided. Eventually he stood looking over dark, slow-moving water, the bank heavily eroded, held together by tree roots and a thick matting of knee-high grass that hung over a steep, sandy drop. Clayton wasn't sure he could get back up if he got himself down there and so worked his way towards the mouth of the creek.

It was cool in the shade and a breeze kept the flying bugs to a minimum. Small red-headed woodpeckers flitted to and from a hollow tree that stood white and full of holes like a chewed bone. The racket of their knocking echoed across the river and back. A fish jumped and splashed into the opaque brown water under the shadowed deadfall of a cottonwood tree. He made a mental note of the spot. As he walked he studied the dark water where it eddied in the line of shade cast by the overhanging trees for more signs of greedy fish and so was almost on top of them before he saw the bodies.

His first impulse was to run and he did, his heart muscle hammering. Weaving in and out of trees and around a clutch

106

of horseweeds he finally pitched himself behind a log. From his cover he listened intently and tried to slow his breathing, but could hear only the woodpeckers and the croak of frogs. The mosquitoes found him, drawn by the heat from his exertions. He slapped at them with little effect. He would have to shift himself. In a low crouch he ran to a tree and sneaked a look back the way he'd come. Nothing. He searched for a stick and found a stout branch, broke off the odd limbs and felt immediately better with something he might swing as a weapon. When he closed his eyes he saw hung bodies again, more clearly now with the help of his imagination. It was not possible to avoid thinking about the book, about what Crusoe saw on his island, the horrific sight of people eating human flesh. He'd been entranced and terrified when he read those pages. The nightmares had kept him up for the better part of a week, until his mother threatened to take the book away. Each time Clayton had found himself watching the very same scene: brightly painted men danced and leapt around a fire with their captives trussed nearby, the whites of their eyes reflecting the flames, and then suddenly the dance stopped and they all turned to look straight at him. When he tried to run their hands were instantly on him and then he was tied up with the others. He woke himself up by straining against his bonds, apparently crying out as he did so.

Curiosity overpowered his fear. He moved as stealthily as he could from tree to tree. The sand allowed him to approach quietly and when he was close enough he risked a longer look at the two headless shapes that hung magically in the air. They were gruesome. The bright colors of the viscera appeared gaudy and out of place here in this brown and green world: the silverskin that enveloped the ribcage, the cartilage protruding from a severed joint, the blood dripping into a trench that had been scooped out beneath. He saw that they hung this way by a rope knotted to a rough-cut beam suspended between two trees, each carcass secured by an iron hook threaded through the sinew and muscle at the base of the neck. They swayed gently in the breeze and splayed as they were he could understand how he'd mistaken the shape for a man. Fresh meat, recently butchered. Not human, but without head, hands, and feet he could see how he'd been fooled.

Though matter-of-fact and measured, the man's voice frighted him half to death.

"You ain't the sheriff, are you?"

Clayton screamed like he had in his dream, the voice so clear and close. He tried to run but his legs would not obey him. Nor was the stick any use as he was too scared to move. Turning his head he saw a man standing not five feet away bearing a load of greenwood with both arms. He appeared to be waiting for an answer.

"No sir," he managed.

The man was dressed in ragged clothes, but not homespun. His light blue trousers were grimed to a blue-brown, a linsey-woolsey shirt had sleeves raveled to an end shy of bony elbows. He was taller than Clayton but not by much. His blonde hair was stringy and if it had been in the water it was not for the purpose of washing it. Above the collar of his shirt he had a nasty red scar.

"Well then if you don't mind I need some help." He carried his load of roughly chopped saplings and broken branches, depositing them in the trench. Then he turned and on his way by said, "Come on now, I need to get a fire on that meat afore the flies eat it all."

The man delivered this in such a friendly manner, as if they'd known each other for years, that Clayton found himself following before he knew what he was doing.

"Name's Furnish," he said over his shoulder, setting a steady pace and forcing Clayton to follow at a trot. "But you can call me Judah."

In a half hour they amassed a considerable pile of wood

chopped with a hatchet, broken off by hand, or, for saplings, stood on and snapped off at the base. Judah set a furious pace and Clayton was out of breath when he dropped his third armload and heard him say, "OK, that'll do."

He replied by stating the obvious. "You know that wood ain't gonna burn, mister."

"I reckon I done this a time or two" he replied. "What'd you say your name was?"

"I didn't. It's Clayton."

"Pleased to meet you. Now come on." Away he went in the other direction with his new helper struggling to keep up.

On the high ground above where the creek opened to meet the river Judah had constructed a dwelling out of split logs and roughcast. It likely kept most of the weather out, but Clayton imagined the look on his grandfather's face at the workmanship, or lack of. In the cleared space to one side of Judah's house there was a fire pit ringed with flat stones from the creek. Beyond this he bent and pulled a piece of dirty canvas back, reaching into a hole to remove several pieces of yellowed wood each the size of a loaf of bread. He put a half dozen of these into a sack, slung it over his shoulder and whisked by Clayton before he could ask what they were doing.

Judah got on his knees and removed the chunks of wood from the sack, placing them at regular intervals at the bottom of the pile of wood they'd gathered.

"Now," he said, "see if you can't find some dry limbs. Break 'em up and stick 'em in amongst this here greenery."

When Clayton returned with his first load Judah had begun nailing deer hides to the cross beam, staking them out at the bottom so that they formed a kind of tent over the dressed deer. By the time he made three trips Judah had finished his enclosure and only his legs stuck out as he lay on his belly working at something.

"What you doin now?"

In lieu of an answer Judah scuttled out backwards, careful not to dislodge the stakes, coughing and wiping his eyes. Smoke trailed out after him and when he had caught his breath he went back down and began blowing between cupped hands.

"If I had me a bellows this'd work a whole lot better. I cain't blow like I used to. Give her a try."

Clayton obliged, taking deep breaths and blowing beneath the edge of the hide, hearing the crackle of flames each time. He started too fast though and after a few lungfuls felt lightheaded and had to stop to catch his breath.

"Easy there my friend. Nice and steady."

"What was it you put in there? It burns somethin fierce."

"Heartwood from a pitch pine. You know where to look for it there's plenty of it, though it ain't easy to get out of the tree."

"I ain't never heard of it."

"Where you from?"

"Up the bluff – "

"Afore that. You ain't from these parts I reckon."

"Alabam and then up Nashville way. We only been here a couple months."

"Winter gets pretty serious around here. You seen where I live. I'm either pretty handy with fire materials or a shivering son of a bitch."

"What's all this meant to do?" Clayton asked, gesturing at the carcasses swaddled now in their cast-off skins, emitting smoke through the imperfectly sealed top.

"I ain't got no place to cold cure or store fresh meat this time a year so I got to smoke it. Keeps it from rot and turns the flies away. Makes it taste pretty good too. Plus I'd have coyotes and buzzards in here after it quick as you please."

"I seen fish smoked thataway. Does it cook all the way through?"

"That's a right smart question. No it don't. You still got

to cook it some, especially any meat with a sizeable bone running through it."

"You need a smokehouse."

"I reckon so but I ain't got around to it. I mostly eat fish and whatever I can trap that's edible."

"You live here by your ownself?"

"Had me a dog but he got kilt a few months ago."

"You always lived out this way? You grow up in that house yonder?"

"I come out here in sixty and five." He hadn't yet met Clayton's eye and now did so only to turn away from the contact, slight as it was. "I don't do too good around people no more."

Clayton lowered his voice to a whisper he could barely hear above the crackle of the greenwood. "Was you in the war?"

Clayton helped Judah tend the fire with his stick, keeping the branches and saplings moving atop the flaming knots of pitch pine. The smoke was acrid and stung his eyes if he let the wind outmaneuver him. They worked this way for some time in silence after Clayton asked about the war.

He had not anticipated the effect such a question would have.

Judah had wiped his palms on his trousers and stared at them. Then again. He flexed his hands as if trying to renew the circulation after bearing a heavy burden. His face bore the guise of a beaten man, hollow and drained of vitality. Clayton had never seen a man make himself smaller so that the world could not get a hold on him. He felt sure he could walk up and push him over without resistance.

"Mister Judah?"

He feared he'd done something very wrong.

Because it was what his father would do, and because it was what his grandfather had done for him this very day, he

111

put his hand gently on the man's shoulder. He could feel the sharpness of his bones. A tenuous smile played across Judah's face but he could not hold it. The corners of his mouth trembled. He looks older now, Clayton thought. When he spoke he sounded far away and faint, like the last notes of a sad song.

"I'm not too good around people. Not any good at all."

He stared at his boots, their wrecked leather the same color as the river. Clayton gave his shoulder a light squeeze.

"Can you help me catch some fish?"

They stood in silence this way in the lee of the question, a kind hand on a distant body. Clayton's burn didn't hurt anymore, he realized. He was glad he'd struck out on his own.

"If I wadn't handy with catchin fish I'd be a hungry son of a bitch."

Clayton smiled.

Beached on the creek bank in the rocks above the waterline Judah's dugout canoe did not inspire confidence. Clayton had no idea how they'd be able to fish out of such a thing without turning it over and he did not fancy having to swim out where the current would drag a body down in the deep channel. He thought about the day he'd been baptized in a similar river far to the south. The light sparkled off the green Coosa at the end of the red clay path. Pitcherplants rose in bunches out of the scrub and a rattler that skittered into a bush was given a wide berth by the procession. It took all the verses of "Shall We Gather at the River" to get there. What he remembered most was the grip of the current below the still surface, as though the rite he was undergoing was solemnized by the grasp of unseen watery forces. He felt the river's strong cold fingers long after he'd risen up for the lord and felt his mama's warm hug on the shingle of gravel.

There was a rope threaded across holes bored in the gunwales of the bow which Judah used to haul the boat into the shallow creek. It bobbed at the edge where the river lapped a curious tongue into the creek bed. The dugout did not appear to have the draft for two but it held them, Clayton hanging on and trying to balance himself on his knees in the dead center of the lurching hull. He figured Judah had gone for tackle but he returned silent and unreadable with a coil of hemp rope, a short wooden club, and a hessian bag whose markings were faded beyond recognition. Concentrating on keeping them level kept his mind off the water and afforded him no opportunity to ask about the technical nature of fishing with the kind of tools two men might employ for stealing chickens.

With a paddle cut and scappled from a length of red cedar, Judah guided them out into the main channel and then downstream a half mile so smoothly that his passenger loosened his grip and began to enjoy the cool breeze and the rhythm of the water lapping the hull. Judah piloted them expertly to the bank. When they touched the muddy shore Clayton stepped carefully out and pulled the dugout far enough that it did not drift back into the current. He expected Judah to get out and wade up to the bank, but instead he said, "At the base of that silver beech yonder is my trot line. Get hold of it and follow it to where it goes into the river. There ain't no hooks, but be careful you don't jerk it any more than you have to. When you get to the edge stay put and hold on to it and I'll collect you."

The overhang was lower here and the big smooth beech was rooted stubbornly in the cut of the bank. The line that girded it was nearly invisible and he only found it after bending back the grass. He hooked two fingers under it and followed until it disappeared into the dull water, where Judah already waited feathering the paddle with deep strokes holding the dugout steady.

"There ain't no hope for you stayin dry if you want some fish. Step on in and I'll come around."

Clayton did so tentatively, feeling with his right foot for a drop off that might send him tumbling. The line in his hand reassured him that he would at least not go far. When Judah brought the dugout to where he could grab the gunwale he was stuck with one hand on the boat and the other on the line, unable to move. Judah regarded him impassively.

"I don't wanna tip the boat over."

"That makes two of us."

"How do you reckon I can get in and not let loose of this here?"

"Pull the bow to you and slip the line over it and let it rest there. Get your leg in and roll over the side and I'll hold us with the paddle."

Clayton did as he was told and found himself miraculously in the bottom of the dugout and not swimming in a panic for the bank. He took hold of the line and they moved along its length out into the river.

"When you get to the first hook you ought to be able to tell if there's a fish on it. You know how to get a fish off a hook?"

"I reckon I done it a time or two."

A wry laugh from the stern.

"Get that sack ready and the club. You get a good sized flathead or channel cat on there you're gonna need it. Knock him in the head and stay clear of his spines. I don't want you bleedin all over my clean canoe."

Judah's trot line had fifty or so hooks evenly spaced across the river. On the third hook there was a lively pressure pulling back against Clayton's hold on the line.

"Got one," he said. Judah kept them steady and guided him through the steps of getting the fish unhooked and into the bag. He didn't mind, since fishing from a listing, narrow boat was a lot harder than being able to step on a fish and extract a barbed hook on solid ground.

By mid-river Clayton had the hang of it. Only one lost and that a small sunfish too small to eat.

As they moved down the line Clayton was surprised to hear Judah begin talking. At first he thought maybe another boat had come up on them and he was making conversation. But when he heard what he was talking about he understood that the Union soldier in what was left of his dirty blue uniform had begun to answer his question.

"Later in the war I heard grape and shell fall like awful music. But not at first. Of that time all I can recall was the screaming. The roar of that first fight was like all the hells you ever reckoned in church. I thought I'd not make it for ten minutes, much less the hitch I'd signed up for. But the thing about war is you don't have any choice. I was too scared to run and so even with my ears ringing and frantic thoughts of getting blown up by the ordinance thudding the scrub field I did what I'd reckon any man would do. Followed those who'd survived for years at it. I looked around and saw my mess mates flat on their bellies shooting at the advancing Rebs. Hell, I hadn't even seen them. We'd been waiting in a little draw that passed through a fallow field gone to weeds. When ordered to advance we did so in a neat line. A quarter mile ahead was a border of trees and behind that a hillock and behind that a heavily forested ridge. Some puffs of blue smoke rose out of the foliage on the ridgeline and I was wondering what it was when I heard the shouted order to take cover. Then that hellfire clamor and I thought well surely I am dead."

Clayton pulled them along hand over hand deliberately, taking his time and trying to go carefully so as not to interrupt the story. He was afraid to look around or do anything to break the spell. When he came to where they'd hooked a white perch he slid his hand down from its head, smoothing down the fins, popped the hook out of its bottom lip and put it in the sack. On they went across the flat of water in the late afternoon sun.

"By imitating my fellows I pulled myself out of the terror of those first moments. My rifle was a few feet away. I picked it up and checked the end of the barrel for mud and the loads to see if they were compromised and crawled up beside whoever the hell had the temerity to shoot back. After my first shot into the enemy's ranks I felt a damn sight better. On that first day in some broken field outside Chancellorsville something clicked in me and I found a way to survive. There was so much mud and blood, noise and pain. You were always sick and half the time about to shit yourself or puke the moldy food. But when the shells started raining down and the lines were formed up then it all came down to moments of clarity. Looking along the sights of a gun barrel was the only time I felt safe. Every single night I rolled up in my blanket I was scared to death."

Several hooks later Clayton thought there was a water snake and nearly dropped the line. He could feel a flash of the terror described by the man in the other end of the boat, the mammal reaction to a dark reptilian shape that might suddenly strike. It was a stick undulating in the current, a trick of the light. They went on.

"I made it that day though I saw many others who didn't. It's different than you'd think, seeing a dead man in a field and not stopping to care or do anything about it. The first one pulls at you, makes you feel responsible. But you can't stop or you may end up just like him, your dull eyes open to the hole in the sky. Then there's another and another and you don't see people no more. Just versions of what you hope to avoid. The dead are so lonely looking.

"We moved on from there after pulling guard over a company of captured infantrymen from Georgia. The poor ragged butternuts had no shoes. Half of them were boys and many carried a look of crazed savagery. Dead enders off to northern pasture. To Gettysburg we went, then back down to Virginia on Lee's trail. Some rest if my memory is right, where we played cards and kept our heads down. I think we got some whiskey that time. At what they called The Wilderness we slept the first night in the woods not twenty rods from the field I just told you about. In that woods a year on was the wreckage of that same Chancellorsville battle. I felt the crack of a branch when I knelt down to knock a stake in for our wedge tent and when I lifted up my knee there were the shattered ends of rib cage bones. We saw caissons robbed of any useful iron, spent cartridge boxes, the shattered remnants of limbers and battery wagons where they'd been shelled and burned, the skeletons of draft horses, pieces of belt leather and uniforms poking out of the sandy ground. Wearable boots and hats had all been scavenged, as had armaments and personal effects of any worth. Some pieces were on the surface and some likely went deeper. No one wanted to pull on anything for fear of what might be under it.

"The next morning we were rousted before first light and General Ward formed us into our line. Sixty rounds of ammo weighed heavy but at the start of the day you always want to go out flush. South of the Plank Road we moved forward none too fast for the poor light and with the leaves come on and all the young trees you couldn't see a goddamn thing beyond the space of a company on either side. We could hear the regiments behind us stationed on the road and once in a while you could glimpse one of the sharpshooters from the Second U.S. out front on skirmish. I peered into the gloom for something gray to shoot at. Suddenly we were right on them. Most were asleep or just waking. They'd built earth and log entrenchments and we nearly fell on top of them before we could shoot or they could surrender. When Ward figured out that we had the advantage he ordered a charge. We fixed our bayonets and ran full tilt yelling. Many Rebs fled and others were shot down before they could fight back. My best friend Johnny McBeth was right next to me. I remember him so clearly ahead of me. He turned around with a ragged grin. Then he was jerked like he'd run into a low branch and I felt his brains and blood across the side of my face. He went down, his bayonet digging into the ground while both hands still held his rifle. God I tried to slow myself but I could not with the minié balls singing over our heads and slapping the trees. I was too afraid to stop for him and I could not help but do as my fellows did and continue to the earthworks where we killed and maimed and captured. All that day we fought. It was hot and at supper time the lieutenant stopped where we were eating cold beans and crackers and told me to get to the surgeon. I'd noticed that no one else in my mess would look at me but I thought it was because I'd left Johnny out there in the woods. He said, because you have been shot in the head. I couldn't feel anything apart from what the lead ball had done to my best good friend. The fifth of May, eighteen and sixty four. Feels like a thousand years ago and yesterday all at the same time."

Clayton had stopped pulling and their progress was halted as he stared petrified into the water, Judah's story alive in the river like a vision. When it was clear that it was finished he began their progress once again on the line.

As they neared the next hook there was a splash as a big flathead catfish yanked the line out of Clayton's hand. He lunged after it and caught it, splaying his legs out to brace himself. He'd seen the head with its black whiskers near the surface right before it flipped over to dive for deeper water, its wide mouth bigger than his own. Judah didn't shout any instructions and Clayton realized that there weren't any apart from *pull*. He did and the cat came to the surface and thrashed, twisting its yellow belly and throwing its head and tail, then holding suspiciously still. He looked it in the eye. Just as Judah said something that he thought was probably worth hearing in the way of instruction he yanked the big fish towards him and they both tumbled to the floor of the boat. Clayton tried to get his knee on him but the mass of its body was too thick and slippery and its writhing made it hard to pin down. The bottom of the dugout was not an ideal place as it had no angles in which to trap something. He grabbed the sack from where it hung over the side and used it to get a grip on its body. Behind him he found the club and began trying to bash it in the head. Judah was shouting something which after a minute or so of flailing he made out.

"Other end."

No wonder his efforts weren't keeping fifteen pounds of muscle from trying to get back to the water. He was hitting its tail. He flipped it around without getting stuck by the spiny top fin and after a few cracks it was still.

"You all right?" Judah asked.

"Yes sir, I believe so."

Clayton loosened his grip on the fish to see if it would commence its flopping, but it did not. He wrangled it into the sack and washed the blood and slime off his hands. The trot line had sunk below the surface and they now drifted with the current, the paddle across Judah's knees. He was looking into the distance.

"Mister Judah, you want me to paddle us back?'

"No son. I'll be fine."

It was a chore to climb the bluff with the hessian sack. By the time he was within sight of the house he was sweat-soaked, covered again in mud, and swollen with mosquito bites. His mama and granny were laboring over the cook fire with their supper. He could see his brothers running through the field at the top of the rise, their laughter reaching him on the wind. As he neared the barn his father came around the corner carrying a block plane and an unshaped oak plank. James stopped short at the sight of him. He looked his son up and down.

"What you got in the bag?"

"A mess of fish."

He wanted to say more, let the whole thing tumble out

about the deer and the fire, the dugout and the fish, Judah and the Wilderness and the war that he'd been too young to understand.

"If you ain't too busy tomorrow you think you could help us put that roof up? Your old granddad ain't any good without you there."

"I reckon so."

"Glad to hear it. Now get on to your mama and granny with them fish. If I eat another bowl of stew I'm goin early to my grave."

Clayton smiled, and went on.

Eleven

The mules they bought in Crawfordsville – a john and a molly – were strong, healthy, and entirely unruly. It took several days to get them into harness. James and Amos made the first attempt at the edge of the field they intended to turn in preparation for a late crop of hay. The john mule was all teeth and hooves, taking the bridle but not willing to let anything touch its shoulders or withers. Amos slid the harness carefully down over his head and as soon as the collar touched him he set to bucking and biting. James yanked down on the bridle, by sheer force taking the fight out of him. Next they tried it in a stall, thinking perhaps the confined, familiar space would work better. He kicked out two boards before they could restrain him. Finally they covered his head with an old seed bag and by repetition and patience persuaded him to accept the collar and the bellyband. When the rattle of the trace chains made him skittish Amos calmed him by whispering through the sacking.

Clayton watched from a safe distance. He had not seen such a thing before and marveled at his father and grandfather's patience and courage. One snap of the molly's teeth into his shirt when they'd arrived had made him keep his distance. Granny named them Samson and Delilah.

An hour after sunrise it was already hot. The grasshoppers jumped in the brittle prairie grass. Clayton was crouching down, his eyes level with the undulating growth of the swale, the hoppers erupting from the earth like broken pieces from an angry machine.

"Clayton, wake up over there boy!"

His grandfather's voice was graveled this early and hardly discernible at a distance.

"You holding that stake straight? I have to come back there I'll jerk a knot in yo tail."

Clayton refocused his attention on the wooden stake he was holding, a notch cut near its top holding a string running to the stake the old man was setting many yards away. In the shade of a black locust his father was harnessing the mules, preparing to hitch to the plough the three of them would draw up. He felt a greater tension on the line and turned his head to see his grandfather staring at him, a look of concentration as he pulled taut and drove the sharp stake in at an angle. The reports from the hammer were softened by the hush of the grass.

He closed his eyes and through the soles of his bare feet felt far-off thunder. He opened them and stared the length of the string until he found the rhythm of his grandfather's stroke. Amos struck the stake firmly at regular beats, but without the force to cause the ground to shake. To the west there was no change in the deep blue of the sky in the cloudless morning. The breeze was light. Closing his eyes again, putting his head down, he heard it clearly, rhythmically, growing nearer.

Riders. More than one, coming on fast.

He yelled but Amos did not hear him, intent on his hammer work. Under the locust his father was nowhere to be seen, the mules shifting their feet in harness, cropping at the grass in the shade. Must have gone to the barn for something. The field they were laying out was across the road and to the west, near to the place where it plunged down the bluff to the river road, in the far corner of their land. It was flat, low, and sheltered by the bluff to the south. A good place to clear and plant. But not to command perspective of the road or the house and the other buildings over the rise.

Clayton let go the stake and ran toward his grandfather, who, seeing the line go slack stopped his hammering in mid-stroke and hollered something the boy did not hear. Trying to yell as he ran did not make his voice carry and yet he did not want to stop to put his hands up to his mouth to do it properly. He felt small and vulnerable and needed desperately to be near someone and not out at the end of a thin piece of string. As he closed the last yards he stumbled in the tall grass and went down. Amos picked him up.

"Calm down Clay. Get yer breath now. Easy ... easy. What is it?" The anger gone, the old man sensing that it was more than childishness.

"Horses. Fast. Riders."

Clayton whirled around and pointed back behind him, up the gradual slope where the road ran unseen from the woods across the prairie to the bluff and down to the floodplain. The unmistakable drum of hoof falls pounded the earth.

"Come on."

Amos could not run as fast as his grandson but managed to keep at his heels through the grass to the rise where they saw horsemen pulled up four abreast a stone's throw away, going down the drive at a walk. The cloud of dust they had thrown up floated on, a gauzy cloak left to twist and dissipate into the loosestrife and nettles. Clayton watched this, fascinated, imagining that they might rejoin it and ride it down the face of the steep bluff like silent specters.

James was walking to meet them, having heard their approach and come from the barn. He carried something at his side that he now clutched in both hands and held in front of him, stopping in their path. The riders checked up and sat their mounts.

James saw his father and son descend the downslope in the waist-deep grass and wished they had gone round to the house unseen to set up some kind of defense of the women and smaller boys. He looked them over. Four of them on well-equipped horses. Two familiar big men, similar-looking, with red-brown beards and long hair beneath sweatsoaked hat brims. Both were narrow-eyed, begrimed, tobacco stains rampant on one dirty homespun shirt, down one side of the man's lip and chin, the other with his mouth locked on a spent cigar which he talked around, never moving it. These two in the center, in charge, flanked by two thinner men, one short and one tall, spindly, Adam's apple prominent in his clean-shaven neck. The short man had a rodent's pointy nose, wore his mouse-colored hat down to the top of his eyes, like a child in passed down clothes. James felt wariest of this man; the little ones always had something to prove.

Protruding from all four saddles was a Winchester. Nice new rifles, hardwood stocks gleaming blood red in the sunlight. Each man with polished sidearms lurid against worn leather. The brother with the cigar had a blacksnake tied to his saddle and a ridiculously large knife strapped across his chest, its bone handle nearly reaching his chin. James was glad to have grabbed the shovel as he'd sprinted out of the barn at the sound of approaching horses, but it did not exactly present a formidable sight.

"Somethin I can do for you all?"

As soon as he said it he knew who these men were. He knew what the voice around the cigar would sound like even before he heard it.

"You can get yer black ass off my land."

His brother turned and spat a mouthful of brown juice over the back of his horse, clearing some room to talk.

"*Our* land, goddamnit," he added. And smiled, dirty gold tooth scarcely visible in a broken line of mottled brown.

Walt and Gene Lecroix. The alley behind the livery, the woman in the yellow dress, the boy, the stock of the Hawken coming down on a head, then into the chest about where the knife now rode sheathed.

"I don't know what you all are up to, but I paid for this land and got the papers to show fer it." He kept his voice level, as calm as he could, held the shovel in front of him and tried not to grip it too hard. It wouldn't do to start shaking.

The brother with the chaw in his cheek laughed. James reckoned by his eyes that he was the younger. He cocked a leg up onto the front of the saddle, tipped his hat back.

"If it weren't for that damn Colegrove you'd – " he started to say, but was interrupted by his brother, who had a less amused look on his face and whose body language was more intent on some as yet undivulged purpose. He put a gloved hand up, which stopped his sentence. Flustered, he spat between the horses and at a look from his elder put his foot back in the stirrup, then said something low and incomprehensible into his beard that James could not hear.

"We come from the land office at the courthouse," the man with the knife said around his cigar. "Turns out that woman what sold you this here land had no right to do that. Made a mistake. It's part of our holdings now, bought for cash money this morning."

"You got papers to prove that?"

"They's bein drawn up as we speak. Be ready in two days, by which time you and yours better have your shit off this place or we'll take it."

"Or burn it," his brother added.

"Or worse," the little rat-faced man said, laughing through his nose.

"This here's fair warning. You get yerselves packed, go to the land office and get what you paid back. Minus rent for the time you been here, of course."

James gripped the smooth hickory handle. He wanted badly to swing it into this man's face at the thought of being thrown off this land, having to leave the work and care they had put into the place. Over their heads he regarded his father and oldest son who had stopped in the grass, the older man's hand on the back of the boy's neck, waiting.

"You hear what I said?" Lecroix asked, leaning forward over the pommel, then back, pulling the long shank of steel out of its scabbard. He pointed the knife at James's chest. All eyes on him. The tall man reached for his sidearm, touching the grip and hammer lightly with his fingertips. "You don't do exactly what I told you I'll gut you like the fucking nigger catfish you are. Don't think we forgot about the alley. I lost a fine piece of cunny that day and my best Colt and my brother reckons you dented his skull permanent. Ain't no coon gets away with that and just goes about his business. You got debts to pay."

In one deft motion he sheathed the knife and spurred his horse at James, who held the shovel higher in defense, preparing to swing it into the muzzle of the closing animal. At the last second he reined hard, turned the horse in the sandy drive. He rode away leaving the other three to turn as best they could, rat-face taking his horse into the grass. They pounded away across the prairie.

When they were out of sight James leaned against the shovel, breathing heavily. The cloud of dust rolled up the slope carried by the soft breeze to where Amos and Clayton stood, but they did not move and it passed right over them, into the green scumble of trees, down the bluff, settling, eventually, quietly into the river.

James was not sure the woman who answered the door spoke English. Wordlessly she led him into a small sitting room furnished with a table, four low-backed chairs, a long bench beneath which slept a dog, and a cradle holding a sleeping infant. She picked up the child and went into a back room through a dark hallway. James waited, hat in hand. The volume of the man's greeting startled him and he dropped his hat, which the awakened dog growled at before rolling back over to sleep.

"This is pleasant surprise, James. How are you?" They shook hands. The expression on James's face gave away his urgency and Cmicky broke off the handshake, putting a reassuring hand on his visitor's thick shoulder. "What is it? Sit, sit." He drew out a chair and yelled for his wife, who yelled something back that James did not understand. The baby began to cry.

"You want a drink?"

"No sir, Cas, I don't think that would suit me right now."

"Coffee?"

"That sounds better. Please."

Cmicky yelled again and though the words in reply were incomprehensible, James knew what she'd said. Get it yourself. Easy domestic translation. The baby was now screaming.

"I put on coffee and we talk outside. More air there, yes?"

He led James to a seat on the narrow porch, returned five minutes later cursing in a low voice, sucking the edge of a burnt thumb.

"Now, tell me, what happened?"

James unfolded the events of the morning. When his visitor finished, Cmicky rose and went back into the house. A crash of crockery. The sound of a kicked dog. He reappeared with a tray that held two steaming cups of coffee, fresh cream, lump sugar.

"You see now what I told you before, yes? These men stop at nothing. You think stupid Lecroix brothers do this on their own? Have money and brains like that? No chance, my friend. As we say in Poland, that is dog that don't hunt."

"Question is, what can I do about it?" James sipped at the hot coffee. Terrible.

"Maybe see sheriff. Maybe go to land office, try to get to bottom of it that way."

"You don't sound like that's worth the walk up the stairs." James looked hard into his blue eyes. Cas returned the stare.

"I think you can guess what it is worth doing. I think as you ride your horse here you work out what will happen if you involve sheriff, if you go to courthouse and speak to fat bastard. I think you already make up your mind."

"You a sharp man."

"It is not all Polacks who is stupid, James. It easy to let people think so. Keeps them from noticing what you are up to if you are up to something."

"I reckon whoever all is behind this will expect me to turn tail. Law or not, papers or not, they won't be no rest till this gets settled. Sheriff Colegrove is a good man, but he can't sit out there and protect us all the time. So I'm here to ask will you help us."

Cas looked down the street, empty but for a pair of women walking with loaded baskets on their arms. He sighed. "It never end, this war." He turned to his guest. "You know about Lecroix brothers?" Before James could answer he went on, gesturing with his mug. "No. How could you? Well, their father was respectable man they say, came up from east Tennessee where it borders Carolina. Proud man, had a good farm in the county someplace. Sons though, no chop off the old block. Get into trouble early, then the war. All four bounty jumpers."

"I don't reckon I know what that is."

"Join a regiment, collect the bounty, say four hundred dollars, then slip out of camp at night and never return. You give false name, say there are no papers. Two were caught and put in jail. The other two brothers go south with some copperhead friends and join Confederates. Killed they say at Vicksburg. Others say they still alive, in Missouri with the thieving gang that killed all those Jayhawkers. We never see them again. The two from the alley were paroled and showed up in town last winter. There was dispute about their land, disturbance at the court house. Sheriff Colegrove hauled them in for a week."

James thought this over. "Cas, I ain't no fighter. Them men scared me and I got family to think of. But you're right. Riding over here I thought about the choices, and they ain't but one I can think of. We got no place else to go. I think it's

128

time we stand up for ourselves. I was hoping you'd give me a good reason to think I'm right."

The women with the baskets had gone into a house a few doors down and there was no one about. A wagon turned the corner and as it passed the driver tipped his hat to them. Cas returned the gesture.

"When I get off boat in Baltimore I speak not much English. This is in spring of sixty four. I find church and priest sends me to Polish neighborhood, but there is no work. I sleep in barn, do odd jobs, make some pennies for food. I decide instead of starving I join army. Fifth regiment Maryland infantry, about to muster out and join Army of Potomac. So you see, at least I was not bored. Middle of June we are at Petersburg. Battles at Chaffin's Farm and New Market Heights – I never forget these names – before we break through to Richmond. I learned to fight and speak English and make coffee. Lucky to not get my ass shot off."

Cas laughed, but James could tell that he was woolgathering, taken away to an earlier, fiercer time when he desperately hoped he'd live long enough to have a wife, a baby, a porch.

"You learn anything might be helpful in this here situation?" James asked. "I mean, besides coffeemaking."

"At the Heights we fought next to the Fourth Maryland, colored regiment. Some of my fellows not too sure about that. I hear many bad things about blacks, about how they lazy and not brave, only fit to be cooks or servants. I tell you, when shooting starts black soldiers fight like hell, hold our line and save many white skins. So be easy in your mind. I can handle guns and horses. Killing too. We will be ready for them when they come, and that day I pay a debt owed for some years now."

Cas took a slow drink of his coffee. James could hear the baby still crying somewhere in the house, the voice of its mother faintly audible. Cas grimaced and threw what remained into the weeds next to the house.

"Fucking horrible." He slapped James's knee. "You go home, be with your family, get some sleep. I round up my men and we come out tomorrow, get things ready. Not to worry. It better this way."

James's shoulders slumped in visible relief. He was worn down and cared less now whether Cas could see it.

"It don't feel better, but all right." He stood up, pulled his hat down firmly. "Thanks for the shitty coffee."

"No fucking problem, my friend."

James rode back as fast as he could manage. The horse was burdened now with two sacks bulging with flour, sugar, and coffee. He didn't want to raise any alarms by buying shot and powder. Better to provision for the unforeseeable future. Pretty damn unforeseeable. He tried to keep his mind on tasks at hand and not allow it to range too far ahead.

After supper he gathered everyone around the table.

They needed to know what had happened and James spoke about what they must do. There was no sense raising boys ignorant of what kind of world they were growing up in; better they face it with their minds and hearts right. Faces grim with determination mixed with fear, they went to their beds. James went out into the night to check the stock one last time, lingered at the well to listen to the night sounds, feel the cool breeze, then in to try for sleep. Passing the room where the boys slept he heard low voices. Clayton talking to his little brothers, the whispers calm, reassuring.

Good little man, his father thought.

The wagon came up the drive slower than it had the first time Casimir Cmicky had visited them. In an effort to keep things going on as normally as possible under such circumstances James and Amos had taken the boys back to plot out the hay field. They helped with the setting of the stakes, the harnessing of the mules, spreading seed. An early start saw them half finished by the time the sun pared their shadows to a nub. They ate a cold lunch in the shade of the locust: cornbread, cheese, slices of apple, rhubarb hand pies. When they had eaten James surprised them by calling it a day. Wordlessly they gathered tools and loaded the wheelbarrow. Back at the barn they cleaned the plow, set the mules to pasture, then polished and hung the harness in the storeroom. When Cmicky arrived in his wagon, another following, they flowed out of the barn and down to the house to greet him.

James was reassured at the sight of these men, felt suddenly as if he had been holding his breath since returning from town yesterday. With Cas's arrival the atmosphere changed. It was hard to stay mindful that they weren't preparing for a celebration.

Sitting next to Cmicky was Moberly, whose head rode his shoulders at the quizzical angle that made him always seem to be watching something that had just flown by. He remained that way even after Cmicky dismounted to deliver a bag of hard candy to the boys and to give the women a formal kiss on each cheek. Even Granny appeared tickled by this.

In the wagon that rolled up behind, a safe distance kept to let the dust pass, sat the imposing form of Fabrizio the Italian, gripping the reins in his hands like a giant holding fishing lines. In the bed of the wagon rode a young man and woman, a couple by the looks of it. They seemed out of place here and James wondered whether they had not been picked up along the river road. Amos spoke to Moberly, the latter taking and releasing the proffered hand without meeting the old man's eye. James greeted the big man as he got down off the heavily listing wagon. Cmicky slapped him on the back, startling him.

"Sorry James. It understandable to be jumpy. Fab you know, but you have not met the Llewelyns. They from Wales. Not like Jonah from the fish but from edge of England." Cmicky laughed at his joke and James smiled politely. The expressions on the man and woman's face remained dour and unchanged. "Anyway, it long story, but they arrive recently. Griff try to open cobbler shop but tanneries close him out when he not play their game. Now he working at tannery and I find he sick of having – "

Fabrizio put his large hairy hand on Cas's shoulder.

"Cas, adesso basta. There is time later. Now wagons." He gestured with his thumb to the beds which were covered with stained canvas tarps. The Llewelyns climbed down without speaking, the man turning and taking the woman's hand as she jumped lightly to the ground. They were short, fair-haired, the woman with ample freckles sprinkled across her sharp nose. She wore a simple gingham dress in blue; both wore well-made black boots. The man looked down at James's worn brogans, then at his wife, whose eyes said no, keep quiet.

Fab took the couple over to Amos and the rest of the family to introduce them, while Cas led James to the back of the wagon, where he removed the tailgate, a two-by-twelve board that fit into channels carved into the side rails, its ends chamfered to allow its slide up and down. When he had wiggled it free, standing on tiptoes to do so, he turned to lean it against the wheel and stopped.

Something was moving beneath the canvas.

James took an instinctive step back, saw Clayton approaching and held out a hand to stop him. The boy froze. Cas gently leaned the board against a wheel. He grasped the edge of the cover and plunged his hand beneath, grabbing and jerking out the form of a boy who slid right off the edge and fell in a heap in the grass. He covered his head and pulled his legs in, as if expecting to be kicked while he was down.

Cas and James exchanged a look.

"Stand up," Cas said.

He stood, hands at his side as though turned out at a muster, head tilted down regarding his dirty shoes and dungarees.

"Hey there June," Clayton said enthusiastically. "What you doin – "

"Clay," James said, "hush up."

"Shitting hell," Cas muttered into his hand, stroking his whiskers. He took his hat off, slapped it against his knee. "What we going to do with him? Sheriff be out here looking maybe tonight or tomorrow and get into the middle of all this. Not what we planned. Not good."

"I'll run him back in on my horse. Be back a tick past nightfall – "

Cas shook his head vigorously.

"No, that no good. What if they come while you gone? This not good risk to take, not part of plan."

"Well he can't stay here. It's too dangerous. If somethin was to happen to him . . . " James looked at the ground.

"I'll take him," Clayton offered. "I know the way and – "

"No," Cas and James said at once.

Cas added, "You too valuable here little man. We cannot spare you."

"I ain't going back."

The boy spoke with his teeth clenched at the edge of tears. His voice tried for the gravity of a man but it did not have the timbre. Their eyes were on him as he raised his head. "I come out here on purpose. To help. Heard you all talking about it back of the livery." He looked at Cas and tipped his head toward the others. "Watched you load the wagons and when you picked up them folks," he pointed with his chin at the couple beyond the other wagon, "I crawled under cover and laid still. I ain't going back."

"Sneaky little bastard."

"Cas."

James looked the dark-headed boy in the eyes.

"Now son, we appreciate – "

"Don't talk to me like a child," he said. "You did me a turn and now I want to do you one. Them men in the alley, they got a reckoning coming and I want to be part of that. My daddy he smokes his pipe and talks a lot but he don't do nothin cept lay with that Lane woman and make me sweep floors." He sobbed once and then they could see him harden and choke down what was coming. He dried his eyes with his shirttail.

Cas had his hat off again, scratching his head hard behind his ears.

"No. No sir. It makes no difference what he say. He can't stay. James – "

"Daddy thinks I'm at the fish camp up on the Tippy," June cut in. "Supposed to be back in two or three days." He looked at James. "I owe you, mister. You know that."

"All right. But you stay with my boys, out of the way. You do what I tell you, or what Cas or the others tell you, or yonder in the loft you go trussed up like a holiday turkey."

He gestured for his son to approach.

"Clayton, take him to the well for some water and make sure your mama knows he's here."

They ate like pigs.

And would have sung and danced and carried on until late had they not serious business to attend to the next morning. Beneath the canvas of the wagons had been provisions, along with a cache of rifles and ammunition and two large rolls of barbed wire. On horse blankets in the barn they organized this material, loading some of the weapons for the night watch. Cas showed James and Amos how to load and fire a Winchester, since all they had ever shot was black powder. The cartridges were different but made reloading a far easier proposition once you got the hang of it.

Dark settled across the woods from the east, the sun setting fire to the prairie, dying to the west behind the tree line. Clayton sat with his father and grandfather around the small fire they'd built in its ring of stones, now burning low and feeble in the warm summer air. He watched his mother and grandmother shepherding his brothers to bed in the house, the boys worn down from all the excitement and company. James imagined them asleep as soon as they hit their beds, breathing quietly and steadily, limbs akimbo, off in that place of peace, a child's dream, a little boy's loosening of soul from heavy flesh. James felt tired and old, expectation sunk deep between his shoulder blades. He looked at his father who sat on a hackberry stump, the orange light playing on his graybeard face, smoking his pipe and watching the last of the sun fall behind the soft curves of the fields. His eyes were bright with the light but he seemed far away. James glanced toward the barn where music began to play. In the twilight he could just make out the pale form of Moberly sitting cross-legged and hunched over, playing the banjo he'd brought. Its tailpiece caught the firelight glare as he rocked with the tune. When he finished, the last plaintive tones fell across the yard and walked on through the corn and high grass leaving them sitting in the human silence of night, its creatures resuming their song.

"That was real pretty Moberly," James said, stretching, trying to work the heaviness out of his bones. "What's that tune called?"

"Booth Shot Lincoln."

In his limited time around this odd man, James had not been able to figure out how some of the things he said went with some of the things others had just said.

Amos beat him to it.

"That the name of the tune?"

That Moberly had a deep-grained southern accent perhaps added to their suspicion of what such a statement might mean devoid as it was of context.

"Yep. Booth Shot Lincoln."

"It got any words?" Amos asked around the stem of his pipe.

"Yep. Didn't you hear them?"

Amos and James looked at one another in the dim light.

"That ain't exactly a upliftin subject right now," Amos replied, passing over what he and his son had not wanted to admit, that they had both been supplying words for such a song, thinking back to where they had been when the news had burned across the South of the President's assassination.

"You learn that in Carolina?" James asked.

"Yep. From the same guy what gave me this here banjer. Chicken Leon."

"Yes, Chicken Leon," Cas slapped his leg and laughed. "Some night we get Moberly to drink some applejack and he recount for us the adventures of Chicken Leon. Very funny." The giant form of Fabrizio shook where he sat with his back against the barn. James hoped such a night would indeed come.

"Play us something else," Amos said, knocking the bowl of his pipe against the stump. "Something more cheerful. You know "Say Old Man, Can I Have Your Daughter?" Starts with, lemme see, *Say old man can I have your daughter, to cook my food and tote my water.*"

Cas's face lit up with delight and he looked at his southern friend expectantly.

"Nope," said Moberly who hunched over again and started picking. It was the same tune as before. No one interrupted, and when he was finished they sat in the quiet.

It was Clayton who finally said, "That was the same one."

No one else said anything. Moberly rocked back and forth. His nearly bald head refracted the light which then shone off his face and his small even teeth. He smiled a pearly smile, like he'd remembered something he'd been searching for all day.

"No it wadn't. That one had all different words."

Twelve

At just after noon they came.

Six riders in two rows three abreast through the high grass, as if they had no need for the road. The Lecroix brothers, the two men who had ridden out with them before, and two more whose features varied little from their comrades: unkempt beards, dirty slouch hats pulled down low, well armed. James noticed they all rode fine horses. Someone else's fine horses, either bought, borrowed or stolen.

They descended the rise, moving into the open space between the house and the garden. James had been standing at an equal distance between these and now moved to meet them.

All morning they had prepared. The first question was whether the women and children would stay in the house or the barn. Lily said to James and Cas that she did not want her boys harmed and would do whatever was best for their safety. James suggested the loft in the barn, but Cas said no, too dangerous. Too much risk of things going bad and the barn and house getting set afire. These buildings go up like that, he said, snapping his fingers, and there no way to stop it. Loft worst place to be. What then, James asked, the pain between his shoulders now like the point of a knife.

The woods.

Cas had a small pistol, which he gave to Lily. James's Hawken was loaded and Clayton, who had shot it for the first time that morning, carried it against his shoulder like a soldier, the gun taller than him by a foot. They loaded one of the wagons with two days' worth of food and water, extra ammunition, blankets. At mid-morning they made their way across the prairie, over the shallow creek and into the woods to the east as far away from the road as they could get. James went along to help find a suitable spot. They walked single file, the light filtering weakly through the trees alive with the racket of blue jays. A crow called rudely to its fellows. A few hundred yards into the dense hardwoods they found a stand of pines. James coaxed the horse inside and they all bent to follow, the sound of the forest dampened by the bed of copper-colored needles. Once in they would not easily be seen by anyone passing through. James hugged each of them and reminded them not to leave the copse until he came back. He shook June's hand, tried to smile. The boy had been none too happy about being left out of the fray, but James and Cas had been vehement. Along with Clayton he would protect the vulnerable, and this was a vital part of the plan. June reluctantly accepted what he could not change.

By the time James got back, Cas had everyone in position. Amos sat in the privy with the Winchester leaning against the wall, the door cracked so that he could see the yard and his son, who would alert him of approaching riders. Cas said it didn't smell too good but at least he could sit and his pipe would make it tolerable. He put Moberly and Fabrizio in the house, where they had nailed boards horizontally inside the windows. In the barn loft went the Llewelyns. Cas opened the hay mow door, forked a high narrow pile across it at the edge, and had them lie down behind it, gun barrels barely poking out. From a distance it looked like dried grass piled haphazardly. Cas saddled James's horse and sat it in the orchard beyond the garden. In the closely packed apple and pear trees he was invisible. His plan was to draw them into the rough triangle formed by the house, barn, and orchard, to pin them down there and relieve them of their weapons when they found themselves surrounded.

"What then?" James had asked.

"Then we give them reasons not to come back."

James looked at the Polish man, a head shorter than himself, studied his face for what this meant.

He was pretty sure he knew the answer to his question, but asked it anyway.

"What kind of reasons?"

"You remember what it sound like when I hit my head on wagon?"

"I do."

"Lecroix brothers have thick skulls, but we see if it the same. James, you know what has to be done. They must learn lesson. Such a lesson cannot be taught to men like this as you would a horse or dog. It must be cruel. We beat shit out of them, others watch, lose stomach for fight, see that we spare nothing to defend what you have here."

"I don't think I can do something like that less it's self defense. I did it before in the heat of it."

"Wait and see how it goes. Brothers maybe give you reasons. You think of pretty wife, those little boys."

James doubted seriously he could beat a man in such a calculated situation, but stayed quiet. He would wait and see.

The ring of bits and bridles and two dozen hooves hammering the earth was more intimidating than James had reckoned. As he stood his ground he felt a stab of fear replace the plumb of worry. He wiped his forehead with his handkerchief as the riders pulled up.

They formed into a ragged crescent and faced him, the Lecroix brothers in the middle, looking the same as they had two days before: short cigar in the corner of Walt's mouth, his brother's left cheek distended in working a cut of plug tobacco. As if they had simply ridden over the horizon, added two men, and ridden back.

Earlier that morning James stopped at the edge of the trees on his way back from leaving the women and children in the pines. He looked over their farm. The men who were coming with their weapons and anger had homes too. Maybe even wives. Certainly mothers. They were people too. Did their wants and needs, pains and sadnesses count for nothing? He knew what a good Christian would do. But he also had no doubt what the outcome would be and though it was perhaps a sin he could not let them take everything. If there was any opening to make peace with these men he would take it. And if not, well, God help him.

Gene spat, looked at his brother. He removed the cigar in a deliberate motion and waved it in a gesture meant to include the buildings, the surrounding fields, and the prairie.

"In the late forties, back in Posey County where we come from, they was some niggers come from Boston or some such Yankee place. Said they was fixing to set up a community or the like same as them nuts over in New Harmony. Them damn Brits who bout starved to death from thinkin that farmin had to do with good ideas. Shit. I seen them plow with suits on when they first set to work."

He replaced the cigar, spoke around it.

"Point is they had no business there. Neither did them niggers that come after, who we run out of town back east where they belonged. This here is *our* land, people like us. Now, it don't look like you all have moved out of here yet. We give you two days, which was plenty. My brother and these boys are gonna drag yer family out of that house along with everything you own, burn it, and then see you off in a wagon with what you can carry. That is if yer lucky and I don't lose control and they commit some mischief on the wife or daughters. You got any growed daughters boy?"

James wanted to kill this man. And felt able to by whatever means he could accomplish it, despite an upbringing that had taught him the wrongness of such an act. He imagined the dead body at his feet, eyes glassed and empty like a spent fish. This allayed the fear he felt from the men facing him and

140

allowed him to concentrate on what he had to do next. One hard look into Walt Lecroix's ugly face and then he turned and walked towards the well.

From where he sat in the saddle amongst the fruit trees, peering between the leaves to keep the scene in view, Cas watched James turn slowly, calmly, moving with even strides further into the triangle of buildings. *Nice and easy James my friend*, he said softly, the horse's ears perking up. *We almost there*. Looking into the loft he spied the barest trace of gun barrel, certain they were invisible unless you knew what to look for. The riders held their ground, looked at one another as the black man walked away from them.

They had not expected this. The older Lecroix's horse took furtive steps forward, then stopped. James was almost at the well.

"Hey!" the younger Lecroix yelled. Cas tightened the reins in his fist and dug his boots deeper into the stirrups. He twisted around and pulled the Winchester out of its scabbard, checked that the safety was off and quietly jacked a round into the chamber. Then his pistols, the cylinders turning smoothly and snapping smartly into place. He pulled his hat down tight and whipped the horse out of the trees, uphill for a short distance and then hard downhill in a curve to bear down on them from behind.

It all happened fast. Cas did not have time to fume about the dissolution of his plan.

Gene Lecroix had his Winchester out and swung it around at the approaching rider, whose hoof falls he must have felt as urgent warnings up through his own horse's legs. When he did so a rifle reported from one of the windows of the house, the bullet catching him from behind high in the right shoulder, shattering his collar bone and grazing his cheek as it exited in a tight splash of blood, bone, and what smelled to him like burnt rope. He managed to hang on to the stock of the gun with his left hand as the impact jerked him forward, the horse twisting under him and rearing slightly which hit his lifeless right arm causing him to scream. All was chaos as their horses, who had been only feet apart, panicked and tried to run for open ground. Each man sawed the reins desperately in an attempt to gain control and get his weapon out, find some shelter or a target. Walt reached to grab the bridle of his brother's horse but could not, instead labored to get his mount in alongside to calm him and keep Gene in the saddle. He tried to say "Hang on" to his brother but his mouth wouldn't make the words when he saw that one side of Gene's face was covered in blood.

Walt heard another shot, the bullet hissing close over his head, looked down to the well in time to see James taking cover and leveling his rifle. He ducked behind the neck of his horse and looked for an avenue of escape, tried to think how he could get his posse organized to take the house or the barn or anywhere they might be able to defend. There were more shots now from other quarters. Movement in the loft of the barn, the lone rider now with a pistol in each hand, puffs of smoke trailing over his head as he emptied them. The tall skinny man was shot in the chest at the same time his horse was hit in the neck, going down twisting in his rider's failing grip, pinning his leg to the ground as he clutched at his stomach. The blood pooled beneath him darkening the trampled grass. One of the other riders, whose name was Grissom, was hit in the leg, then in the foot. He howled in pain and shot back at the house with one arm as he struggled to control his horse.

The shots splintered the wood above and next to one of the boarded windows. The rat-faced man was low behind his animal's neck, the reins clamped in his teeth, firing both pistols at James, his horse inching down the slope towards his target. This exposed him to the fire from the windows of the house, and by the time he had shot the cylinders empty, pinging off the thick fieldstones and the wood of the bucket carriage, he was shot in the side, the impact nearly taking him to the ground. He tried to breathe and felt suddenly like he was drowning, then another bullet hit him in the jaw where the muscle and cartilage holds the bone, and he saw a red flash of vapor cover the pale mane of the roan before he slid off into the grass.

Truth be told, Cas was not a very good shot with a pistol. In the first minute he emptied both guns without hitting anything other than the roof of the house and one of the shutters next to a window. He prayed to God it did not penetrate the wood and kill Moberly or the Italian, reassured himself that no bullet could go through a log and do any damage to that big hairy bastard. He almost laughed but his horse skittered and he nearly fell off, sending a shot far over the barn. Still, he kept them from riding back across the prairie, which was his job, his shooting discouraging the horses from bolting their way to safety. When his pistols clicked empty he threw them down and pulled the saddle gun free, shouldered it, and dropped the man on the far left out of his saddle. He was much better with the rifle. With his knee he coaxed the horse to the right a few feet in order to get a bead on the little man moving down the slope towards James at the well, but could not as the chaotic mass of men and animals moved in their confusion into his line of sight. He shot into the group and must have hit Gene Lecroix's mount in the hindquarters. It careened out running full tilt through the garden heedless of the chest-high corn and across the prairie towards the woods. Lecroix was badly wounded. He slumped in the saddle clutching his gun with his left arm, his right hanging loose like an empty sleeve. He shot and missed. Cas considered chasing him but thought it a bad idea to leave a clear path back to the road. At least *someone* ought to follow the plan.

Amos didn't like guns and found that when the shooting started he had no stomach for it. He stood in the outhouse at the first shots and poked his rifle out the half moon of the

143

door at the mass of horsemen on the downslope. His son was crouched behind the well so he aimed over his head and fixed his sights on the big man in the middle. It was not in him, he found, to shoot a man this way. Maybe face to face if he was threatening his wife or others in his family, or had a hold of one of his little grandsons. Then, thought Amos, I would do some damn horrible things. But not this way, no. He kept the notch at the end of the barrel firmly in the groove of the front sight, centered on the man's brown-shirted chest no matter where he moved.

Just in case.

When the bullet came through the door Amos thought he had been punched in the stomach. His lungs were empty and he tried to draw in a breath but could not. An enveloping coldness stiffened him. His body of a sudden held no hollow space for air or blood or motion. His head went forward against the wood pushing the rifle out of the hole all the way to the trigger guard. He looked at his feet but could not move them. Again he tried to breathe but captured only a shallow breath before it stopped abruptly, as though some mechanical piece of his breathing mechanism had snapped. The stock of the rifle felt reassuringly smooth and warm. He took small, halting breaths, the icy tendrils spreading from his toes up his legs through the thick trunk of his body into his shoulders and down his arms until holding the gun made him shake with the effort. Through the cut in the door he saw riders down, scattering horses, the chaos of shot men and animals, rifle and pistol smoke. The crackle of gunfire was now all around him growing louder. With what strength he had, a small place of warmth lodged precariously inside the clawing spread of cold, he leveled the rifle with tremulous hands, sighted, and shot the big man off his horse.

Cas saw Walt Lecroix tumble backwards, his head hitting the wide rump as the animal darted forwards at the slack in its reins sending his limp body cartwheeling in a heap into the grass. He reloaded low in his saddle, pinching the mare with his knees and whispering to her in Polish as his mother would have done to him when he had a fever. Peering around her neck he saw only two men left on horseback. The others must have run out of ammunition too since there was a lull in the shooting. They looked at their fallen mates, shouted at Walt who did not respond, then spurred in the direction of the house and around up the drive and into the road leaving a diminishing trail of dust and gun smoke.

If not for the flies, James thought, the bodies looked like poorly crafted dolls left out in the weather too long. Grimacing, gaudy with blood and piss stains or the purple wall of an intestine protruding from a ragged chest hole. Six staring eyes made of colored glass.

"Deader n hell," Moberly said, looking at something far away in the blue blue sky.

"Nothing to be done about the two that got away," Cas said. "Ain't nothing they can say or do anyhow."

James agreed, having no desire to chase anyone to town. He looked down at the bodies of Walt Lecroix, the rat-faced man, and the longer, wiry form lying alongside him. They stood in a line with their rifles slung muzzle down. No one spoke. They passed the bucket and ladle of sweet cold water from the well down the line. At the moment it occurred to James that no one had been hurt, and that this seemed miraculous, he realized that his father was not there. He turned and noticed the privy door open partway but motionless. Not right for a spring-loaded door. Then he saw the end of a rifle barrel poking out of the half moon window at an angle. He clenched his teeth and ran.

"Let's get him into the house. I don't want none of these goddamn flies on him."

145

James had fetched a rectangle of tattered canvas from the barn and with Fab's help they moved Amos's body gently onto it. They carried him into the kitchen and scraped the long table across the hardwood, laid him down and stood round. The impact of loss settled into them. From a bedroom James brought a wool blanket and they helped him cover his father with it. The bulge of a body made a strange shape in that domestic space. The Llewelyns stood just beyond the threshold. The woman came through the door, stepping lightly as though amongst sleeping children. She approached James who stood with his hands folded in front of him. She touched his arm and said in her soft Welsh accent, "If you like I'll wash him and put fresh clothes on him while the lot of you deal with that mess outside." She waited for him to answer as the others held their hats and moved out of doors. With her hand on his elbow she pressed him to go, whispering, "Go on now, I'll look after things." He wanted to let her do this, to feel that his father was being taken care of as if only sick, as if too tired to get up, as if knocked out.

Something temporary.

Only sleeping.

As if.

If only.

James felt himself taking the first steps on a path that would require some time to traverse and he felt heavy and alone. He wondered what they were doing here and why he had thought they would get through this. Only then did he think of his mother and his wife, the children, out in the trees.

"That's mighty kind of you ma'am, but my mother will want to do that her ownself."

"I understand," she said, then bent down and put her white palm on Amos's forehead, closed her eyes, and spoke a quiet valediction in a language James could not understand.

Near the well they gathered again in a half circle, looking down at the bodies. James put on his hat in the bright sunlight

146

and joined them. Cas rubbed the whiskers on his face and seemed about to make an announcement when they heard the drumming of a rider or riders coming fast in the road. They scattered for cover, training their guns up the slope of the drive.

Charles Colegrove rode his gray mare toward the house and saw that he was marked by five guns. Keeping hold of the reins he raised his gloved hands. The Polish delivery driver stepped out from the side of the house as he drew up to one of the shade trees that grew there.

He had not expected that. Who were the others?

He dismounted and looped the reins around a tree limb, felt inside his shirt for his pipe. Joining Cmicky, each carrying a rifle, were the big Italian and the pale queer fellow from down South who sold eggs and pullets. He couldn't remember their names. Odd that neither James nor any of his family was visible. In the cradle of his hands he lit his pipe, drawing on it deeply while scanning the area between his fingers. Nothing looked amiss, but he could only see part of the side of the barn and the corral. Standing shoulder to shoulder he had the distinct feeling that they did not want him any further around the house.

"Didn't expect to see you out here Cas. Afternoon."

"Good day to you too Mr. Colegrove. I was thinking same thing. What brings you out to the county?"

He paused, released blue smoke into the air. "Where's James?"

"He working. We come out to help him with some things."

"What things?"

"Carpentering," Cas replied, slowly, with difficulty across the syllables. Colegrove took a long pull on his pipe.

"Those don't seem like carpenter tools, you ask me. Now why don't you tell me what's going on out here and stop fucking me around." He lowered the pipe and his left hand came to rest gently on his sidearm.

147

From around the side of the house James emerged with a shovel over his shoulder, its heart-shaped blade dark with recently turned soil. The sheriff looked him over, checking for signs of duress, but if the big man was in some kind of danger he did not sense it. He appeared tired and worn-looking. Probably the hard work. Plus his three boys, crops to mind, sick livestock. This was one of those moments Colegrove was glad to be a sheriff; he preferred his trouble disease- and weather-proof.

"Afternoon James."

"Mr. Colegrove. You pretty far out of town today. Somethin we can do for you?"

"Maybe. I come out here looking for my boy. Supposed to be up on the Tippy fishing but I found out this morning that he never showed up. I also heard a rumor at breakfast that Walt Lecroix and his brother rode out this way with some of their friends. You all know anything about any of that?" He tipped his hat back and scratched at his hairline, put his index and middle finger over the bowl of his briar and puffed in quick succession, reviving it. The aromatic smoke wafted over them.

"Now sheriff – "

James wondered what Cas was going to say, what sort of tale he would tell that might keep this man from investigating, from finding the bodies lying beside the well, the other beneath his blanket on the kitchen table growing cold as any stone.

Successive shots from the woods interrupted his thought and sent everyone's head around in that direction. James dropped the shovel and loped around the house to see if anyone had emerged from the tree line. He saw no one as the others came up behind him. When he turned the sheriff was looking down at the three bodies, his face careworn. James picked up the Winchester he had leaned against the round of stones, checked the loads and set off

148

at a trot for the trees not bothering to see if the law was at his heels.

Gene Lecroix could barely hang on from the agony. His shattered arm blinded him with pain as the severed ends of the bone ground against one another with each step of the horse. He knew he had to make the trees.

After what felt like hours he was in shadow, the horse slowing without a visible trace to follow. The black gelding stopped, its ears pricked for sounds in the deeper dark ahead. To a town horse the woods did not make any sense. Lecroix clicked his tongue and with his heels urged the animal forward, forcing it to pick its way through the undergrowth. Over slim saplings craning for scant light he stepped, snapping dry brush, crunching a hesitant rhythm in the fallen leaves. On they went, the wounded man's thoughts only about how to slip away from his pursuers, find a place to rest, check his body, get some water in him. Maybe find a creek, sleep a little. If he could locate the bluff he could likely feel his way to town or make it down to the road. Walt would be there and would know what to do, would make things come right.

Each time he thought he heard the sound of water whispering over smooth rocks he straightened up in the saddle. The horse, easily spooked, tried to pause but was compelled forward. His arm ached intolerably. He was glad for the poor light so that he could not see his blood or the wound, perhaps something sticking out of it. If he fainted he was dead. He swallowed with effort and wondered how long he could go on with the pain draining him so.

His desire began to play tricks on him. First it was the sound of running water, then the laughter of a girl, then the banging of pots and pans, as of a busy kitchen.

When he saw the boy he thought he must be dreaming. The familiarity would not resolve itself and it occurred to him that it was himself he was seeing, younger, whole, unimpeded by

149

suffering, free to have adventures in the woods with forked branches, a slingshot carved from a wishbone of ash, traps and snares concocted out of spare wire, springs, the discarded tines of a hayrake. The horse whinnied and checked against the bit, throwing its head, nearly sending him sideways to the ground. When he gained control the boy was gone, but left in the space where he had stood was his image, and Gene Lecroix remembered exactly where he had last seen him. It made about as much sense to him as the appearance of the big negro had in the alley that day. That yellow dress, the womansmell, those soft white thighs.

Despite the pain that took his breath and gave it back to him in shallow gasps he pulled his rifle from its scabbard and laid it across his knees, gathered the reins in his good hand and pointed the horse at the line of evergreens directly in his path.

The boy could help him get back to town.

Or maybe just shoot him for revenge.

He'd have to see how he felt.

June ran crouched and careful, silent on the bed of needles between the low-lying branches of the firs that edged the small clearing. This instantly interrupted the conversation Clayton was having with his granny, their familiar question-and-answer about her girlhood on the big plantation south and east of Meridien, Mississippi, as well as the card game between Lily and the boys, hands over mouths to keep their laughter in check. Five heads turned in his direction, a fan of cards falling to the ground. June put a raised index finger to his lips. At the wagon bed he leaned over and whispered.

"It's one of them. On a horse. Wounded, but he's got a rifle. I . . . I think he saw me."

Silence as this sunk in.

"We'll be all right," Lily said quietly, looking into his eyes

150

and putting her hand on his shoulder. "He won't find us in here if we quiet. The good Lord wouldn't let – "

"Dammit mama, no," Clayton hissed. "We got to do something. Hide in the trees or move the wagon or – "

Clayton felt the sharp sting of his granny take a handful of his hair.

"Boy, you watch that mouth. I don't care if them devils has a gun pointed right at us. You'll show respect to your mama."

Clayton bit his lip, hoping this was not going to lead to a lengthy lecture, certain they did not have time for it.

"Now," she continued, "here's what we do."

When Gene Lecroix's horse passed through the last branches of the close-grown pines he saw a wagon hitched to a bay mare. It rested unmoving at the far side of a broad clearing of sandy soil, the prairie grass holding back the trees. The afternoon light lay warm and sallow, made hazy with gnats and gauzy swarms of midges. The mare's head came up from her grazing and she looked at him, ears registering the bare jingle of his harness. It was after a few seconds of surveying the open space for trouble that he noticed the tiny old woman sitting erect on the seat. Her body in profile no thicker than a distant tree. He nickered the horse forward, holding on with his thighs. His working index finger felt through the guard for the trigger's cool steel grooves. When he neared the wagon he swung the rifle around until it ran along his leg for support, the stock pinned against his hip.

Twenty yards. Birds dipped out of the trees, the grass a din of crickets. The sun brightened and he had to squint to keep the old woman in focus. He was thirsty. He feared he might be too dry to yell.

"Hey!"

The old woman did not turn, nor betray any indication that she had heard him. He leveled the gun at her and shouted

151

again. Nothing. He wheeled the horse to get closer and move into her line of vision.

She was eating a peach. He could see now that she was toothless, gums gnawing at the soft flesh, the juice running down the front of her homespun dress. This careless savoring, the nonchalance with which she sat before him, heedless of his hurt and of the force that lay tense against his finger enraged him so that he extended the gun as steadily as he could and shot her in the head. The trees exploded in doves and starlings, the bareboned dark body thrown with the force of the impact nearly off the seat to hang over its edge. The back of her head dripped blood into the grass. The half-eaten peach amassed flies on the footboard. The horse and rider sat motionless, waiting for the ringing of the shot to end and for the woods and its clearing to return to its languid hum of life.

The unmistakable sound of crying came from a low stand of sumac that fringed the far side of the clearing, a green patch at the foot of the border of trees. Lecroix shifted his concentration, trying to make out a person in the thicket. He would find the boy cowering there, would compel him with the rifle and the example that now lay slumped in the wagon seat to drive him to town.

"Put the gun down."

The voice surprised him and he nearly dropped the rifle as the horse tried to wheel. He jerked the reins but the horse, still spooked from the shot, stumbled wide-eyed and fought his weak hand.

He closed his eyes. The pain in his arm came sharp with each heartbeat. Behind him. Not a man's voice, and not the one in the sumac. He let the muzzle of the rifle fall so that it pointed straight down. With pressure from his left knee he turned the horse. When they were perpendicular, his gun side obscured, he would raise his weapon and face the boy down.

Easy as pie.

The white boy from the alley, arms extended, aimed a small

caliber revolver at his chest, the narrow bore proportionate to his size. It was either getting heavy or he was scared. Or both.

Then there were two of them.

The black boy, taller but bony in his threadbare overalls, came out from his leafy cover holding a black powder rifle, its bore gaping darkly in its octagonal barrel. Heavy, hard to load properly, harder yet to shoot straight. One shot. After a dozen seconds the wounded man was amazed that it still steadily marked him.

Lecroix could see that he was crying.

"I said to drop the gun," the white boy said. The pistol danced a little, but did not waver outside the frame of the rider's body.

"Boy, you and your nigger get those fucking guns offa me or I'm going to kill you dead in the grass."

No one moved. Gene Lecroix tried to judge the effect of his words, decided he would shoot the white boy first, since he had more shots and an easier gun to fire. The other one would not be able to handle such a heavy weapon, would have nothing once he'd shot it high into the trees. Then he would face him down, wound him if he had to. It was still possible to get to town flat on his back in the bed of a wagon.

"I'll count three," he barked, using his command to mask the weakness he felt. "You see what I did to that old bitch yonder in the wagon? To drop the both of you like I did her ain't no extra trouble."

The barrel of the Hawken dipped as Clayton adjusted his grip and Gene Lecroix swung the Winchester across him, his finger on the trigger already applying soft pressure for the moment when the bead of the front sight fell upon any substantial part of the white boy.

June stood transfixed, fingers white on the grip of the pistol. He looked into the reddened eyes of the man on the horse and waited for the impact, already seeing his father's

153

disapproving shake of the head as he stood over his son's broken body.

The sound of the gun going off deadened June's eardrum, and he stood still with arms extended as the dumbshow played before him.

The fifty-caliber bullet caught Lecroix beneath the chin at the base of the jawbone and blasted a path up at an acute angle through the back of his throat, his sinus cavity and brain, exiting in a wash of pink matter, blood, and bone, the sum force of the impact pulling his feet out of the stirrups and depositing him on his back on the croup of the horse which bolted, leaving him to fall in a graceless heap.

Clayton dropped the rifle and held his shoulder which felt badly bruised, maybe knocked out of joint by the recoil. He could hear June sobbing now, and was surprised to see him move deliberately forward to stand over Lecroix's prostrate body.

June aimed the revolver.

"No," Clayton said, breathlessly, without conviction.

Book Two

LaFayette & Tippecanoe County, Indiana

1868-1901

Thirteen

Granny had not reckoned a man would shoot an old woman without talking to her. Or without at least trying to force her to help ease the pain from his wound.

"I'll promise him remedy and a comfortable ride to a nearby doctor," she said. "And while we're conversin you boys ease around and get your guns on him."

That was her plan. The peach had been meant to ease Lecroix's mind. And anyway, she'd added, I'm about starved. While things had not gone as intended, her sacrifice allowed Lily and the boys to live.

Clayton helped bury his grandparents in a spot James staked out next to the orchard. They held a service and the family was honored that Sheriff Colegrove, June, Cas, Fab, Moberly, and the Llewelyns all attended, coming from town dressed in their Sunday finery. Cas asked if he might say a few words and spoke of Amos and Clara's sacrifices on behalf of future generations of McGhees and all other freedom-loving people in the county.

In recurring dreams Clayton held the sight on a man and shot him off a horse, off the roof of a house, out the window of a tall barn, from the branches of a tree hung with strange fruit. Sometimes he called out and would wake up to his mother or father holding him and whispering that it was all right, he was safe.

Clayton and his brothers began attending the little school over in Granville. The schoolteacher was a Quaker and welcomed them even if the other children did not. Of the three, Clayton was the apt student, finding genuine pleasure

157

in his school work, especially literature and history, while his brothers chafed at being kept indoors, impatient for adventure and mischief. Clayton fought in fields and backyards, made friends, coveted books, learned to farm and make things by hand as James and Amos had before him. In the new year they began attending church in town where they joined the tiny community of black folks who were happy to have them added to their number. At Second Presbyterian Clayton met girls, held their cool hands in his sweating one, kissed their soft lips in the hush and privacy of side yards after Sunday suppers. Then met Sara Beall who would have nothing to do with him. Turned out it wasn't him but her shyness, which he spent two years overcoming. She was the oldest in a large family and had the caretaking of her siblings. This lengthened their courtship, as she was unwilling to leave her mother, who was often ill, and her father, who worked long hours as a cook and night porter. There was so much to do and she was not about to abandon them. Clayton admired her for this though it sorely frustrated his desire to set up on his own and start a family.

In 1879 they got married and Clayton moved in with Sara and her family. He worked for a time at a factory that made chairs. It soon became clear to him that factory work was not carpentry. He turned one chair leg after another on a lathe, each the same as the next, until they gave him a new pattern and he copied that for a few weeks. It wasn't hard but he could not abide the tedium. Guilt about quitting plagued him and he stayed on, earning his pay and keeping to himself. Then his brothers set off west, leaving only a note and taking his aging father's best three horses. James came to town with the news. It was clear to Clayton that his father was not going to be able to care for the farm on his own for much longer.

Two weeks later he moved back to help set things right.

The first day he could see that his brothers had not been interested in the work. Many tasks had gone undone and others had been accomplished without patience or perhaps even skill. He could not tell which it was, realizing that he did not really know his brothers as well as he ought. Elder brother had assumed his father would not tolerate any nonsense, but he understood now that it had all been too much for the old man.

After supper that first night, once James had gone to bed looking exhausted but smiling at the return of his boy, his mother confirmed what he'd suspected.

"It hurts me to say it," she said, looking at the floor, "but it was best the boys left. Now that you're here," she added, meeting his eye, "things will get better."

Clayton wore out the River Road going back and forth to see Sara. It was a strain but neither knew what else to do. Many times he planned to deliver an ultimatum or pick a fight about it, but he was always too tired and too glad to see her. And anyway, he knew it wasn't her fault.

One day he and James were working in the far field when a wagon rattled up from the bluff. They stopped and shielded their eyes against the sun and damned if it wasn't Sara being driven by Casimir Cmicky. He ran as he had those many years ago when it was armed men in the road, but this time smiling and waving his hat.

Cas, now well into his sixties, descended the seat of the wagon more deliberately. Still, he had the suitcases out of the bed before Clayton could get there to help. His grip had not changed, nor had his good cheer. He laughed as Sara was lifted down and swung around by her husband. He left them, walking up the drive to greet James whom he had not seen for months.

Sara planned to stay for a few weeks but never moved back to town. Each Sunday the four of them went to church and then ate dinner at Sara's parents' place. The Beall house was full of people and music and food and Clayton would remember those days as some of the best in his life. Judah went with them once in a while. When they got down to the culvert bridge on the river road they might find him standing ready, his hair slicked back and face clean shaven. He wouldn't go into the church and they never knew what he did to pass the time. When the service let out he was always at the wagon keen to go for a meal and to hear the spirituals Sara's mother and sisters sang. While they ate he kept his attention on his plate and spoke only if spoken to, but a transformation came over him when the music started. His old friend had never seen him so happy and attentive.

On rare occasions June would appear at the house. This caused Clayton a great deal of anxiety as June would either be badly hung over or, worse, still drunk from the night before. He invariably smelled like liquor and Sara's teetotal, deeply religious parents struggled to tolerate his presence. More than a few times Clayton had to make him leave, walking him home and putting him to bed. One freezing December day June took a swing at him, catching him on the shoulder, and before he could think about it Clayton had knocked him senseless. Fortunately, this happened in the alley behind June's house and no one was there to see it. He dragged his unconscious friend to bed, slapped him awake, and told him he was no longer welcome at Sunday dinner. Nevertheless he showed up three weeks later and though he didn't say much was fed and welcomed, if not enthusiastically. He had simply been too drunk to remember.

Clayton and Sara wanted a child but the years passed with no success. She had two miscarriages, the second one nearly killing her. Then she gave birth to a boy short of full term who fought for his life for three months before he died in his sleep. Clayton enlarged the little picket cemetery and they had a quiet service with a Bible reading and prayers. He replaced his grandparents' wooden crosses with proper headstones, buying a smaller one for the boy. Soon after this James insisted they build an addition to the house to make room for any new McGhees that might come along. He told his daughter-in-law such a project brought luck to a young couple, but Clayton could tell by the way he said it that he was making it up. It sounded exactly like something old Amos would have said. Yet soon after the new rooms were completed she got pregnant again. Clayton was terribly worried he might lose Sara this time. The baby came in 1887 and they named her Clara, after her great-grandmother. She arrived healthy but until she was a year old they never felt safe.

James and Lily died within a year of one another in 1892. Again he cut the fence and made the plot a little bigger to accommodate two more graves. Cas came for the service, looking like a real old man now, Clayton thought. He never thought he'd see him surrender his air of impishness, but this bent gentleman, despite the sparkle in his eyes and his easy smile was a diminished version of his former self. Judah came too, bringing two burlap bags of smooth river stones from the sandbar below his house. They outlined the graves with these and Clayton was touched by his friend's solicitude for the dead.

As that summer came to a close they had some of the fiercest thunderstorms anyone had ever seen. Judah asked Clayton for help rebuilding his house, which had been damaged by a falling tree and leaked badly. They settled on what they would need and agreed to a day at the end of August.

Clayton was laboring to maneuver the wagon off the road and onto the track that led to the river when suddenly there was a man with his hand on the bridle. Judah, who had the disconcerting habit of appearing out of nowhere, coaxed the reluctant animal down the embankment and across the drainage ditch. The horse did not care for the water but managed it with only a toss of its head. Clayton was relieved to be able to concentrate on the wagon's descent. He did not want to get stuck and have to lift it filled as it was with lumber and tools. The springs creaked and the frame flexed just enough that they got through it and into the field. At the woods they unloaded onto a skid which the horse pulled with ropes along the narrow path to Judah's cabin. Three trips saw them sweating but finished.

They worked until the light gave out.

Judah had patched the damage the fallen tree had done when it punched through the wall and roof. Once this was removed it was a matter of marrying new materials to old ones. The alternative was to knock it all down and start over. That was Clayton's first thought when he was up top leaning on the chimney.

"What you think?" Judah asked. The day was bright and he shielded his eyes under the brim of his hat.

Clayton sighed. In his mind he saw all the steps he ought to take to do the job right. Peel back the moldering shingles. Pull up the rotted decking, maybe even the joists if the water got in far enough. Re-set the walls or even replace them, depending on how bad the wood had weathered. The chimney looked solid at least. If he had his way they would use a sledge and a spud bar until it was the only thing standing. But there was no time for that. He would have to do the best he could to make the place habitable. He consoled himself with the thought that Judah was not used to a properly constructed dwelling anyway. Two full days of work ought to see them through.

After a dinner of catfish, potatoes, and pickled cucumbers they sat in front of a good fire. Judah brought out a jug and they sipped at his homemade hard cider. "I forget how nice it is to have company," he said.

"You know you're welcome any time at our place. Maybe this winter – "

"Stop right there, Clay. You know I ain't leaving the river. I'm thankful for the offer but I'm fine right where I am."

"You will be if I brought enough boards and nails and tar," he replied.

"I been rained and snowed on before. Long as the larder don't go empty I'll get to spring. Which reminds me. You bring those seeds I asked for?"

Clayton stood up and stretched. The satchel was near the door and he rustled in it and brought out a sheaf of small brown envelopes. He checked to see if anything had spilled out of them. "Here you go," he said. Judah pulled spectacles out of his shirt pocket and read each one. "Pinto beans. Runner beans. Green peas. Yellow squash. Punkins. Radishes. Oh," he rattled it next to his ear, "those are some tiny sons of bitches. You get peppers?"

"I meant to tell you that," Clayton said. "I accidentally threw out the ones I saved for you. I'll pick some up in town next time I go. No trouble."

Judah passed the jug over. He noticed Clayton holding something. "What you got there?"

"Since Mama died I took up the good book again. Reading it some before bed every night. Thought I'd tote it down here and see if you'd care to listen. No one at home cares for me to read it to them."

"I'd rather you brought a piano but if that's all you got go right ahead. I can't think when was the last time I heard someone read from the Bible."

Clayton started at the beginning of Luke. He thought it the most riveting of the Gospels.

When he got to the parable of the mustard seed Judah said, "Hold up there now. That reminds me I wanted to grow some collards. And hell, I might as well grow mustard greens too. Can you see if the co-op has seeds for those?"

"We get to the Last Supper," Clayton said, "I'm gonna have to start taking notes."

"Let me ask you something," Judah said, picking his teeth with a match. "You believe all the miracles and whatnot in that book? I mean, we ain't in church so you can be honest."

163

He thought about it. Judah was the only person he knew who asked him questions he lacked a ready answer for.

"It's probably not a Christian thing to say, but I believe in the stories. I can say I've felt the power of the spirit in church when the choir is singing, but I don't talk to God like my granddaddy did. I like what the stories tell us about how to live and how to treat one another." Clayton closed the book, holding the place with his finger. He stared into the flames and thought about Amos and Clara. They always appeared to him when there was a question of right and wrong. "How bout you? I suppose plenty of men carried a Bible during the war."

"Come to think of it I did take one when I mustered out. Mama made me. I can't recall when I lost it but I had it then I didn't have it. At first I prayed all the time. I was so scared I would have done anything to stay alive. It made me feel better but after a while the silence was more powerful than my ability to believe there was anyone out there. I know as well as any man why we need that but I came to depend on other things. Other people, mostly."

"And guns and liquor," Clayton replied.

Judah's eyes were bright in the light. "I am a right infidel, ain't I?"

They passed the jug and Judah smoked a pipe he had carved out of cherry wood. When Clayton came to the end of Luke his companion was snoring quietly. He put a blanket over him and set the pipe where it couldn't do any mischief. He stoppered the jug. As quietly as he could he slid Judah's chest out from beneath the bed. Tomorrow when he said his goodbyes he would tell his old friend that he wanted to make a gift of the Bible and when this was refused he would shake his head and say, "It is too late for that you rascal. It is where you will find it if you have a mind to do some reading."

And he did.

164

Fourteen

The decade of the 1890s brought scant evidence of what would later be called the Gilded Age though plenty of tarnish beset LaFayette and its businesses. The Panic of 1893, the Pullman railroad strikes, and the miners' strikes that made coal expensive and, briefly, scarce, led local factories to lay men off and lower wages. The only businesses that seemed to prosper as the century ground to a close were land speculation and cattle. For a few men in LaFayette, this meant buying thousands of acres in the counties to the north and west and importing the makings of a large herd fattened on the prairie and then shipped up to the sprawling stockyards in Chicago. Since these men had also invested in the railroad they made profits coming and going.

One of the most successful of these speculators turned Middle West cattle baron was Henderson Jeffries, who well into his 80s had a keen appetite for investments. He started out in the grocery business, soon founded a wholesale firm and then plowed his ample profits into banking. In the 1880s he wisely diversified, at first following a business partner into land and cattle and then buying out his share and minimizing his exposure in the bank. When the Panic struck his material investments paid handsomely while the bankers took to drink and poison and high windows. At his death in 1899, on the cusp of the new century, he left a fortune to his wife, Sylvia. His son, Peter, had become weary of living in his shadow. And even wearier upon not receiving his inheritance. The ever imperious Sylvia Jeffries kept hold of her husband's considerable wealth with a tight fist.

Peter Jeffries made his living practicing law. Early in his career he observed that being a successful attorney required being a good actor. This led him to work at perfecting the demeanor of a character he had seen in a stage play in college. An urbane, yet sensible trial lawyer, the fellow had captured Peter's attention by his ability to anticipate what would happen next in the narrative. Like a fortune teller. But even better, he made the story that he controlled. In the play the lawyer was one step ahead of everyone else, discovering the truth and the details of a case of murder and the cover-up that followed. He had observed that people, including his father, a man of means and accomplishment, reacted to life as it presented itself. Before him opened the possibility of another way. He chose law so that he could perfect his role as the man at the center of events.

Peter stood at just over six feet, taller than most at the courthouse, and had a barrel chest which he accentuated by holding it towards any interlocutor. With his gold wire spectacles and slicked-back dark hair he resembled the photos in the LaFayette Courier of Teddy Roosevelt, whom he by turns cursed and worshipped.

In the early summer of 1901, he was approached by some of his fellows in the Chamber of Commerce and asked to join them in investing in a new venture. While railroads were well-established across the Midwest, hauling freight and passengers via coal and steam, they did not with any frequency serve the fast-growing towns that now dotted the map between Chicago, Cincinnati, St. Louis, Cleveland, and Detroit. Into this breach rolled the new electric railroad, called the interurban. These were single passenger cars that ran like an urban subway line but between towns and small cities underserved by locomotives. In order to establish an interurban line, investors had to survey the route, secure the right of way, ensure the proper grade, construct the track, build the powerhouse, hire workers. All this took a large chunk of capital, raised from

166

private sources. Once this little task was accomplished they had to entice people to ride. It was a risky proposition. But Peter Jeffries considered himself a modern thinker and a man who looked to the future. The invitation and its opportunity excited him much more than his moribund law practice. To be the economic engine of a brand new mode of transportation, one that would change the face of the country and bring what had so recently been the wild frontier into the modern age at the dawn of a new century.

"Think of it," he said to his wife, Annabelle. "This could make us a fortune."

She laughed. "Wake me up when you can think of a reason anyone would want to go to Peoria or Danville." He had suspected he might be wasting his time talking to her about it.

Peter met with his mother and put the whole thing to her, wondering whether she would see the potential and give him everything he asked for. He was stunned when she turned him down flat, scoffing at the very idea of the little trains moving people from backwater to podunk for a pittance.

"Why," she asked, "are the railroad barons not already doing this?"

He had no answer. "Lack of vision," he offered, but she was having none of that.

She pointed her arthritic finger at the ceiling and informed him that "a fool and his money are soon parted."

He stood and, red-faced, asked her to leave.

When his friend Cassini showed him, in secret, the plans for the line that went west and then north from LaFayette, he noticed that the route passed along the top of the bluff before turning away from the river towards Chicago. There was a farm up there, smack in the path of the rail line, owned by the negro who had shot a white man some years ago. Peter had been just a boy, but so had the shooter. In fact, there had been several killings that day if he remembered right. He would have to stop by the Courier and see McCutcheon, have him look that up in the archives. His father had wanted passionately to dispossess those negroes and played some part in the scheme that had gone so badly. Peter had overheard his parents arguing about it. A plan formed in his mind, though he said nothing to Cassini. Two birds with one stone, if he was not mistaken. Acquire the farm, get rid of the negroes, make a tidy profit from the right to run rails across his land. Perhaps he'd even start a settlement or put an inn there. Yes, he thought. Possibilities.

Turned out George McCutcheon, editor of the Courier, knew a lot more about the events of 1868 than Peter Jeffries would have guessed. On one of the large work tables in the newspaper's archives he arranged the relevant articles. The editor pulled out a wheeled chair and gestured for his guest to sit. He did so, setting his hat down next to a full ashtray.

When Peter had read through them he let out a low whistle.

"That's about as wild a story as I've ever heard. Add Wyatt Earp and Luke Short and you've got a nickel weekly hot seller. You know anything else about this?"

McCutcheon gathered the pages into a neat pile.

"My old man was deputy sheriff in the '70s. Never tired of telling tales of what he called the 'wild west'. Said Tippecanoe County was like Dodge City. Said the sheriff had told him about a slew of heinous goings on during the war and after, with bounty jumpers and escaped slaves, deserters, thieves robbing women whose men had gone off to fight for the Union. Train robberies too. You heard of the Reno Gang that robbed and terrorized folks down around Seymour?"

"Hell yes. Lynched finally, weren't they?"

"They were indeed. First train robbers in the whole world."

"Is that right? Jesus."

The editor carried on. Peter suspected he could tell these kinds of stories all day.

"School for negro kids was burnt down in the '60s, windows

broken out of the little synagogue on Seventh Street, Irish in the south end constantly worked over. This was a tough town at the sharp edge of a growing country." McCutcheon scratched at his neck beneath his shirt collar. "Come to think of it I ought to write something about that. Make a good column. "Old Tippecanoe" or the like."

"So," Peter asked, tapping the stack of newsprint, "this shootout was a race thing?"

"Not entirely. Maybe those Lecroix brothers went out there to do some such mischief, but according to the sheriff the whole thing was engineered by the men who ran this town and the county."

"Like my father?"

"Oh lord yes. You ever meet an associate of his, fat man, on the short side, worked at the Courthouse?"

Peter shook his head. "Not that I remember. But he didn't bring his business home. I remember his secretary, but every time I visited his office it seemed as though nothing was ever happening. Until I was older I imagined he sat there all day looking at papers."

"Man's name was Tumwater," McCutcheon said. "I don't think Henderson Jeffries brought men like him to his home nor to his office if he could help it. Tumwater was his cat's paw. It was him arranged that little posse led by Lecroix and his brother, and nearly went to prison for it. Colegrove, the sheriff, pressed him to turn on your father, but he would not. Shortly after that he and his wife moved to Kentucky and were not heard from again."

"Wait. Colegrove?"

"Yep, he was sheriff for a lot of years. You remember his son? Three or four years behind us in school. Fell pretty far from the tree, that one."

Peter laughed, picked up his hat.

"You got that right. Thanks for your trouble, George. I owe you a drink."

169

Peter Jeffries, son of the Henderson Jeffries who had tried to get the McGhees off their land, dead or alive, and who had nearly caused a wounded Gene Lecroix, if somewhat indirectly, to shoot two little boys dead, did indeed know June Colegrove. They frequented the same drinking and whoring establishment on Wabash Avenue in the south end of town and had places there in a regular Sunday night poker game. On more than one Monday morning they had taken breakfast together at the Lahr House Hotel. Not friends, but friendly.

Peter found June at a bar on the north side called The Squirrel Cage, whose atmosphere and clientele was proximate to its name. Scruffy loiterers and raffish old timers, a few whores on the weekends, more on the first of the month when the Monon Railroad paid out and the boys had ready cash. Even the light coming through the polished windows looked dirty.

June had two modes of drunk. The first was dandified, practiced at restaurants and hotel bars, designed to draw in a higher class of friend or female companion. The second was on evidence as the sun slanted through the mullioned windows, throwing shadows against the liquor bottles and the mirror behind them. June had his hat pulled down to his eyebrows, his chin resting on the rail of the bar with his elbows out and hands folded under it. In front of him a shot glass filled with amber liquid and an empty one upturned over a stack of quarters. The place was empty apart from the bartender who left off polishing glasses and cocked his head at his new customer.

"What's he drinking?" Peter asked.

"Rye." He looked the lawyer up and down, noting the cut and quality of his suit. "The cheap stuff."

"Brandy then."

The barman was heavily muscled beneath the long sleeves of his white shirt and was missing his right front tooth. He put the cloth over his shoulder and began rummaging beneath the bar. He shifted a tray of pilsners and one smashed to the floor. Muttered curses. June did not move, though Peter could see that his eyes were open, focused on the glass and its contents.

"I'll have to go in the back, mister. There ain't – "

"Just put it in a shot glass. It's too fucking early anyway."

"Yes sir. Next one's on the house. Four bits."

He fished out the coins and took a seat one stool over from June. He sniffed at the brandy and took a sip. Not bad, actually. The benefit of low expectations, he thought, running a finger along the bar to see if it was safe for the arms of his jacket.

Without looking up June said, "What brings you to this dump?" The barman was down sweeping up the broken glass so he raised his voice. "Sorry Reg, but it's true."

"You ain't gettin no argument from me," they heard him say.

Peter smiled. "Loose ends, thirsty, in the neighborhood."

"Should I pick one?"

"Suit yourself."

He disliked drinking in the afternoon, but the brandy tasted good. The first one would clear his head. June sat up suddenly alert and rubbed his face. He tried to straighten his tie but found he wasn't wearing one. Reached into his pocket and drew out wrinkled silk, barber pole stripes, past care. Thought better of the bother and pushed it back in. He placed his hands upright on either side of the full glass, as though he were going to catch a fly on a bet, then with his left swiftly seized it and drank it off in one motion, snapped the glass back in its place and shouted, "Reg!"

The barman had done this before and was quick with the bottle. June felt again in his pockets, came away empty, looked confused. Reg lifted the other glass and took a quarter from the stack. "Right," said June. "Good man." He tried to lean his arm on the back of the stool that stood between them

171

and nearly crashed to the floor. "Now, you fucking pettifogger and cardsharp, what the hell do you want? You're in the wrong part of town for coincidences."

He sounded amazingly lucid for someone with so many drinks in him.

"Got a question about a friend of yours. You involved in that business back in '68? Up the river bluff with Lecroix and those darkies? Must have been one hell of a fight."

"Why you asking?"

"Paper said your father shot Gene Lecroix before he could shoot you. Figured you'd remember something like that. Occurred to me you either went out there with the sheriff or you was already out there. Don't make much sense. Wondering if maybe you spent time – "

"McGhee."

"What?"

"Negro family. McGhee. Nice people. Nicer'n some others, that's for sure." He looked Peter right in the eye then turned back to the bar and leaned on one elbow.

"So you know that boy lives out there now?"

"Since I was in short pants."

"You think he'd sell that farm to me?"

"He may be black but he ain't stupid. There's pretty much nothing out there they didn't build by hand. You'd probably have to kill him to get him off it."

They drank their drinks.

Peter opened. "I have a business proposition for you. You interested?"

"Depends. I got irons in other fires."

"I want that farm. I have plans for that land and they won't wait."

"Likely buy yourself other land up there."

"I need that land, specifically."

"*Specifically.*" June laughed. "Now this conversation is getting interesting. What for?"

"Can you keep a secret?"

"Depends who I'm keep it for. Specifically."

Peter was starting to regret this course of action. If he had any other choice he'd take it, but there wasn't time, and beggars with rich selfish mothers can't be choosers.

"Well," Peter looked around histrionically, June aping him as there was no one who could hear them with Reg smoking at the far end of the bar, "the new electric train line is going through there and that land is going to be valuable for right-of-way. The county will declare eminent domain if it's McGhee land, unless I'm mistaken. But if I own it they won't dare. Not only will I make a tidy profit, I plan to get a station there and put in a business. An inn or tavern. The county is growing, Colegrove, and I want a piece of this modern transportation."

"What's in it for me?"

"If you can get McGhee to sell me that land for a good price I'll give you a finder's fee of a thousand dollars."

June considered this, or at least Peter thought he was thinking about it. He watched him turn in his frumpled suit, set his hands again equidistant from the glass of rye, then pluck it neatly, this time with his right hand, downing it as deftly as he had before. How he kept from throwing the liquor out of the glass he had no idea. Practice, he supposed.

"Since we're telling secrets," June said, still facing his glass, "I'll admit to always wanting to own that farm. I spent some fine times out there and I'm sick to death of living in this town. Maybe we can work us a deal where I can buy it, or part of it, say the house and barn and whatnot, with that thousand as a down payment." He slapped the bar. "Reg! You asleep or what? I'm dry and get my partner here another of what he's having."

Peter knocked off the rest of his brandy and closed his eyes tight against the burn. Reg poured him another, then a rye for June, to whom he sent a smirk that said if you'd like me to break your loud mouth for you so I can have some new teeth from the damage that can be arranged.

June put his hand over his heart and flashed a wide smile. "Oh Christ, *Reginald*. Loosen up my friend."

The barman took the rest of the quarters and the shot glass. June's thumbs-up went unacknowledged.

"I think we can find a solution that suits us both," Peter said in his best courtroom tone. "Tell you what. Why don't you have a chat with your friend and I'll start drawing up some papers. Come see me at my office as soon as you've spoken with him and we'll go from there."

Peter put his hat on, took a small drink, and shook June's hand.

"Glad I ran into you, Colegrove. I think this might work out nicely."

"Lucky I was here. Be seeing you."

When Jeffries was gone, June reached and with two fingers slid over his almost-full glass. He held it up to the light and then drank it slowly, letting the finer liquor ease its own way down his throat.

"Clayton McGhee," he whispered. "My dear old friend."

Fifteen

Late the next morning, after an ample breakfast and coffee into which he tipped a little pick-me-up, June rode out to talk with Clayton. He would leave out the part about always wanting the farm, of course, and of the profit to be made off the land. It would be no easy task, but his plan was to persuade Clayton to move up to Chicago or down to Indianapolis where there were other black folk. Think of the girls. Think of Sara. Let on that trouble is brewing like when they were kids. The shooting of Gene Lecroix had been playing nightly in his dreams and no matter how much he drank the sight of the ragged wound blossoming out of his chest would not cease bedeviling him.

He got as far as the bridge over the river before his massed thoughts got the better of him and he turned for home, intending to unsaddle his horse and go in search of a drink. It was no use trying to argue with Clay about the farm. No use at all. He needed to think.

But there was no time. Jeffries had been clear on that score. And given that Clay might have to be worn down he couldn't hesitate now or the opportunity might be lost. He turned the horse again and kicked it into a trot.

An hour later he surprised Sara hoeing along a row of pepper plants, a handkerchief tied around her head to keep off the early afternoon sun. Without taking her eyes off him she stopped, leaned on the handle and spoke to the little girl sitting in the dirt playing with a collection of dolls.

"Well look here, Birdy. Some kind of stranger come to visit. Must be he's lost. What do you reckon?"

175

The girl shielded her eyes and squinted up at him. "I ain't sure, mama. He looks familiar. Might be he's a salesman."

Birdy loved the tinkers and traders with their laden wagons. For a child who'd seen the inside of a store only a handful of times, the wonders to be found there seemed infinite.

"You see any wares, child?"

"No ma'am," she replied, looking him over intently and then standing and peering out above the grass as if maybe a wagonload of toys and candy were waiting just out of sight.

June said, "I could fix you up with some all-purpose cough elixir. Guaranteed to cure what ails you and eliminate the hitch in your git-along."

"I bet you could. Birdy, say hello to Mr. June and run tell your daddy he's here."

She gathered up her dolls and ran along a worn path that skirted the well then led to the house.

"Child!" Birdy stopped in her tracks, dropped a doll, picked it up roughly as if she would admonish it for carelessness. "Now, what did you forget to say?"

Looking down at her feet she said, "Hello Mr. June sir. We are sure glad to have company." She laughed and turned and ran.

Sara barked at her again. "Child, he out past the barn, the other way," and Birdy turned once around the round of stones and up the gentle rise disappearing behind the shaded side of the barn.

"How long's it been?" asked Sara.

"Not sure . . . couple years?"

"Since you been out *here*."

"Oh, more than that. Half a dozen. About the time that little one was born I'd say. Thank the good lord she got her mother's looks."

Sara laughed. "You terrible as ever, Mr. Colegrove. How you been keeping? I expected to get an invite to your wedding some time ago. What happened to that lady professor you took up with?"

"Well," he tipped his hat back and adjusted himself in the saddle, unused to being in it for so long, "that's a pretty long story. I'm not sure my behind can tolerate this saddle for that long."

"Mercy, where are my manners. We don't get too many visitors and I'm out of the greeting habit. Get down off there and come to the house for something cold to drink." She shouldered the hoe and gestured for him to follow. "There ain't no liquor but they's lemonade and sweet tea and cold water in the bucket. You hungry? Ain't no trouble to – "

"No ma'am, thank you. I'd have a lemonade if it isn't too much trouble. Hate to sound ungrateful, but I need to see your husband and get back to town before dark."

He got off the horse and followed her, stopping at the well to drink a dipper from the bucket.

Sara leaned the hoe against the porch rail and paused with the screen door half open. "Go on up to the barn. Get your horse some water and oats. Clay will find you there and I'll bring up the lemonade."

June had never seen a more well-organized barn. Tidier than my house, he said to the horse. There were stalls along one side, some with sliding doors, some hinged, the last one larger to accommodate several animals or a birthing. On the other side were implements: plows, a harrow, a hay rake, a rack of hand tools. Beyond these were neatly piled spools of twine and bags of seed, a collection of wooden buckets, baskets, and crates, and on the wall a two-man buck saw, oiled and sharp-toothed like some rich man's hunting trophy. Below it were pruning saws and shears, post-hole diggers, and a small rack of long-handled hammers, axes, and mauls. He'd seen dry goods stores less well stocked. In the far corner was a room walled off with a narrow, closed door. More storage or a workshop, he supposed. Its roof was the floor of the loft, where the hay was kept and where he'd spent many an hour working and napping as a youngster.

"I'll be damned." June jumped, startled at the voice. He hadn't heard or seen Clay but there he was silhouetted in the far open door. He was holding a scythe with its blade up, gripping it near the top. Behind him, peering around his leg, was Birdy. "Thought this child was tellin me a tall tale. Said to Birdy I don't know no one by that name any more."

"Hello Clay. Barn looks nicer than a hardware store. If I didn't know you I'd say you were a gentleman farmer who never used any of this gear."

"Let's get that horse some water and feed. Can I get you anything? I expect Sara's on her way here with something, but I can always send my little runner." He put his hand on Birdy's head and she smiled shyly, ducking back behind him.

Clay set the scythe in its place in one of the racks and took the horse, leading it into one of the stalls. He forked it some hay and threw several handfuls of oats in a trough, then filled another trough with water from the barrel near the door.

"You can leave the saddle on her. I need to be back by sundown."

"What brings you out this way?"

"Do I need a reason to visit my old friend?"

Clayton ran his hand along the mare's withers, down her leg, stepped across and picked up the hoof. He inspected it, drew a pocket knife out of his front overalls pocket and dug around the shoe.

"This old girl needs to be trimmed and re-shod. I could do it but you won't get to town afore nightfall."

"Leave it. Farrier up in Five Points owes me three dollars. I'll collect it in trade." June felt his breast pocket for the flask but thought better of it. "You didn't answer my question."

Sara came in bearing a tray with a pitcher wrapped in a towel, glasses, a small sugar bowl, and cookies. She looked for a place to set it down but there were no flat surfaces among all the angular tools and equipment. Bringing it straight to her husband she held it while he filled two glasses, handed one to June, and selected a cookie. June demurred on the sweets. Birdy hovered, swooping in when her mother handed her the cookie plate and told her to take it to the house and share with her sisters.

"Can I get you all anything else? Well then, I'll get back to my garden. Holler if you need me, or help yourself."

"Much obliged, Sara," said June with a tip of his hat.

When she was gone he brought out the flask and darkened his lemonade with rum. He wiggled it at Clayton who shook his head. "Got more work with sharp edges to do before the end of the day." He fetched two crates and they sat in the shade inside the wide double doors, looking down the slope at the house and the fields that rose and fell to the road and then to the tree line in the distance. It was a fine view.

"I'm glad to see you, June. What is it you want." Clayton said this as a matter of fact, not as a question.

"I got a proposition for you. What would you say if I told you this farm would fetch a very good price?" He put up his hand before Clayton could respond. "I'm not talking about the end of something here, but the beginning. On my way I couldn't help thinking about your little girls. What kind of life is it all the way out here? Don't you want a better future for them? Don't you think they should have the chance to be around other kids?"

"We ain't that far from town. Look – "

"Hear me out." But June was already running out of arguments. Each point he had lined up was essentially a variation on the same theme. He thought they might add up, becoming weightier as he dropped them on the scale. But they were too similar. Soft, identical waves lapping against unrelenting stone. "There's a group of business men, men with money and influence, who have big plans for the county. Now, I can't divulge the details, but suffice to say that they are going to start buying up land soon. The highest prices are going to go to the ones who sell early. If you hold out, there's a chance they'll get rights to use your land anyway, and you won't see a plug nickel."

"That don't really make sense, June. Wouldn't the last to hold out get the most? I admit I ain't no expert on such things."

"No, you aren't. You gotta trust me on this thing. It's business."

"What they want with land in these parts? Railroad runs well east of here. Ain't no gold or coal, or other such things, least not that I know of."

"It isn't like that. I can't tell you what they're planning."

"It don't matter anyhow. You know damn well I'd never sell this place. We paid too much sweat and blood to leave now. We got us a good life."

"I don't think you are hearing me," June replied, his voice raised. He took a drink straight from the flask. "They are going to take it *anyway*."

"That don't make no sense. I may be black, but I got rights. This ain't Alabama. Ain't no Klan here, no Jim Crow flyin up this far north."

June was angry now.

"You sound like old Amos. Naïve as hell. Yassuh, nossuh. No idea what these men are capable of. Like a goddamned field hand."

He shook his head and looked June in the eye. There was silence between them.

Clayton broke it. "You about finished?"

"No, I'm not." He took a slug from the flask. "You told me yourself how your daddy had to convince the old man that fighting fire with fire was the only way to keep what you all had worked so hard for. What I'm telling you now is that you gotta be smart, stay one step ahead of this kind of financial venture. *That's* the kind of fight you're in."

Clayton took a long drink of his lemonade, held it against his forehead. He waited until he was sure his question would come out calm and measured. "So, what's in this for you?"

June's answer came lightning-fast. "What do you mean? Damn it, we've known each other for – "

Clayton could read an angry man. It was always the same with hotheaded people. Whatever provoked them was the key to finding out what they wanted. Sometimes they didn't even know it, but he did. His father had a little of that streak in him and when it came to the surface you waited and then you could steer a surer path to what was really going on. Arguing back only hardened the defensiveness. He knew from June's response, and what would surely follow it, that his visitor was looking after his own interests. Thus his appeal to the past, to their friendship that had always been Clayton's responsibility, and his pathetic reasons that even he didn't believe. These were all clear signs that it was June Colegrove who was most likely to benefit from whatever deal was in the works.

Clayton McGhee prided himself on being a good friend and an honest man. He didn't shy away from a scrap, but he didn't pick them. It was one thing to have to save June some embarrassment or get him out of trouble. But beneath the mask of opportunity was a warning, and the man sitting next to him was content to hide his face while profiting from his family's loss. Now it was his turn to get angry and he fought to master it. Nothing good could come of a fight. Or humiliation.

"I appreciate you coming all the way out here, June, and we've known each other for a long time, as you say. But I don't have any intention of selling this place. You know why as well as any man, so I won't insult you by trotting out the reasons."

"Like I insulted you by asking?"

He was angry again and Clayton almost felt sorry for him.

"I didn't say that."

"You didn't have to." His voice edged toward hysteria. "You've always had everything. Your parents loved you and took care of you, taught you how to make things and live off the land. You got this perfect farm and a pretty wife and it all just fell right into your lap. You don't have any idea how hard it's been for me."

Before Clayton could respond June stood up and kicked his crate which rolled awkwardly and sat broken on the downslope. He took out the flask and was about to hurl it out toward the orchard when he stopped himself, took a drink, and put it back in his pocket. The air went out of him and his face was set, the grimace of a man who knew he'd fooled only himself and thus been the fool twice over.

From the doorway Clayton watched what passed for his friend stomp over to a stall, pull his horse's head out of her feed, get himself with some effort into the saddle, wobble there until he found his balance, then ride slowly out of the barn without so much as turning his head. The expression on his face bore no trace of anger or determination, or even of concern. It was the vacant stare of self-absorption. He could almost hear the wheels turning in that inebriated head, and they turned as they always did in service of the next plan, the next angle, the next advantage. June Colegrove's thoughts revolved around June Colegrove with mathematical certainty.

Clayton shielded his eyes against the late day sun. The horse passed the well and as it neared the garden he could hear the faintest trace of a human voice as Sara offered some kind of farewell. Horse and rider did not slow down, nor was there any change to the angle of saddled posture. No tip of the hat nor words spoken. There would be neither anger nor other passion spent on someone who had nothing to do with the future betterment of the dead sheriff's only son.

And it occurred to Clayton out of what was indeed a clear

blue sky, arced across by purple martins, that they had gone through something like this the last time they had spoken. It made him laugh a little, though with sadness, that he had forgotten. Since now it was as obvious as could be. Such a paradox. What his grandfather would have called a vexation. He thought now about the particulars of that day and what he'd learned about June and about how funny a world it was. Funny and sad. And dangerous.

It started with a letter.

Sixteen

Clayton looked over the letter several times but it became no clearer to him what his friend was talking about. June had contacted him before without making any sense, but this time there was an urgency that nagged at him for the remainder of the day and into the evening. At some godforsaken hour in the middle of the night he'd gotten up and dressed, made his way out to the barn and started a fire in the potbelly stove he'd set up in a little room he was calling his workshop. He had cleaned out a corner where they'd stored an old broken plow, hauled by wagon and sold to a farmer in Montmorenci, and built an enclosed room where he could work in the winter and in all seasons out of the weather. There was always something to be fixed or, when what he needed couldn't be bought or afforded, made. The truth was he enjoyed his little space with its window, the workbench and stool, his tools, and the stove. He even kept books on the top shelf when he had a mind to use his head instead of his hands.

He moved his favorite hammer, an awl, and the piece of leather he'd been working on, then unfolded and spread the page on the bench. There wasn't much light with the oil lamp, but he was used to it. When he couldn't sleep he came out here to read a little and listen to the comforting sounds of the farm. Usually what he read made more sense.

Dear Clayton,   29 April 1899
I don't think I can go on like this any more. She left again yesterday and I thought maybe this time I would be able to let her go. But no, I am off the wagon, entirely fallen, and

can think of nothing but her. It seems each time she goes I ~~get~~ become less able to resist demon drink. You suggested once that she was too good for me, though that was not ~~what~~ how you put it. I knew what you meant. She is educated and while I am too there is a whole chasm between what we have done with it. She has her career and her fancy office and I have my ~~fuck~~ pathetic picture business. I never had the courage to do anything with my photography. My daddy told me it wasn't work and I told him to go to hell and then proceeded to believe him. I didn't, really, but I couldn't stop ~~from feeling like~~

Aw fuck, Clayton, you know me and you know what kind of man I am. Everything I touch turns to shit. And now this. No. And now this <u>AGAIN</u>.

I'm writing to you because no one knows me better than you do and no one has as much good common sense. You have always succeeded where I have failed. You have a beautiful wife and children and a grand farm and your parents loved you every day of their lives. I never figured I'd envy a colored man, but then again there's a lot of things I never figured. Get them to knock that into my tombstone for me.

Please come and see me at my house. Best to come of a morning as I will likely be sober. No promises. I have a ~~business~~ proposition for you. I wrote business there as you can see but Jesus Christ it ain't even dignified enough to call it that. ~~There~~ I just do not know what else to do and I am desperate.

Your Friend,
June

There was a stain at the bottom, something brown Clayton assumed to be liquor. It was also crumpled and appeared to have been rescued and flattened out before being folded and sent via rural free delivery. When he fished it out of his new mailbox he already knew it would not be the kind of pleasant reading he usually received there in the form of mail order catalogs or news.

It would be Saturday morning in a few hours. He couldn't go today. Too much to do. Tomorrow would be good for Clay but bad for June after what he expected would be an eventful Saturday night. Monday morning then. Sara would need some things and he could turn it into a useful trip. He wondered if one day would be better than another, but decided he had to take his chances. A friend in need and all that.

On the way to town he thought about how far he and June had come since they were boys playing on the farm. June always returned to his father reluctantly. He grew into a fun-loving but moody teenager, his behavior swinging from gregarious to morose. His late mother's Crawfordsville family paid for him to go to Wabash College, assuming wrongly that this would bring him closer to them. After four years he managed to receive his degree without becoming any more familiar with his extended family than he had to. His grandfather expected his grandson to follow him into the practice of law, especially given the tuition funds he had shelled out. But June had no interest in it. The old man dismissed him with the observation that his grandson was just like his daughter: attracted to the wrong side of the law. He had never forgiven her for marrying a lowly sheriff.

At Wabash he took a photography course out of curiosity and immediately fell in love with it. Impatient with so many other things, photography absorbed him fully. He learned the collodion process, using wet plates of japanned iron for making ambrotypes, then moving on to tintypes with glass plates. Wet emulsions, dry emulsions, experiments with different materials. It was the supreme expression of art and science his mentors assured him. Clayton knew that prior to graduation, June borrowed money from his grandfather on

186

the premise that he was purchasing some photography equipment in order to earn money to supplement his study of law. The old man saw nothing wrong with such a harmless hobby and his wife was delighted to be supplied with free images of her family for posterity. She was a patient, if uninteresting model, and June used her to practice his technique.

In the end, June spent far more than he was supposed to and set himself in business before anyone knew what he'd done. For the first year or so he worked hard, making portraits and taking pictures of babies, capturing local civic events, and selling pictures of houses to their wealthy owners. He felt the art slipping away and grew bored with the science, drank too much, fought with his father. Every few years he would rally and find a new appetite for picture-making, but never seemed able to sustain it. Or was unwilling. Or was betrayed by the drink and his temper.

It took patience to handle and manipulate the glass plates then in use, and Clayton recalled a day he'd dropped in to the photography studio to find June face down amidst a wreckage of glass and chemicals, bloody, stained, and near dead from liquor poisoning. A week later he checked in on him, finding him still bandaged but otherwise content, working on framing a print from his new Kodak camera that used film instead of plates. This process will probably save my life, he joked, gesturing at his stack of unspoilt glass.

He tied up in the street in front of June's house, hoping to find him still asleep, or at least home. No one answered his knock so he pushed open the unlocked door. June was sitting in a rocking chair fully clothed, rocking in slow motion, fast asleep. Clayton had observed him in such a state before, either leaning against something or holding an object as though perfectly awake. It was as if instead of going to sleep, sleep went to him. He seemed often taken unawares by it, part of him staying just beyond its reach.

"June. Hey, wake up."

His eyes snapped open. The rocking chair stopped on the backswing, then resumed. June smiled.

"You want a drink?"

"No. It's too early."

June's face said that was a matter of dispute. The look made it clear he felt sorry for someone who inhabited such a narrow range of possibility. On a three-legged stool next to him sat a tall brown bottle of unidentified spirits, a short, straight-sided glass, and an ashtray long past overflowing. Butts littered the floor around it, as did spent matchboxes. The room smelled dank and sour.

Clayton sneezed. "Mind if I open a window?"

"Go right ahead. Got yourself a cold I see."

The window would hardly budge and gave several inches just when he was about to give up.

"Thought that was painted shut. I owe you one. Now, what can I get you?" He picked the bottle up and gave it a shake, frowned when there was none. "I'm afraid provisions are somewhat scarce. We may have to go out if you're hungry or thirsty."

"I'm fine," Clayton said, moving a stack of sheet music from the seat of a battered upright piano. He sat on the edge and asked, "What did you want to see me about?"

"What do you mean?"

"Your letter. Some trouble with Lida . . . you drinking . . . a business proposition. It wadn't real clear but that's the gist. Sound familiar?"

"Did I send that?"

Clayton patted his coat pocket. "Got it right here you want to have a look."

"I remember. Truth is, Lida left me a couple months ago. She'll be back. They always come back." He closed his eyes and his rocking became slower and more rhythmic.

"June!"

He opened his eyes again, spoke without missing a beat. "I

got a proposition for you. Met a guy at the Lahr, fancy fucker from Kentucky owns race horses. Thoroughbreds. He's got a two-year-old he needs to sell to pay off some debts. He needs fast money and says if he can get some collateral and a place to pasture the horse he'll sell it far below what it's worth. Now – "

"What collateral?"

"Well my house isn't worth all that much, but with that plus your farm, I think he'd agree."

"Agree to what?"

"Letting us have the horse till I could buy it clear."

"Where you gonna get the money for that?"

"That's the beauty of it. I'll race the horse and use the winnings to buy her."

"What if you don't win?"

"I'm telling you, this horse is the real deal, the golden goose."

"What's its name?"

"The horse?"

"Yes, the horse."

"Well, Golden Goose, as it happens."

"That ain't a good name for a horse."

"That's how they do it with race horses. Anyway, what would you know about it?"

"You know how many colored fellas rode the winning horse at the Kentucky Derby in the last twenty, twenty-five years? No? Better than half."

"You don't say. Well, that is something. Anyway, I have to meet the fellow by Wednesday or he'll be gone and the opportunity with him."

"I ain't signing the farm away for no horse, no matter how fast it can run."

With a crash the door burst open, kicked by the biggest boot Clayton had ever seen. It stuck open on the warped and uneven floorboards. The man wore a long black duster and

189

a bowler, giving him the appearance of a tower topped by a dome. Someone stood behind him but Clayton could only make out the color of his suit, a yellowish-green tweed. The man-tower stepped aside, in profile no slimmer than before. The well-dressed man entered as if coming into the lobby of a hotel in which he expected to be received with anticipation. He stopped in the center of the room and looked about. His eyes passed over Clayton without pause, took in the shabby furniture, the framed photographs that nearly covered the walls, and fixed his gaze on June who had ceased rocking and sat still.

In an Irish accent he said, "I'm just off the train from Chicago to visit me brother and to collect what's owed me. You will render to me my horse or my money or I shall have Samuel drag you from this house and beat you until you do." His voice was much deeper and commanding than his stature would suggest. "Understand me, boyo?"

He spread his feet and held his hands behind his back, looking as though he were getting comfortable for however long he might have to wait. June sat unmoving. Clayton was trying to figure out what was going on.

"If this is the negro you spoke about last week at the Palmer House," he continued, "I am surprised at the modesty of his size." He flicked his glance over and then back at June.

Clayton was puzzled. Size? Since June gave no indication he was going to speak, Clayton felt obliged to state his case. "Look Mister, I don't know what terms you discussed but I have no intention of signing over my farm for any horse." He stood up. The tweed gentleman faced him, pivoting as though executing a military maneuver.

"As I already possess the note for your farm, I fail to understand how that is relevant. Before you get it into your nappy head to coerce me to drop my demand for what is legally mine, I would point out my protégé beyond the doorway. Mr. Colegrove, if you would kindly – "

190

"I beg your pardon Mister – "

"It's Lanahan, boy."

"Mr. Lanahan, if I could ask what note you mean?"

"The promissory note with your signature writ on it. In my goddamn traveling trunk at the Lahr. Handed over by your friend there." He indicated June with the first and middle fingers of his right hand as if he were shooting him. "I've come for the balance of payment or for my animal. Absent one or the other I'll be forced to call Samuel in to assist me. Despite some fine braggadocio by the rocking chair king here I don't give you much chance against him. I've never heard of you. And after horses, Terry Lanahan's favorite subject is boxing."

Clayton wondered if he could get his hands on June before Samuel could knock him senseless. He looked again at the mass of man blocking the light from outside. He doubted it.

Later, Clayton would wonder how he had missed it. Maybe he'd been more frightened of Samuel than he'd realized and was in shock, or perhaps he was so angry he'd stopped paying attention to the still figure in the suspended chair.

With an astonishing agility June leapt from the rocker and in three steps was through the bedroom door. There was a faint squeak of mattress springs then a crash of window glass.

The room grew lighter as Samuel disappeared in pursuit, the whole house shaking with his passage across the porch. Lanahan did not move. He removed a small pen knife from his trouser pocket and pared a fingernail.

"Well I'll be goddamned," he said.

After a few minutes Samuel reappeared in the doorway and shook his head. Lanahan sighed. He turned to Clayton. "You should probably know that your friend there had quite a few things to say about you that I expect were exaggerations, to be charitable. You don't look like a fighter and my guess is this scheme was none of your making. I also have grave doubts about whether you have grown up a child of

191

privilege and ease. Reports of your ferocity, selfishness, and megalomania appear to have been greatly exaggerated."

Clayton, not knowing what to say to these astonishing pronouncements, said nothing.

"While I see that I will have to rip up the note to your farm, as it is clearly a forged document, I would urge you to limit your dealings with this man in future. He does not have your best interests in mind. In fact," and for the first time a smile marched its way across his face, "I suspect he is using you because he envies what you have."

Lanahan touched his fingers to the brim of his hat in a kind of farewell salute, turned on his heel, and was gone.

Seventeen

Peter Jeffries' office was on the third floor of a building that faced the courthouse square. He'd chosen the higher floor not because it was cheaper but as a deterrent against unannounced visits from his mother. What he had thought a clever idea gave way to disappointing results. She appeared less often, but stayed longer. Whether this was, as she claimed, because her feet were ruined by the stairs, or, as was more likely, in order to torment him, only God knew.

The secretary told June to have a seat and he did so while she informed her boss that he had a visitor. Expecting to be shown right in, he was annoyed after fifteen minutes and angry after thirty. When the door opened and no one exited he brushed past Jeffries and his phony smile without saying a word. He sat in the right-hand chair and lit a thin cigar with a match from the desk.

"Thanks for keeping me waiting. I thought you had someone in here."

"I'm a busy man, Colegrove. I don't get to work only when I feel like it."

June ignored the dig. "Let's get down to business. I went out to McGhee's farm and spoke to him about our business proposition."

Jeffries' eyebrows went up at the pronoun's plurality, but he let it pass with an "mm hm."

June went on: "He is a stubborn man and it took every bit of persuasion I could muster. At first he flat refused, then – "

"For Christ's sake get on with it."

"I thought you'd want all the details."

"I want the details that matter," Peter said, sitting back in his chair. "Now, please come to the point."

June wanted to walk around the desk and take the lawyer by the hair and mash his face into the desk blotter until he showed some respect. In his expensive suit and crisp white collar he sat impassively, and June hated him for it. Instead, the lie that he found himself telling came as easily as a razor in an assassin's hand. Or so he reckoned. He could not abide the sight of blood.

"He'll do it, but he wants cash up front, said he needed money for a business opportunity in Chicago that was about to expire. If you're willing to trust him then he'll sign the papers and do the deal."

Lawyers, in his experience, always overestimated the power of signed documents.

"Sounds like I'd be trusting *you*."

"Look, if you want to get this done, you'll give him ten thousand now. I'm telling you. He gets this thing up in Chi, we're going to roll him on the overall price. I guarantee you're going to be happy with the way this works out."

"I'll give him five thousand. He can take it or leave it. And I'm putting a lien on your house as collateral. And yes, I know the place isn't worth that much. But since it's all you own I'd at least have the pleasure of throwing you out of it."

June rubbed the back of his neck. "I don't know about that. What keeps you from just taking my place once you get McGhee's?"

"The law, you simpleton. It's a hedge against any grift you may be running. I'll draw up the papers and explain them to you before you sign. That's more security than I'm getting for my risk."

"Fine. Get the papers."

"I can't do it right now. It will take time to write it all out and make copies. Tomorrow afternoon, say 4. Anyway, won't you need to ride out to McGhee's and ask him if five thousand is enough for his Chicago deal? If not, what's the point?"

"Yes, you're right. I'll do that first thing. Though I expect he'll take it without any trouble."

"And you will arrange for him to come here and sign the paperwork for the sale of the farm?"

"Of course."

It pained June to act so dense in front of this man who overestimated his own cleverness. But he reminded himself that it was necessary. He owed money he had borrowed against the house and his lease was expiring on his shop. It was time to get out of this town. Five thousand dollars would get him pretty far. Maybe even buy him a little farm of his own somewhere west.

For his part, Peter Jeffries suspected that something was not right. But he could not stop thinking about the business opportunity that awaited his possession of the land. And if he lost money he would get it back, one way or the other.

The next day, June spent the morning packing all the belongings he could fit in a hired buggy. He made a list of items he needed that could be put on credit: a new suit, a long coat to wear against the weather, a sidearm and rifle to replace the guns his father had left him, canvas and poles for sleeping out when he had to, provisions, whiskey, and the horse and buggy. Since he was not coming back, he saw no reason to pay for these things. He was supposed to be out at McGhee's making a deal, but as this was all a ruse he happily found a seat at the far end of the bar at the Squirrel Cage, pulled his hat down low, and whiled away the afternoon getting good and drunk.

Peter had court early, then meetings with clients. It was noon before he had time to draw up papers for the farm sale as well as the earnest money and the lien on Colegrove's house. He worked through lunch on these and when they were ready he walked across to the Assessor's Office on the second floor of the courthouse. When he entered he heard the usually cheerful Marjorie Lane yelling at someone on the telephone at her desk. She shouted goodbye as he eased the door closed.

"Oh, Mr. Jeffries. I hope I didn't startle you."

"No, but it sounded like somebody got the edge of your tongue."

"I was trying to make myself heard is all. A lady who wanted to know about her property tax. I tried to give her the correct number but either she was hard of hearing or we had a bad connection. I hated to have to holler, but she just kept saying "pardon, pardon" over and over. I can't say the telephone has been a blessing in this office. Much better to see folks in person."

"I couldn't agree more. My wife made us get on the telephone and I wish I'd never said yes. Damn nuisance." He put his papers on the counter and arranged them into two neat piles.

"What can we do for you today?" She tilted her head to get a look at what he brought. He spun the paperwork around so she could start reading.

"Two things. First, I'm in the process of purchasing a farm west of town. The price has not been settled, but I wanted to get the preliminaries going so that we can close this quickly. If you could pull the relevant documents and prepare a file, that would speed things along. Second, I'm using a go-between with the seller and in order to guarantee my earnest money towards the purchase, I need to put a lien on his property."

"A lien on the farm?" she asked, pivoting from one stack of papers to the other, her brow furrowed.

"No, the house of the go-between." He put his finger on the page. "Here, the third party."

"Why don't you negotiate with the seller directly? This is a lot of complication for – "

"I'm sure you can understand that there might be reasons

I would rather not disclose." He smiled as though he were doing her a favor.

"Yes, of course." She flipped to the end of both documents to see who the other parties were. The shape of her mouth went from concentration to concern. "McGhee farm. June Colegrove? Am I to understand that you are buying Clayton McGhee's farm with June Colegrove as your agent? I find that hard to believe, Mr. Jeffries. Why on earth would he sell it?"

Peter thought Marjorie might cry. He'd never seen her act anything other than calm and efficient. As a teenager he had thought her beautiful and always accompanied his father on any errand that might take him to the courthouse in hopes of seeing her. Now, nearing 60, she was still slim and attractive, even if she'd lost her youthful appearance.

"As they say, Miss Lane, every man has his price."

She shook her head. "But you just said you hadn't worked out a price yet."

"That's correct," he replied calmly, hoping to defuse the situation. "But I'm willing to spend whatever it takes. As for Mr. McGhee, I have it on sound authority he has a business venture in Chicago for which he needs the capital. I would suspect further he is seizing such an opportunity for the sake of his family. Living out there cannot have been easy for such people."

She laced her fingers on the counter and took a deep breath. He could see her control her breathing as the cross that hung on its bright gold chain rose and fell. "It was not *made* easy for them, as you may know. With all the work they have put in I just can't believe this. It's over thirty years they've been out there. And what's more, I've known June since he was a boy. I . . . I was close to his father. But I must warn you he's not a reliable man."

"I appreciate your candor Miss Lane, but I can assure you – "

197

She put up her hand to stop him. "Let me show you." She went to one of the tall file cabinets at the back of the office, opened the top drawer, picked across the tabs until she found the one she wanted. The drawer closed with a sharp click. From the file she drew two papers which she presented for his inspection. As he began to study them she said, "The first one, from fourteen years ago, shows that one-third of the purchase price was put up by June's grandfather. The other, dated just last year, indicates that he borrowed against the house. Two thousand eight hundred dollars. Of which he owes . . . .hold on," she rummaged in a different file on her desk, "twenty one hundred dollars."

"How would you know that? That's the bank's business."

"It would be were he not in arrears. June hasn't made a payment in six months. The paperwork came in last week. They're putting a lien on the house for lack of payment. Now, Mr. Jeffries, you know I'm not one to involve myself in other people's business. But something seems amiss here. I'll start a file for the McGhee sale if you'd like, but I can't put a lien on the Colegrove house."

Peter leaned against the counter. He had no idea what to do now. Marjorie was right. There was no use in arguing. Imagination had gotten the best of him; he'd wanted so badly to be part of the interurban project, to make a name for himself as an investor in the future. And now a picture-taking drunk thought he could swindle him out of his money.

"We shall see about that," he said aloud.

"Pardon?" Marjorie replied.

"Nothing. Look, I've decided to clear a few things up before I do anything official. I'll stop back when I've gotten everything sorted out. I thank you for your time."

"It's my pleasure, Mr. Jeffries. Best of luck."

On the way back to his office he realized he needed a drink. He also needed to talk to Colegrove as soon as possible.

Not finding June at home or at the photography studio, which was closed, he had a good idea where he might be. He almost didn't recognize him, hewing low to his drink at the far end of the bar, busy with men just off their shift at the railroad depot. It stank of stale tobacco and grease. He was careful not to touch anyone. As he made his way through the crowded bar he saw Reg, who had recognized him and was holding up a small snifter. Peter tipped his hat and nodded and Reg reached to the top shelf of the bottles along the mirror for the good brandy. The lawyer wedged himself in a tight space next to June. Reg set the snifter on a napkin. June's hand crept slowly across the polished wood for the glass, like a cat stalking meadow mice. Peter snatched it up before he could reach it. Perched on the bar's edge, chin resting on his fist, he turned to the brandy's owner.

"Jesus Christ, I can't go any fucking place without seeing you." Then, in mock bravado, "Sir, have you been hired to shadow my movements?"

"I came here to check – "

"I read a Wilkie Collins novel that started out this way," he said, interrupting him.

"As I was saying, I came here to check on *our* business proposition."

"Good novel. Gripping. If memory serves, though, the chap who I most identified with came to a grisly end."

Peter sipped his brandy, which was excellent.

"I hope your trip out to see McGhee was a success?"

There were shouts and the sound of a chair turned over from the direction of a card game in the far corner. Men hushed conversations then craned their necks to see about the commotion. It ended as quickly as it began and the room resumed its hum.

June tapped the bar with a forefinger knuckle. "Ah, business. Yes. Well, I'll tell you, it was touch and go out there. McGhee was damn angry you only offered half of what he'd asked for. I thought he'd run me off his property or do me some harm. What he called you I will not repeat. I can say that it was aimed not only at you but your entire family."

Peter laughed. "I've been insulted before. I'd be worried if it were otherwise. You want a brandy?" He gestured at Reg with his glass. The barman produced an identical snifter, sluiced in a measure of brandy, and set it in front of Peter who pushed it over.

June put both hands around it as if warming them. Then he took a gulp, sucking air between his teeth. He said, "I have to be straight with you. McGhee is getting cold feet. I think the whole deal is falling apart."

Peter acted as though he were crestfallen. "No. That is terrible news." He wondered how Colegrove would try to play this out.

"I know. But I have an idea." He sat up, swayed on the stool, searched his pockets but did not find what he was looking for.

"I'm all ears."

"When he was running you down and saying some pretty awful things about your father, it occurred to me that he needed to be taught a lesson. If something were to take him down a notch and put some fear into him, well, then I think he would change his tune."

"What have you got in mind?"

June beckoned Peter closer and said in his ear, "Burn down his barn. Send a clear message. Get out or your house, with perhaps your family sleeping in it, is next."

Peter extricated himself from the handhold on his jacket. He took another drink while June drained his off in a single long swallow. He could guess what Colegrove was playing at. Something personal or a new angle on the money. Burning down McGhee's barn, though, was an idea he was surprised not to have entertained himself. Regardless of the drunk's motives, Peter saw an opening. With his property burned and his family threatened McGhee would surely seize the opportunity to sell and move.

Lost in his thoughts, Peter felt a finger poke him in the chest.

"And I know precisely the men to do it."

"Acquainted with a band of ruffians, are you?"

"No," June replied with a cocksure smile, "but you are."

Peter Jeffries belonged to a shadowy organization formed by men who had tired of the way the county was being run. They had been shut out of the group Peter's father had founded, comprising wealthy merchants, bankers, and factory owners – which controlled much of the commerce and most of the local political offices. The Chamber, as that group was called, operated at the highest levels, making sure any new business, any expansion of public services, conformed to their idea of progress. Their methods only extended to violence when they felt it absolutely necessary. This frustrated men with little patience, whose desire for results was made even keener by inaction. The precipitating event occurred when a stranger ran over a little boy and killed him on Main Street. The law would not satisfy them. The Chamber would not force the sheriff to give the man up. This group of vigilantes locked Colegrove in a cell, took the man to the edge of town and hung him by the canal. These men called themselves the Horse Thief Detective Association after a national organization of the same name. Dissatisfied with Charles Colegrove's idea of the law and unable to interest the Chamber in backing their acts of open aggression, they would act on their own.

Peter became a member soon after his son Henderson was born. His marriage had been happier then. Annabelle was temperate and mostly cheerful, they had nice friends and a vibrant social life; their parties were the talk of the town. But times began to change. At home, his wife began taking nerve tonics, then moved on to more intoxicating substances, prescribed and not. Domestic strife was soon mirrored by societal friction. There had always been immigrants who found their way west, came down the canal, settled where there was work and land. But now LaFayette was growing fast and the new population was almost exclusively foreign. Peter had no use for his father's clubby approach to politics and business. He was determined to be a force in shaping his town and the county.

When he was invited to join the HTDA he accepted with the zeal of a man who felt certain he had it all figured out.

Peter was no fool, but he was out of options. Any chance of simply going to McGhee to lay it all out for him was gone the minute he sent June out there. So when June suggested the HTDA for the barn burning, Peter was pleased with himself for his ability to think two moves ahead.

"Yes," he had replied, "I do know the fellows for the job. And you're going to join them."

Eighteen

Henderson Jeffries sat on the soft curve of the bathtub's edge and tried to remember how to tie the knot. The length of silk appeared dark blue in the light of the high window, its distended caterpillar shape wryly hinting at the wings of a butterfly. There had been a lesson conducted without patience. Henderson had contributed to its superficiality by answering every question of technique too hastily with "yes sir." His mind had been elsewhere, lost in a complex scenario involving a riverside greensward, a blanket, and the imagined flesh of Betsy Hansen. Now his attention was firmly on the tie and the dim memory of his father's explicit instructions. Any minute the front door would slam and he would have to descend the stairs bearing his insufficiency.

Better to get it over with.

In the kitchen he aimed a halfhearted "good morning" at his mother, who leaned against the frame of the back door, blowing smoke through the screen where the warm breeze disposed of it. She angled her head until it touched the molding, looking into the yard where the lilacs waved at the edge of the herringboned brick walk that curved out under high oaks. Her patterned housecoat, aqua satin with pink and orange flowers, vaguely oriental, advertised a cheer unendorsed by the tangle of her red hair.

To his surprise, breakfast was arranged tidily in serving bowls on the table, the smell of coffee almost obscuring the acrid tang of the thin cigarette. There was bacon, scrambled eggs, sliced tomatoes, half-moons of muskmelon; the toast had even been cut, buttered, and neatly stacked. It was the spruceness of the setting that gave him pause. The leap of imagination it took to square the woman standing in the doorway with such a spread announced some design. She had prepared this for him, the props for a scene staged in anticipation of whatever his father had in store later on. If persuading her husband to let their son make up his own mind had failed – if she had even bothered to make the attempt – then all that remained was to influence the outcome by other means. If he was right she would play her customary role as The Poet Queen, ever the contrary to his father, who was typecast as The Bully King.

Henderson was uncertain about what specific paternal plot, and what maternal counter-plot, had been prepared for him, but he knew the genre. It never wavered.

"You know he can still smell it, even if you blow it out there."

Henderson took a plate from the cupboard and filled it with toast, three servings of eggs, and bacon, crispy the way he liked it. She was a good cook, though it was hard to imagine her holding her attention to such a mundane task.

"When lilacs last in the dooryard bloomed," she said, her voice catching, the last word graveled out. She coughed and to suppress this took a deep drag, blew more smoke through the screen.

"Long live the Queen," he mumbled through his food.

"What?"

He swallowed egg, poured cold milk from the pitcher, made a show of sniffing the air.

"I said, I don't smell lilacs."

She tried on a smile, then took it off again.

"You know as much about poetry as you do about life."

He responded in the flat intonation of a schoolroom recitation: "In Whitman's masterful elegy, blooming lilacs represent death, while the drooping western star suggests Venus – "

"You see, right there, you think you are mocking the teacher, but you are missing the seriousness of what the poet is saying. It's not a mere elegy for a murdered president. It's urgent. It's about regret, about missing opportunities."

"Mother, I'm sixteen. What do you expect me to do? Run away to France? Marry an old widow for her money?"

"This is a warning to you to be mindful of the decisions you make."

"I'm eating breakfast, wearing my best suit, you recite poetry, I'm now at some precipice. This is worse than school."

She turned from the door, blew smoke out of the downturned corner of her mouth vaguely toward the screen.

"I'm afraid I can already see him in you, appearing one Jeffries feature at a time. Sixteen is old enough to start knowing the difference."

He forced himself to eat, knowing that if he did not he would be sick later and couldn't afford it on a day like today. The bacon had no taste. He looked at it, but it was just bacon. Blameless, symptomatic. So many things ruined by moments like this.

"What diff – "

"You would never do any of those things. Some day you'll realize that men live in a fantasy put before them by other men. Their tragedy is not to notice, their comedy not to care."

"And women?" He had heard this one before, with variations, and knew it was better to help get to the end of it.

"Their tragedy to care, their comedy to pretend not to notice."

"Their farce?"

"When they are alone, and say to themselves that they are free to do as they wish."

"What does that have to do with Whitman?"

She turned her eyes on him and Henderson thought she

would smile, offering a bridge over which he might cross some of the way towards her. But her lips registered nothing. Her expression allowed him no ingress, no fellow feeling.

"Desire. He's the poet of desire, and of love without regard."

"Without regard to what? I don't have anything against love. In fact, once I get out of this suit – "

"That is *not* the kind of desire I mean, and don't change the subject like a stupid schoolboy. I mean without regard for what others think or expect of us."

The fierceness of her tone caused him to look beyond the kitchen to the hall to see if his father stood there in the gloom quietly listening, the unacknowledged interlocutor invoked by her words.

"If you are trying to warn me about something, you might just say what it is."

She smoked and let this opening close without comment.

He reached to the sideboard for the coffee, poured it into a china cup, added sugar. His mother opened the screen door with the toe of her shoe and flicked the snipe of the cigarette neatly into the bushes. She came into the kitchen and took his plate from the table, scraped it into the trash bin and left it on the white enamel shelf next to the sink for the woman who came in later to do the cleaning.

"The bacon was excellent," he said, blowing on the surface of his coffee.

"Is that why you only ate one piece? Could you at least try to be honest about the goddamn breakfast food?"

He looked at his coffee, hoped it wouldn't taste like ashes. She was bad today, worse than she'd been in some while. She straddled a chair and sat looking at him. Her eyes were ringed with dark circles. When she blinked, slowly and deliberately, it looked painful. All simple things required effort.

"What's keeping him, do you think?" Henderson asked. Not, certainly, a neutral subject, but a different one.

"I have no idea, but you can bet that if he's late there will not be a smile on his face when he comes through the door. And if there is it will not survive his notice of the tie you are wearing."

He was surprised she remembered this detail. In his pocket was the bow tie and knotted around his neck, for all the good it would do him, was a recent birthday gift from his aunt.

"How much do you know about what we're doing today?"

She kept her head still as if posing it, leaned forward so that her chin came lightly to rest on the top of the straight-backed chair.

"Very little," she replied. "The *affairs* of your father are best left mysterious. I've been reliably informed that they are none of my business."

On the other side of the house a door slammed, followed by the reverberating steps of a determined gait. Peter Jeffries understood perfectly his ability to effect an entrance, to project himself into places to which he had not yet arrived. He strode confidently across the living room secure in the knowledge that his wife and son would have stopped what they were doing, acquiescent to his presence and its demands before he set foot in the room with them.

"How is everyone on this fine morning?" he asked, bursting through the swinging door. In the immediate silence, the hinge protested with a croak, then subsided. On his face, to his family's surprise, was a smile below his thick waxed mustache.

Henderson drained the last of his coffee, his mother having returned to the frame of the back door at his father's approach, leaning there, preparing the room for him.

"Well, are you two still asleep or what?"

"Please stop picking the goddamn flowers in front."

His father did indeed have a just-opened red rose in the buttonhole of his lapel. He ceremoniously bent his head, grasped the fabric between thumb and edge of forefinger, and inhaled deeply.

"By any other name, my dear, even a blasphemous one, it still smells sweet."

He looked at his son, furrows appearing on his brow.

"Why are you wearing that tie? Where's the bow I told you to wear?"

"I thought Aunt Tessa would be pleased to see me wearing my birthday present," he lied.

"You *thought*," he shook his head, reaching over and pulling the knot of the tie down, wrenching it and the boy's neck, forcing Henderson to put his hands on the table edge to keep from hitting it with his face. He felt the tie slip around the collar, silk hissing on starched cotton, then pull free, releasing him. Peter folded the tie neatly and set it in front of him on the tablecloth.

"Now, get up there and put on the tie I laid out for you. And do it quickly." He spoke in a low voice, his anger coming under control, and now the smile returned. Henderson pushed the chair back and got up to do as he said. His mother said nothing, stood leaning still, arms crossed, her eyes fixed on him. The only movement that betrayed her feelings was a slight shake of the head.

"Tessa," his father spat, as he poured himself a cup of coffee.

He managed the knot, but it took some time to get the wings even. He was beginning to sweat, and he could not help but imagine his father looking up through the ceiling, muttering to himself. The phrase "fearful symmetry" kept running through his head and he wished his mother had not started up with the poetry this morning. It was, he reassured himself, better than some of the alternatives.

Downstairs in the now quiet kitchen, his father grasped him by the shoulders, rooted him in place, and adjusted the tie. As Henderson knew he would. He tried to hold his breath but could not, and smelt the grown-up staleness, cloying cigar sweetness, that he so hated. It was conspiring with his breakfast to make him sick.

Annabelle Jeffries had grown up in Philadelphia and in the wake of quiet left by the departure of her husband and son was reminded how strange this part of the country still seemed to her. The Middle West was like the middle ages, she figured. It had been of necessity invented by the East, as the medieval had been by the Renaissance, as a more primitive place, mired in religion and habitually violent, so that bankers in New York and newspaper men in Boston and Baltimore would have something to define themselves against. She couldn't be sure about the age before Shakespeare and Spenser, but she was certain that this part of the country held a fundamental brutality. She was afraid for her son and his entry into its inner sanctum. He was running out of time. They were all running out of time.

Her father, like her husband's father, had been a banker. Until she was twelve they lived in Chestnut Hill in a large Queen Anne on a street with others like it. There were many children of or near her age and she had two sisters. Her childhood was a time into which little alteration came to interrupt the pleasant flow of days. When her father's bank went under they held on for a summer but by the time the leaves began to turn they had moved into the city into a small apartment above a hardware store on Panama Street near Rittenhouse Square. That summer under the enveloping elms everything stayed the same for the last time. When she was grown up, Annabelle often drifted back to those final days before her sister and mother died and the family came undone.

She tried not to think about what her husband was getting Henderson involved in. If she stayed in the house there would be no avoiding it. She changed into a light dress, dropped a few essentials into her purse, and took an umbrella from the stand on her way out. On Main Street between Seventh and Eighth she stopped to watch through a smudged window a jeweler's fingers burnish a tarnished length of silver chain. There was dust everywhere. It could well have been a museum in which a lonely figure toiled at his precious metals in a room without time, there being no end to the work of removing what air and elements could do. The dust was perhaps lapidary, the cast-off of gems and scoured metal, the residue the emery left in smoothing a ring or perfecting a clasp. Or it had settled over the years where no hand cared to disturb it. Where such dust might come from she had no idea. She considered tapping the glass to see if the scene would change, but thought it better to walk away and wonder whether it ever would.

Down the block short of the corner was a shop that made photographic portraits and sold various prints and paintings. Annabelle never understood why people would allow themselves to be displayed this way, their families made into advertisement. In the window a faded print of two men squared up in a roped ring caught her eye, the almost motion of it, the sense of symmetry of strong arms poised to inflict pain and the stillness the camera had caught. She got as close to the glass as she could and made out shouting backers with round mouths and black hats, the din rising in the theater of her mind. And though the jeering, shrieking men called for blood, the echoes rattling her inner glass, she held her fighters still and made the punters suffer.

If it were just her and the windows in the world she would have confessed to being content. There were things you could control and things you couldn't. That was easy to conclude. There was no arguing that a choice lay there for the taking, but she knew that even this separation of the multifold into two discrete ways of acting was a feat she would never accomplish. It had always been this way. At least it seemed so. It was possible this was a result of the deaths she had experienced at such an early age but when she untangled the skein of her life and drew her attention back to those years she could not find a thread where it was otherwise.

She was startled by a child pulling a clacking toy on a long string, running along the sidewalk past her. He glanced at her all smiles and tiny perfect teeth in a little sailor outfit just like Henderson had worn. Oh, Peter had hated that blue and white get-up with its beribboned hat and made a face of disapproval every time he saw his son in it. Which had been often. Annabelle remembered the raucous laugh her friend Frances unleashed when she told her that never had a woman gotten so much enjoyment out of a sailor without catching something.

Where was Frances now? She could not say. Christmas cards had come back unopened two years in a row, stamped Return to Sender, and so she stopped sending them.

On the little boy ran, his mother trailing him with a swaddled baby in a pram. She crossed the street and at the slanted bookcart browsed the spines to see if there was anything of interest. A book on beekeeping, a thin Guide to Vincennes, several outdated almanacs, a well-thumbed Bible with a thin leather cover foxed by rain or devotional tears, a French primer. Her sister had loved books. Loved them like they were some miracle greater than words on a page. How many times had she sat and watched Rachel read, riveted by the drama that possessed her. There was a witchcraft at work in that girl when a book was in her eyes.

Without making a purchase she continued down Main, crossing Fourth as the streetcar passed, slowing across from the Courthouse. Impulsively she hurried forward and boarded the car as the conductor clanged the bell. She paid her fare and took a seat near the back. Among the handful of passengers she noticed a woman in a stylish business suit reading a book which she annotated with a pencil.

Annabelle wondered why someone would do that.

211

At the last stop before the bridge she moved up two rows, close enough to see her making marginal notes, underlining an occasional word or phrase, but not close enough to identify the book. As they crossed the bridge she had a clear view downriver. A barge laden with wooden crates had cast off from its moorings and was straightening out into the current. In the distance a sternwheeler was disappearing around a bend which made it look as though it were plowing into the trees to continue on land to its destination. The woman did not take advantage of the view or even raise her face into the pleasant breeze that kicked up over the water. The route took them across the river onto the levee, up State Street hill, continuing on State to the University. She looked too old to be a student. When she got up Annabelle did too, following her through a gate and across the grass beneath a line of shade trees that ran along one edge of an open square. On three sides were brick buildings, students pouring out of one of them, pooling around benches and the lawn in small groups, many lighting cigarettes. One performed a mockery of a cartwheel to a chorus of laughter from his fellows. The woman with the book tucked it into her shoulder bag and made a bee line through the grass toward the far building on the square, ignoring the paved walk. Annabelle did her best to feign nonchalance though she felt conspicuous treading the virgin green mere steps from a perfectly serviceable path. Despite living only a few miles away she had never been on the campus grounds. Undetected she reached the building just behind her quarry, the door whispering closed. Without a plan of action she went inside and as her eyes adjusted saw her ascending the broad stairway. Annabelle took the stairs as quickly as she could and was out of breath by the time she reached the second floor. Light spilled from the fourth office on the left. By the shadow cast into the hall it was clear someone was inside.

The floorboards squeaked. She was reading the placard

next to the door – Paola Benvoglio, Instructor of Latin and Romance Languages – when an accented voice said, "come in." The woman was reaching for a book on a shelf above her head and had her back to the door. When she turned and saw Annabelle in the doorway she said, "Oh, I thought it was a student. Is there something I can do for you? Are you lost?"

In the uncomfortable silence Annabelle thought of all the things she would like to say about poetry, about the books and articles she had read, about her desire for conversation and a connection to a world of words. There was no place to begin and she was afraid she would not be able to leave off if she got started. She turned and fled the way she had come, walking as quickly as she could down the stairs and out into the bright sunshine. From the grass of the square she stopped and looked back at the brick building, searching the line of second floor windows. She saw nothing but the reflection of the clear blue sky.

They got into the buggy and Peter took up the reins, clicking the bay into a walk. Independence Day was two days away and the street was festooned with banners. The sun was already making for a hot day and Henderson put a finger in his collar to let some air in. They turned from Ferry Street, where they lived, onto Fourth Street, passing along the courthouse square. Workmen in slouch hats swept the sidewalks and clipped bushes along the wrought iron fence where another crew was applying black paint over the rust. It would get crowded with people coming in from the county and surrounding areas to see the fireworks and hear the bands play. The men would filter into the taverns while the women kept the children, talking amongst themselves, those from further out in their finest, glad for the company. The oldest son, if there was one, would later be sent to find his father, to drag him by any means necessary back to his family so that they might set off and get to bed at a decent hour.

There would be work to do on the fifth. Many of these boys were met with rough treatment and returned crying back to their mother, who was obliged to enter the tavern herself, causing men to turn away or at least avert their glances, until she found the elbow of her husband and he drained his mug, shrugging off the touch and then following as though he'd only then decided he'd had enough.

They continued on past the State Bank on the corner of Fourth and Columbia, a solid block of squat limestone, where on the sidewalk three men in brown suits stood talking and smoking. The buggy stopped abruptly. Henderson held the horse while his father jumped down, greeted the men, one of whom wore a small inscribed gold bar over his breast pocket. The bank manager. Peter shook hands and put his arm around the smaller man, his pale skin pocked like the inside of an orange peel. He was saying something animated. The bank manager and the third man, older, as nondescript as that age of man always is to someone of Henderson's years, leaned in, beginning to laugh well before the punchline. Using his free arm to accentuate the story he had the men doubled over and roaring in under a minute. His son timed it with his watch. He noticed that the smaller man laughed less, eventually twisting out of what was now an uncomfortable position beneath his father's prodigious arm. Back in the buggy a merrier Peter Jeffries pulled a handkerchief out of an inside pocket, blew his nose and dabbed his eyes. He slapped his son on the back and told him to drive on.

At Alabama Street they pulled up in front of a wide brick building of recent construction, the bricks and mortar still bright and unoxidized. It had a long, shallow roof line, like a barn pressed down, and extended back from the street for a hundred feet or so. A door on the right side appeared to lead into the office portion, where there were windows and a hitching rail, the rest of the front taken up by massive sliding doors that allowed large wagons to move in and out of the interior. The sign over the office said LaFayette Tent and Awning, Salvatore Cassini, Est. 1877. Cassini was from the little village of Santa Croce in the Val Bregaglia and had married a Swiss woman from over the border in Soglio. In his passion for her he had converted and, in the way of so many apostates, came to regard his cast off faith as an abomination. He was an occasional dinner guest at the house with his wife. Henderson had met them before being sent to eat upstairs. The man had the biggest hands and forearms he'd ever seen, having watched him personally help with the installation of a voluminous canvas tent for a party his father had thrown the previous summer. He wielded a three-pound sledge like a character from a song. Peter had come up behind his son and said in his ear, "Those fucking Italians know how to build, boy. Doesn't matter what it is. Finest masons and craftsmen in the world."

"Go around the corner and up a block and tie up," his father said. "I'll be in the office. Meet me there." His father climbed down, buggy yawing and righting, adjusted his vest, brushed off the seat of his pants as best he could reach and went inside. He tied up under a spreading maple. As he crossed the street and walked along the building his stomach clenched like a fist. He had to stop and take several deep breaths.

Henderson hesitated, not sure whether to knock or go on in. He decided to be bold, aware of himself as on the verge of greater responsibility. The uninhabited office was small but well-lit by large windows, with a pair of cluttered desks, a file cabinet, a gramophone on a stand, and a narrow-bellied stove in the corner. At the far side a door to the interior stood ajar. He waited. Nothing. Perhaps he'd misunderstood. He moved slowly, between the desks covered with papers rife with sketches of polygonal structures, numbers on each side, each angle, vertices calculated, square footage of canvas noted, stakes numbered. He paused to pull the arm

215

of a sophisticated adding machine, the paper tape advancing unmarked. He put his hand on the doorknob and listened, hearing distinctly a murmuring from the larger space beyond, closing his eyes better to make out what sound this was.

Henderson heard a man's voice say "Ah, Jeffries!" and opened the door by reflex, as though he had been called out. The long vaulted room, supported overhead by curved joists of layered, bent timbers, lit by an array of high transom windows, was alive with ghosts.

At the far end of the warehouse, where they stored materials, prepared structures and coverings permanent and transitory, he could make out rolls of canvas, bins containing stacks of wooden poles and slats, coils of rope on wooden spools, a rack of stakes. Milling around the center surrounding an unhitched flatbed wagon were several dozen forms in white, appearing headless in the gloom. Suddenly torches were lit in the wings and two men mounted the wagon up steps set against the back, fixing them into holes drilled into its deck, four in all. These cast a yellow, flickering light revealing men standing in small groups dressed in white, bareheaded, talking to one another quietly. Some were smoking and passing around a bottle. He tried to make out his father but could not. He tried to retreat back into the office but could not tear himself away.

One of the white forms detached itself and came toward him. He moved to the frame of the door and stood with one hand on it. Peter Jeffries did not look pleased to see his son and upon reaching him put a hand on his shoulder and spun him through the door, nearly knocking him down and then nearly falling on him as he stumbled over the threshold.

"Goddamnit what did I tell you? To *wait in the office.*" He composed himself, straightened his robes over his suit, adjusting his collar. He looked down at the toes of his black shoes, one of which was scuffed badly in front.

"Take off your tie."

216

He did as he was told.

"Now give it to me and turn around. You will at least *pretend* to be surprised at the appropriate moment if you know what's good for you." He tied the bow tie firmly over his son's eyes, spreading it in front so that it did not allow him to see under it.

Henderson was turned back around and felt his father's hands on his shoulders from behind. His voice whispered, "Now you see why Tessa's stupid present was insufficient. Lousy for blindfolding."

Nineteen

The murmuring stopped. It reminded Henderson of the subsiding of crickets as you walk through the woods in the evening, a quietus near and a chorus further away. He had no idea how far he'd been marched, but after a minute or so could hear the guttering of torches. A hand on his shoulder guided him until he was stopped and his father's voice said "Step up." He did so tentatively, ascending until the voice said "Stand still." He did, wondering if he were at the edge of the wagon, not wanting to take a misstep and fall face first to the ground.

A few paces in front of him a man cleared his throat. His voice was pulpit clear and piercing, a tenor if he had sung it.

"Brothers. Welcome. This morning we gather for one of our most solemn rites. The choosing and initiating of a new member is the very wellspring of our organization. We cannot survive without new blood. My brothers, there are many who use the word *vigilante* as a term of vilification, preferring to ignore what an organization such as ours does in the public, Christian good. Without us the citizens of this county would be at the mercy of the government, who neither knows our interests nor cares, given that it is rife with the corruption of Jews, niggers, and agents of the Pope. Here in our county seat we see it every day: Catholic policemen, a Jew on the city council. Those of you who've been up to Chicago and seen the tenements . . . I ask you, is this what you want? Is this what the good people of our county deserve?"

Massed voices rose in agreement.

"What some people forget is that we have chosen to stand

vigilant against forces that would drive us from our way of life. In our work we must fight a constant battle against these forces. I come to you today to remind you to be strong. I can see by your numbers that you are so and are intent on remaining so. I have been asked to perform the initiation ritual, so that your leader can stand by his son and perform the rites properly. Let us begin."

There was a shuffling of feet and a shushing of cloth. Something heavy clumped the deck of the wagon, which pitched slightly. A hand on Henderson's back gently pushed him and he took two cautious steps. He could feel the void in front of him. Fingers searched the back of his head for the knot. He braced himself, gritting his teeth as with the rough untying of the blindfold came some of his hair. Then he saw only a wash of yellow light, white below and dark above, resolving slowly as he blinked it away. He resisted the urge to rub his eyes. Like a boy would, he thought.

Below him lay a sea of white, like spilled milk on a table, each man wearing a hood cut with oval eyeholes, peaked at the top. Their white robes bore an insignia on each man's left breast and what looked like a word embroidered below it which he could not make out. Someone turned him to face what appeared to be an altar, a cross set in gold on the side facing him. There were two hooded men on the stage, one barrel-chested and tall, who he knew immediately to be his father, and the other shorter, slimmer. Henderson could now see that the insignia was a red shield on which a figure in a white robe sat a rearing horse while wielding what looked like a burning cross. The horse, he noticed, was also robed and hooded. Below this were four letters, but the angle of his father's jutting chest made them hard to see. The first letter was H, but then he could not be sure. Henderson flinched as the slender man began speaking loudly from the altar, unrolling a piece of parchment which he ceremoniously removed from the sleeve of his robe.

"We are called here today by the bond and oath of our association for the most sacred performance of the swearing in of a new member." He opened a large Bible to a place marked by a cross made of sticks.

"The Book of Lamentations says: "Thou has seen all their vengeance and all their imaginations against me; thou hast heard their reproach, O Lord; the lips of those that rose up against me, and their device against me all the day. Behold their sitting down, and their rising up; I am their *music*. Render up to them a *recompense*, O Lord, according to the work of their hands. Give them sorrow of heart, thy curse unto them. Persecute and destroy them in anger from under the heavens of the Lord."

"Amen."

The hoods all nodded and repeated the word. He licked a finger and turned the pages, this time stopping where the pink ribbon sewn into the binding held the place.

"Thus sayeth the Book of Ezekiel: "Make a chain: for the land is full of bloody crimes, and the city is full of violence. Wherefore I will bring the worst of the heathen, and they shall possess their houses: I will also make the pomp of the strong to cease; and their holy places shall be defiled. Destruction cometh; and they shall seek peace, and *there shall be none*."

In unison the men put their right hands over their hearts, palms on the shield with the horse and its hooded rider, and then assembled into orderly rows. This they had clearly practiced, as the men in front were shorter while those in back taller, the columns rising as they receded. Each peaked hood with its cutouts framed eyes glistening in the torchlight higher than the one before.

The slim man turned to Henderson.

"Place your hand on the Bible."

He raised his right arm, stiff from holding it rigidly for so long, and took a step forward, placing it on the closed book.

"The other hand, son," the man said in a whisper. He

220

quickly changed hands, as though playing a child's game of handslap.

"Now raise your right hand and repeat after me."

Henderson was asked to repeat an oath of loyalty that required him to forsake the world of selfishness and alienation and emigrate to the delectable bonds of the Association. Would he defend his race, his nation, his religion, and his way of life against any and all who came against it? Would he? He decided to reply more resolutely. I will, he said, plighting what troth he had, certain that this invitation to the world of grown men was the means to leaving boyhood. As he repeated the words and replied his affirmations he saw the letters clearly now: HTDA.

He had no idea what these stood for and ran the acronym through his mind to no avail. Hoosier Defense . . . no, wrong order. Home Truth Defenders . . . no, too abstract. It was not until the final step of the ritual that he found out.

"And so I pronounce you a provisional member of the Horse Thief Detective Association."

It took several seconds for the words to sink in.

I would never, Henderson thought, have guessed that.

The man then took the cross he had used as a bookmark and lit it at one of the torches, holding it carefully above his head and waving it flaming at the crowd in their robed lines, whereupon they each touched their shoulders and said "In body," then their foreheads and said "In mind," then waved their hand in a circular motion over their head and said "In spirit," and then with both hands made a circle at waist level and said "In life."

He held the burning cross aloft again and asked, "Is there any man in this posse comitatus who will not accept this new member?"

A hushed silence. Henderson, hand still on the Bible, its leather cover slick with the sweat of his palm, wondered how long he would wait, hoping that the silence would not provoke someone to raise an objection. The cross was extinguished with a hiss, the man dropping it in an unseen container behind the altar. He turned to the new provisional member.

"Welcome to the posse," he said.

After they congratulated him, shaking his hand and saying "Welcome" or "Glad to have you aboard," the white-robed figures moved to the back where the stored rolls of canvas allowed them a place to sit as they disrobed and straightened out their clothes, smoothed down hair, put hats back on. Henderson noticed that all manner of men were present. As they filed back by twos and threes to the stage area, he could see some in suits, others in farm clothing or worker's togs, cleaned and pressed but worn, clothes worked in and not wardrobe hung. A few men he knew. The grocer from the little store over on Salem Street, Yeager the druggist. There was the doctor who shared the office with his mother's doctor, who wore a solemn black suit and string tie and had bushy sideburns and a thick, waxed gray mustache in the old style. Each time he saw the man Henderson thought of pictures of U.S. Grant at the surrender table at Appomattox, chair pushed back, leaning on one elbow. He'd look fine on a piece of money, he once said to his mother as they walked to the apothecary after one of her visits.

His father instructed him to sit on the edge of the stage while men went to another part of the building and began bringing in folding chairs which they formed into circles. Peter Jeffries went to the office, poked his head in and stood back as Cassini emerged and they began talking. Chairs assembled, the men broke up their little groups in which they had been conversing, some quietly and some with back-slapping animation, ribaldry there by the sound of the laughter. His father returned with Cassini and Henderson jumped down and greeted the Italian who offered his enormous hand with a toothy smile.

"We go to groups now, eh?" he said in his accented English, giving Henderson's shoulder a final squeeze.

"What do I do?" he asked, feeling it safe to venture a question.

"The circles each have a task in the larger association, and you'll be assigned to one of them soon, when you're a full member. For now, you'll come with me to the executive circle and listen."

For the next two hours Henderson sat in the circle listening attentively to the business of the leadership. He had always wondered what went on when his father was away, what grown men did together that drew them so willingly from family and home. Now he was seeing right into it. His father had shown faith in him and Henderson was not about to let him down.

When the meeting was over Henderson brought the wagon around. "What say we take a spin up towards Five Points and see what there is to see up that way?" his father asked.

"That sounds fine," he replied. Henderson could not remember seeing his father in such good humor in a very long while, perhaps not since he was kitted out to go on a hunting trip to the Upper Peninsula of Michigan. On the morning of his father's departure Henderson woke up at three o'clock unable to sleep. Wandering downstairs he found him at the kitchen table cleaning one of his English bird guns, running a round patch of felt through the bore with a steel rod. His father had smiled at his son's appearance and, humming quietly to himself, went about his task contentedly. Henderson poured a glass of milk and pulled out a chair, sat down, drank it slowly. They did not exchange a word. The son was glad to be near his father in his happiness, the aura of his pleasure encompassing him. They sat on as the grandfather clock in the hallway chimed its metallic toll. Peter rubbed the gun thoroughly with an old diaper oiled by use, bringing a deep luster to the bluing of the barrels, then another diaper with linseed oil for the stock. Henderson was shaken awake by his mother hours later, the sun up and streaming through the kitchen window, birds going in the lilacs, having fallen asleep beneath the table curled around the pedestal. His father was gone, far across the state line by then.

On the left they passed the jail. Made of bricks and rough-cast it squatted low and silent, its narrow windows barred and opaque. As if the light had no business there. At South Street they turned right, the horse coming around obediently to its master's "Gee now, Ruth," short for Rutherford, a chestnut gelding they'd had since a colt. Though his father constantly complained about them – their decisions foreign and domestic, taxes, lax immigration policies – he liked presidents. They passed buckboards from the county laden with produce, straw, manure, pigs caged and grunting headed for the slaughterhouses at the foot of Union Street on the canal near the gas works. There were smart phaetons, black lacquer and brass, a coach bringing travelers in on the road from Indianapolis or Fort Wayne, its driver laboring to keep the horses in check. Henderson resisted the urge to yell over to ask where they were in from. He had done this with his friends many times as they'd loitered along South or Main on a Saturday. Occasionally they got a Louisville or Champaign. Or they would walk across the bridge to Chauncey Village and wait for the Chicago coach, trying for a look at the passengers, most passing through to the capital or to points south, coaxing the occasional penny out of a gloved hand.

They crossed over Fifth Street and the rail tracks, the horse stepping gingerly. Here were row houses of brick and limestone and a scattering of older timber-framed homes that had not burned down or been bought up and replaced by the money that dominated this part of town. Mostly now there were the big Victorians and Queen Annes: three stories, floor to ceiling double-hung windows and long wrap-around verandas. These were families who owned the businesses around the courthouse square and along the river: breweries, the tannery, shipping and warehouses along the canal, the boiler factory, sawmills, and dry goods stores.

At Seventh Street, stopped at the corner and waiting to enter the stream of traffic, was a beaten-up chaise with a hood of black canvas, like an old umbrella stretched over the two men who sat in its shadow. They wore dark suits and hats, round and shallow-crowned, and had heavy black beards. Henderson could barely see any skin and could not see their eyes at all.

"Interesting," his father said.

"What?"

"The men in that shandrydan. Jews, and out on a Saturday. Must have some reason. Their temple is down there on the left," and he pointed down Seventh. Henderson knew this, had seen it in one of his many forays up this way with his friends, the six-pointed star carved into the limestone above the front doors, wondering what the strange letters meant on the lintel of the oddly-shaped building. His father had warned him years ago to stay away from it, that if he got taken in there he'd never come out. His mother had snorted derisively.

At the intersection with Ninth Street was another set of railroad tracks, the rail bed high-banked to counter the slope, providing a level purchase for the trains that passed along for Richmond, Louisville, Cincinnati. Henderson leaned forward as they crossed to see how far he could see along the twin rails which hove off to the right in a gentle curve. After Ninth Street the climb steepened.

Henderson noticed a crowd of people up ahead below the church. They wore best suits and dresses, the ladies in elaborate hats and lace, crinoline umbrellas up against the sun, the men in top hats, flowers in buttonholes. The women who stood along the first two landings made a bouquet of pinks and yellows, powder blues and creams, even a few violets and one conspicuous in deep burgundy. The black suits gathered round the sidewalk at the bottom of the long set of steps, spilling over the grass and onto the edge of the street.

A wedding. Lined up along the other side of the street, facing downslope in front of the St. Ignatius Academy, Henderson could see the coaches and buggies, a new brougham decked with carnations and crepe streamers, a blanket of bright yellow flowers draped over the horse's back. Most were tied to rails while others were held by smaller boys, each suited and looking resolute in what they found an important job, hoping for a nickel tip.

The bells of the church began to ring, mellifluous through the oaks and elms, the bell tower of St. Mary's impossible to see through the overstory of leaves. When they were ten yards from the group of men furthest out into South Street, Peter aimed Ruth directly at the crowd. One man bent to laugh at the joke of one of his friends then took a step back. The horse missed him but the wheel of the buggy struck him in the hip, sending the hat off his head and knocking him down hard onto the cobbles. He rose quickly, hands clenched into fists, an enraged scowl cutting his face below a dark mustache. His oiled hair was undone and stuck up like raised hackles. The horse paused, sensing the commotion and Peter let the reins go, reached his offside hand into his coat pocket. Henderson wondered why his father would purposefully hit someone. The man pointed his index finger.

"Jeffries, you goddamn son of a bitch." The other men took a step back. Heads turned, the ladies on the stairs squinting beneath their hat brims.

"Why don't you get your ass out of the street, Lanahan." Henderson looked down, saw his father's hand close around something in his pocket.

"You go straight to hell," the man replied, this time with less volume. He rubbed his struck hip. "I will not," he drew out slowly, "sully my niece's wedding by thrashing the likes of you, which I could do and you damn well know it."

226

"Come and try if you'd like to get peppered. I'd be happy to let all the blood out of that red face of yours."

There was movement through the crowd along the stairs as people were jostled and made way for someone. At the lower landing the ladies moved aside and a priest in black cassock and white surplice stood at the top step. His fine, sandy blonde hair wisped up in a tangle, as though he'd just taken off a wool sweater. He surveyed the scene. Two men locked on one another. Violence in the air. The man who had so much practice separating bloody-nosed boys across the way in the play lot of the St. Ignatius Academy raised his voice to the assembled.

"Gentlemen, please." Though slight of build, Father Bernard knew he had a voice that made people listen. He had trained it to effect what his appearance could not.

"Bride and groom will be out here any minute and I ask that you not send them on their life's journey with such poor behavior." Neither man moved nor looked up at him. So Father Bernard did what he so often did across the street, beyond the arrayed carriages in the playground beneath the climbable though forbidden limbs of the ancient white oak.

"Would it not be more fitting to let men whose profession violence *is* settle your dispute? There will be the boxing match Saturday next and we will have all the sport we need then." A murmur from the crowd as heads tilted to whisper to those who did not know, who were few, and those who shared their eager anticipation of a local event of such magnitude. Which the priest wagered would turn the mood of the whole and distract them from the man in the buggy.

And it did. The men closest to Lanahan, one of them his brother, put their hands on his shoulders and he let himself be turned and led up the stairs to where two ladies took his arms. His head swiveled back to regard the figure in the seat of the buggy, still leaning forward in an anticipatory posture.

227

Lanahan saw him slowly take his hand out of his pocket and gather the reins.

"Git up, Ruth. Hah!" Many turned to watch him snap the leather lines and the buggy lurch off up the slope.

Bernard stood thinking of his work across the way at the school, sitting at his desk in the cool quiet beneath the opened sash as down purled the sounds of children's games, of laughter, of surprise, until the moment that came once every week or two of a puncture in the delight. He saw the boys first push each other while the crowd gathered properly, the sounds of their play silenced, focused now on greater sport. They would jockey, testing the other's seriousness, to gauge whether it was to be a test of resolve or something more: honor, a buried hurt, the compelling inner voice of a drunk father or mad uncle, and sometimes that rare frightening occurrence of the love of the fight, the taste of blood in the mouth and the sheer joy of giving way to the deepest instinct. Without sex, Bernard thought, they would find ecstasy only in letting their little bodies go to violence.

When the noise gathered to a melody he would rise, take his polished leather strap off its hook, and go into the play yard. Other men would sigh just now. But he never did, feeling each time a bated anticipation. They always parted smartly for him and he relished the moments before he separated the combatants, flailing often without skill or guile but with everything they had in their spare limbs. When he had them by the backs of their necks the heat always came off them and they breathed and quivered in his hands.

The priest turned aside as Lanahan passed, smelling his anger, noting the perspiration above the band of his high white collar. He smoothed his hair down, interlaced his hands before him and tried to suppress a smile. The consistency of little boys, he thought, pleased with himself. It also occurred to him that he must remember to get a ticket to the match, certain that many at the reception would offer him one gratis, as well as a ride, a meal, perhaps a nip afterwards. Rice flew and there was a shout as the young couple moved crouching out the door and through the crowd, looking confused as to what had been occurring outside but too carried away by the immensity of the day. As they came down the steps he loosened the muscles in his face and fixed them with a grand smile, placing his palms together to bless them as they passed. He was smiling long after they had gotten into the brougham and were driven away.

Truth be told, Father Bernard loved a good fight.

Twenty

With the house emptied of menfolk Annabelle poured herself a cup of coffee and sat on the back step. The day was beginning to build its heat out in the grass, along the bricks of the walk, shimmering across the tarpaper roofs of the houses and outbuildings along the alley. The breeze when it reached her in the shade was warm and florid. She poured the coffee into the bushes. Bitter. She considered saying this out loud. Her father used to talk to himself and it seemed to placate whatever troubles he caused himself when alone.

She had hoped this morning would be different and smiled at entertaining such a thought. In her mind's eye Henderson rode along proudly with his father, into the company of men just like him: overstuffed, haughty, fat-fingered, smelling of talcum and alcohol. Besuited babies all. But dangerous too, and insatiable in their desire to control and possess. She tried to reconstruct her path to this place and, as always, failed. Philadelphia, the leafy college north of Chicago where she had immersed herself in poetry and music before dropping out. Getting pregnant. The cold doctor's office, alone, decisions to make. Then the promises from Peter, notes tucked into bouquets, his sudden arrivals with gifts of silk and silver, a diamond, a woman's thoughts of a big house full of children. A grown woman. What her mother would have been like. Her father's silence. Her unreturned telegrams, telephone calls, carefully plotted letters. The cruelty of a check for a hundred dollars without a note. When Peter seemed relieved that her East Coast people, as he called them, wouldn't be coming to their wedding, she was relieved that he didn't protest. Briskly married, soon a mother, neither friends nor family nearby, the beating heart of the city concealed behind doors open only to convivial company.

Why had he married her? With his family's money he could have paid her off, sent her packing, or shut her out of his life altogether. She suspected his commitment had to do with a desire to strike back at his parents. His failure to do this directly, to provide for himself a measure of independence, found a catalyst in this banker's daughter who understood how to meet and frustrate expectations. Her ability to charm his father and avoid his mother's claws had amazed him, and he saw in her an ally. Dreams of escape and adventure gave way not, she knew, to the necessities of parental duties, but to Peter's own inability to break free of the role into which his family had cast him. Into which he had cast himself, truth be told. His inability became an unwillingness, which he rationalized by blaming his wife and child for his lot in life.

Each day her son grew more like his father which she countered by waging a patient war to win him back. She read countless books to him, kept him at the piano, bought him a cello, brought in a French tutor. Peter scoffed at the books she chose – hefting *Waverley* and joking that at least the boy would build his muscles – held his ears at Henderson's musical efforts, breaking the cello one night when, drunk, he attempted to dance with it. She'd fired the tutor after she found them sitting knee to knee, Peter whispering in her ear. She had not become a poet nor was she playing in an orchestra, but it seemed possible that her son might. This could save her. Something had to.

When Henderson was still a small boy her doctor had prescribed a tonic for her nerves. That this was part of her history she knew but again she could not reconcile it with the years that had passed. She looked at her toes, now in the sun that crept over the roofline. They appeared to her like a girl's toes. They wiggled like a girl's toes. The tonic, the doctor had said, would make her feel like a girl again. But it had not restored her energy or put her in a better mood, nor had it allowed her to wiggle anything with any enthusiasm. It was soon hard to get out of bed. She became unaware of the subtleties of day-to-day life; seasons passed and she found that she had been doing things without thinking. She would go slowly down the stairs to the kitchen and find it a mess, dishes and cutlery piled in the sink, food left to spoil, the icebox bereft of staples. Then she would wake up at the kitchen table having fallen asleep on her arm, unsure of the hour but knowing it late by the terrible silence that fell across the house. The counters and fixtures had been rendered spotless, the whole room so clean that it appeared never to have been used. She was certain a day would come when there would be no need for a draught from one of her bottles, or a few pills in the afternoon, or a little something to help her sleep; but there were always more maladies and for each a remedy that made promises she believed. It was science, wasn't it? Hadn't Byron and Shelley done the same? True, she had stopped writing poems, but she would get the voices to cooperate soon. Any day now. There was plenty of scientific poetry on her nightstand, in fact: Dr. Williams Pink Pills for Pale People, Dalton's Sarsparilla & Nerve Tonic ("A Scientific Combination of the Best Alternatives in the Known World"), Dr. Blendigo's Celery Tonic (Peptonized), Primley's Iron and Wahoo tonic. There were setbacks too. Lillybeck's Tasteless Chill Tonic was neither tasteless nor chilling. Despite the promise that Dr. Williams Pink Pills would cure "all forms of female weakness," the only tangible result was mild constipation. In response the lady at the apothecary had recommended Mull's Grape Tonic whose label touted its ability to "cure constipation." It was only when she was home and her bowels had routed her to the toilet did she read the paper inside that claimed the tonic would "cure constipation permanently." Peter's response to this when he found her asleep in the bathroom was that the Mull's people had a bad business model.

Henderson was either being lost or was lost altogether. He had a quick wit and she was pleased that he'd talked back to her, but there was inevitably a moment when he began to play along. That was not what she wanted though perhaps she was guilty of it herself. This initiation business had been on her mind all week, coming and going when she was sharp enough to know what was nagging at her. Now she felt the full weight of it and realized she ought to jump to her feet and go after them. There would be a riding outfit handy that she could change into, vaguely masculine with a hat she could secure under her chin, a short riding crop, and she would barrel out of the barn on a small fast horse to insert herself into whatever rite was making her son forever his father's little man. She had read a scene exactly like this in a novel. Whose story was she in now? She willed herself to concentrate, to form a realistic plan that gave Henderson a chance. Arguing with him had failed; he wasn't that kind of person and this was something to be glad about. A ray of hope. An opening in which she might exploit the strength her husband thought he held over her. He did hold it over her. But it wasn't herself she was trying to free and she might use this as leverage.

Annabelle was startled by a ferocious knocking at the front door, as if someone was hitting it with a stout cane or a stave. It announced itself through the length of the house and swept the birds from the alabaster bath. She stood up and clutched her dressing gown. Quietly she made her way through the kitchen and down the hall, careful to stay to the wall so that she could not be seen from the narrow window running alongside the door. A shadow blocked the light and she froze, holding herself still and listening for any sign of who it might be. She fought the urge to run to her room and lock the door. There was a barely touched bottle of laudanum in the top drawer of her dresser, hidden in the back corner.

A few drops and she could dull the fear brought on by this unknown visitor. She stood unmoving, pollarded against the wallpaper.

"Peter!"

The shadow withdrew. The rough knock again, rattling the heavy door's brass hardware.

"Annabelle!"

She tried to slow her breathing. Closing her eyes did not help and she picked out a spot on the far wall and concentrated on it, listening acutely for any sound that would signal the visitor's departure.

The silence was becoming unbearable.

Annabelle Jeffries slid to the floor, unable to remove the image of her son in a blue suit, with a large bunch of flowers, a cigar in his mouth, laughing at her. She began to shake all over and to cry in embodied sobs, overcome with the force of a helplessness that gripped her with an old grief. She knew she could not save her son. She held one clear thought: should she? Would he be better off with me or without me?

"Annabelle?"

She knew the voice and what it meant, what it was there for. It called to her across the years, across the span of her life that now felt like loose knots unraveling a frail net. She could see the old lady standing beneath her flowerpot hat, busy with its small birds and aigrettes, the bulge of her bustle perched above brocaded petticoats too heavy for summer weather. The jet beads of her handbag's passementerie would chatter to one another about the wealth hidden there. She knew which stick she would bring on such a day, its grip a sleek hound carved into ebony. Her driver would want to come to the door to help and she would turn to him and wag her chin no, stay back.

When there had been no answer at the door, Sylvia Jeffries made as much racket as she could getting back to her carriage.

She hammered her stick on the porch and then down the stanchions of the handrail. Like a spoilt child, her daughter-in-law thought. She didn't have to peek through the curtains to know that the old lady would stop and turn at the wagon's step, petulantly shooing away the helping hand of her driver in order to take her time staring balefully at the house. It was her way of yelling "I know you're in there!" without having to risk any loss of dignity by actually doing so. The driver would, when given the appropriate knock from the all-purpose stick, urge the horses into a walk, leading them directly to her son's law practice on the courthouse square. The driver did not have to be given instructions. Once there she could not be stopped from entering Peter's office, no matter what he was doing or with whom he was meeting; if he was out she would lower herself into a chair, remove her gloves and scarf, and wait.

Later that evening Annabelle was on her third old fashioned when Peter bustled in. He looked bedraggled. It was approaching dusk but she had not bothered to turn any lights on. She stood in the hallway, leaning back, the glass of a hanging mirror cool against her neck.

"Hard day?"

He jumped, startled to see her there so near the front door. He sat down his valise, dropped his hat onto the bench, and loosened his tie.

"It was actually. Any interest in making me a drink?"

"Slim, bordering on none, but I'll get through it."

She went into the drawing room, where there was a bar and a formal seating area, rarely used anymore. She handed him the glass and sat in one of the heavily upholstered chairs, her legs angled over one of the arms.

"How's Sylvia?" she asked.

"She sends her love."

"I bet she does."

"Why didn't you come to the door? She knows you were here."

"Now I shall ask you a rhetorical question. Where did you and Henderson go yesterday?"

"It's really none – "

"Rhetorical means you don't answer, counselor."

He held an involuntary memory of cocktail parties long ago, some in this very room. He could almost hear the clink of glassware and smell the perfume. She was good at that, he mused, once upon a time. He killed his drink and moved behind the bar to make another.

"She has some ideas about Henderson."

"Ideas."

"She wants to help out with his schooling, and – "

"What, college?"

"No, well perhaps, but that's not what she was talking about." He took a long pull from his drink. "She thinks he ought to go to boarding school. There's a military academy, Culver it's called, up in Marshall county. She actually went up there and looked it over. Quite taken with the place, she said, right on Lake Maxinkuckee."

Annabelle laughed, sliding her hand over the top of her glass to keep from spilling.

"That sounds entirely invented. What that woman gets up to."

"She was also taken, from the sound of it, by the man who runs the place, a Colonel Alexander Fleet. He had a middle name but it escapes me. Apparently he showed her around the grounds and was a complete gentleman. The kind, and she was emphatic about this, you just don't get around here these days. She was pleased as punch to find out that he had been a Confederate officer during the war."

Annabelle sat up at this.

"You *are* serious." She put her feet on the floor, dug the cherry out of her ice and bit it in half.

"You know how she loves the golden age."

"Yes, 'before the war when people knew their place'. I've heard that a few times."

"She even quoted to me what the founder said their mission was. Here." He reached into his jacket pocket and drew out a piece of stationary, folded once. He handed it to her.

"For the purpose of thoroughly preparing young men for the best colleges, scientific schools and businesses of America." She refolded it and dropped it to the carpet.

"Hear me out," he said, gesturing with his highball glass, but she already had her hands up as if they might make a screen beyond which his words, and the argument she knew they would contain, might not pass.

"No."

"She is willing to pay for this academy and then for college, but it has to be a package deal."

"I'd say *over my dead body*, but then Sylvia would get everything she wants in one throw."

"This might be precisely the thing Henderson needs. The boy could benefit from the kind of structure this place can offer." Annabelle could hear his joints pop as he bent and retrieved the piece of paper embossed at the top with his mother's initials. She remembered a much thinner, sprier version of him moving around this very room as though he were on ice skates. "It says right here, "the best colleges and scientific schools." I thought that's what you wanted?"

"You left out the part the Jeffries care about most. What your mother wants is a little tycoon to emerge out of some factory fueled by her money, one that stamps little Vanderbilts or Morgans, or a Carnegie without the largesse. Oh yes, the captains of the Confederacy molding captains of industry. I can see it now – "

"Oh for god's sake Annabelle."

"I am prepared to accept the fact that my son is not going to grow up to be a poet. How could he, coming from such a place." She made a sweeping gesture with her drink that slung its remnants across the room. "Perhaps Whitman was wrong. Perhaps the America he heard singing didn't make

237

it this far west, the voices drained out of the people who spent themselves settling this land, throttling the life out of the natives then everyone who came after them."

"It's also a school. It's not the actual army. Anyway, look at this in the longer term. He has two more years of high school and then he's off to college. There won't be any restrictions on his choices. I figured it all out once I was at university and so will he."

Indeed, she thought. You figured it out all right: your cold imperious father and harridan of a mother gave you all the rope you needed to hang yourself. And you did, one school tie, one secret society meeting at a time. There were ripostes to Peter's assertions, to his insincere proffering of his mother's desires shrouded in his own. Annabelle knew too well that her husband had long ago convinced himself that he was his own man. Assertions to the contrary had become tiresome. And what was the point? Beyond the sport of disagreement, what good would it do to try to best him in a contest in which she played from a position of such weakness? No good at all. For her. But for Henderson, perhaps, she could channel the force of her will and make a cunning move in a game her husband had not imagined to be afoot. He could be convinced to go away. Chicago or New York, or even Philadelphia. Where there were cafes and booksellers, museums and opera houses, places he might frequent long into the night where people argued politics and history and the affairs of stage actresses. He could make friends with the sons of professors and anarchists, eat at communal tables and play billiards with immigrants who would still be alive with the spirit of 1871 or at least aware of how 1898 had been less than a nationalistic triumph. How much money did she have hidden? This had to be plotted carefully but she felt so shaken, so wan with fatigue that she could not rouse herself. A few pills would be just the thing.

"Annabelle?"

She offered no reply. Needing time to think, she closed her eyes and removed herself from the conversation, from this room filled with spectres.

Her glass hit the carpet with a dull thud. The streetlamps cast a pale light through the sheer curtains, revealing only the side of her face, the rest of her in deep shadow as if the chair were swallowing her.

"I'm going out. There's some business I need to take care of."

When there was no answer he retrieved his hat and eased the door closed behind him.

Twenty One

In the trees it was the cicadas' time. From buried stillness they clawed their way up into invisible perches to fill the air with the sound of late summer. Around the gas lamps moths danced against the heavy glass. Along the sidewalks young men and women walked in pairs. One couple stopped to look up, startled by a large beetle ringing the globe like a dull bell.

A wagon clattered down the street behind them and pulled up sharply. Two figures jumped down and approached the couple who had turned, arm in arm, to see about the ruckus. They were startled at the approach of men in dark clothing with handkerchiefs tied around their faces. One grabbed the young man by the upper arm and the back of the neck and compelled him roughly towards the wagon where he forced him over the lowered tailgate while the other held the young woman firmly but respectfully by both shoulders. Her face registered confusion and a twinge of fear, unsure whether this was serious or some boyish prank. The hands that gripped her were strong and there was nothing she could do but watch as two other men, similarly clad and disguised, pinned the young man down with their knees. She made no struggle nor did she give chase once released, her captor vaulting the wagon's edge at a run. The reins snapped and the horses dug for the end of the street where they turned and faded into the night.

"Henderson?" she said, in a whispered voice, and walked home quickly before her parents began to worry about her.

In the wagon there was laughter and the smell of sour liquor. A face pressed against Henderson's, its breath stinking of booze.

"You scared yet?"

"See did he piss himself, Cor."

"I don't feel nothing down there, no, wait, I think he's got a stick of wood hid in his drawers." Laughter. "Must have been a hell of an exciting walk along the promenade son. You get your elbow up there in her titty, did you?"

Henderson struggled, trying to throw them off, to get an arm free so he could fight back. More embarrassed than scared.

"Cor," the driver yelled back over his shoulder, "let him up and give him some shine, but don't let him jump out."

The knees and restraining hands came off him slowly. The four figures retreated to the edges of the wagon and removed their handkerchief masks. Ensconced in the corner hard by the driver's seat was an unmasked man who was older than the others. He could tell this by the way he sat, reclining hatless with a piece of straw in his mouth. Henderson brushed himself off and could see that they were out of town, the humpbacked moon hanging halfway up the eastern sky paling the dirt road ahead. They passed a large frame house, its windows dark. A dog followed them without barking then stood in the settling dust as if curious about the commotion at such an hour. One of them handed Henderson his hat, which he reshaped and put on snugly against the dark.

The biggest one handed him an unstoppered gallon jug. The white stoneware glowed in the moonlight and without hesitation Henderson hooked his finger in the ring, slung it over his arm to steady it, and slugged a drink. It hit his throat like fire, lighting the insides of his closed eyes so that he expected to open them to daylight. He opened them on all fours, gasping, the jug safely grabbed away from him before he went over. There was general appreciative laughter, a hand slapped his back, an "atta boy." The driver yelled, "Don't let him puke in the wagon Cor, else you're gonna clean it out."

They drove in silence, passing the jug around in a circle,

every other round bisected with a pass to Henderson, who drank more modestly. It hurt his throat but warmed him in a way that had nothing to do with being cold.

The man in the corner kept his eyes on the prisoner, as if trying to judge his value. Henderson felt his gaze and wanted to ask what the hell he was looking at but was unable to muster the courage.

"If I'm not mistaken you are Peter Jeffries' boy."

When he did not answer the man kicked his foot. He took the straw out of his mouth and asked, "Is that the case?"

The driver turned and replied, "Yes goddamnit, now cut the chatter and hand me up a drink."

The man replaced the straw, looked at the driver's turned back and snorted a dry laugh.

"Ain't that a hell of a coincidence," he said to himself.

It was Henderson's turn at the jug and by the time his breath returned from the sting of the liquor he had forgotten to ask what he meant.

When the road passed through heavier woods it was nearly full dark and they were quiet, attentive to the sounds of nightbirds. Hands slapped at mosquitoes. At first there was an occasional house along the road, each somber and mutely dark. As they drew away from town the farms were set further back, the buildings picked out by the moonlight square, angled amongst the rounded and diaphanous shadows of shade trees, an orchard, rows of staked vines. The newly shingled roof of a barn shone in the distance on a low rise, a rectangle held aloft by a blankness, a trick of reflected light. Likewise the whitewashed ribs of a corncrib, its keystone shape stark against a line of cedars. Henderson could smell them, like an opened drawer, but supposed it a conceit of memory. The moonshine could do that to you he reckoned.

In a thick stand of trees, hemmed in by a pulsing insect chorus, the driver said "Whoa now," in a soft voice. Henderson raised himself up on his knees looking forward, where the faintest glow of woods' edge appeared thirty yards in front of them.

"Cor," the driver hissed back.

Cor eased his large form over the side gracefully for such a large man, his passage in the roadside weeds a barely audible swish. After a couple of minutes he returned and whispered something inaudible to the driver. Henderson could sense the shape of the driver turn in his seat.

"OK fellas, let's get to work."

The others pitched over the side and Henderson felt his way to the edge, had a leg cocked over the side feeling for the wheel when the driver brought him up short.

"Not you boy. You get up on this seat and keep the reins in your hands and the horses steady. You got a watch on?"

"Yessir," he felt for the Hamilton beneath his shirt and jacket.

"You got any matches?"

"No sir, I don't – "

"Shut up. Take these."

He took the handed-over matches, put them in his pocket.

"In exactly thirty minutes from when I get down off this wagon I want you to drive out of the trees yonder, go a ways till there's room to turn around in the shorter grass. Turn back the way we come and stop in the road. You got it?"

"How can I read thirty minutes on my watch in here?"

"Them matches ain't for picking your teeth with."

"Yessir, right." Dumb, Henderson thought.

"Thirty minutes. You don't do it like I said Cor'll be real upset. He don't take to oath-breakers. You do something foolish like leave us and well, hell, I wouldn't even try to say what he'd do to you."

He reached into the bed for the jug, smacked his lips and jumped down, wading into the weeds around the horses. Henderson raised up into a crouch and watched him advance toward the light then disappear into tall grass. He stepped over the seat and sat down, feeling for the reins. Alone now, the time seemed to tick away with impossible slowness. Calm down, he said to himself. Do your job and it will come out right.

Suddenly it occurred to him that he would not be able to measure an exact thirty minutes unless he knew what time it was when he began the count. With his right hand he rummaged in his pocket for the matches. He removed one and struck it on the rough sole of his boot as he'd seen his father do many times. It broke smartly in two, the head falling away and leaving him with a short piece of wood.

"Shit."

One of the horses whinnied softly.

Henderson realized he might be a little drunk.

Again into his pocket, this time more carefully holding the match in the middle. It flared and the horses shuffled their feet.

"Easy now," he said reassuringly. He turned his left fist over and pushed up his sleeves against his thigh, bringing the match down close enough to read the hands on the watch. The cuff of the shirt was caught on the winding post of the watch and would not give way. He tried to use the last two fingers on his right hand to pry it up. Doing so tilted the match too far and it winked out.

"Shit."

The horse whinnied again, louder. He shushed it, aware that this was likely to be ineffective on a horse.

In his pocket he counted two more matches. He still needed one for later, to tell when a half hour had passed. Or would he be able to see the hands in the moonlight? Should he run up and hold out his arm to check? What if the horses bolted? What if it got cloudy? What would Cor do to him if he messed up his instructions? He smelled the hot breath again and felt the steely grip from those strong hands. In a sudden panic he realized that he had no idea how much time had elapsed since he had been left alone. The darkness and the screech of the bugs, an owl hooting somewhere in the trees, all suddenly pressed in upon him, as though he were in deep water and running out of air.

He pulled another match out, struck it against his boot and it snapped off.

"Fuck!"

Which came out louder than he intended, a consonant explosion against the soft night sounds. Which spooked the horses, who bolted for the light at the end of the narrow road. Which sent Henderson, reins slipping cleanly through unready fingers, over the short backrest of the seat and into the wagon bed. He landed in a sprawl hoping it would stop before the whole thing tipped over or the horses broke loose, either of which would result, he was certain, in his being torn to pieces by Cor.

Horses being horses, he was lucky. Upon reaching the light, like souls come to salvation, they slowed, and smelling the ample grasses they stopped. He climbed back into the seat, his heart pounding violently. He checked his watch and found that he could see the hands clearly. It must have been ten minutes or so since the driver had gone he reckoned.

He was at the edge of a wide prairie, undulating away on all sides in the light breeze. Ahead the road ran straight for a hundred yards, a pale cut through tall grass grayed in the moonlight. It then curved off gently to the right, running at a slight incline down, then up again and into the far tree line. To his left the prairie went as far as he could see. He was unsure whether the horizon in that direction was a distant line of trees or just a lack of light. There were the unmistakable shapes of a farm: house, barn, outbuildings, rectangle of vegetable garden, even the vague shape of the outhouse. He could make out by texture rows of corn, beans, tomatoes, plants staked and low to the ground running off mounds, an orchard of short, heavily-laden trees, a line of bee boxes. It all looked so peaceful, Henderson thought, like a model you might build for display of what a farm in the Middle West ought to look like.

Part of the outhouse shadow detached itself and ran to something round and squat. A well? The shadow melted into other shadows and all was still. Is that where they'd gone?

In the next twenty minutes he saw other movements. Pieces of the dark broke off to move until joined again, but he could not be sure it wasn't a trick of perspective. Or the liquor. As quietly as he could he coaxed the horses into a walk, their heads pulled reluctantly from their foraging. He turned and halted the wagon twenty yards from the woods. Henderson had no idea whose farm it was, nor did he know anyone who lived this far out of town. For the first time he thought about who it was that had abducted him. It surprised him now that he had not been more afraid. He had only drunk whiskey once before and had thought it noxious, but tonight he had done so willingly. It was the doing of it he enjoyed more than the taste, if taste it could be called. His tongue felt burned, his mouth metallic, as though he'd bitten split shot for a fishing line. They were older than him, he knew that, and the driver had said something about an oath. When he'd said it Henderson thought it a figure of speech, but now it occurred to him that there might be larger forces at work, that this could be his first, post-initiation action in the HTDA. Were they out here looking for stolen horses? Was this innocent-looking farm a den of thieves, outlaws, stone cold killers? In his mind he saw a picture from one of the penny dreadfuls he had read of a train robber, handkerchief covering his face, gun extended, steady blue eyes betraying neither fear nor mercy.

Of a sudden he was glad he had gone along without fighting or crying. He had made good account of himself so far during the ride and now handling the wagon. This was a chance anticipated for a long time. He imagined his father coming in to breakfast, looking at his son and giving him a small wink or sign just between them, indiscernible to his mother, that let him know he could see him, that he considered him a part of his world. After that, school and chores and uncertainties about girls would not seem so important and would not cut him to the quick as they had done before.

Something flickered in his peripheral vision. A single cloud had scudded across the moon and the prairie was cast into a deeper darkness. Something was going on down near the house. Beyond it where the barn rose up a flash on and off. The flicker resolved into a glow, yellow visible for the first time in all that gray and blueblack, a tongue of flame licking up over the eaves, orange fingers grasping at the roof. Henderson sat back as though singed, blinking. Lines of color became visible between the structure's vertical slats. It must have been burning fierce in there and was now consuming the whole, taking off and getting out into the night.

A figure moved suddenly around the corner, disappeared, then one side of the double doors opened and light spilled out into the space between house and barn, picking out the shapes of both buildings, one a black shadow the other a mass of brightness. The screams of animals reached him, horrible from even this distance. Whether of horses or cows or something else he could not tell. Something charged out of the door aflame, the beast tossing its head and running into the tall grass setting it ablaze in its wake. Enough dew had settled to keep the field from going up. Passage through the damp grass put out the fire as whatever it was burnt out and was gone. The grass at the field's edge smoldered, revealing details: a harrow lying on its side, a well, a clothesline hung with sheets and pillowcases, a single pair of trousers.

Henderson thought it odd that there was no resistance, no men pouring out of the house guns blazing. As if to oblige him there were flashes at one of the windows and the delayed report of gunfire. He instinctively ducked and the horses flinched, their trace chains rattling like his nerves.

247

Then he heard the screaming. At first he thought it was a woman, its pitch high, but then realized it was the pain that made it so, and perhaps youth. How I'd scream, he thought, if I were shot or on fire.

Henderson tied off the reins to the brake handle, setting it as tight as it would go until he thought it would snap. He searched the bed of the wagon and found a loose coil of light rope. Maybe they had planned to tie him up if he resisted too much. Over the side and onto the road he moved around the port side horse, his hand on its flank letting it know he was there. Its feet danced and for a moment he thought they would bolt back to the safer dark of the woods, but he grabbed hold of the bridle and calm returned. He made sure they kept their eyes on him and not on the growing brightness across the prairie. With the rope he hobbled both horses as best he could. Thank god for *Last of the Mohicans*. He had read it twice, mesmerized by its lore and the way in which the hero could do anything to survive. It was hard to tie a knot without being able to see, but he finally got a loop secured and clinched so the rope could be untied with a pull. He left them munching contentedly and plunged into the chest-high grass.

Running was difficult and he fell, his foot going into a depression sending him down. He spat out chaff and felt for his hat, which he found and replaced. It was pitch dark near the ground, and dead silent. The screaming had ceased while he was at work on the horses. He sat still on his knees listening.

Nothing.

On his feet all he could see was grass, with what looked like a glow ahead and to the right. He went as quickly as he could, trying to part the grass with his hands, the backs of which began to itch fiercely. Five minutes of this felt like an hour. He was tempted to check his watch but thought better of it. I must be close now, he reckoned. At the sound of two quick shots he dropped. Something was making a ticking sound and he put his hand over the Hamilton but realized it could not be that loud. It was coming from up ahead. The crack of burning timber.

He stood up. Forty yards to the house, which stood dark and silent, obscuring his view of the burning barn. Over the roofline there was a glow. Once at the edge he parted the grass and made sure there were no men at the windows, no gun barrels poking out. He wished he was armed. He wished he knew how to shoot a gun.

Staying in the grass for cover he bore left, then broke out of it to hide behind the outhouse. From there, low as he could manage, he ran to a line of staked tomatoes at the back edge of the long vegetable garden. The tomatoes smelled good, earthy-ripe, and he tried not to think about his mother standing in the kitchen slicing one, humming some aria or other to herself. He tried to keep her back to him. Did not want to see the look on her face when she turned around with the knowledge of what he was doing. Maybe he could persuade her that it was worth the risk, that law and order had to be preserved. He remembered the words the man at the initiation had spoken, about who they were fighting against, but he could not imagine any foreigners or suchlike all the way out here. This must be about thieving. He would have to hold her gaze and explain it to her. As a man.

He quick-crawled on elbows and knees along the row of tomatoes until he reached their end. The barn was engulfed in flames. The wind was from the west, behind him, and was taking the smoke in the other direction or he would have sensed it earlier. Everything was bathed in an orange light and washed in a low rumble of consuming fire, cracks here and there from pockets of super-heated air or moisture, a crash inside of falling beams and rafters.

Where was everyone?

Between the house and barn lay fifty yards of open ground.

On the far side of the yard, before the border of high corn, was a tall shade tree, beneath which hung a swing. He could also make out a table and some chairs and a long bench. Nearer to him was the well and on it lay the prostrate body of a man. It must have been some slight movement that drew his eye. Over the edge of the flat stones his head lay toward the barn and his blonde hair glowed red in the light. By the slightness of his build Henderson thought sure it was the wagon driver. He wondered whether he was shot or had been burned, whether the screams had been his, or if they had been human at all. A pig could scream like that, his friend the butcher's son had said. Raise the hair on the back of your neck.

Something about the posture of the form on the well looked unnatural. A wounded man would not lay like that. A gun blast sent him sprawling, face into the dirt, fingers digging in. It felt close. Henderson caught the muzzle flash out of the corner of his eye from the back of the house, from one of the windows darkened beneath the sheltering eaves. A shotgun, he guessed. Then he saw three figures, keeping low, run along the far side of the open space beneath the tree and around the table, plunging into the rows of corn. The shotgun reported again, caught the top of one of the ladder-back chairs and sent it over backwards in a hail of splinters.

The man on the well moved his head. He considered making a run over to him, calculating that he would then be invisible to anyone in the house. But to get there he would make himself vulnerable to a shot from the window. Thirty yards and he would be in the light. He waited. Wasn't sure why he felt he had to look at his watch, clawing back his shirt cuff, feeling the button pop off, getting his fingers on its face and angling it toward the fire. Before he could work out what time it was the back door of the house opened and a man filled the doorframe.

He was big and held the dull mass of the shotgun at an

angle across his chest. The firelight picked it out as a dark slash over his union suit, which was either a dark red or appeared so. Henderson scrunched down lower behind his tomato blind, feeling the man's eyes roving, sweeping across him. He felt suddenly exposed. A boy hiding behind vegetables. The man stepped out, leveled the gun. In the open Henderson could see that he was not a white man. His face bore a sheen of sweat that caught the light like one of the slate slabs of the courthouse sidewalk after rain. He had not expected that. He had also begun to wonder where all the horses were. Shouldn't they have set them loose, stampeded them down the drive or into the grass? And where were the gunman's confederates? Did they send him out alone?

The man approached the barn with measured steps, taking him away from the garden towards the tree and the shot chair. He continued to the edge of the cornfield, stooped down and picked something up, dropped it. No pockets anyway, Henderson thought. No more than two shots then, he reckoned. One for each barrel. Not a very comforting thought.

He shifted the gun to port arms and walked in the direction of the barn. Flames licked above the burnt-out roof. The walls still stood, their tops jagged, skeletal beams hanging inward, thinned and enfeebled, beginning to collapse on themselves in showers of sparks. When the man went far enough around the barn Henderson saw that he could get to the well and crouch behind it unseen. Before he could think about what he was going to do when he got there, or how he would get back, he was running full tilt. He dove headfirst behind the ring of flat stones into the shadow thrown toward the house. Only when he came to rest did he realize that if there was another gun in a window he would be an easy target. He froze, hands laced over the back of his head. A moan drew him up into a sitting position, his back against the solid surface. He inched around until he could see the bottoms

251

of the man's boots, drawn together as if he were lying at attention. Reaching up he grabbed one and whispered, "Hey, it's Jeffries." There was no reply but he thought he felt the foot move. He sneaked a look around the curvature of the well but saw nothing of the man with the gun. Taking a deep breath he got to his knees. It was the driver.

Even in the poor light Henderson could see that he was badly wounded in the legs. The right leg had taken the brunt and was a mass of blood, the fabric of his trousers blown into the flesh. The left leg had been hit on the inside and the lead had gotten the knee. A piece of loose flesh had pulled away and Henderson could see the white of a ligament, awash in dark blood.

"Goddamn," he heard himself say, his hands out as if he were falling.

"How bad is it?" the driver whispered between clenched teeth.

"Pretty bad. You think you can stand, walk maybe? We get into the grass yonder we might make it."

"Don't know. Untie me."

His legs had been wired together at the ankles. He bent over and tried to twist it free. Henderson shuddered at the thought of being shot and bound. The driver groaned in pain. He threw the freed coils into the well and looked toward the barn. Still clear. He got him to his feet though he made an agonized cry when his feet touched the ground. Henderson could feel him shaking, could see that his eyes were glazed. Afraid the man would pass out he put one of his arms around his shoulders and said, "Come on, we got to go." They took two steps together, Henderson bearing the weight awkwardly, a macabre sack race pair hobbling toward the garden and the curtain of grass beyond.

When the sound of the shotgun blast hit them he thought he could feel the lead bore into the back of his head and expected to fall. Instead, another shot boomed and his burden became so heavy and unbalanced that they went down in a heap.

"I ain't gonna say it again." The voice was deep and the man sounded out of breath. "You stop right there or I'll shoot you."

Henderson tried to feel for the driver's pulse but could not find it.

"Put them hands behind your head."

He did so and felt a foot between his shoulder blades pressing him down along with most of the air from his lungs. A hand felt up one side and down the other, ranging around to the front of his trousers.

"Awright, sit up."

Henderson did as he was told, trying not to cry. He knew the man was out of shells, but he could still beat him to death with the gun or with bare hands. The driver lay as he had fallen, unmoving.

Some quality of the light and its low roar changed. A new brightness picked out the black man's face in a hellish glow. He followed his gaze and looked toward the barn. He could not believe what he saw.

From the wide open doorway of the burning building walked a man on fire. He had tried to cover himself with sacking but whatever he'd poured on the burlap had accelerated its incendiary force. In trying to free himself his clothes went up and he staggered forward beating at the flames with his hands. He screamed but the words were an animal cry of desperate fear. Henderson rose to one knee, then stood and tried to run to him.

A strong hand gripped the collar of his shirt and he was wrestled down. A knee in his back pinned him painfully to the ground. "You stay right where you are," the man said in a fierce whisper.

"He'll burn to death," he managed, but wasn't sure the black man could hear.

Henderson saw it was the older fellow from the wagon,

the one who'd recognized him. Engulfed in flames he fell to his knees and seemed to regard them with curiosity. He reached out a hand, the arm a sword of flame, then fell face down. His back side burned and smoke lifted from him into the night air.

"Why? – " Henderson began, but had to swallow hard and clear his throat to gain enough composure to speak. "Why didn't you let me help him? He . . . he was alive." His voice trailed away to nothing at the thought of it.

Clayton had no answer for this boy, whoever he was. The Clayton McGhee who wished he could have caught the burned man unharmed and took him to the law walked around the well, past the outhouse where his grandfather had been shot to death, beyond the garden his grandmother had dug with her bare hands, and into the high grass they had sweated and died for. The piece of him that was untouched by rage, that would have taken the fire from his friend's body, went with him. June had destroyed his property, killed his livestock, threatened his family. That he was burning had a rightness to it he had no desire to explain. The Clayton McGhee who remained stood still. He would go on.

Across the years he heard Cmicky warn his father and grandfather. Whoever was behind June's attempt to buy the farm then burn him out had to be stopped.

"What's your name, son?" Clayton asked. He had to start somewhere.

"Why didn't you at least shoot him out of mercy?" Henderson asked.

Clayton raised the gun as if he would strike him.

"You talk to me about *mercy*? Why you want to burn my barn out?" He shook with anger, pointed the stock of the shotgun toward the house. "I got three little girls in there scared to death. Why cain't you all leave us be? What we ever do to any of you?"

Henderson saw it all now for what it was. Clearly. There had been no stolen horses, no thieving gang, no threat to law and order. A negro family living way out here, farming on the prairie, coming into town only when they had to or to visit with one of the dozen other colored families there. Maybe go to the AME church on Sixth Street in its little white building, take the children past the Lincoln School for coloreds to have a look at where the girls might go if they could manage it.

Still the man stood over him waiting for an answer that would not satisfy him, could not, since this boy at his feet had no intentions to reveal. Before Henderson lay two paths, clear to him now at what might be his last moments. His father's way, that of authority and power, a rectitude based on color and status, a way of organizing the world that brooked no introspection. Then there was his mother. How long had she questioned such unmitigated righteousness, clawing away at the façade of propriety with her reason, interrogating her husband and what he stood for? But for what? What had she ever *done*? His father the man of action and his mother the woman of languor; the dull juggernaut, seeing little but assured of direction versus the sharp wit and tongue without will. What was it going to be, motion or emotion?

He wiped his face with his sleeve and looked the tall dark man in the eyes. He stood up, swayed a little, found his feet. The man backed up a step. Henderson bent down to see if the driver was breathing. He was, his breath coming in shallow gasps. The shots had been in the air.

"My name is Henderson Jeffries. I didn't come out here to burn anything. I'm sorry about your barn. But you shot this man here pretty bad and he's going to bleed to death if something ain't done about it."

"I wouldn't a shot him if he hadn't come too close to the house. A barn I can rebuild, but my family's in there and I'd kill any man – "

255

"OK, fair enough. You lend me a horse I'll get him to town. Won't no one have to know how he got this way."

Henderson saw that the man was thinking it over. He released his grip on the stock of the shotgun and set it on the ground, holding it now near the end of the barrel. His face was lined, the furrows in his forehead and below his eyes deep, as though carved into grainless wood.

"I'll fetch the horse."

He crossed the garden where Henderson had hidden and disappeared into a row of low trees that marked the edge of the orchard. He had gotten the horses out of the barn with what other stock could be saved. There were crashes as the barn burnt down and collapsed, reduced to heaps of wrecked timbers. In the open space where the doors had been the body smoldered.

The man returned with the horse. He cinched the latigo on a saddle whose fender and cantle were singed and blackened, the stirrup charred but intact.

"He'll get you to town, no biggern the two of you are. Name's Ulysses. Uly for short. Only horse I got now."

He didn't say whether this was due to the fire or not.

"Hold onto him. I be right back."

He went into the house, resting the gun against the door frame. After a few minutes he emerged with a woman holding what looked like a sewing basket. The look on her face made Henderson want to hide behind the horse. At his fear the animal whinnied and stepped back, shaking its head against his hold on the bridle.

"Hey," the man said sharply, quieting the horse.

The woman plied the driver's wounds with some kind of salve and bandages, which she tore off in sheets, wrapping then tying them around his legs. He neither moved nor struggled, having passed out, which was fortunate since she was none too gentle. She had no more regard for his pain than she would have for a Thanksgiving turkey she was trussing for the oven.

He couldn't say he blamed her.

Without a word she picked up her basket and went back to the house. Between them they got the driver lifted, the man hauling him onto his back as he would a sack of seed corn. With Henderson holding the horse he managed to get him onto his belly behind the saddle.

"You'll have to hold him. Think you can manage?"

"Not much choice, is there?"

"I reckon not."

"One more thing Jeffries," the black man said, taking hold of the bridle and scratching the horse between the eyes. "Tell him I ain't never gonna sell this place. Never."

"Tell who?" Henderson asked.

"I don't know, son," Clayton replied, leading the horse up the drive and then pushing him on his way, "but when you find out, you can also tell him to go to hell."

Twenty Two

"This thing with Lanahan is not a problem. I get some of the boys to pick him up. He work late, sidewalks quiet. No one notice. We tie him to a chair and leave him in the dark." Cassini gestured with his long nose over his shoulder. "He get plenty nervous back there with no light and the mice."

"Mice?"

"We never get rid of them with all that canvas and wood. You stand back there in the middle of the night you hear them. Sound like *un corteo funebre*, but faster and with more feets." The big man shivered and rubbed his hands together. "Probably shit himself before you even get there."

Peter Jeffries sipped at his short glass of grappa. Always grappa when you talked in Cassini's office.

"It good eh?"

"It's terrible." He held it up to the light. How could something so clear be so noxious? "You know I hate this shit."

The Italian spoke with both hands: "*Chi beve solo si strozza*, my father always said. He who drinks alone will choke."

In response he set his glass down and fetched one of his dark cigarillos from an inner pocket. He lit it and blew the smoke over the Italian's head.

"This way we both choke."

Cassini took the cork out of the tall, slender bottle and refilled his glass.

Peter watched him enjoy his drink contentedly and hoped like hell he couldn't read his mind. No telling what he could do to me with those stonemason hands of his.

In the companionable silence Jeffries wondered if he could trust Michael Lanahan. He recalled their conversation in his office two months ago. It had been the end of the day and his secretary had knocked and stuck her head in to say that he had a visitor. She said he wouldn't give his name. When he saw Lanahan sitting with his hat in his lap, working a matchstick back and forth in his mouth, he sent the girl home, locked the outside door, and invited him in. Before he said a word he'd checked his lower right-hand desk drawer to make sure the revolver was there. He left it open an inch. After he'd inquired of Lanahan just what the fuck he was doing in his office, the Irishman wasted no time telling him why he'd come.

"I've got what you might call a business proposition, like."

"I'm not taking any clients."

"This don't involve lawyerin. I got me one a those already. What I'm wonderin is would yis like to make some money. A lot of money."

"I'm an officer of the court. Breaking the law . . . you know about the law, yes?"

"Oh aye, I know all about it. This is in what you might call a gray area. It ain't strictly speaking legal, but if it's a crime I'd be hard pressed to find any victims in it."

As much as he disliked Lanahan, he had been keen to know what the man was talking about. The summer had gotten off to a dull start.

"There's a wager we could make, if it were managed properly, that could see us both atop a pile of greenbacks."

"I like a wager. But what I don't like is risk. Get to the point if you please. What's the venture? I'm guessing you don't have a tip on a horse."

Lanahan had then gone on to unfold the story of his brother Terry – who held some unspecified place in the Chicago underworld – and his connection to fight promotion. Now that boxing was illegal there, the money men were looking for venues before all their business began moving away to Detroit or New York. The brother had made it clear that LaFayette was a prime candidate for a bout. He told him about the fighters they had in mind, about their ethnicity (an Irish Catholic, an Englishman) and reputations, about the swells and gamesters that would follow them down from the city, of the kind of money they could make if they bet on the right man.

Peter recalled how excited his visitor had gotten at this point.

"Think of it," he'd said, flicking his hat onto the desk so that he could gesture with his hands. "The whole town riled up. National pride at stake. Emotion will win out over sense when it comes to the betting. Me brother laid out the whole fighting part of it and it come to me how we could make it even grander."

"Fix it, you mean."

Lanahan's face lit up with a smile, innocent as a schoolboy.

"It's already fixed. It's but now to capitalize on it."

"What do you need me for?"

"You're the man what controls the establishment around here, or at least a fair part of it. We have Moran the City Attorney, and it won't be long till we have a chief of police, but for now yous have things well sewed up. And there's also your little night-time outfit there, with that big apostate Italian and all."

Jeffries smiled.

"Our social club, you mean?"

"Sure, real social, I hear. Real friendly like."

"You need my connections. Let's see," with the toe of his shoe he closed the drawer with the pistol, opened the drawer above it and drew out a fresh legal pad, unscrewed his pen and made notes. "Venue, police cooperation, lodging, and . . . sundries. We'll sort out the details once I've made a few inquiries. Your brother can arrange to front expenses?"

"Yes. Get me the numbers and I'll pass them along. Shouldn't be a problem."

"Now for the important part. What did you have in mind for the wager?"

"You'll give me ten thousand in cash and I'll double it for you."

"That's a lot of money."

"That's a lot of money to double for having a few meetings and making a few simple things simpler."

"How do I know I can trust you?"

"You're a smart man, Jeffries, and so you reckon there's risk even where it's supposed to be a sure thing. I'd do the same. The difference between gambling and doing business though is that we leave chance for the punters. Guessing is for poor people. Do we have an understanding?"

Lanahan stood and carefully replaced his hat. He ran his fingers around the brim and snapped it down in the front. He held out his hand.

Peter Jeffries took it but held on, catching the other man's eyes and holding them.

"Who's taking the dive and when?"

Lanahan returned his gaze and his grip with perfect steadiness.

"You'll find that out when you give me the money."

Cassini startled Peter out of his reverie by abruptly standing up and stretching.

"I like you Peter. You know how to keep your mouth shut. My wife, she like the talk all the time. I can see this trouble with the Irish is heavy on your mind. Don't worry. We take care of it. I have the boys meet me here Friday – "

"No. We'll wait on that. I want to give it some more thought."

"Suit yourself *amico mio*, the mice ain't going nowhere. Let yourself out, OK?"

"Goodnight Sal."

In the empty office he went over the progress of Lanahan's scheme since their meeting. He had spoken with the appropriate people around the courthouse. Arrangements were made. Promoting the match in town proved too expensive on the front end and riskier for having to include the cops. Instead of paying them off and answering a lot of questions about how Peter Jeffries came to be associated with a boxing match out of Chicago, he secured a venue in the county. Preparations there were almost complete. It had been Peter's idea to raise the profile of the match by ratcheting up the ethnic rivalry. Terry Lanahan had thought that this would take care of itself, but he didn't know LaFayette. In the Star City something was smoldering and while every once in a while it would catch flame, it needed some fuel, something incendiary. The brother agreed that if the crowd was big enough, the tempers raw enough, more money could be made. Lanahan added that Terry also pointed out that the eruption of what he called "afters" would go some way towards getting people's mind off their losses and how such losses had come about. So Peter went to see his friend George McCutcheon at the Courier. He slid an envelope across the desk and said, "This should help if no one buys that novel of yours." He looked inside at what Peter was offering, thumbed the fresh bills, and nodded. The editor sat back in his chair and steepled his fingers in front of his nose.

"The paper," he declared, in his best imitation of a judge they both knew, "has become deeply enthusiastic in both sponsoring the bout and publicizing it."

"A clash of peoples," McCutcheon continued, framing the large type with the brackets of his soft newspaperman's hands.

"Now you've got it," Peter replied.

After that it had only remained to plan something personal, something that would give them both cover in their communities. The confrontation on South Street, at Lanahan's niece's wedding, had been no accident. The Irishman had played his part perfectly. There was no one in town of any significance who believed that Peter Jeffries and Michael Lanahan could be in business together.

He snubbed out his cigarillo in the ashtray and checked his watch. Late. Time to be getting home. Henderson had done pretty well at the initiation yesterday, but still, his father thought, there were questions. The boy was still far too liable to go the way of his mother. She peeked out of his face when he was thinking and Peter could see that he had her habit of getting lost inside an idea and finding pleasure from that. And worse, he couldn't be sure whose ideas they were. The more he thought about it the more agreeable he was to the idea of this military academy. He made a mental note to buy his wife some flowers.

As he locked the door he felt a stab of fear about Lanahan, wondering again if he could be trusted. A thought he'd had too often since he saw him sitting in his office with that matchstick and smug mick look on his face. He hated to use Cassini and the others this way but it could not be helped. He would throw a party and make it up to them. Anyway, it was business. And of course they would enjoy themselves at the sport. They liked a little blood and they loved to fight the Irish. And once he got the ten thousand from the bet he'd get the McGhee farm, invest in the interurban line, and bring Cassini in on some country business venture.

On the way out he stopped and listened intently. If there were mice anywhere about on their little funeral procession feet he could not hear them.

It was dark on the road, the moon almost gone in the tree line. If the horse had not been able to see its way in the woods they would have had to turn back. Henderson could see nothing. The liquor and adrenaline, the fear and crying had scoured him clean. Now all he wanted was to get into his bed, pull up the covers and go to sleep. Several times he nearly fell off the horse, coming awake with a start, summoning quickly the memory of why he was twisted around holding reins in one hand and the back of a man's belt in the other.

To stay awake he sang. This made the horse walk faster and so he kept it up. He ran through hymns, his school song, and a number of tunes that his mother sang at the piano, the words learned off the sheet music she bought as soon as it came available. The horse seemed to like the latter best, perhaps since they were jauntier. He sang "Hello Ma Baby (Hello My Ragtime Gal)" and "There'll Be a Hot Time in the Old Town Tonight" twice each. The cover of the sheet music for both had always intrigued him. Though his mother was meticulous about these thin, elegantly printed booklets, the cover of "Hello Ma Baby" was missing and he could see that it had been carefully removed. She never gave an answer to his question of what had become of it. "Hot Time," as his father called it, was the only song that caused him to put down his paper and tap his foot. On this song's cover was the picture of a woman who looked decidedly like a man. Like a man in a dress. His questions about this had likewise gone unanswered.

The wagon had not been at the edge of the woods waiting for them, nor had he seen any sign of it on the long ride back to town. His passenger made a few murmuring noises but did not awaken. Henderson followed the road, bearing at the few crossroads in the direction he thought town to be. He felt lucky when he saw rail tracks sweep in since they had to be going in the right direction. By the time they came to houses that were close enough together to indicate a more urban disposition he had nearly fallen from the horse in fatigue several times. Each time he shook his head vigorously to rouse himself. Still, sleep found him and he instantly dreamed of a man digging a hole and rolling a body into it. The sound it made when it hit the bottom startled him awake. It was near dawn. The birds were coming awake in the trees to tell him the day was close.

He knew where he had to go but had no idea what to do once he got there. One advantage of being so tired was that he did not care.

The horse drank from the trough while he got the door of the carriage house open. He made his way as carefully as he could by the buggy, feeling his way in the murk into the center aisle, through a double door to where the horses were kept. There were bags of oats at the far side beneath the bench upon which tack was worked, where his father had taught him how to repair a harness. He opened one of the bags by touch, took a wooden scoop off its hook and sunk it into the feed, careful not to let the awkward mass fall over. The scoop emptied into his hat, he went back the way he'd come and put the provender onto the foot rail next to the trough. He figured that a feeding horse would not move in his absence and so gave Uly a scratch between his ears and hurried through the gate, across the back yard along the brick path, between the lilac bushes to the back door.

Where he smelled cigarette smoke.

He froze, not sure how quiet he'd been.

"It's very late," she said, more matter-of-factly than he expected.

He could hear his shoes squeak as he shifted on the balls of his feet.

"I need to have a talk with you."

He had been reaching for the door but there was an urgency in her voice that brought him up short. He kept hold of the handle and said, "This isn't a good time. Later."

"No. No." Her voice rose in pitch, causing him to look over his shoulder into the gloom in fear they could be heard. "It has to be now. Your grandmother, goddamn it, and your father, they are – "

"This has to wait. I need to speak with him *right now*. Where is he?" His tone surprised him, as though it had issued from his father himself. He pulled at the screen door but it would not budge.

"Unlock the door mother. This is serious."

The tip of her cigarette glowed red. She exhaled and he smelled her strong tobacco. As tired as he was he felt a new measure of fatigue at having to join in this game. Henderson wanted no part of it after what he had endured tonight.

"You need to listen to me, Hen. There isn't much time. They are going to send you away."

He let go the handle.

"What? Where?"

"Boarding school. A military academy."

He was alert for telltale signs of the kind of disjointed talk that told him it was the laudanum or liquor talking, but she didn't sound like that. Frantic, yes, but not hallucinating or speaking with the voice of a young girl. Or calling for her mother. That was the worst. The kind of thing you just had to wait out.

"Father wouldn't do that. He has plans for me here."

"If he were in charge I might well agree. But Sylvia has him in the palm of her hand. I'll let you guess whose idea this was, who's paying the bills."

Henderson loved his grandmother but he did not have to be reminded that she was a stubborn woman. When she became fixed on a course of action there was no stopping her.

"Hen, you have to go away. I've been thinking about it and I have a plan. There is some money your father doesn't know about. You can go to Chicago or New York, maybe even west. Finish school and see what's out in the world. Meet new people. Painters and actors and, I don't know, anyone who isn't trying to sell people something. You have so much potential and this place is turning you into a monster. Dreams die here, Hen."

266

She was crying. He pictured the shot-up legs of his passenger back in the alley, saw the man aflame, and he wanted to cry too. This is too much, he thought. To get away, though. That would be something. He would have to think about it. But to become like her . . . that would be the risk. It struck him that the extent of her plan was likely no more than what she'd just said. She wanted to send him away to become who she had failed to be. But one man's monster is another man's hero. Perhaps he could free himself from all of this and have it both ways.

But not now. He had to find his father and get his help. The concrete necessity of this crowded out abstract deliberations of what lay ahead.

"Please shut up and listen. Open this door before I rip it off the damn hinges. We'll talk later about all this." He had never spoken to her this way. She was silent but he could feel her on the other side of the wire. "There is a man out there bleeding who needs help now. I have to talk to father. He'll know what to do."

Which, being true, would take the fight out of her. Until this moment they had shared the resignation of not doing, of arguing and bantering. Roles known, steps practiced, the dance familiar. But now Henderson was too tired to keep up the act.

His father never hid inside himself. Henderson had often wondered whether there was any place in there to hide.

The bolt slid back with a snap.

"Mother?"

No answer.

When he flung the screen door open she was not there.

"There's a man bleeding to death, maybe even dead already, out in the alley." He waited to see what effect this would have. His father looked sleepily at him, as though he was unrecognizable.

Peter Jeffries sat up on the sofa, tried to rub the sleep out of his eyes.

"Come on," he said, and went across the dark drawing room, into the kitchen and outside.

"Jesus," his father said in a low voice, putting three fingers on the wounded man's neck. "Get Ruth hitched to the buggy and throw some horse blankets in."

"There's something else."

"It'll have to wait," he said sharply, steadying the horse.

"There was a man who died. He was on fire."

Peter turned and looked at his son. "Who was it? The negro? That might just – "

"No, the black man had a shotgun. But he wouldn't . . . It was the older fella. He knew who I was but I didn't get his name. He must have been trapped in the barn. I . . . I don't know what happened."

Peter took Henderson by the shoulders and looked him straight in the eye. "You will say nothing about this. *Nothing*. You hear me?"

His grip tightened until Henderson said, "Yes sir." Then he added, "The black man wanted me to tell you something." He'd figured it out now. At least the general idea. "Said he'd never sell his place. Said you can go to hell."

Peter released him, a rueful smile playing on his lips.

"I expect it will be one or the other."

Henderson opened the carriage house door, pulling it along on its steel track. His father lowered the man from the horse and gently placed him on the ground. There was blood on the front of his white shirt.

He went through the barn as he'd done earlier, this time to one of the stalls. In the darkness he put his hand on Ruth's head and spoke to him, receiving a whinny and bob of the head. He knew this meant Ruth was awake and wanted to go out. More like a dog than a horse sometimes. He swung open one of the big doors at the end of the barn and led the horse out into the alley where he pissed a torrent. It took a few extra minutes in the bad light to hitch him but he got it done and had the blankets on the floorboards by the time his father hefted their cargo onto his shoulder. They got him down onto the floor, his back against one of the sides so as not to bend his legs, covering them with one of the blankets.

Peter drove, lighting a slim coffin-nail cigar with a lucifer he flicked to the side as they exited the alley. They rode without speaking, the sprung seat jostling them together, Henderson making a concerted effort to stay awake and aware. When they pulled up to Cassini's he was not too surprised. There was a light on in the office. His father said to wait, went through the door without knocking. A minute later he emerged and gestured towards the big double doors of the larger part of the building where the initiation had taken place a week before. He steered the wagon across the threshold and pulled up next to the wagon that had left them out on the dirt road.

Henderson sat in Cassini's office drinking coffee. It warmed him and beat down the hunger pangs. The warmth and a fuller belly made him drowse in the chair. The door opened and the man he guessed to be Cor, tall and broad-shouldered, entered and passed through the room followed by a doctor carrying an unmistakable black bag. Cor gave him a little nod. He stood and stretched, set his mug on the nearest desk. Cassini had praised his courage after he had told an abbreviated version of the night's events and his father had put his hand on his shoulder, as if claiming him in a dispute. Then there had been talk between the two older men about niggers with guns, about needing to set some things right, about gathering their forces. Henderson felt his kinship with these men, knew he belonged in a way he hadn't when he had picked Betsy Hansen up from her house what seemed a week ago.

269

His father called his name. The lights were on in the cavernous interior now. They revealed a table covered with white canvas, blood in various streaks and shapes of red down the side. The wounded man lay still in the brighter light of held lanterns while the doctor worked at removing buckshot from his legs. It was so quiet he could hear the lead hitting the bottom of the metal tray. His father handed Cor his lantern and the big man held one up in each hand like a sturdy human lighthouse. He stopped Henderson before he got to the circle of light.

"You get on home now. We'll handle it from here. Take the buggy."

"Is he gonna make it?"

"It looks like it. Birdshot. Doc says it didn't do as much damage as it could have if it were heavier. Missed his whatever-it's-called artery or he'd a bled out right there."

"OK. I'll walk though." He turned, suddenly overcome by a wave of sadness, of a sea change that he did not have the legs for. He walked away in tears he would not have his father see.

"Son."

"Yeah," he replied over his shoulder.

"Good work tonight."

It was faster to take the alley and go in via the kitchen as he had done before. He had his hands in his pockets and head down, trying to get home without being seen. The horse was still tied to the rail at the trough. His hat lay on the ground no doubt licked clean inside.

Ulysses. Damn.

There was nothing to be done but put him away. He led him around and into the center aisle, backing him into the stall next to Ruth's. He left the animal chewing contentedly on a sack of oats and trudged toward the house, feeling like the other Ulysses come home to Ithaka, hoping the insomniac Penelope would not be waiting for him at the door.

270

In the half light of the kitchen he heard her voice as if from a great distance.

"Where have you been now?"

"To seek my fortune," he said, neither stopping nor even turning his head, placing one foot in front of the other until he was fast in his bed.

Twenty Three

Someone was shaking him.

"Wake up, son."

His clothes were still on, the counterpane twisted over his lower half. He forced his legs out from under the cover to the ground. He took a quick look at the pillow to see if all the saliva had leaked out of his mouth. His father stood in the door wearing a crisp white shirt without collar and tie, gray trousers, the light behind him obscuring the expression on his face.

"How you feeling this morning?" he asked, reaching for his watch. He noted the time and snapped it shut. "Good," he went on. "Then as it's nearly over get yourself cleaned up and eat something. Meet me in the barn."

Henderson made straight for the toilet. Why does he need me in the barn, he wondered. He pulled the chain and remembered the horse.

When he entered the tack room his father had his back to the door, working at the tool bench where typically he mended and polished harness. They could easily have afforded to hire someone to work as groom, to see to the horses and their maintenance. But Peter Jeffries, his son knew, insisted on doing these things himself. Out of pride for a job well done, yes, that was part of it. But his father was also a man of privacy, insisting on doing things for the sake of knowing their completion as well as the complementary isolation that attended this.

His father continued with whatever it was he was doing, unaware of his presence. The bond that had stretched between them the day before felt fainter now, but alive, a gossamer cord that Henderson felt he might strengthen through boldness.

"You wanted to see me?"

Without turning, his father said, "Evidence."

Henderson was not sure he'd heard him. "Sir?"

"Evidence. You got about nine hundred pounds of evidence in that stall back there and I was wondering what you planned to do about it."

"Well," he paused, hoping something would come to him or that he'd be interrupted by the answer, his father often asking rhetorical questions in this manner. The older man continued working at something Henderson could not see on the workbench.

"Well what?"

"I suppose I could take him back out there, tie him up where they'd see him or let him wander toward home. I'm pretty sure – "

"And that's it? You'd feed him like he probably hasn't been fed in months, hell, in his whole life, and then ride him out pretty as you please and drop him off like a parcel? You sure you don't want to rub him down or tie some fucking ribbons in his mane?"

He turned to face his son, throwing something into the rag bin beneath the worktop.

"Have you already forgotten Tab Wordlaw's legs like ground meat from being gunned down out there? Maybe I should have made you help the doc pull shot out of him. It's a wonder he's not dead."

Peter Jeffries made a visible effort to gather himself.

"Come here."

Henderson crossed the low, murky room, its light from a bare bulb over the bench aided weakly by the oddly placed window near the corner. His father's umbrous shape blocked the light, muting his features. He would give much to see the

273

look on that face, to read there the direction of things. This room had always smelled so good to him, its aromas of leather and hay, the sharper tang of the oils and polishes in their tins and soaked into soft cloths, his father working contentedly, often humming as he did so. When he was within two paces he stopped. The pistol registered as a dark space at the end of his father's white cuff and pale hand, indistinct yet massive.

"You take this, ride him out there, shoot him in the road."

"But what if someone sees me on him, puts it together with – "

His protest was cut off by a sigh and his father's body language, pistol clapped hard against his leg with the strain. Henderson wished he'd hit him with it. Such a task would be easier if he had a reason. His father's effort to compose himself was palpable. He spoke slowly and deliberately.

"That nigger will drag his horse off the road, dig a big hole, and bury the son of a bitch and count himself lucky that it's the only goddamn thing he's putting in the ground."

He tried to ride slowly but Ulysses knew the way once they were out of town and at every opportunity quickened his pace. A jerk on the reins checked him, but only for a little while. His father's final words played in his mind. He'd left out the man who had burned to death. Henderson had not corrected him.

The sun went in and out of high wispy clouds. Red-winged blackbirds screeched at each other from the fence rows, riding cattails where the ground was marshy. He trotted along until the fist of what lay ahead hit him in the stomach. Henderson thought about an impending after-school fight with an older kid he'd had and the feeling of dread, its weight bearing down on him all day, crowding out the present moment and filling it with images of blood and pain and smashed teeth.

He tried not to look down at the horse's head, and especially not in his eyes, big and liquid brown and alive with intelligence. He tried, and failed as with all these efforts, not to look at the leather bag tied to the pommel containing the gun.

The day advanced as he rode between green fields of chest-high corn, past single farms with penned dogs carrying on behind split rail fences. The farms on their low rolling hills neatly squared and rectangled eventually gave way to the slopes of ravines. He rode past a last whitewashed frame house, turning back to see it amongst elms and willows, its green roof blending in as though it were waving too in the summer breeze. Ahead, the light green of the corn changed to the mottled, black-green of a stand of hardwood forest as far as he could see, the road plunging into it darkly.

He was reminded of the cover of the Grimm's Fairy Tales his mother had read to him as a child. If he remembered correctly things had not gone so well in there.

Ulysses again picked up his pace and this time was unhindered in his desire to bear them more rapidly. In the tunnel made by the trees there was little to see. When the light grew stronger ahead he slowed the horse and looked closely at the weeds on the left-hand side of the road, where he thought he could see a trampled line but could not be sure in the poor light. He considered dismounting and looking for spent matches in the roadbed, but thought it better to get on with his undertaking. This had been the way, surely.

Once out of the trees Henderson squinted against the afternoon sun and gripped the horse tightly with his knees. He could see clearly what in the moonlight had been only dimensionless dark and gathered shadow. Ahead the road stretched out between tilled fields, disappearing then visible rising across a flatter space. He could just make out where it ran alongside the far tree line before disappearing down to the river valley. Between the forest he had traversed and the wooded face of the bluff stood, he reckoned, nearly a half mile of good ground. On his right grew knee-high grassy crops he could not identify. Oats or barley maybe, but he didn't think it was wheat. It had been a long time since he had ridden out into the county with his father of a Sunday to look at the farms and ask about plants, trees, animals, the use of implements, what someone was digging, the name of a bird. To his left the land folded gently then flattened out between two tongues of woods. A farmhouse and outbuildings were visible amongst shade trees, the ordered rows of a garden, and beyond, an extended rectangle of orchard. In contrast to the white of the house and other well-kept structures the barn was a mass of charred timbers, some sticking up like rotten teeth. The collapsed roof had fallen to the side. A partially burnt joist protruded at an unnatural angle.

Henderson sawed the reins so the horse could not see his home. He patted him on the neck to soothe him, dismounting slowly. He ran his left hand up Ulysses' head, between his eyes, stroked his ears as he pulled him down to the grass at the edge of the road. He didn't need this big animal sensing where he was and bolting for home. From the pommel he untied the bag and withdrew the pistol. When he was twelve his father had brought it on one of their country rides and had let him hold it after shooting at some cans placed on a stump. The next week he had begged to fire it and was shown how to hold it. Given its weight he could barely keep the barrel level, much less line the sight with anything in the distance. He had fired it into the limbs of a tree, the recoil throwing him back in a stumble. The barrel dug into the ground and his father snatched it away in a fit of anger.

He was not happy to see it now, the oiled blue steel, its smooth grip crafted from wood so blood red as to appear black. It was still too heavy for him to handle. He let it angle down to rest partially on his thigh as he clicked the cylinder out to check the loads. All chambers full, he snapped it to, thumbed the safety on and stuck it with difficulty in the back of his belt. It was just like his father to own such a damn big gun, a Colt Walker, when he might have sent him off with something more suitable. But then maybe that was the only thing that could kill such a large animal. He sneaked a look at Ulysses, contentedly munching away, his eye reflecting the high blue sky. His ears perked up as if spoken to. He took the reins and walked him to where the drive cut into the field toward the house.

When Clayton came out of the woods he was drenched in sweat, filthy from shoveling ashes and dirt during a sleepless night of watching to make sure the fire did not flare up and spread. He had gone into the trees at sunup with an axe to mark timber for cutting replacement boards for the barn. They would have to buy most of it at one of the sawmills on the river since there was no way Clayton and his girls could do the job of felling and shaping by themselves. They could, he thought, sinking the bright head of the axe into the true trunk of a high white oak, at least rough out enough boards that they would have some money left over to eat. It felt good to swing the sharp blade into the grasping green wood, letting the rage out one blow at a time. But after two hours he could barely lift the axe as the strength went out of his body. He felt like curling up around the stump of the tree he had just chopped until it wasn't true anymore, until his barn was standing and they were simply a family minding their own business, too insignificant to bear noticing. It was times like these he most missed his grandfather. He tried hardest to conjure up his voice so that he could hear the wisdom of what it would say. *Come on now Clayton, you ain't gone give up over some rickety barn. You wanted a bigger barn for some cows anyway. So you can hang your head and mope or take hold of what's got to be done and do it. You alive and ain't no man to tell you what to do. Don't let them ignorant white people own you by making you forget that. Without*

277

your fear they have to kill you to stop you getting on with your life. You hear me?

He ran his forearm across his forehead and felt the grit, the pieces of bark clinging to his skin and his hair, and nearly smiled. That old man's voice so strong and sure. He could always see his father's face when he needed to, the set of his jaw and his grim determination. In that man's image he stood up for himself. He had done so many times in town and on the road along the river when they went to market. James's carriage came down to him without his having realized it until he saw himself do as his father would have: refusing an unfair price, looking a man in the eye and telling him to check his scale again, taking a firm grip of a white man's hand and holding it. But it was his grandfather's voice that stayed with him when he felt this waver, when he felt seen through or unable to blend in when he had no stomach for confrontation. There was a strength in the timbre of it that filled him with confidence and a sense of his being. The craft that his grandfather and father had been so proud of and had carried with them in every nerve, cell and sinew of their strong bodies had come to him as the gift of understanding himself as an individual, as more than what others allowed him. They could call him what they liked – and they did – spit in front of him on the street in town, repeat their stupid ideas about what kind of man a black man is, but they could never touch what he had been given by those two men, by his granny, by his mother. Of this he felt certain. He would raise a new barn. All this would pass as if it had been some natural disaster. But of his girls he was less certain. How they were supposed to get on here when they were grown he had no idea. The way Sara had looked at him when he'd fetched the axe and was headed for the woods told him that they would be talking about it directly.

He came out of the woods determined to bring his family some assurance that things would get back to normal soon enough. Coming down the drive, perhaps a hundred yards away, he saw a figure leading a horse. He stopped, crouched, then raised up as he recognized it.

Ulysses.

Years later, Clayton would read the fat book of Cervantes and in his mind would see this image of man laboring with horse each time Quixote struggled with the rackabones Rosinante. The thin figure struggled to keep hold of the animal's head as the horse tried to get the bit in his teeth, the desire to run the last distance to his berth strong in his bones. As the pair tussled their way onto the downslope an even smaller figure emerged out of the tall grass. She must have been playing in the dirt at the edge of the barley, her mother having sent her away from the burned barn. From that distance Clayton could see them confront one another. He tensed and froze, tightening his grip on the haft of the axe.

Nothing moved.

Clayton strained for any sound that might reach him. He heard the little man yell and wave but his daughter did not move. She had her hand over her mouth as she always did when she was frightened. When the figure reached back and pulled the pistol out of his belt he began to run.

When he was close enough he tried to yell but his breath was too short. The scene ahead appeared frozen, then jerked into action. The horse tried to wrest its head out of the man's grip, its strong neck too much for him, the pistol silhouetted against the sky, the figure lurching, regaining his composure, trying to bring his right arm up to level again. When he heard the high-pitched sound he thought it was his lungs whistling from the pain, or maybe the horse, but as he got to within steps of the edge of the field he recognized it was his daughter screaming. He could see the cornflower blue ribbons tied at the bottoms of her braids. He could make out the pattern on her yellow dress, recognized it as a hand-me-down from both older sisters after starting its life on a Tennessee white woman Sara had cleaned house for. Then the gun went off.

The force of the Colt's kick launched the shooter's arm up and then down like a shot bird. The horse bucked wildly tearing its head out of the man's grasp, lunged into the field and galloped away. The brown blur broke once into the light and disappeared into the orchard. Clayton continued without pause brushing past the small yellow form straight into the slight man's body without regard for weapon or technique. Bowling him over in a heap he grabbed a handful of hair and ground his face into the dirt. Beneath his knee he could feel the hard, angular shape of the pistol the man had not let loose. He heard sobbing and a low-pitched sound like a cornered animal might make, turned to see how badly his daughter had been scared but she was not there. It was the one under him crying. His chest heaved, laboring against the bigger man straddling him. Clayton realized that he was the one growling, gritting his teeth and pushing the head down as though he would plant it in the unyielding earth.

The two figures remained that way until the little girl parted the weeds from her hiding place. She had been playing house, trampling down a square in the grass, setting rocks in the shape of a woodstove, table, chairs, sideboard where she stowed pebble dishes, twig cutlery, plucked upturned lilies-of-the-valley cups, her cornhusk dolls turned towards her for instructions and conversation. She saw Ulysses get away and her father jump on the man, thinking it best to retreat to the safety of her house. Her granny doll told her to go out and see what the noises were, that it would be ok, that her daddy would be there. She went carefully to her father who was making a noise deep within his chest unlike any she had ever heard. His face was covered with dust and bits of grass. She wiped his cheek with her fingers. He slumped down, pulled her to him and whispered in her ear for her to get on to the house.

All right, she said, but don't bring that man with you.

He nodded, placing his forehead against hers, as he always did at bedtime. She turned and ran all knees and elbows down the drive.

"Get up."

The figure wore dark gray trousers, baggy over skinny legs, brown scuffed boots, a white muslin shirt rolled to the elbows, soaked through with sweat and dirt stained. The gun lay conspicuously where Clayton had kicked it, using the toe of his boot to prise it out of the limp hand.

"I said get up."

He tried to roll to the right but stopped abruptly, groaned, tried to press his forehead into the ground and by this means pull his knees up under him but could not manage it. Using his left hand he levered himself onto his side, bent his legs and with great effort sat up, his right arm dangling, teeth clenched in pain. It was the Jeffries boy from the night before. Clayton was too tired to think clearly about the events that had transpired since the last time he'd put his head down onto the soft feather pillow next to his wife.

"What you doin back out this way? You come out here to shoot me for puttin some birdshot into that barn burner's legs last night? Ain't no way that's fair trade. Ain't no way he died of that, less you didn't get him to town or he fell off my horse and broke his neck."

Clayton knew he was asking as much as telling. He peered closely into the white boy's tear-streaked face to see if any of what he said registered.

"My arm's broken. I can't move it and it hurts like fire."

"What you come out here for?" Louder this time. "You tell me that first."

"Return your horse," the boy croaked.

"What you got that pistol for, highway robbers? You tell me the truth I might help you. You keep lyin I'm gonna pick up that Colt and beat the hell out of you before I shoot you and bury your ass in them woods."

281

The boy had white flecks of spittle at the corners of his lips and tried to lick these away. "Shoot your horse, teach you a lesson."

"A lesson?" He laughed but there was no humor in it. "What kinda lesson you all think I need that burnin down my barn didn't teach me? I know we ain't welcome here, but we got no place else to go. You think that horse any different from any other? He a darkie horse? That little girl some kinda threat to you or your town or all what you white folks got?"

Henderson rose to one knee, looked up and into the black man's eyes which were red with exhaustion.

"I came out here to shoot your horse and would have done it too. I didn't mean to scare the girl but she wouldn't leave. As far as I'm concerned it's just business."

Just business. That was it. He had found a path out of this emotional dead end, set with the wreckage of hope, littered with excuses, empty bottles, the fog of bitter liquid on the tongue.

"A boy sent out to do man's work," Clayton said, more to himself than anyone. "Well, I got a barn to build, so if you'll scuse me."

He turned toward the house, bent to retrieve the axe lying at the edge of the drive where it had fallen in the channel that drained the downslope. Behind him he heard a hoarse voice.

"What about my arm? You gonna help me or not?"

Clayton wanted to turn around. It wasn't anything to pop the boy's arm back in its socket, make his walk to town less jarring. He thought of the big pistol in that unsteady grip, his daughter's cool fingers on his cheek, the grim determination of the mask the boy had put on to inform him of his purpose. He'd looked younger and vulnerable, involved in something he wasn't sure of, then his features had set themselves. Clayton had seen it before. Likely he would again. He also knew that Jeffries might very well faint from the pain on his return.

Despite his desire to let him suffer it did not seem a good idea to risk having him die someplace close. More than the barn would go up then.

Henderson waited. When the black man turned he could not read the look on his face. It passed through his mind that he might kill him. He put up his left arm and tried to turn away. He was told to hold still. He kept his eyes closed as the sole of a boot was set flat against his hip. The pain in his shoulder when his arm was pulled out set the world on fire. A roar went up around him and as he felt himself buffeted by this, lifted and tossed, carried into the air light as a blown dandelion, he felt a pop.

He sat stunned in the dirt. His shoulder felt massive with stung nerves. Into the base of his neck crawled a deep penetrating ache. The man stood over him, his shadow cast along the drive that of a giant.

"Thank you," he managed. He coughed, choking on the dry air.

"Wadn't nothin. Just business."

Henderson watched him go with the glinting blade of the axe over his shoulder. It hurt to get up and he thought simply lying down and sleeping would be nice. No, got to get home. Pinning his right arm to his side with his left hand on his elbow he got to his feet, then took several deep breaths for fear he would faint.

In the dirt and scattered rocks lay the purposeful form of the gun. He stuck it in the front of his belt.

He made it to the woods by singing "Frère Jacques," a song his mother had sung to him as a child, rocking him in her lap when he was ill or had some hurt. By taking a step every other beat he set up a rhythm and tried to stay focused on setting one foot in front of the other. Dusk was coming on, stealing the light from the prairie. In the distance a slice of pale July watermelon with the seeds picked out, a trick of his thirst. The dark green line of the trees against the pinked evening horizon looked impossibly far away at first. After uncounted steps he could pick out individual trunks and shades of leaves. Finally knew he would make the opening.

Stay asleep, brother Jacques, he said to himself. *I need this song for a while.*

Having no choice, he went on, singing the song in his head round and round, gripping his arm tight against his body. He stopped at woods' edge, realizing he might take off his belt and use it to strap the arm down. But when he tried to take it off the pain was too much. Plus it held the gun. The belt cinched tight again he went on.

Time stopped inside the enveloping pain which alternated between sharp and dull. In the pallid light he tried to judge the size of his shoulder. It felt enormous. He was glad that he could not see it, afraid it might be so blood-engorged that it would fright him beyond his ability to continue.

He walked some way out of the woods before he was aware of being in the open. The frail sliver of moon in the east silvered the road ahead. He stopped to blink, thinking mistakenly that his eyesight was failing. The night bugs churred more softly. It was almost possible to synchronize his song to theirs, and he was pleased when *din-din don, din-din don* matched the syncopation of the crickets. As he was considering whether to mash down some weeds and have a liedown he heard the hoof falls of a horse. Well, he thought, it can't get any worse than this. He stood his ground in the middle of the road.

Whoever it was, outlined by a hole in the night, was big. Whether this bade ill or fair he could not reckon. The strength was spilling out of him all at once and he went down, wondering where his legs had gone. Leaning his head back he could see the sky. He heard the rider dismount then bend over him. The small explosion of a struck match lit up the face. As big as a store-bought pie. It was the man from the night before who held the lanterns in the makeshift operating theater at Cassini's. Cor, his name was, potential throttler of unskillful getaway drivers.

"Cor," he gasped.

"Sorry bout the light, Jeffries. Wanted to make sure it was you is all."

Henderson would have laughed had he been able. Wished he had the strength to make the joke lying in wait: Who the fuck you think would be lying out in this road hurt in the middle of the night? You come across other ones on the way? Big dumb dangerous sonofabitch.

He did manage to approximate the word "water" and Cor fetched a canteen and splashed some into his mouth. Henderson felt himself lifted up and onto the horse. With the big man's thick arm around his middle they rode to town in the darkness. He hummed his song to the hoofbeats of the trotting horse, heard the morning bells descend over the waking city, saw Brother Jacques open his eyes as he passed out.

Twenty Four

That night Clayton came as close as he would ever come to packing Sara and the girls into the wagon with everything they could fit and leaving for good. The first part of the plan was easy. Getting away from trouble, from history, felt so good you were liable to forget about the next part. Where do you go? That was the hardest. How do you recoup the sweat and blood you've forced out of yourself to raise up children and shelter, crops and livestock? When he remembered that Ulysses had run off he had to laugh.

Hell, he didn't even have a horse.

Sara came in with a last bucket of water and poured it into the washtub in the middle of the kitchen floor. They had eaten an early supper and the girls would have a bath. Then he would read them a story and they would fall off to sleep and he would be free to think of something more constructive than abandoning their farm.

"That water's gonna be mighty cold."

Sara looked at him petulantly and started to say something. She had been upset about the barn burning, unsure whether they would live through the flames and the shooting. Clayton had calmed her down. But this had not scrubbed her memory of the feeling of helplessness. It was only intimidation, he'd said. He'd lived through it before. They would rebuild and raise the girls, work on the place, live peacefully. He had crafted a narrative of their future long into the night and she fell asleep determined to put one terrible event behind her.

And then today a man with a gun. It didn't matter to her that he had been not more than a chap. The gun was still a gun and Birdy could be lying dead on the table under a clean white sheet right now for all that mattered.

"It'll have to do for tonight."

He got up from his chair and caught her as she opened the door.

"Hold on." He folded his arms around her from behind and she let out a sigh. He kissed her neck and her cheek, bit her earlobe softly, took the bucket out of her hand.

"Get off to bed," he whispered. "I'll see the girls get clean and tucked away."

"No – "

"Yes. You dead on your feet, woman. Now get on upstairs and leave it to me."

He wished he hadn't said "dead," but she was so tired she didn't notice. With any luck she'd be asleep when he climbed into bed and they wouldn't have to talk about what had happened out in the tall grass.

The moon was nearly full and he steered by its light to the well where he replaced the bucket. The fieldstones were still warm from the day's heat and he leaned there for a minute in the cool air. It was quiet but for the bugs and a gentle breeze high in the treetops. Clayton loved to sit and listen to the night sounds or walk the place in the moonlight but there was work to do inside.

Still, there was a lot to think about.

Sara had not seen June's burned body and he did not say anything about it. He knew he should tell her but could not bring himself to say the words. It would likely be too much for her. Or maybe it wasn't her he was worried about. He held at a distance the fear that if he permitted himself to think about getting away, by taking up the offer to sell, he might just do it. Clayton knew he could not live with himself if that came to pass. He reckoned the law would be out any day to investigate the shooting of the young barn burner or the whereabouts of one June Colegrove and that would settle it somehow. The body lay even now in the smokehouse on a makeshift table. He'd wrapped him in a square of waxed canvas he used as an awning to work out of the rain and carried him over his back, the smell of burned flesh nearly overwhelming. Never would he forget the blackened face, eyelids burned away, the lips burnt back, teeth sticking out in a gaudy leer. Those staring eyes.

It was time to act. If he waited he'd only be fooling himself. Whoever wanted the farm would not stop just because an unreliable man who owed money around town had disappeared. No one but he and the boy knew June to be dead and not lounging aboard a riverboat or westbound train. If anyone had information about the buying and selling of land in the county it would be Marjorie Lane. He'd go see her. Then he'd pay a man a visit about a horse, and a barn, and three terrified little girls. To make it crystal clear what the consequences would be for any further trouble.

His daughters were waiting. With the deliberate gait of the weary he went back inside, glad he did not believe in ghosts.

The girls were playing quietly with their dolls in the dollhouse he had made for them. It had two floors like their own home and was hinged so they could open it up and maneuver the small figures into each of its rooms. On any other night in which they were left to themselves they would have been rambunctious, with Lucy, the littlest one they had always called Birdy because of the way she meticulously pecked at her food, ending the fun in tears. The sisters shared the room downstairs he and his brothers had slept in. From the doorway he watched them and thought of how he had felt on this very floor at the end of a day of trouble come on sudden and terrifying. He knew they had a good idea that something had happened and he didn't mind them knowing such things occurred; but he would be sure they first understood that he was there to protect them. The sun would come up in the

288

east tomorrow and they would put their faces into it and go on with their lives. Being afraid was a luxury he was not interested in anyone getting used to.

"It's bath time young ladies," he said, getting their attention. "Put the toys away proper now, so your mama don't have to fuss around tomorrow."

"Where is she?" Eliza, the oldest, asked. "Why can't she do the bath?"

Clayton admired his oldest daughter's cleverness. She knew the bath would be quick at this late hour with their mother so tired from a long day. They liked a wash in the creek when it was deep enough, but a washtub bath was a different experience. At least she got to go first in the clean water.

"She's in bed already so you all keep it down while we get cleaned up and ready to meet the sandman."

"Daddy I don't wanna take no bath. I had one the other day."

"Birdy, you was out in the dirt all afternoon. I can smell you from here."

She laughed. "You can *not*."

Her sister smelled her.

"What you think, Hannah? She smell like Ulysses?"

Birdy twisted away from her sister's attempt to get her nose into the arm of her dress and Eliza was just about to hold her littlest sister down. Thirty seconds to tears.

"Let loose of her Eliza and come on. Hannah, back for you in a jiffy."

After he threw out the dirty bathwater he took a rag and wiped the floor. When he was finished his back was sore and he was happy to sit in the rocking chair he pulled up next to the girls' bed. Birdy was in between her sisters and they were hushed with anticipation. He had a book on each knee. It was their habit to choose from one of two books they read at the same time, progressing in a story until they wanted to move over and see what was happening in the other. Sara thought this ridiculous and though he didn't contradict her, he thought it perfectly fine that his daughters couldn't just stick to one story.

"Whose turn is it to pick? Hannah? What's it gonna be?"

Hannah rose up on her elbows to look at her choices. *Treasure Island* or *Uncle Remus*. Her brow furrowed in thought as she tried to remember where they were in each.

"While you thinking maybe you all want to hear how I bought my first book. Or how I caught a hunnerd pound catfish with my bare hands." In his best imitation of his grandfather Amos, lost on the girls who had never met him, he stroked his chin and went on. "In eighteen and sixty seven, I believe it was, or sixty eight, it might have been. Mercy, now I plum forgot the year. Hold on now, I get it in a second."

Giggles from the gallery. The threat of a true story never failed to elicit a choice. Hannah's finger came down solidly on *Treasure Island*.

"Good choice." He meant it. If they ever let him actually tell the story of Setliff's bookshop they'd know how partial he was to islands, pirates, and all such maritime adventures.

As he read he glanced at his audience to judge their attention. Birdy was always first asleep and took a few sharp elbows when she drifted off on the first page. After a half hour, right as Jim Hawkins came ashore with Long John Silver's crew and then ran for the woods, he was the only one lost in the story. He would happily have continued but he knew he ought to put the light out and let them sleep. He turned down the wick in the lamp till it sputtered out and shut the door behind him.

He slid into bed gingerly, trying not to wake Sara, whose breathing held steady as he settled in.

"They give you any trouble?"

"I thought you was asleep. You a crafty woman Sara McGhee." He rolled onto his side and they made spoons. She

290

felt warm and soft and he was instantly sleepy. "They was fine. Birdy splashed water in my eye but I kept from cryin."

"You a brave husband." She took a deep breath and let it out slowly and he felt her expand and contract with it. "I don't know, Clay. Most time I feel safe out here, but when I don't it about scares me to death. Last night I didn't think I could bear it and when I went out and saw that man on the ground I wanted to kill him. But then I thought about what we would do if we left this place. Maybe go to a city or find somewhere so lonesome no one would know we was there. I don't see how that would change things. And the worst of it is I know you'd never be right anywhere else. Hell, burnin up that barn ain't no way to get rid of no McGhee. He just commence to plannin how to make the next one better."

He chuckled into the base of her neck. "I was already makin a start when that fella come out with Uly."

"They'd have to kill you to get you off this place. But you'd still be here. Your granddad is still here. And Clara and James and Lily. You all changed this land and most everything on it and there ain't no one can take that away."

He pictured his parents and grandparents as they'd looked the day they arrived here. Even his daddy had a hopeful look on his face.

"I was recollectin ol Amos a little while ago. I'm sorry you never got to meet him."

"Me too. At least I get to hear him tell those awful stories."

When he tickled her she giggled like her daughters. He made his voice low and scratchy.

"I ever tell you bout that time I caught a fitty pound flat-head with one hand?"

"Why I reckon I ain't heard that one."

He started telling her the story but she was asleep before he even got into the boat.

So he told her about that summer day when Gene Lecroix killed his granny in cold blood and then he and June shot him dead off his black horse. How James had come running followed by the sheriff. The feeling of having the heavy rifle pried out of his aching fingers. June writhing out of his father's grip and screaming until he lay quietly in the grass. He unfolded an account of the scene back at the house, his grandfather, kind and gentle old Amos, lying on the kitchen table as still as a statue. And in the faintest whisper he described seeing June emerge from the barn on fire and told her as best he could why he would not help him. He held his breath as Sara breathed, waiting for her to say something in the darkness, but she lay still sleeping. So he went on and told her about June's scorched corpse in their smokehouse. He asked her how many days he ought to wait for the law before he buried him. When she didn't reply he listened to her rhythmic breathing. He reckoned the answer would come to him. And he said that he was sorry, terribly terribly sorry, but there was nothing he could have done. I'll put June in the picket graveyard with mama and daddy, Amos and Clara, and the baby, he said. They'll look after him.

Twenty Five

Annabelle's doctor, who thought of himself as progressive, had blushed heavily when asked for his opinion of vibrators. A magazine advert had caught her eye, she ordered it, and when it came in the post she hid it in the bottom drawer of her dresser. Not, she realized later, because she was embarrassed, but so that she could anticipate its pleasures. There could never be enough things her husband didn't know about her. The first time she'd used it she nearly flopped off the bed. Life experience had taught her that something this good had to have consequences and so out of desperate curiosity she asked Dr. Goodloe whether the vibrator was too good to be true. She would have readily admitted that she also asked him out of pure titillation. The only thing that rivaled a good vibration was the flushed cheeks of a supercilious general practitioner. She laughed that day for the first time in weeks.

With Peter and the others out looking for Henderson she needed a way to relieve the tension. There was bourbon. There were nerve tonics and the tincture of laudanum, which Goodloe had so sternly warned her about. But these were stronger than what she needed now. It wouldn't do any good to pass out and miss her son's return. She needed her full complement of wits to press him about her plot for his escape.

She relaxed on the bed, thumbed the switch on the little machine and it whirred to life. She turned it off. Too angry. Goddamn Peter Jeffries anyway. She needed to be in the right frame of mind for this kind of pleasure. If she wanted to have a lackluster orgasm while unhappy and distracted she could just let her husband have a go. She thought about what she'd yelled at him when he had gone out so hastily to find Henderson. And to escape her, she knew. At first, Peter could barely get the words out when she'd forced him to tell her where her son had gone. Reminding him of how stupid and irresponsible he was had no effect on him nor did she have much enthusiasm for the tedium of this repetition.

She put the vibrator back in its box, then secreted it in its drawer. This reminded her that while she had the house to herself she needed to retrieve the money she'd set aside. Several years ago she'd read a novel in which the heroine had kept a contingency fund in case she ever had to leave her husband and make her way in the world. This had seemed a very good idea. There were accounts in both their names, but these joint monies would not be readily accessible to her if she needed to get away in a hurry. Peter's relationship with bankers and lawyers was comprehensive, and his reach was, she guessed, considerable. This was something she needed to be able to control. So she began skimming cash from the household accounts that were under her management. Peter never had much patience for these affairs and was more than willing to provide her with amounts she demanded with little question. Since she had scant reason to access these accumulated funds they grew to a sizeable amount. Eight or nine thousand dollars, she figured.

Her hiding place would have pleased her sister Rachel, who had died when she was eleven and had in Annabelle's imagination stayed that age. They had played hide and seek in their house in Chestnut Hill and then with greater exuberance in their building after they moved to the flat on Panama Street. Alongside the basement stairs hung a small landing where they kept potatoes, onions, and root vegetables in small bins. It was dark and the temperature was relatively cool and constant. Behind one of the bins she had placed the money in an empty tin of Johnson's Baby Powder, which was not only the right size but gave the bills a pleasant aroma. She retrieved it and sat at the kitchen table to count the money. The writing on the can proclaimed that its contents were "Best for baby, Best for you." Clever people those Johnsons.

It was empty.

She sat it on the table and tried to collect her thoughts, or at least get them to run all in the same direction. She screwed the lid back on and went to the bedroom to lie down. She had to think. Peter had done this, surely. Question was, what was she prepared to do about it?

She must have slept because when she heard the ruckus down in the front hallway she started up and had to wipe the slaver from her cheek. When she got to her feet the can bounced against the baseboard and came to rest on its side. She put it in the drawer with the vibrator. Everything secret had been spoiled.

Henderson was carried in by a big man Annabelle did not know. There wasn't any blood that she could see but his eyes were glassy and his head lolled back nearly hitting the hall tree.

"Be careful for God's sake." She moved to support her son but before she could get there Peter took her firmly by the upper arm and pushed her into the darkened drawing room.

"You stay out of the way until I get things under control." He shook her. "You hear me?"

Annabelle looked him in the eye and without wavering from her husband's gaze said, "You are going to regret all this."

He released her arm. "As if I didn't already," he said, turning to go.

She took a handful of his sleeve. "Where – " she had to keep herself from slapping him. "*Where* is my goddamn money?"

He laughed contemptuously, looked down at her feeble fistful of fabric.

"*Your* money. That's rich. You know exactly whose money it is. In future I will account for it more attentively to prevent any such confusion."

He pried her fingers from his arm.

"I was going to offer it as an alternative to your mother's meddling," she said. "You can invest it or something and use it, all of it, for Henderson."

He opened his jacket deliberately, as if he were performing a dumbshow on a stage, put his hand inside its inner breast pocket and retrieved his wallet. It was made of oiled calfskin, a gaudy present from Sylvia, and like her it was stuffed and fat. He held it in front of her, full to bursting with filched bills, and then replaced it as theatrically as he'd drawn it out. Never had Annabelle found the smell of baby powder so infuriating.

"I will, in fact, be doing exactly as you suggest, tomorrow. A rare investment opportunity has presented itself and I will be taking full advantage of it. Now if you don't mind I would like to see what has happened to my son."

Peter had no intention of telling her that he would be finding other purposes for his prize fight winnings. Such as buying a tidy little farm out by the river. He would give her a thousand to shut her up, to placate her against the day Henderson had to go away to his new school. From what he could gather, the boy was in certain need of what a military academy could provide for him. And with the old lady willing to pay? All the better.

Henderson opened his eyes to soft light on the ceiling. Late morning. His shoulder throbbed most at the apex of each breath. It hurt, but nothing like before the big man had collected him and brought him back to town. His memory of taking those steps from the failed execution of McGhee's horse and across the prairie, through the dark woods and out unfolded in his mind's eye in indistinct scenes.

The impression of having sung returned to him.

He had regained consciousness when handed down from the horse. The doctor cut his shirt off while his father pinned him down. A wrap secured his shoulder and he was given something in two teaspoons that made him gag. All the while his mother stood in the doorway, hands clutching the front of her robe. Once he swallowed the second spoonful he wanted badly to say, "a drowsy numbness pains my sense, as though of hemlock I had drunk" for her amusement but he could not get the words out. Now that he was more lucid he realized that Keats was probably neither funny nor reassuring.

Whatever the doctor gave him left him feeling as though he floated in warm water. As he drifted off he heard the sounds of a violent argument beginning downstairs. His mother screamed and his father responded in a tone he could barely hear, forceful but measured. Heavy footsteps, a door slamming, the shattering of glass, horrible crying.

Sleep took him down.

He could not tell how much time had passed when he awoke again, so thirsty he felt barely able to breathe. Pulling his knees to his chest he patiently kicked at the sheet until he had it bunched at bed's end. A pale lavender. His bound shoulder appeared to be normal sized. Damn did it hurt. Like a mouthful of toothaches. With his left index finger and thumb he gently probed it, finding it less sore than he'd anticipated. It seemed of a sudden a wonderful thing how the arm could move in so many ways, twisting and turning and doing one's bidding so. He moved his left hand elaborately gracing the air like a dancer. Perhaps the sleeping potion had not worn off.

As he braced himself to swing his legs around and test his head in standing he saw her leaning against the doorframe. Still wearing her robe. Her eyes were deepset, dark with fatigue and a greater thing, some draining force that seemed always on her worst days to claim her for some other place or time. A war on two fronts.

Henderson had the urge to cry. He could give in and admit his mistaken path. It could be undone. Succumb to her and take the great risk. To do what? That was the question. He had thought this settled out on the prairie when he had spoken resolutely to the black man, holding his tone and leveling with him about the way things stood. But his mother's look said peacetime required further choices, with less distinct parameters.

When she spoke her voice came in low and fast. Nothing like what he expected.

"Are you proud of yourself?"

He closed his eyes and sighed.

"It is customary to ask a person in such a condition if they are feeling any better, or perhaps if they need anything from the uninjured."

"Do you see any uninjured?"

That was too easy. He tried a faint smile.

"And what is your *condition*, Henderson? I look at you and see a stranger. On second thought, no. You are perfectly recognizable to me, the brutal half of you that has throttled your other half is clear as could be. It's all starting to sound disturbingly predictable and biblical. Cain, the father's son, always kills his mother's Abel – "

"Mother, stop. That's not fair. Please don't." The tears would come now.

"Fair." She spat the word at him.

He swung his legs around, clenched the edge of the mattress and stood facing her. From her eyes he tried to extract some tincture of tenderness, a softening that would signal the game. But she was not there, not really. Not the part that mattered to him. He could not stop the next lines from Keats' poem dancing across his brain, the lines that he would have held back before – "Or emptied some dull opiate to the drains one minute past, and Lethe-wards had sunk." His mother had sunk into that obliviating river some time ago and he could no longer save her. Her silly plan for him to get away and start over struck him as a bitter joke. What would leaving accomplish? Then again, he wasn't sure; distance might be a kind of cure.

No. For now he would drink his hemlock. It would at least be his choice.

"I would rather be decisive than hide in the dark. I can't do it. *You* made it impossible."

This garnered no immediate reaction. The tension in her face eased, replaced with blankness and for a brief second he did not recognize her. Her antagonistic self had turned and walked away, receding further into shade. Without another word she was gone. He heard her door close.

It took some effort to get dressed. He pulled a loose-fitting shirt over his immobile arm, tucking the empty sleeve into his belt. For a full minute he stood quietly at the door to his parents' bedroom. He held his breath and willed himself to hear some sound through the oak.

The knob would not turn. He could not bring himself to knock.

Weak with hunger and thirst he went down to the kitchen. The milk tasted sweeter out of the bottle. There were biscuits on a plate and he took these out of the icebox then a jar of blackberry preserves. The butter was on the table next to the gun.

He had not noticed the Colt when he came into the kitchen. Standing there with the plate in his hand he felt its presence, tried to think when and where he had seen it last. Hadn't he left it in the dirt where it had fallen? Hadn't the man taken it from him? He put the plate of biscuits down on the table and pushed the heavy weapon over with it. It felt like it weighed fifty pounds. He had no idea how he managed to bring it back.

With difficulty he halved a biscuit, buttered it, then shook out the seedy, dark preserves without bothering to use a utensil. It wasn't easy to ignore the gun while he chewed. When there were only crumbs left he put the plate in the sink. He had worked out that it was Saturday and that his father had gone to the fights at Tecumseh Trail Park. Something he had been looking forward to for most of the summer but had forgotten. He sighed when he remembered that he had also agreed to take Betsy, imagining her even now looking through the lace curtains of the front window expecting his arrival. There would be no doing that in this condition. He sat down heavily at the table and with his belly full felt the dead weight of his weariness. The desire to be in a crowd, to make the trip across and along the river, to cheer, had all left him. There had been enough battles for one week. The Courier would have full coverage and he would console himself with reading about it. That would do fine. As he nodded off to sleep it occurred to him that his father had left the pistol in such a conspicuous place on purpose. He would never have done so carelessly. There was dirt caked in the grooves on the cylinder and on the grip, an ochre dust along the bevel of the front sight and in the mouth of the bore.

In the shop he gathered the oiled rag, bore brush and the gun's holster. Back at the table he burnished the blued steel until it wouldn't take his breath. This was a chore with one hand. So was scouring the length of the barrel with the brush, but he managed. It felt good to have a task to concentrate on. He left the pistol leaning rakishly against the stiff leather of the coiled holster and belt in the exact center of the kitchen table.

No way he could miss it.

He went straight up to bed and without removing his clothes lay down and dreamless slept. As if of hemlock he had drunk.

There would be no meeting in his office this time.

Peter proposed Cassini's. Lanahan countered with the Public Library. He acquiesced, wanting to get this over with

300

so that he would have plenty of time for other errands before going across the river for the fight. Sixth and Columbia was close enough that he could walk. The library and the high school had for ten years shared a building, the thinking being that housing books and students in the same place would lead one to the other. He had thought this economical but naïve. There was no one about; curious for a Saturday. The custodian informed him that the library had moved in the spring to the old Reynolds home at Fifth and South Streets. This was only a few blocks. As he walked he found it difficult not to put his hand over the bulge in his inner pocket. He hoped he would not run into anyone he knew.

The Reynolds house sat on an entire city block, a squat two storey behemoth with a prominent belvedere perched on its flat roof. He entered, ignoring the matron's smiling face which said "How may I help you?" in that unmistakable dowager manner that reminded him of his oldest sister. They had agreed to meet in the main reading room. He found Lanahan ensconced behind a Chicago newspaper.

"You best be careful. You'll ruin your reputation if anyone sees you in here actually reading something."

There were perhaps a dozen people scattered across the well-lit room, which must have once been a dining hall. He was shushed by an old woman indistinguishable from the one he'd encountered upon entering. He turned and looked back the way he came but could not see her. This was not his kind of place. Lanahan folded the newspaper and gestured with his head towards the high rows of books at the back of the room. In the far corner their voices were muffled by the volumes that immured them on both sides.

"Right," said Lanahan, "we'll have to whisper quiet like or we'll have one of them ladies over here before you know it. They're silent as ghosts and twice as sneaky."

"We should have met in a tavern, for Christ's sake. This is unnerving."

"You bring the scratch?"

He looked over his shoulder and then tapped his chest.

"Give it over and let us count it."

"I want the information first. Fighter and round."

"Well, about that I got good news and bad news. The bad news, at least for your part of town, is that Lewis wins in the eighth by a knockout."

"And the good news is I make a considerable amount of money."

"That and one other thing. Lewis is about as Irish as you are. He's English. But you best not cheer for him or your mates will probably murder you."

"You had better be sure about all this. And I had better get my money or I will make you very sorry."

"Relax my friend. My brother was plenty happy with the arrangements and you're gonna be pleased with the payoff. It's good square business all the way round."

Peter handed over the thick sheaf of bills and when he had counted them to his satisfaction Lanahan said, "I'll meet you here at noon on Monday then and *you* can do the counting. Now, you go ahead and linger a bit. Wouldn't do to be seen together now would it?"

"Are you going to place the bet now or out at the park?"

"That ain't any of your business. Before I do anything though I gotta go see a priest about a secret." He tipped his hat and made his way down the shadowy aisle.

Fucking superstitious bastards, Peter muttered.

Clayton waited on Fifth Street in the shade beneath a striped awning, pretending to admire the hats and scarves in a shop window. The young attendant, his blond hair slicked back, looked up from his work on a display of cuff links in a glass case, but made no effort to coax him into the store. Which was just as well, since in the reflection of the plate glass he was able to watch Peter Jeffries walk into the Public Library.

He had not figured the lawyer for a reading man, especially not of books that could be freely borrowed. Nothing to do but wait.

Uly had reappeared two days after he'd galloped off at the discharge of young Jeffries' pistol. Clayton found him at sunup grazing contentedly at the edge of the orchard. The saddle had twisted but it was still intact and the horse had no marks from his ordeal. He brushed him down and fed him, told Sara he had to go to town to see the farrier. At the courthouse he found Marjorie Lane and asked her if anyone had been in to ask about his farm. The look on her face told him indeed there had been. In a quiet voice she related the visit by Peter Jeffries and her surprise that he would consider selling. He assured her he had no intention of doing any such thing. He asked if they had a city directory in the office. She found it beneath the counter and pretended to busy herself with some papers as he looked up Jeffries, Peter, memorizing his home and business addresses.

He tried his law office first as it was nearby, but only got as far as the news stand on the corner of the courthouse square before he saw Jeffries come out of a building that matched the address. It had been about ten years since he'd last seen him, on a visit to the Saturday market on Fourth Street with Cmicky, who had pointed him out with contempt and not a few profanities. No one put a finger on a son of a bitch like Cas. He followed from a distance, not wanting to catch up with him where so many people were about. Better to wait until he was on a side street or even near his house. And so now he waited, moving to a cigar store, where he admired the Indian and then fished deliberately in his pockets for a penny for the scale next to it. Above the slot for the coin was a mirror, which Clayton used to scrutinize his face to see if it bore any trace of calculation. He pulled the brim of his hat down in front to mask his eyes but overall he found nothing to suggest that he was anything but a man innocently strolling the downtown. He pretended to want to know his weight exactly and made a show of peering at the needle that swept across the numbers. When a man in a dark suit exited he thought it was Jeffries and got off the scale so he could follow him in the shop window. But this fellow was shorter and had black whiskers. He laced his hands behind his back and was feigning serious interest in a hardware store when Jeffries emerged into the sunlight.

Clayton stayed on his side of Fifth Street and followed him, wishing he had something to carry that made him look less conspicuous. He had no idea what to do with his hands. Jeffries walked as if he hadn't a care in the world. He appeared to be whistling. A faint tune mingled with the sounds of wagons and commerce. At Ferry Street Jeffries turned right and Clayton realized he only had a few blocks to intercept him before he reached his house. As nonchalantly as he could he ran after him until he was a few steps behind. The whistle was indeed the attorney, who was oblivious to his being the object of pursuit. I could have clubbed him over the head by now, Clayton thought, and wondered if perhaps he ought to have. There was no more time to waste.

"Mr. Jeffries." No break in his stride. "Sir," he said louder, with what he meant to be an accusatory tone. This stopped him and he turned with a smile under his neatly trimmed brown mustache.

"What can I do for – " but his genial mood was broken by his astonishment at being addressed in person by a man he had not thought of as real. And if real, at least not proximate.

Clayton regretted the "Mr." and "Sir" as soon as he'd said them, but he was unused to casual address for men he did not know. He knew himself to be slow to anger but the look on Jeffries' face threatened to accelerate the process. It registered a superiority that guaranteed he would lie with impunity to any questions put to him. Summoning the image of Sara and his three little girls huddled together in their nightdresses, scared half to death at the terror of flames and screaming animals, of their father rushing into the night, of having no idea of what they had done to deserve such a thing, he approached and clenched his fists. With no regard for his family this man had burned his barn without even leaving his fancy house. Now his blood was up and he badly wanted to put his fist into that smug look and turn it into pain, into wages for sins committed. As a wordless warning for the future: you even think about us and I'll make you bleed. Maybe next time your son will never find his way back. Plenty of places to put a body such that no one would ever find it. You all ain't the only ones can skulk around at night with mischief on their mind.

"Jeffries," he said, pointing his finger, "if you ever do anything to my family or my farm again I will make you sorry. You're lucky I'm a peaceful man." He didn't feel peaceful. Nor did he care right now about the consequences of a swift and violent retribution. A wagon went by loaded with crates and the driver tipped his hat to Peter, looked at Clayton. Whatever he saw there made him twist around in his seat. As if he'd miss something if he didn't. Jeffries had his hands out and took a step back.

"McGhee, hold on a minute. I understand from my son that there was an unfortunate incident out at your place, but surely you don't think I had anything to do with it. I'm an officer of the court and a respected citizen." He let this claim hang in the air as he felt for something in the inside pocket of his suit.

Clayton took a step back.

Jeffries took out a flat silver case and snapped it open. He put a small cigar in the side of his mouth with a quaking hand. Clayton saw the tremor. You noticed these things if you were unused to being around a lot of people. Especially when you had to gauge the weather of a situation in which you had no status as a person.

Clayton had dropped his accusatory finger; now he pointed it again. "I know damn well you're behind this. You can stand there and lie, but I didn't come here to argue. I came to make you understand that any more trouble and I will do something biblical to you. Do you know the Old Testament, Jeffries? How about Paradise Lost?"

Jeffries' eyebrows went up and Clayton caught this with a smile.

"That's right, *the nigger can read*. And he's got the book of revenge carved into his memory like only the son of a slave can. You've got a lot in this world, but I swear I will cast you out of it and bury you in the ground."

Jeffries smoked but his hand was no steadier than before. When he spoke it was more conversationally, as though he were a child trying to talk his way out of being punished.

"Look, it was your friend June's idea. The barn burning. He forced me to send my son and insisted he lead them. I tried to stop it but there was no reasoning with him. Did he give you the money I gave him?"

Clayton shook his head. Jeffries went on, talking faster now.

"No? Well there you go. He took my money . . . thousands of dollars . . . and burned your barn out of spite . . . I mean, he resents you, said you'd always had it better than him, had what he never had. He hates you, or at least wants your land more than he cares about the consequences for you and your family. And where is he now? Gone. Probably halfway to New Orleans or Kansas City. We're the victims here."

"That ain't what your boy said."

"Henderson? What does he know about this? He – "

"After I took his gun away we had a man to man talk. I think you'd be surprised what he knows."

Twenty Six

Father Bernard sat in the vestibule of the rectory on a narrow bench and read from the missal he kept in his inside pocket. The horses would clatter up on the cobbles any minute and in the silence he tried to concentrate on what Saint Mark was saying about love. It was no use. His brain would not absorb the sense of the passage. He was too excited about the fights.

Lanahan's face betrayed nothing of his own state of mind. Once Bernard was seated he snapped the reins and the identical black beasts set off at a brisk trot. It suited Bernard fine that his companion was predisposed to silence so he took off his hat and angled his face forward into the last vestiges of cool late-morning air. They rolled along Second Street in that part of the south side people called The Towpath, paralleling as it did the old canal. No more than a ditch now, filled in where buildings had risen, the path a memory of mules and shirtless men and the packet boats that had allowed the town to grow before the railroad. Lanahan broke the silence.

"What is it we'll see today, do you think, Father?"

"If I were a betting man I'd lay my sovereigns on the Irish boy," Bernard said, pleased to be able to show off his knowledge of the sport. "Though with caution, as the Englishman is experienced and knows the science. A powerful thing, experience in the face of youth. The lure of glory often sends a young man where he ought not to be, his chin forgotten by the confidence of his fists until flat on the canvas, the angel of mercy counting out his tally."

Lanahan nodded his large head in agreement.

"I'm just after telling the wife the same thing but without your eloquence. The kid's got brass to be sure, but it's not a mere game of fists is it? He's got to have a plan and use his craft against his man there. Otherwise, as you say, it'll be full bull to the knacker's hammer if you know what I mean."

Second Street sloped down, then flattened, then sloped again until it reached the broad rail tracks. Lanahan coiled the reins and took a firmer grip, sitting forward slightly, checking the horses against the descent. They slowed.

"It wouldn't do to come careening down the hill with the priest in the buggy would it now Father? My old mother bless her soul would have the skin off me for that."

"I suppose not, Michael," Bernard replied, holding on to the seat and laughing.

"Can I ask you something Father?"

"Absolutely."

"When me brother was down for the wedding he brung me what's called *The Pugilist Gazette*, published up in the city, full of all manner of numbers, stories about fights and fighters and venues, rumors of matches and such like. You see?"

"Yes, a boxing magazine. It's a popular sport in Chicago. I hear thousands at each bout."

"Exactly so. Brendan says the same. Crazy fer it. Anyways, I came across an article on the top welterweights, and it gave a preview of today's match, believe it or not."

"You don't say. All the way down here. Well." Father Bernard tipped his hat to the postman, trying to think if he'd seen him at church recently. "Were you going to ask me something?"

"I'm getting to that. It give the date and time and described the grounds, how to get down here on the Big Four train, then it had what it called 'bios' of the principles. Accounts of their lives and careers, you see."

"Yes, from the Greek."

"Greek? Who? No no, that's close. You've come near it

308

you have, a sharp man the Father I said to myself. Ask him and he'll have an answer."

"I meant the word, but no matter. Go on."

"Yes, well." Clearly flustered he jerked the reins to catch the drift of the horses, leading them to the center of the lane. "These two lads, Jack Britton and Kid Lewis, they . . . well, they aren't really who people think they are. That is, the posters about town and the Courier have been building this up as The Irishman versus The Englishman, and that's not the case. Or if it is, not all there is to it, like."

They were nearing the livery where they would leave the wagon and walk to the restaurant to meet the others who were going to the fight. A few drinks and lunch and then catch the electric streetcar operated by the LaFayette Street Railway Company.

"What do you mean? Are Britton and Lewis not fighting?"

"Yes, no, it's not that."

Lanahan pulled over to the curb half a block short of the livery. He looked at his watch. From his inside pocket he retrieved a thin cigar, gesturing with the cheroot to the priest out of politeness only, as he knew his companion did not smoke. He inhaled deeply and continued.

"Jack Britton is Irish."

"What?"

Lanahan let this sink in. "His real name is William Breslin and he's from Chicago. The Stockyards neighborhood. Apparently when he was a boy he moved from Connecticut, a place called New Britain, and so they called him 'Britton'. He lives in New York now and what with Tammany and the Nativist machine going there he found himself well supported, if you know what I mean, as an English fighter."

"Well now that is interestin'."

"That ain't all. The Kid, Ted Lewis, is from England. Yeah, that's right, moved to America when he was in short pants. You want to know *his* real name?"

Lanahan tipped the ash from his cigar.

"Gershon Mendeloff." He waited for the expression on the priest's face to change, indicating that he had registered the gravity of this. "That's right. A feckin sheeny."

Lanahan reached behind the seat and produced one of the posters for the fight that had been plastered all over town. In bold letters were the two fighters names, first Britton and then Lewis. Below that were likenesses of both men facing one another, bare fists held up like the fighters of another era. Beneath each man a symbol: a Union Jack snapping in an invisible breeze for Britton and a harp for Lewis. It had been like this since the match had first been announced in the Courier. The paper, it had declared in a bold-type headline, would sponsor the greatest sporting event in Tippecanoe County's history. It could do so, it told its readers, due to the boxing ban in the city of Chicago that swiftly followed in the wake of the infamous Gans–McGovern fight of December 13, 1900. The Big Fix, the paper reported in mock concern, could be healed by a Big Match, a square deal in a fair city. The Gem of the Prairie's loss, the caption below the fighters read, would be The Star City's gain. And there, so that no one could miss it, was the star atop the name of the paper. The Courier was committed to scoring a big success and had been loudly promoting the contest as more than simply a major sporting event. This would not just be two men vying for a belt and a purse but a clash of peoples. If the many would turn out to see good sport, a multitude would turn out for a cause.

Lanahan rolled the poster up and put it back. He flicked the nub of his cigar away and turned to Father Bernard with a serious expression on his broad face.

"Did you not know any of this Father?"

"I did not Michael, and I'm surprised by it. A little shocked even." Bernard rubbed his smooth chin. The bigger man continued looking straight into his face, unmoving.

"Being an enthusiast, like, I thought you might've known and I couldn't risk that. The question, now that you do, is what next?"

The priest hesitated. "Well I'm not sure, not sure ... it would perhaps be best to tell some of the boys at lunch and then get word round at the grounds. Maybe the lads from the south end can be persuaded to back Britton – " He could see this was the wrong answer. The malice in the bigger man's look was clear.

Lanahan fastened his large hand on the priest's shoulder and the narrower man could feel the strength in the grip through the tightly woven wool of his cassock and the thin cotton shirt beneath it. He could smell Lanahan's breath as he was drawn forward, stale with smoke, his front teeth yellowed where they came together unevenly.

"You will do no such thing," he said, squeezing the priest's shoulder until he felt him try to draw away. He spoke now slowly and distinctly, enunciating every word and never taking his green eyes off the priest's brown ones. "You will not say a fucking word about this to anyone. You will keep this to yourself and let the fight happen as it will. It'll be our little secret."

Father Bernard closed his eyes. Lanahan felt the wind go out of him and patted him on the back.

"Buck up, father. It's going to be a grand day."

Twenty Seven

Father Bernard wondered whether there was anyone left in LaFayette. If there were shops open it would be the milliners or the dressmakers. Even these would be hard pressed for custom, as he saw many ladies in their finest summer attire under trim parasols, fanning themselves energetically.

The South End Irish occupied a corner of the second floor of the pavilion. Father Bernard joined them where they stood at the rail in animated conversation. Below on the first floor gallery the crowd jostled for a space from which they could see the ring. They had secured prime seats for the action. Above them in the octagonal tower spectators were visible in the open windows. Two women in nearly identical broad-brimmed hats leaned out recklessly, laughing and holding onto one another, their red lips and rouged cheeks looking to Father Bernard like the splash of color on an exotic bird. The sun shone through a tissue of high clouds and a breeze off the river made it an exceptional day.

Oh Father, he said to himself, you do love a fight so. A minor, minor sin.

Across the makeshift fight ground Bernard spotted Peter Jeffries, looking bigger and certainly happier than he had that day in his buggy on South Street. He had a plum seat near the ring and was conversing with friends, all men and neatly dressed, their boaters signaling semaphores of anticipation.

He turned and looked up at the tower to see if he could make out who had managed to command such seats if it wasn't the fancy lawyer and his fellows. In his mind's eye he saw well-dressed figures eating peeled shrimp and drinking champagne, could picture clearly the subdued chatter of society who would be aware of those below them with less fortunate seats. Across the way Jeffries had his hand on a smaller man's shoulder regaling him with some story or other.

Heads in the crowd turned toward the far side of the pavilion as a tightly packed cortege made its way toward the ring, the people parting and then closing behind them. At the center bobbed a hooded figure in a white robe with a Union Jack longways down the back, his gloved hands resting on a stout bald man. The announcer saw this and took his cue.

"*From* New York City by way of fair *Al*bion weighing in at one hundred forty-six pounds, the battling Brit Jack Britton!"

The other side of the stands erupted in applause and cheering, hats raised and fists pumping the air to urge on their man, followed by a chorus of "Jack Jack Jack Jack" and an unsuccessful attempt by a number of enthusiasts to sing "God Save the Queen."

The announcer waited as the noise abated and as Britton, his manager, the cut man, and his corner assistant climbed into the ring. Britton kept his hood on and danced in place, periodically shadowboxing and then dropping his hands to his sides and working his neck in slow circles.

A murmur arose from the crowd on the other side as they craned their necks, wondering where their fighter was. When he emerged all heads swiveled and a great cry went up that resolved itself into a chant of "Kid Kid Kid Kid," which gave way this time to a more organized version of "Danny Boy" due perhaps to the crowd's having heard the English song fail so. It got as far as the pipes calling, uttered clearly and forcefully in the felicitous acoustics between pavilion and treeline, but by the word "mountainside" was overtaken by clapping and earnest cheering for the green-clad figure moving steadily at the center of his own retinue.

Father Bernard could barely make out the top of the

green satin hood as Lewis passed through the close-packed spectators.

"*From* Chicago Illinois fighting in the colors of the Emerald Isle, weighing in at one hundred forty-five pounds, Ted Kid Lewis."

The cheering persisted through the instructions, both men receiving the referee's dictates with hoods on, shifting fluidly from foot to foot. It was not possible to see whether they looked one another in the eye or not. The crowd chanted names and national slogans, began songs that fell short of completion, raised banners quickly brought down by obstructed viewers. A scuffle broke out where one set of supporters met another in the fringe of disorganization on the pavilion side of the ring but was stopped by cooler heads.

The fighters shed their robes. Each man stretched from the ropes with his back to the other and then turned to shadowbox aggressively, sizing up his opponent as he made his way through his combinations. Father Bernard stood on the tips of his toes and imagined that if the crowd was suddenly rendered silent he would hear their fists cutting the air.

The referee brought them to the center of the ring where they touched gloves. The bell sent them circling, covering up and coming together to jab and feel their way into the contest. Britton wore white trunks and stood at just below average height. His dark hair was oiled and shined in the sunlight. His fighter's body caused him to look odd in his stance, with his short legs and long torso, arms longer than seemed proper. Lewis had the build of a fighter from a lower weight class, taller and thinner than Britton. His punches came from leverage, using footwork and misdirection to catch his opponent coming in with his weight committed and no way to avoid the collision. The puncher Britton and counterpuncher Lewis. Britton's engaging style committed him to wearing down the other man, to get into his body, close an eye and pound that side of the head from the shadows, set an ear ringing or bruise a kidney so that it hurt him in his guts. Against this was Lewis's science of slipping straight rights and left hooks that took energy to throw, following them with stinging punishment that made frustration a weapon. It invited the impetuous to spend himself in finishing what became incrementally less enjoyable, less controllable, less feasible in hitting what was there and then impossibly gone with a pop to the side of the head to remember it by. The first lesson of the gym was that few fighters fought well angry.

Lewis opened the first round with his jab, sending his glove out to disrupt Britton's comfort and rhythm. A minute in, Britton threw a left hook that missed, the Kid backing away and slipping it easily, then bobbing down and to his left flush into a right uppercut. Britton looked surprised when the fighter in the white and green trunks staggered back into the ropes, blood beginning to run down his cheek. Lewis could see the dark stain on the leather when he wiped at his eye. He shook his head. Britton hesitated, then the roar of his supporters awakened him to his opportunity. He stepped in to cut off the ring, pinned the Kid against the ropes and landed a flurry to the body before missing with a straight right. Lewis slipped this, wheeled and planted a left hook solidly on Britton's ear.

The crowd erupted on all sides. Now they had blood. The punch to the ear had hurt Britton, causing him to cover up while Lewis got his feet under him and darted his jab at the space between his opponent's guard. Encouraged by the blood smeared across the Kid's forehead, Britton bulled his way past the jab and tried to open the cut further, pounding at the raised gloves. The blow to the ear distorted Britton's hearing, but at least he could see. He hammered with his right until Lewis was gone.

Not down as he hoped but beneath the ever widening arc of his punches grown careless with repetition, made clear to him when the Kid's left smashed into his right temple. Britton

315

staggered forward, caromed off the ropes and nearly went down as the bell sounded shrilly and the referee grabbed him and sat him in his corner. Three glorious minutes for those assembled.

Father Bernard looked around. This had indeed become a fine day. He did not give a good goddamn where anybody was from. Good Christians every one, he whispered, and crossed himself just in case.

Rounds two and three saw the combatants more cautious. They clutched and exchanged ineffectual attempts to put together combinations. The Kid circled, threw his jabs and danced side to side, light and brisk, tried to keep intact the two fingers of Vaseline that sutured the deep gash in his eyebrow. Britton took the sting of the Kid's left and concentrated on getting his wind back and his breathing under control. He used his footwork to cut off the ring and worked to angle his opponent into an ever smaller space in order to get at his body. If he could hurt him there he might get his legs out of the match. Toe to toe Britton was sure he could damage Lewis's eye further, maybe even get to the jaw. He'd feel better if he could bring some claret out of the fast fucker's mouth.

Neither fighter did any damage through round six. The cut stayed for the most part closed, leaking a little and mixing with sweat to turn the waistband of Lewis's trunks pink in the front. Britton's ear was red, but then so was most of the rest of him. Over successive rounds the jabs had begun to exact a toll from his right eye. He knew that he looked more hurt than he was.

A minute into round seven he looked asleep. With his guard up higher than usual he stayed in the middle of the ring and took punches into his forearms and gloves, content to clinch after absorbing a flurry of punishment from Lewis. The Kid was happy to provide it, sweeping in to deliver double and treble jabs, combinations to the

316

side of the head and then between the gloves when they came apart. Britton's corner urged him on. His manager, fat and short-legged, his hat worn far back on his bald head, slapped the canvas repeatedly trying to snap his fighter out of this slothful spell. With thirty seconds to go Lewis caught Britton with a straight right flush in the mouth and as he dropped his gloves to regain his balance was set on and punished with combinations to the head. The crowd rose and the murmurs became cheers as those backing Lewis sensed an opportunity for a knockout.

Britton, saved again by the bell, fell heavily onto the stool positioned by the cut man who almost didn't get it under him in time.

Father Bernard craned his neck and stood on tiptoes in order to look into Britton's corner. He tried to read their lips but to no avail. As a student of the fight game Bernard did not share his fellow spectators' certainty that present circumstances neatly foretold future events. His skepticism emerged not from his Catholic belief in God's mysterious ways, though these he well understood to work fully and inscrutably. No, observation of the human animal had taught him that if it looked too good to be true it probably was. The fighter with the British flag on his kit had not taken nearly enough punishment to warrant his abrupt decline. Father Bernard, for one, was having none of it. If we were in England in the last century, he thought, where they bet each round separately to changing odds, I would put something significant on the sagging fighter in the right-hand corner. He turned round and again looked up at the tower rising above them. Framed in the open window, a cigar clenched in his teeth, Michael Lanahan leaned against the sill and stared directly down into the crowd on the other side of the ring. Bernard followed the line of sight and saw that Jeffries' head was turned to face him. Their gaze was connected as if a wire passed between them and could be traced, electricity running back and forth crackling in the afternoon air. He would not be surprised to have smelled ozone or burning flesh.

The Kid answered the bell like a terrier after a rat, attacking Britton not two steps from the spilled water in his corner. If the stool was still available he looked ready to sit, it being as good a place as any to take a beating. Lewis drove lefts and rights into Britton's forearms, beneath his elbows low into the ribcage, hammering punches into his sides where there were fewer muscles to protect his lungs. After the initial flurry he danced back, shook his arms out and used his left hand to try to pull down Britton's guard, punching over it with his right in an attempt to batter him in the face. Union Jack's fans were noticeably quiet. They were finding little joy in witnessing the Pride of Albion getting the shit pounded out of him. The banners no longer waved. The shouted encouragements were sparse and desperate-sounding. A vicious right hand to the temple sent their man almost down. He went into the ropes out of balance the Kid hard after him nearly hitting him in the back of the head. The referee came in and looked into Britton's face for signs of recognition. He clinched immediately and Lewis's fans booed energetically between cupped hands.

Father Bernard reckoned the round was a bit past halfway and was studying the tie-up closely. "Now," he said to himself.

Britton had worked Lewis's tired arms down beneath his armpits, putting the top of his head against the thinner man's breastbone. This straightened the Kid up and gave him a sense of security and the chance to rest a little from his efforts. His mouth was open and he breathed heavily from the strain of all that punching. Between the time it took Britton to drop the arms and step back in a low crouch, in the second before he exploded up and forward into the Kid's jaw, the priest just had time to smile in admiration. Britton's straight right hand had all the force of his weight behind it as he used his legs to smash it into Lewis's unguarded chin.

When Kid Lewis's back hit the canvas it was the only part of him that wasn't in the air and so fast did this happen that his fans were still screaming for a knockout. They quieted quickly when Lewis showed no signs of getting up. Britton stood menacingly over him until the referee shepherded him to the opposite corner. Britton's faithful jumped and hugged one another and waved their heavy flags. Below him in the seats the air went out of the Irish. By the count of ten Bernard could hear some begin to weep as if over the body of a dead child.

Lewis did not rise.

Bernard scanned the crowd over the ropes and finally picked out Jeffries. He was now much easier to find because he was standing rigid as a statue, as though a spell had been cast over him. It was an unreal sight, the men around him jostling one another, slapping backs and pumping each other's hands, while he stood unmoving and expressionless. Bernard was further amazed when Jeffries stepped down out of the seats to ringside, went around the apron to the aisle that passed through the Irish spectators, then up the steps to the same floor of the pavilion on which he stood. He backed away from the rail and tracked him as he crossed through the still bewildered crowd to the door that led up into the tower. Bernard had no idea why Peter Jeffries would have greeted Britton's win with such anger, or what now possessed him to stalk so determinedly towards Lanahan. He looked up to the window in the tower and there stood his countryman with his arm around a man who looked enough like him to be his brother. They were both smiling broadly.

Father Bernard could not have said how, but he knew there was about to be trouble. And not only in the tower.

The crowd around him seemed not to know what to do with themselves. They had been so sure of victory that now they had a fervor with no purpose. They would gladly spend it in violence. Father Bernard had the sickening realization that he was about to be in the midst of a great riot. The faces around him looked as though they would fight friends and family. Two men down the row already had one another's lapels in their fists trying to free a hand to strike a blow. Surely order would be restored in getting everyone out of the ground and to their transport. It was then he realized there were no police this far out of the town.

Beyond the stands that stretched out below the pavilion terrace where he stood there was an open space of graveled walks and greensward with a fountain at its center. Something was happening in that direction. He saw the crowd begin to turn that way, then move as though it were suddenly the only avenue open. He tried to see what was happening there but could not make anything out over the heads and hats that blocked his line of sight. The mass of people had no sense about them. Along the row they went, up the aisle and over the apron of the stands where he could no longer see them.

By the time the priest managed to push his way through, the area around the fountain was a melee. He thought first that it looked like his school playground but with all playfulness removed, shouts of glee and youthful abandon replaced by screams and the dull sounds of struck flesh.

He whirled around and pushed back the way he'd come, determined at least to get into the tower to make what peace he could. Bernard got himself through the door and into the half-light cast down from a small stained-glass window set high in the well. Jeffries had reached the top of the steps and was rattling the door which was locked fast. Father Bernard shouted "Jeffries!" as loud as he could but did so at the exact moment the latter threw his shoulder into the door and smashed his way in. The wood splintered and spilled light down the stairwell. He could better see the steps and took them by twos grasping the rail. Up he went as fast as he was able, trying not to stumble. He heard angry shouting and a woman's scream. Then he was in the doorway.

Michael Lanahan was silhouetted against the light, a dark figure with hands raised in a gesture of surrender. The shadow of smoke from his cigar curled up and out into the open air. A man who resembled him, though shorter and thinner, had retreated and stood behind a tall-backed chair. Bernard thought Lanahan must be mocking Jeffries until he stepped into the small octagonal room and saw the pistol in the lawyer's fist. Jeffries looked quickly at the black-clad priest who had appeared as if from nowhere. If he was surprised or concerned he did not show it.

"Stop this," Bernard said in his best level voice.

"You get the fuck back down those stairs. This is no business of yours." Jeffries did not look at him directly as he spoke, merely tilting the gun a few degrees to emphasize his point.

"Stay, Father," Lanahan said in a voice that betrayed mild amusement, "and see what this officer of the court is about to do in cold blood. He'll need you after."

The priest looked around. There were perhaps a half dozen people in the room, all kneeling down and covering their heads save the man he guessed now to be Lanahan's brother.

"I want my fucking money you thieving mick bastard."

Lanahan slowly reached for the cigar in his mouth. He ashed it on the window sill behind him, balanced it on the edge carefully, and put his hand back up.

"Look Jeffries," he said, "things didn't work out too good with the fighter. These things happen in the sporting racket."

After his conversation with Lanahan earlier in the day Bernard could guess what the dispute was all about. He noticed that even though he held the gun, Jeffries seemed the more nervous one.

"I am not interested in your excuses. I told you that if you crossed me you'd be sorry."

"You aren't going to shoot me in front of all these witnesses, are you?"

"I guess that depends on how much confidence I have in the local legal system. I'd say claiming self-defense is a strong possibility."

Lanahan's brother pulled out the chair he had been standing behind and sat down on it, crossing his legs on the tabletop. The scrape of the chair caused the gun to waver before it was centered back on Michael Lanahan's chest. The brother said, "Look friend, put your little gun away or in two days a couple of associates of mine, one of whom is a giant of a man with a terrible temper on him, are going to get off the afternoon train, walk over to your house there on Ferry Street and kill your family deader than shit."

"Terry."

"No Michael, I warned you about these small town duffers. And I told you I should have brought Samuel with me." He pointed his first two fingers at Peter. "Yer money is gone pal and we're skint so it'd be best if you reversed yourself back down them steps and left us be."

"We'll see about that," Jeffries replied, stepping abruptly towards Terry Lanahan. The sudden move brought the pistol swinging back and, afraid he was going to shoot, Father Bernard launched himself in an attempt to grab it before Jeffries could fire. The roar of the gun going off in such a small space was deafening. The bullet splintered the oak planking at the base of a table leg. A woman who had been crouching beneath a window screamed as Jeffries grabbed the priest by the back of the neck and threw him down.

The brother went over backwards in his chair. Jeffries kicked the chair away but before he could get to him he heard the priest say "Michael, no," and turned to see Lanahan pulling a derringer out of his coat pocket. He saw the Irishman trying to thumb back the hammer, aimed his revolver and shot him in the neck below the line of his coarse black beard.

There were more screams and one of the men ran stooped low to the door, got it open, and disappeared down the stairs.

Jeffries trained the pistol back on Terry Lanahan who was in a crouch, gathering himself to rush this man who had likely murdered his brother. Lying prostrate Bernard could see everything clearly: Jeffries with the gun leveled, Terry Lanahan poised to take action in his fury, Michael Lanahan slumping down the cream-colored wall beneath the window, a bright smear of blood tracing his path to the floor. He held his neck in what looked a desperate effort to keep the breath or the blood in or just to find the source of the pain. In the brief moment of silence Bernard could hear the air bubbling out of the wound and see that his face had gone waxen, the color draining out of a hole he could not see. He crawled to him to offer last rites or any absolution there was time for, not caring whether Jeffries told him to stop or even shot him next to his parishioner.

But Peter Jeffries had eyes only for the living Lanahan. He steadied the weapon and said, "I will shoot you dead right now if you move. I'm sorry about your brother but he would have done for me and you know it. All I want is my money and I'll be on my way."

Terry Lanahan considered his options and decided that he had no desire to bleed to death in this godforsaken place even if he could get the gun and turn it on this man. The lawyer was dead anyway. Not today or tomorrow, but a day that would come soon, before the leaves on the trees changed from green to gold. And when that day came being dead would be the least of his worries. He indicated with his index finger that he was going to reach inside his jacket.

"Go slow. I don't trust you one goddamn bit and I might make a mistake you'll regret."

"Take it easy mate. Me wallet is right here." He retrieved it with finger and thumb and gently opened it, offered a stack of bills.

"Reach up and put it on the table. Then sit down with your back against the wall, hands behind your head."

As he did so Jeffries looked over at the priest who was kneeling next to the dying man. He had one hand on his forehead and in the other held his rosary, praying in a whisper. There was no getting him to count the money for him, so he gave it a cursory manipulation, like fluffing a deck of cards, and figured it was about the same size as what he'd handed over in the library. He folded the bills and stuffed them into his trouser pocket. He backed up carefully and opened the door. Before he went down the stairs he stole a glance at Michael Lanahan's face. His eyes stared black and wet and without recognition.

Twenty Eight

Peter Jeffries pulled the buggy to the curb on Fifth Street beyond the bright lights that announced the main entrance into the Lahr House Hotel. A quick nip at the bar and then straight home. He needed to think things through, perhaps shut his eyes for a bit before he called at Cassini's house to see how the remainder of his afternoon at the fights had gone. There was also the matter of arranging his defense, assuming the county sheriff's investigation could not get to him until Monday. The Italian would be essential for strategizing and making the initial moves in what was going to be a complex, and expensive, negotiation.

The bar in the hotel – the Knickerbocker Saloon – was thankfully sedate. Only a few patrons, neither of whom he recognized. No one interested in the player piano which sat forlorn against the far wall. He took a seat at the end of the long el of the bar and ordered a rye neat with a water back. There was a good view of the door from here in case it became necessary to duck out the back. It felt good to smoke and drink in the quiet. He could not arrest the thought that came again and again like the chorus of a catchy song: I shot a man dead. The piano probably held that very refrain somewhere in the rolls of its memory. He weighed the experience, remembered calculating what the derringer could do and how long it would take a man to pull its hair trigger, rubbed his index finger with his thumb but felt no mark there of the metallic convulsion it had set in motion. The stricken look on Lanahan's face when the bullet found him. The little gun dropping out of sight. Not as much blood as he'd thought.

But his eyes. They still stared at him and when he closed his they appeared impossibly black and bright. Three rounds effortlessly became four, then five, until he had to put up his hand to say no. He left a generous but not conspicuous tip and went out the front door keeping his hat pulled down.

"Flowers?"

He said "No thanks" out of habit and was two steps down the sidewalk when he turned and went back. He fished carefully in his pocket, peeling off a bill without bringing the wad into the light, handing it to her while indicating the biggest bunch she had.

"I'm not sure I can change this right now mister. It's been a slow evening." She rummaged around in a leather purse but she only had coins. "I'll have to go into the bar. Back in a second."

He had no desire to be left standing there alone with a gigantic bunch of flowers. "You know what, you can owe me. I have a feeling I'm going to need quite a few flowers in the next week or two and so how about you put it on account?"

"I'm happy to do that. It's Jeffries, isn't it?"

"Yes it is, and thank you."

"Thank you Mr. Jeffries. A good night to you sir."

On the way to the buggy he thought how much easier these kinds of transactions were. Had anyone ever shot someone over a bunch of flowers? He guessed not.

Once home he took his time unhitching Ruth, gave him a thorough brushing, and filled a bag with oats. On the path to the house he realized he was a little drunk. Should have eaten something.

He was rummaging in the icebox with little success when he heard her behind him.

"Who are these for? Let me guess, you liberated them from a whorehouse."

He clicked the door shut and turned to face her.

326

"My dear, is it so surprising – "

"What's surprising is that you would have the gall to think you could use flowers to smooth over what you did. Are thousands of dollars hidden in here?"

She picked up the bunch and tore at the shiny paper, shedding pieces of it till she was down to the stems. They were held together by thin-gauged wire and she untwisted each strand until she had them separated. Then she systematically threw them around the room, some hitting the cabinets, some striking her husband who put his hands up to ward them off, others landing on the stove, the buffet, and on the floor. She did this silently and methodically as though she had visualized a perfect distribution that she was now putting into practice. When they had all been scattered and no more remained she stood breathing heavily. He was sure she would cry. Instead she looked at him coldly and asked, "Where is my goddamned money?" in a voice that to his ears sounded so much like his had in the tower room that he took a step back and leaned against the counter. A sweat broke out on his forehead. He had a feeling that he did not recognize and it alarmed him. It was a kind of panic caused by the realization that he had no idea what was going to happen. This had never occurred to him in this house nor with the woman standing in front of him.

"Well?" she said. "Where is it?"

"I'll give you a thousand. That's all there is. Anything else I have is tied up in a legal matter that I assure you is more important than whatever use you have for it."

He remembered a tin of saltines in the cabinet behind him. He opened it and snapped off a row.

"In fact," he continued, "if you make me a sandwich I'll give you eleven hundred."

This was better. He was beginning to enjoy himself now.

She held him with a steady look that betrayed nothing of her emotional state. For many years he had been forced to diagnose her mood and the pills, powders, and liquids that supplemented it. There was something different here. Whatever she was on had her as tightly wound as a coiled spring.

"I need that money." She held out her hand and he almost laughed. "It's not for me. It's for Henderson."

"For Henderson?" He did not believe this for a second. This was about their argument over the school and his mother. "I've made up my mind on that subject. It's best he goes to this military academy. My mother was right. The boy needs guidance."

She still had her hand out but it was not as steady. Nor was her voice.

"Best for whom?"

Here comes the deluge, he thought.

Annabelle knew she could not hold it together much longer, which made her feel desperate. There was no telling how she would get Henderson to go away if she missed this opportunity. She imagined him asleep upstairs warm in his bed. Her boy. Damaged and vulnerable and with a flickering sensitivity she was determined to preserve. She was going to have to make a sacrifice. She had briefly considered going with him but it would be better this way.

Annabelle had entered the kitchen to find her husband rooting around in the icebox like a starving animal. On the table she saw the gun propped against its belt and holster. The symbol of all that was violent and depraved about men such as Peter Jeffries. It made her sick to think she had his name, had a son who carried it further. The flowers symbolized something too but she could not decide what. They were the kind of thing that lent themselves out to any situation that would have them. Their coyness made her want to rip them apart. Before she knew it she had spoken out loud to him and he had turned.

Now here she stood with her hand out. For the last time, she thought, as she calmly pivoted and reached across the table. The Colt was so heavy she had to slide it to her and then she got both hands on it and with all her strength raised it level with the center of his chest.

He put his hands up. Then he smiled.

"Come on. Give me that."

She closed her eyes and pulled the trigger with two fingers.

Click. She opened her eyes and squeezed again. Squeeze-click . . . squeeze-click . . . .

The hammer dropped on empty chambers. She lowered the gun.

Peter stepped around her to the table and with his thumb-nail pried a shell out of the belt. He took the Colt from her hands and slid it into a chamber, spun the cylinder, thumbed back the hammer and gave it to her.

He felt drunk but he felt good. Really alive and perhaps even proud of her. These were all new sensations and the room had the atmosphere of a stage drama.

"Come on," he said, tapping his breastbone. "Right here."

Annabelle took a deep breath and raised the heavy weapon.

Henderson bolted upright as the sound of the shot echoed through the dark house. He got quickly out of bed and held as still as he could, listening. In the hallway the soft tick of the Regulator clock counted the time. It was dark but he had no idea how late. At the door to his parents' room he paused but heard nothing. Halfway down the stairs he put his hand on the banister, the worn walnut cool then gently warming to match his hand's temperature. He negotiated his way down carefully, feeling for each step, pausing before he reached the bottom to lean over and look down the hall. A faint glimmer of light in the sitting room.

There were lights on in the kitchen then.

He went as silently as he could manage, placing his bare feet warily and holding his shoulder for fear of striking it against something. Someone was in the kitchen. He closed his eyes better to discern the sound. A clinking of metal on china or porcelain, glass maybe. His mother who seldom ate would not be up at this hour doing any cooking. His father could not have kept this quiet doing anything.

What had he heard? He was too practiced at hearing doors slam for it to have awoken him this way. No, it had been too loud and reverberant for that. An out-of-doors sound come inside. He saw in his mind a bull in a china shop. Such a cliché but he could not help but feel the muscular violence of the pent-up animal, thrashing its deadly horned head and lashing out with blind hooves amidst bits and pieces of ruined finery. At the foot of the staircase he turned and checked the front door to see if it was locked. It was. He wasn't sure why he did this. He resisted the urge to throw the door open and look outside. With his hand resting on the knob he cocked his head and could faintly make out the metallic sound.

The dining room was dimly lit and neatly arranged since they seldom used it. Places were set for four. Henderson could not have said whether this habit of his mother's was one of optimism or desperation. He had more than once come home after school to find her sitting alone at one of the places, hands clasped in her lap. The glow from the kitchen marked a long rectangle on the hardwood and he stopped at its edge. The sound he'd heard was clear and unvarying, a dull striking and faint scraping. He sniffed. The air was florid and putrid at once, like perfume mixed with sulphur.

Taking a deep breath to steady himself he walked into the kitchen. His mother stood with her back to him in her red robe, concentrating on something at the counter. She was humming quietly to herself. Strewn across the floor were flowers: amaryllis, orange and white lilies, delicate sprays of baby's breath, honeysuckle, a single red rose flattened as if from a book of mementos, and a lilac branch with its heart-shaped leaves and pale violet flowers crushed. Beyond the breakfast table he could see his father lying on the floor, his head leaning oddly against the baseboard molding, hatless, his eyes staring straight ahead.

"Mother," he said sharply, trying to get her attention. She continued at whatever task she was performing, the sound it made still unfamiliar, his presence in the room and his speaking having no effect on her. She hummed on. He willed her to turn and say the words "dead drunk," but knew she would not and that they would not make it so. He stared at his father's chest and willed the buttons on his vest to rise and fall.

On the table the leather belt and its holster sat exactly as he'd left them. The gun was gone and it was not visible on the floor nor in his father's hand. He moved forward and knelt beside him. In a plaintive voice he whispered, "Daddy." His eyes were fixed and lifeless. Only then did he see the dark stain on his vest wet with blood, the brass buttons blown in or off altogether. He put his hand on it and pushed the warm wound trying he could not say how to put it all back. There must be some trick to start his heart, to set his eyes sparkling, to spring him to his feet and gather spilled flowers. Then his mother could turn and smile. He would have given anything for that smile even if it saw past the flowers to the deception. One of nature's lures. The gaud of spring. The bauble of desire. The bright proffer of dark intentions. The reek of their insincerity made him feel sick. He stood and wiped his hand on his trousers.

He looked over her shoulder to see what she was doing. She had the heavy Colt pistol in both hands and was using the end of the barrel to crush and stir herbs in the large white porcelain mortar she kept for this purpose. He reached over and wrapped his hand around the cylinder. She resisted then allowed him to stop its motion, not turning her head or acknowledging him. He lifted the gun out of her grasp and set it on the counter. As if this had been all that was holding her together she collapsed against him. With both hands he steadied her, the pain in his shoulder making even her slight weight a chore to steer to a chair. Her face was lined. Deep pockets of fatigue girded her eyes. He pulled out a chair and sat facing her.

"What happened, Mother?"

She smiled but her eyes did not register his presence.

He took her by the upper arms and shook her.

"Come on. Please."

"When I was a tiny little girl they shot the President. Daddy took me to see the dead train pass. It rolled slowly, darkly by, car after car. All around grave-faced people threw flowers at it. The train's windows were black. No one waved hello or goodbye."

He released her.

"And now he's gone there will be no more, no more . . . " She put her palms to the sides of her head. "I can't remember. How does it go?"

Then in a pretty voice she sang: "When lilacs last in the dooryard bloomed, and the great star early drooped in the western sky in the night, I mourned–and yet shall mourn with ever-returning spring . . . " She trailed off, a puzzled look on her face. "No, that is not it at all. It isn't a song."

Henderson felt the panic rise in him. She regarded the floral debris that littered the floor. She was drifting away and he needed her.

"Mother!"

She looked at him with a sudden fierce expression.

"What are you doing here? Pack what you can carry and get out. I can handle things." She looked around the room and then down at the body. "I'll cover for you when he gets up."

Henderson considered this. Perhaps he could leave now before his life became marked forever in the memory of this town. He could go west, start over, make a new life for himself.

332

"Take this," she said in a whisper.

Her cupped hands were empty.

"This ought to be enough to buy you passage to wherever you want to go. Don't worry about me."

He pretended to take it from her and put it on the table. She nodded towards it.

"With what's left you can get settled and then I'll join you." She glanced at the body of her husband. "He and I are through. I tried to tell him that you'd never be like him, that you were my son and he had nothing to offer you but pain and suffering. They were going to send you to that Confederate school and then what would you be?"

For the first time in many years she looked happy, her face like a girl's. The lines around her eyes disappeared and she smiled broadly. A further look of recognition passed across her face, as though someone long expected had entered the room. She placed the palms of her hands carefully together as if in prayer.

Henderson felt it all slip away. From a viewpoint above the dim kitchen, the floors and walls of their house rendered transparent, he saw himself in a triangle whose points were no longer connected. His choices were now dictated from this other place, a perspective from which he would always view his life. The son in thrall to a father and at play with a mother would never again be a luxury he could enjoy. Henderson never expected his childhood to end so suddenly. Now that it had its withdrawal left him with far less certainty than he'd reckoned.

He thought of the plan she had proposed to him before. If farfetched, there was something to it. He might have done it instead of being sent away. But now what she thought would free him had trapped him here as surely as if he had done it himself.

His father lying dead. His mother a murderer. To what end had he aspired to manhood? Was this the freedom he'd imagined for so long, plotting for his father's attentions and avoiding his mother's contempt? The worst of it was that he had no one to confront, no one to rebel against or run away from, no one from whom he could meaningfully distance himself.

He had read plenty of melodramas and he could think of no other example in which the main character sat in the final scene with a woman who had lost her mind, a dead body at their feet, a gun on the table, and flowers strewn about, yet without anyone to revenge or kill or love. Or, indeed, run away with.

Annabelle Jeffries moved to the floor and began to gather up the flowers. She sang to herself in a quiet voice. He could not get her to speak to him and realized that the why no longer mattered. Neither the why nor the how. There would have been nothing unusual about his father returning home from a day of sport with a mass of flowers to find his wife unresponsive to his mood. But due perhaps to her son lying injured, their relationship strained to the breaking, his Abel spirit ravaged, she had taken the heavy gun in her two bony hands and pulled the trigger. He knew he had left it unloaded and could hear his father's sardonic laughter as she squeezed and the hammer dropped on empty chambers.

Henderson tried in his mind's eye to see around the bend where she had gone but could not. Nothing could change what had happened. He understood this and could more readily see stretching out before him a changed life, one marked by this event so fresh he had but to breathe through his nose to sense it.

It would be a long, long time before he would be able to stand the smell of flowers.

There was a decision to be made. Something would have to be done and he was the only one fit to do it. Clearly he ought to fetch a policeman and let the authorities take over. He would go to live with his grandmother or one of his aunts. His mother would be taken eventually to Logansport to the state mental hospital. He tried to imagine the stigma that would attach to his father's name and to his mother and to himself even if he were in another town. With his toe Henderson touched the lilac branch where it had been cut. His mother sat holding the gathered bouquet, whispering to herself, rocking back and forth.

It came to him clearly though he did not welcome the realization. In no hurry he saw each step and made a mental list of the things he would need. Plenty of night still remained.

At the end of their street he had to pull the reins to the left to check the horse's habit of turning to go downtown. It threw its head none too happy at having been awakened from sleep. They needed to get over the bridge and on their way while the streets were empty. Henderson turned to make certain the blanket had not moved. In the dim gaslight there appeared no human form at all. No body, neither spade nor shovel, nor wrapped in a tea towel the cold Colt Walker pistol.

It hurt but he snapped the reins.

"Git up Ruth."

They passed along the cobbles to the bridge and across to the other side, turning south on the river road. He imagined the look he'd find on Clayton McGhee's face when he answered the door, probably holding a shotgun in his off hand. He thought it best first to remind him of the secret they shared, of June Colegrove's body lying buried somewhere on the farm. And then he'd lay it all out for him, ask for a favor, hope Clayton would help him with what he could not change.

Epilogue

Tippecanoe County, Indiana

October 1928

It was time to gather at the river.

Not as they had when he'd been baptized in Alabama, nor with the members of the Green Hill Church of Christ on a gravel bar down near Black Rock at the twice yearly revival. It was time to gather up. And to say goodbye.

The leaves would soon begin to turn and fall. In a month's time the far slope of the ravine would be visible, its floor coppered with deadfall. Now all Clayton could see in his descent in the wagon was thick forest. The road was managed by the county and so over the years had become much easier to negotiate. At the bottom he checked the horse, looked and listened carefully for automobiles, then turned onto the river road. The bridge over the creek remained in poor repair. He slowed down out of habit. It probably didn't matter but he felt safer. What had once been open prairie was now cultivated. It flooded some years but the farmer did well in the rich soil with corn and broad beans, a small patch of pumpkins. Between two of these fields was a track that paralleled the creek. On either side was a drainage ditch and he was careful not to let the wagon wander. At the tree line he could smell the river and feel the difference in the breeze, the air somehow damper and fresher at the same time. He tied the horse to a sycamore and let her graze the narrow strip of sedge grass that bordered the field.

There was no visible path in the trees but he knew the way. Besides, with the river on your left a body could hardly get lost. He was nearly on top of the smokehouse before he saw it. The honeysuckle had grown over two of its sides and a thick stand of young sassafras trees grew all the way around like spindly sentinels. Their green stalks and fat trident leaves reminded him that it had been too long since he'd had a cup of sassafras tea. The door had blown or fallen in. He pushed his way to where he could see inside as far as the light let him. Something probably lived in there. When he detected the barest of charred smells he closed his eyes and pictured cured hams, a flitch of bacon, a brace of venison loins. He backed away, proud to see that it still stood, though in a diminished condition. Building it had been a hard job of work but the salary in smoked meat and fish had been well worth it.

Other landmarks presented themselves. The giant chestnut tree that had held a rope swing where they flung themselves into a dependable swimming hole. The rope was gone but the notch that circled the branch was still visible as a poorly healed scar in the bark. He found the ruins of the little chicken house. The pine had not weathered well and once the roof had gone Clayton could see how nature had got herself in and claimed it. The stones they had hauled from the creek for the foundation marked out a rectangle, but even these were grown over with joint grass and clumps of bluestem, putting him in mind of a grave site. The cellar they dug for fruit and root vegetables eluded him. It had a banked entrance and a swinging door but he could not locate its distinctive shape. Perhaps the wind and water had worn it away.

Judah's house stood just where he expected it to be. He would not have been surprised to see him sitting on a stump tending a cook fire and singing to himself. The hymn came back to him unbidden in the version he'd taught to Judah who liked to hum the tune while he worked. He could hear him singing the only complete verse the man could ever remember: *At the smiling of the river, Mirror of the Savior's face, Saints, whom death will never sever, Lift their songs of saving grace.* The smiling of the river. Judah had been skeptical of that line and for a long time harbored a suspicion that Clayton had made it up.

The house had fared pretty well. It did not have any windows, so barring a roof collapse there was nothing that could compromise its structure apart from a falling tree. It had escaped this fate, though just. A hackberry had smashed through the undergrowth on its way down on the creek side not too many yards away. The door opened with the pressure of his shoulder and a lift of its handle; it had always slumped in the frame and needed to be squared before it would unlatch. He swung it cautiously, his imagination active with supposed inhabitants. Somewhere mice skittered about and several squirrels squeezed through an opening in the eaves and scrambled over the roof to escape into waiting branches. In order to roust any other animals he shouted "Hello!" and felt silly that he used a human word in this place. I wonder if this is how the mailman feels at my house sometimes, he thought.

With the door open wide the light reached nearly the whole interior. There was not much to see. A table with its top warped and cracked from water dripping through the roof's broken shingles. The dark void he knew to be the hearth. Two chairs laced with spider webs and a third with the back broken off. A stand with a basin. A bedstead. Over the basin would be a small mirror but if it was there it did not send him a reflection. Beneath the ropes that no longer held a mattress or a tired body would be the chest. In the middle of the room he clapped his hands and stomped his foot twice to flush out any other residents, though on the dirt floor this had little effect but to startle a haze of dust. Nothing moved. He should have brought a candle or his old headlamp though he could not say where it had gone. Feeling warily under the bedframe his fingers lighted on something solid. It took both hands to wrest it out and get it to where he could see. There was a lock but the key was in it and it turned more smoothly than he would have believed. With the lid open it smelt strongly of cedar. There was a tattered wool camp blanket of indeterminate color folded into a tidy square on top, which he took out and sat on. His knees were hurting. Secured by a length of faded violet ribbon were a dozen or so tintypes: men in uniform, a family in which he could not identify Judah, and two of a woman, or perhaps two women who were sisters. One of these was mounted in a stiff cardboard frame that opened to reveal an image of a young Judah Furnish with neatly trimmed hair and winsome mustache. He stood at profile with his arm resting rakishly on a high-backed chair, wearing a tailored frock coat and high polished riding boots. Clayton returned these to the chest and removed a small pistol with ivory handles wrapped in a silk handkerchief. He put this back and after lifting out a pair of spectacles with only one lens, a hand-carved chess piece – the knight – and a bayonet, he finally found what he was looking for.

The Bible was just as he left it. The marker was still at the end of Luke. He recalled the circumstances after his mother's death when he made a present of it, leaving it in the chest beneath the bed. Unbidden a memory had come into his mind of reading to his granny and the rest of the family. Then he had remembered where it was. Thinking of it forever lost in a dark chest in a falling down cabin by the river suddenly made no sense to him. It needed to be gathered up and sent along to his daughters with the story of its place in the family. So it had occasioned a visit to his old friend's place in order to set it on its path once again.

Judah had disappeared in the spring of 1907. Clayton had not made many visits that winter. When there was no one to be found on a clear March day he reckoned him to be out on the river or hunting. He waited but at dusk there was no sign of him nor was he there the next day nor three days later. What bothered him most was that there was no one he could talk to or seek help from.

Sure of his eventual return, Clayton had dutifully looked after things at the river place. The dugout was gone and so he could not run the trot line. He felt bad for the fish hanging off the hooks, stranded without hope of discovery, though it consoled him that fish didn't seem to be too aware of what was going on anyway. He considered attempting to heroically follow the line in the water, clinging to it against the current, stuffing what fish he could into a bag and releasing the rest. But he decided that it would be an awful dumb way to drown. It wasn't worth risking Sara's tears for a sack of fish.

The months became a year. Clayton finally told Sara. She asked whether he had kin nearby. Clayton told the story of Judah's time in the war, about the battles and marches, the sickness, the death of friends, the terror, the scar on his neck. He'd known the man ten years before he mentioned the scar, and then Clayton had wished he hadn't. Clayton promised to ask the sheriff about him next time he was in town, but added his doubts it would come to anything. Sounds like a man who didn't want to be found, she remarked. Over time he made his way down the bluff once in a while to fish and to look around for signs of Judah's return. While he used the river road often enough, he found less occasion to turn off and make his way to the mouth of the creek.

He stood up with considerable effort and put the Bible in the front pocket of his overalls. With all the items returned and the blanket shaken out and replaced over its contents, he closed the lid and maneuvered the chest to its resting place. The door latch caught with a reassuring click. At the bank of the river he gathered himself and tried to imagine his old friend out there somewhere, maybe singing a happy tune, enjoying a thick steak in a fancy restaurant. Perhaps even living in a town somewhere in a well-built house on a pretty street, with a coal chute and milk delivery.

It felt good to see him that way.

He looked out across the brown water and thought of the endlessness of its passage, the way it always flowed, no matter what people did to themselves or one another.

It goes on. We go on.

The smiling of the river.